W9-BZA-338

# THE RODS AND THE AXE

# BAEN BOOKS BY TOM KRATMAN

*A State of Disobedience*

*A Desert Called Peace*
*Carnifex*
*The Lotus Eaters*
*The Amazon Legion*
*Come and Take Them*
*The Rods and the Axe*

*Caliphate*

*Countdown: The Liberators*
*Countdown: M Day*
*Countdown: H Hour*

WITH JOHN RINGO
*Watch on the Rhine*
*Yellow Eyes*
*The Tuloriad*

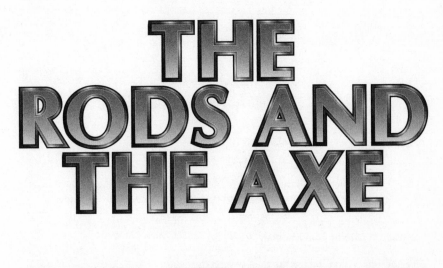

# THE RODS AND THE AXE

# TOM KRATMAN

THE RODS AND THE AXE

This is a work of fiction. All the characters and events portrayed in this book
are fictional, and any resemblance to real people or incidents is purely coincidental.

A Baen Book

Baen Publishing Enterprises
P.O. Box 1403
Riverdale, NY 10471
www.baen.com

ISBN: 978-1-4767-3656-3

Cover art by Kurt Miller

First Baen printing, July 2014

Distributed by Simon & Schuster
1230 Avenue of the Americas
New York, NY 10020

Library of Congress Cataloging-in-Publication Data

Kratman, Tom.
 The rods and the axe / Tom Kratman.
    pages cm. -- (Carerra ; 6)
  ISBN 978-1-4767-3656-3 (hardback)
1. Space warfare--Fiction. I. Title.
 PS3611.R375R64 2014
 813'.6--dc23
                                        2014013092

Printed in the United States of America

10 9 8 7 6 5 4 3 2 1

# CONTENTS

To my living aunts,
Lucy Farulla and Grace Chandler.
They were *always* there for me.

# ACNOWLEDGEMENTS

**in no particular order:**

Yoli and Toni who, in their different ways, put up with me, Steve Saintonge, TBR (the Kriegsmarine contingent of the bar), Ori Pomerantz, James Lane, Jack Withrow, Tom Wallis, Thomas Mandell, Jasper Paulsen, Matt Pethybridge, Conrad Chu, John Becker, Patrick Horne, Sam Swindell, ARRSE (even if they don't know it), Bill Crenshaw, Andy and Fehrenbach at old Cambrai-Fritsch Kaserne, Dan Neely, T2M, Henrik Kiertzner, Greg Dougherty, Keith Glass, Leonid Panfil, Ernest Paxton, Chris Bagnall, Jeremy Levitt, Bruce Cook, Sheinkin, Keith Wilds, Krenn, Charles Krin, MD, Mark Bjertnes, Alex Shishkin, Robert Hofrichter, Ned Brickley, John Biltz, Seamus Curran, Emeye, DanielRH, Tom Lindell, Arun Prabhu, Jacob Tito, Nigel the Kiwi, Joseph Turner, Dan Kemp, Robespierre, Jon LaForce, John Prigent, Phillip "Doc" Wohlrab, Chris Nuttall, Brian Carbin, Joseph Capdepon II, Mike Watson, Michal Swierczek, Harry Russell, James Gemind, Mike May, Guy Wheelock, Paul Arnold, Andrew Stocker, Nomad the Turk, Paul 11, Geoff Withnell, Joe Bond, Rod Graves, Mike Sayer, Jeff Wilkes, Bob Allaband, John Jordan, Wade Harlow,
    If I've forgotten anyone, chalk it up to premature senility.

# WHAT HAS GONE BEFORE

**(5,000,000 BC through Anno Condita [AC] 476):**

Long ago, long before the appearance of man, came to Earth the aliens known by man only as the "Noahs." About them, as a species, nothing is known. Their very existence can only be surmised by the project they left behind. Somewhat like the biblical Noah, these aliens transported from Earth to another planet samples of virtually every species existing in the time period approximately five hundred thousand to five million years ago. They also appear to have modified the surface of the planet to create a weather pattern and general ecology suitable to the life forms they have brought there.

Having transported these species, and having left behind various other genengineered species—apparently to inhibit the development of intelligent life on the new world—the Noahs disappeared, leaving no other trace beyond a few incomprehensible and inert artifacts, and the rift through which they moved from the Earth to the new world.

In the year 2037 AD a robotic interstellar probe, the *Cristobal Colon*, driven by lightsail, disappeared en route to Alpha Centauri. Three years later it returned, under automated guidance, through the same rift in space into which it had disappeared. The *Colon* brought with it wonderful news of another Earthlike planet, orbiting another star. (Note, here, that not only is the other star *not* Alpha Centauri, it's not so far been proved that it is even in the same galaxy, or universe, for that matter, as ours.) Moreover, implicit in its disappearance and return was the news that here, finally, was a relatively cheap means to colonize another planet.

The first colonization effort was an utter disaster, with the ship, the *Cheng Ho*, breaking down into ethnic and religious strife that annihilated almost every crewman and colonist aboard her.

Thereafter, rather than risk further bloodshed by mixing colonies, the colonization effort would be run by regional supranationals such as NAFTA, the European Union, the Organization of African Unity, MERCOSUR, the Russian Empire and the Chinese Hegemony. Each of these groups was given colonization rights to specific areas on the new world, which was named—with a stunning lack of originality— "Terra Nova" or something in another tongue that meant the same thing. Most groups elected to establish national colonies within their respective mandates, some of them under United Nations' "guidance."

With the removal from Earth of substantial numbers of the most difficult portions of the populations of Earth's various nations, the power and influence of transnational organizations such as the UN and EU increased dramatically. With the increase of transnational power, often enough expressed in corruption, even more of Earth's more difficult, ethnocentric, and traditionalist population volunteered to leave. Still others were deported forcibly. Within not much more than a century and a quarter, and much less in many cases, nations had ceased to have much meaning or importance on Earth. On the other hand, and over about the same time scale, nations had become preeminent on Terra Nova. Moreover, because of the way the surface of the new world had been divided, these nations tended to reflect— if only generally—the nations of Old Earth.

Warfare was endemic, beginning with the wars of liberation by many of the weaker colonies to throw off the yoke of Earth's United Nations.

In this environment Patrick Hennessey was born, grew to manhood, and was a soldier for many years. Some years after he left service, Hennessey's wife, Linda, a native of the Republic of Balboa, and their three children, were killed in a massive terrorist attack on Hennessey's native land, the Federated States of Columbia. The same attack likewise killed Hennessey's uncle, the head of his extended and rather wealthy family. As his dying testament, Uncle Bob changed his will to leave Hennessey with control over the entire corpus of his estate.

Half mad with grief, Hennessey, living in Balboa, ruthlessly provoked and then mercilessly gunned down six local supporters of the terrorists. In retaliation, and with that same astonishing bad judgment that had made their movement and culture remarkable across two worlds, the terrorist organization, the Salafi *Ikhwan*, attacked Balboa, killing hundreds of innocent civilians, including many children.

With Balboa now enraged, and money from his uncle's rather impressive estate, Hennessey began to build a small army within the Republic. This army, the *Legion del Cid*, was initially about the size of a reinforced brigade though differently organized. For reasons of internal politics, Hennessey began to use his late wife's maiden name, Carrera. It was as Carrera that he became well known to the world of Terra Nova.

The legion was hired out to assist the Federated States of Columbia in a war against the Republic of Sumer, a nominally Islamic but politically secular—indeed fascist—state that was known to have supported terrorism in the past, to have used chemical weapons in the past, and to have had a significant biological warfare program. It was widely believed to have been developing nuclear weapons, as well.

Against some expectations, the *Legion del Cid* performed quite well. Equally against expectations, its greatest battle in the campaign was against a Sumeri infantry brigade led by a first rate officer, Adnan Sada, who not only fought well but stayed within the customs, rules, and laws of war.

Impressed with the legion's performance (even while loathing the openly brutal ways it has of enforcing the laws of war), and needing foreign troops badly, the War Department of the Federated States offered Carrera a long-term employment contract. Impressed with Sada, and with some of the profits from the contract with the Federated States, Carrera likewise offered to not only hire, but substantially increase, Sada's military force. Accepting the offer, and loyal to his salt, Sada revealed seven nuclear weapons to Carrera, three of which were functional and the rest restorable. These Carrera quietly removed, telling no one except a very few, *very* close subordinates.

The former government of Sumer had a cadre and arms for an insurgency in place before the Federated States and its allies invaded. In Carrera's area of responsibility, this insurgency, while bloody, was contained through the help of Sada's men and Carrera's ruthlessness. In the rest of the country, however, the unwise demobilization of the former armed forces of the Republic of Sumer left so many young men unemployed that the insurgency grew to nearly unmanageable levels.

Eventually, Carrera's area of responsibility was changed and he was forced to undertake a difficult campaign against a city, Pumbadeta, held by the rebels. He surrounded and starved the city, forcing women and children to remain within it until he was certain that every dog, cat and rat had been eaten. Only then did he permit the women and children to leave. His clear intention was to kill every male in Pumbadeta capable of sprouting a beard.

After the departure of the noncombatants, Carrera's legion continued the blockade until the civilians within the town rebelled against the rebels. Having a rare change of heart, Carrera aided the rebels against rebellion to take the town. Thereafter nearly every insurgent found within Pumbadeta was executed, along with several members of the press sympathetic to the rebels. The few insurgents he—temporarily—spared were sent to a surface ship for *rigorous* interrogation.

With the war in Sumer winding down, the Federated States, now under Progressive rather than Federalist leadership, unwisely fired Carrera and his legion. And, as should have been predicted, the terrorist money and recruits that had formerly been sent to Sumer, where the Salafi cause was lost, were instead redirected to Pashtia, where it still had a chance. The campaign in Pashtia then began to flow against the Federated States and its unwilling allies of the Tauran Union.

More than a little bitter at having his contract violated and being let go on short notice, Carrera exacted an exorbitant price from the Federated States before he would commit his forces to the war in Pashtia. That price being paid, however, and in gold, he didn't stint but waged a major—and typically ruthless—campaign to restore the situation in Pashtia, which had deteriorated badly under Tauran interference and feint support.

Ultimately, Carrera got wind of a major meeting taking place across the nearby border with Kashmir between the chief of the United Earth Peace Fleet and the emir of the terrorists, the Salafi *Ikhwan*. He attacked and in the attack and its aftermath killed thousands, captured hundreds, and seized a dozen more nuclear weapons, gifts of the UEPF to their terrorist allies. One of these weapons Carrera delivered to the capital of the major terrorist-supporting state of Yithrab. When detonated, this weapon not only killed the entire clan of the chief of the Salafi *Ikhwan*, but also at *least* a million citizens of that city. In the process, he framed the Salafis for the detonation.

That destruction, seemingly at the hand of an Allah grown weary of terrorism, along with the death or capture and execution of the core of the Salafi movement in the attack across the Pashtian-Kashmiri border, effectively ended the terrorist war on Terra Nova.

The price to Carrera was heavy. With the end of the war with the terrorists, and having had more revenge against the murderers of his family than any man ought desire, he collapsed, physically, mentally, and emotionally. Recovery was slow and guarded by his second wife, Lourdes.

Unfortunately, he was still needed by his adopted home of Balboa. Having arranged for Carrera's wife to be disarmed, Legate Jimenez and Sergeant Major McNamara ultimately persuaded him back to active duty. There followed a vicious no-holds-barred-and-little-quarter-given war with the quasi sovereign drug cartels of Santander, along with an attempted *coup d'état*, by the treacherous Legate Pigna. This was ultimately foiled by Lourdes, with the help of the Volgans of 22nd Tercio. In the same coup, the rump of the old, oligarchic Balboan state was reabsorbed into the rest of the country, the oligarchs and their lackeys being driven from the country or killed. Very nearly the last remaining scion of the oligarchs, and the man who had set up Carrera for assassination, Belisario Endara-Rocaberti, had fled to Hamilton, in the Federated States, where he'd done everything up to and including giving the use of his wife to the president of the Federated States to get the Parilla regime overthrown. But, while the president of the FSC was more than willing to make extensive use of Mrs. Rocaberti or, indeed, pretty much anything in a skirt, he really had no interest in getting the FSC into a war.

As uninterested as the president of the FSC may have been in fomenting war, an easily winnable war against Balboa on the part of the Tauran Union was precisely what High Admiral Wallenstein wanted, on the not indefensible theory that such a war would serve as a catalyst to turn the Tauran Union into a real country and a great power. That war came to pass, though not by the high admiral's doing and not to the result she wanted. Instead of defeating Balboa and changing its regime, the Tauran forces went for high-value targets that turned into bait for a country-wide ambush. When the smoke had cleared, thousands were dead, and almost twenty thousand Tauran troops were prisoners of the Balboans.

All was not good for Balboa, however. In the course of the battle one of its double handful of stealthy coastal defense submarines managed to sink an aircraft carrier of the Navy of *Xing Zhong Guo*, New Middle Kingdom. This would have been fine, had the carrier actually been involved in the attack on Balboa. It was not; it was evacuating Zhong noncombatants from the fighting. No one knew how many thousands of innocents—men, women, and children— burned or drowned in the attack. And, while at some level the Zhong understood that mistakes can happen and that the fault was partly their own, at another level the popular demand for vengeance has overcome their normally philosophical outlook.

Meanwhile, given the war she had tried to foment, High Admiral Wallenstein was doing her not inconsiderable best to bring the Zhong into it on behalf of the Tauran Union. Inexplicably, the commander of the Balboan *Legion del Cid*, Patricio Carrera, seemed intent on helping her.

# MAJOR DRAMATIS PERSONAE

## in order of appearance:

**Marguerite Wallenstein.** High Admiral of the United Earth Peace Fleet, a fleet of observation in orbit above the Planet of Terra Nova. She acquired her position largely through the actions and intervention of Patricio Carrera. The high admiral is Reformed Druidic Faith, repentant for her previous ("and they were many, oh, *many*") sins. Still, she has a duty to her home planet to keep the barbarians of Terra Nova from breaking into space and trashing her system of government, even though she detests that system.

**Omar Fernandez.** Legate in the *Legion del Cid*. Chief of Intelligence, which includes counterintelligence. Crippled and wheelchair bound by a would-be assassin's bullet. A widower, Fernandez's only child, a daughter, was killed in a terrorist attack. Utterly ruthless and utterly loyal to his country and its war chief.

**Patricio Carrera, Born Patrick Hennessey.** Former officer in the Federated States Army, retired, moved to his late wife's—Linda Carrera de Hennessey's—native country of Balboa, raised an army to avenge the death of her and their children at the hands of Salafi terrorists. Currently commander, or *Dux Bellorum*, *Legion del Cid*, a former private military corporation, now the armed forces of the Timocratic Republic of Balboa

**Jan Campbell.** Captain, intelligence officer from the Anglian Army. Female, and highly decorative. Female, and "more deadly than the male." Campbell authored a report, the Campbell Report, which advised, correctly, that the legion was dangerously

9

tough and large. Ignored then, her star is likely to rise with the
perceived accuracy of her report. Rather, it would except that
Campbell is currently a prisoner of war along with—

**Kris Hendryksen.** Cymbrian Sergeant Major, intelligence, seconded to
the Tauran Union, and captured during the last battle in
Balboa.

**Ricardo Cruz.** Sergeant Major, Second Cohort, Second Infantry
Tercio, *Legion del Cid*. Highly decorated. Battle hardened.
Rather young.

**Khalid.** Druze assassin and spy working for Fernandez, on assignment
to the Tauran Union. Like Druze, generally, Khalid is loyal to
his adopted homeland of Balboa. Pretends to be a Moslem,
most of the time. Good friend of Ricardo Cruz and Rafael
Montoya.

**Achmed Qabaash.** Sumeri, Brigadier, Army of Sumer. Legate, Pro
Tem, *Legion del Cid*. Qabaash commands a brigade in the
Presidential Guard of the Republic of Sumer, which brigade,
sent to help Sumer's ally, Balboa, is appointed Forty-third
Tercio, *Legion del Cid*. Most Balboans who know him would
agree, "Qabaash . . . mean motherfucker . . . glad he's on our
side."

**Bertrand Janier.** Chief of Staff, Tauran Union Combined Staff.
Effective commander, Tauran Defense Agency. Former
commander, Tauran Union Security Force-Balboa. Janier was
once rather overbearing and arrogant. Events have muted
those defects, leaving a superior general officer in their wake.
Why, he's even begun to treat almost like a human being his
long suffering aide de camp.

**The Khans, referred to as Khan, the husband, and Khan, the wife.**
They are members of Wallenstein's staff, highly valued, very
capable. They have some rather odd views of marriage and sex,
by Terra Novan lights, but quite within the mainstream culture

of Old Earth and not all that far out of some subcultures of twenty-first century Earth.

**Blanco.** A black lieutenant of the police in Balboa's neighbor, Santa Josefina. Educated at the military academy of another central Columbian petty state, Blanco is about as military as it gets in demilitarized Santa Josefina. Serves occasionally as a military advisor to his president—

**Angel Calderón.** President of Santa Josefina, Balboa's eastern neighbor. Having no particular vices or virtues, being neither perfectly honest nor unutterably corrupt, he was probably as good a choice for president as had been on offer, for normal times. Sadly for the president, the times are not normal.

**Claudio Marciano.** Tuscan general officer, retired but called back to duty as a compromise candidate to command the Tauran Union Security Force in Santa Josefina. Capable and cynical, he detests most things about demilitarized Santa Josefina and rather admires his official enemy, Balboa. Much loved by the soldiers of the multinational TUSF-SJ, his task is a forlorn one.

**Judy Tipton.** Anglian military wife. Her husband is a prisoner of Balboa. She is, perhaps unwittingly, an asset in the propaganda war between Balboa and the Tauran Union.

**Lydia Gordon.** Anglian military widow. A definite asset in the propaganda war between Balboa and the Tauran Union.

**Rigoberto Puercel.** Legate, commanding Eighth Legion and the *Isla Real*.

**Roderigo Fosa.** Legate and admiral, commanding the *classis*, or fleet, of the legion.

**Rafael de la Mesa.** Sergeant. *Tercio Santa Cecilia*. De la Mesa is crippled and wheelchair bound, and leads a small team of Down's Syndrome affected troops on what is essentially a suicide task, to man a fixed tank turret, defending a portion of a beach, on the *Isla Real*.

**Esmeralda Miranda.** Freed slave from Old Earth. Admiral Wallenstein's cabin girl and stand-in daughter. Very young. Lover of Richard, earl of Care and captain of the UEPF *Spirit of Peace*. Likes Richard. Loves her high admiral as a mother and more. *Hates* the Consensus that rules her planet and *hates* the clan that rules her home province.

**Xingzhen.** Of indeterminate age but painfully beautiful. Empress of *Xing Zhong Guo*, or New Middle Kingdom. Real ruler of the Kingdom. Rather despises most men.

**Raul Parilla.** Old soldier, retired. Former figurehead commander of the *Legion del Cid*. Now the genuine president of the Timocratic Republic of Balboa.

**Marqueli Mendoza.** Wife of Warrant Officer Jorge Mendoza, Ph.D. Author and philosopher in her own right, and, with her husband, one of the two main intellectual architects of the Timocratic Republic. Seconded to the propaganda ministry for some educational work in support of the war effort. The essence of pure feminine charm in a very compact package.

**Richard, earl of Care.** Captain of the UEPF *Spirit of Peace*. Foisted on Wallenstein as a sop to the ruling class of Old Earth. Fairly competent but advanced too young and knows it. In love with the ex-slave girl, Esmeralda. Much cared for by Wallenstein, because fundamentally decent despite the class that bore him and raised him.

**Cass Aragon.** Warrant Officer, intelligence, assigned to Santa Josefina. Female, tall, slender, and light skinned, she blends in perfectly with the Santa Josefinan norm.

**Hamilcar Carrera.** Cadet, Twenty-ninth Cadet Infantry Tercio. Seconded to Thirty-seventh Cadet Cazador Tercio. Son of

Patricio Carrera and Lourdes, Patricio's second wife. Worshipped by a tribe of pagan Pashtun as "Iskandr," the reincarnation of Alexander and a god in his own right. He has already fought and bled for the cause, though quite young. "I am not a god, Pili . . . I'm just a boy."

**Pililak.** Also called, Ant. One of Hamilcar's twelve Pashtun wives. Very gutsy girl, defiant to a fault, but dedicated to her god.

**Victor Chapayev.** Legate, commanding the *Academia Militar Sergento Juan Malvegui* (now become the Twenty-ninth Cadet Infantry Tercio). Ex-Volgan para, who came over with Colonel Samsonov and the Three-fifty-first Tsarist-Marxist Guards Airborne (now Twenty-second *Paracaidista* Tercio, *Legion del Cid*). Fought with Carrera in Santander. Son-in-law to—

**Muñoz-Infantes.** Commander of the Castilian contingent of the old Tauran Union Security Force-Balboa. Defected, with his battalion, to Balboa.

**Lourdes Nuñez de Carrera.** Carrera's second wife. Tall, slender, huge eyed, multilingual. An independent thinker and brave; she is a she bear in defense of her family. She, personally, foiled a coup against her husband and Parilla.

**Alena Cano, AKA, Alena the Witch.** First Pashtian of her tribe to recognize Hamilcar as Iskandr. Married into the legion at a young age. Husband is Tribune David Cano. No one, least of all she, knows if she's a witch or just supremely insightful. Dedicated to her Iskandr.

**Ignacio Macera.** Tribune, *Legion del Cid*. Serving in *Tercio la Negrita*.

**Ricardo Salas.** Legate, commanding *Tercio la Negrita*.

**Matthias Esterhazy.** Legate at large. Former Sachsen *Fallschirmstuermpioniere*. Signed on with the legion early. Has a very full plate: alternates between diplomatic duties, comptrolling, investing for the legion, and doing occasional engineering work.

**Larry Triste.** Senior Balboan intelligence operative. Legionary rank unknown.

**Wu Zixu.** Major. Imperial Marines, *Xing Zhong Guo*.

**Liu.** Captain (Naval). Commanding *Xing Zhong Guo* Dynasty-class attack submarine, *Mao Zedong*.

# PROLOGUE

**High Admiral's Conference Room, UEPF *Spirit of Peace*, in orbit over Terra Nova**

Wallenstein sat at one end of a conference table crowded with computer terminals manned by intelligence and communications personnel. Behind them sat the Zhong empress, aboard ship officially as a courtesy. Still other Old Earth spacefarers updated old-fashioned maps and charts temporarily affixed to the conference room's walls. Between the latter, and above the screens and heads of the former, a wide screen Kurosawa television, purchased below and mounted here as better than anything Old Earth was likely to produce, showed split images of the action taking place below.

Tall, slender, blond, blue-eyed, and rather pretty, Wallenstein looked maybe a sixth of her roughly two centuries of life. She'd have looked younger still, except that sleep had come hard of late; hard, light, and often interrupted. There was just too much to fear.

One of the images of the planet below was relayed by the UEPF ship, *Spirit of Harmony*, a sister to *Spirit of Peace*, and one of only four in the spirit-class of starships. This image was of the waters and islands off the northern coast of Balboa.

Wallenstein concentrated on a ray-shaped island, the centermost and largest of the group, the *Isla Real*. It was swathed in smoke, some of it from explosions though more of it came from the smoldering, splintered trees and ruined, charred buildings of the island fortress. Some, too, came from the flickering wrecks of vehicles, many of which had been identified and destroyed despite the defenders' best efforts at concealing them. There were also two freighters, small ones, sunk in the island's shallow coastal waters, where they'd been delivering defensive materiel. The fires in these had burned out, or, rather, been put out by the Balboans as they recovered most of the materiel the freighters had been carrying and ferried it to shore.

Though Marguerite Wallenstein could not, of course, smell it, much of that smoke carried with it the aroma of long pig, done to a turn.

The Zhong, whose invasion fleet was massed to the north, had quite limited ability to launch airstrikes against the fortress, amounting to no more than two and a half sorties per plane, per day, from their two small carriers' compliment of eighteen, each, Sergeyevich-83s. Even that was reduced by the three dozen's ready rate of about sixty-six percent. A mere fifty tons a day was all the Zhong could deliver to the target.

Wallenstein knew for a fact that the Zhong had enquired with the Federated States as to buying one of their old mothballed battleships, the last in the world. "It'll make a great tourist attraction and hotel," the Zhong had insisted. The FSC hadn't bought a syllable of that, but had instead pointed out that restoring one of the old behemoths to active duty was a matter of years, not weeks, while training crews from scratch could take years more, given that no Zhong in history had ever even sailed in one. "No, having had some long deceased old man on deck for the surrender of Yamato doesn't count."

Beyond the Zhong's meager fifty tons a day, more, much more, came from the Tauran Union. Their combined air forces had flown several hundred of the most modern combat aircraft out of Santa Josefina, to the east of Balboa. About two hundred sorties a day, each day's carrying nearly a thousand tons, had been devoted to reducing the island over the last six weeks.

Wallenstein had her doubts about the effectiveness of either Zhong or Tauran efforts. Yes, they'd managed to do some damage, she conceded. But . . .

*But that island is like they took Old Earth's Maginot line, anchored one end on Hill 287, then wrapped the entire line around the island in a spiral.*

Still, the aerial attack wasn't a complete waste. She could see the tilted or peeled-open wreckage of eleven of the sixteen triple-gun turrets that had come under attack. These turrets, mounting three 152mm guns each, had been salvaged from mostly worn-out Volgan heavy cruisers, then mounted atop a series of concrete positions ringing the island on all sides. Three to four ammunition bunkers, connected to the guns by light rail, complimented each turret. The rails, in turn, connected to the island's light railway, a 600mm gauge system that had originally been thought to be merely a cheap way to move troops to training, but had proven its worth in other respects as it contributed to final preparations to defend the island. The rail was a twisted ruin now, too, marked by shattered ties, cratered substrate, and the rusting wrecks of steel bridging. That said, the rail had run through a concrete revetted trench protecting it. This had made wrecking it several times harder than it would have otherwise been.

*The son of a bitch built it,* fumed Marguerite, *intending that it be used to beef up a defense. He was preparing for this all along, for at least ten years. He wanted this war, or needed it, more even than I did. And that preparation, as ruthless as any in human history, has us behind the power curve. I'd say he's been out-decision cycling us except that I know that he sneers at the concept. No . . . he's just had the initiative, even when it looked like we had it. And that's not quite the same thing.*

Again Marguerite turned her attention to the wrecked triple-gun turrets. There was no doubt that they were out of the fight. Nor was there any doubt about targeting them. The only real question had been whether or not they should have taken out the five facing the city.

Janier, in Gaul, had explained it thusly: "In fact, while there is no doubt a fire direction center for each of those turrets, the turrets don't need one; they can always direct lay. Second, even if they did need it, it's either under the guns or out in one of the bunkers, or hidden somewhere completely different. In short, we cannot with certainty render the guns useless by going after their FDCs.

"Another option is to go after the ammunition bunkers. The problem there is that the guns almost certainly have some ready ammunition in well-protected magazines below them. Then, too, the ammunition bunkers are camouflaged, hence harder to see and harder to hit. Worse, they are better protected than the turrets, which are only well armored to their fronts. Yes, the Balboans poured some concrete on top. Trust me here; it's not enough. Finally, there are more of the ammunition bunkers. You can waste four sorties to get all the bunkers with individual deep penetrators, or one to get the guns.

"Go for the guns."

*Which is all well and good and logical*, thought Wallenstein. *But in dealing with Carrera we have always done the well and good and logical. And it never worked out. I do not think that's because he is a genius, exactly, so much as he's a ruthless son of a bitch with some foresight, while we are idiots. We just don't think the same way, not even Janier who is part of the same general culture as Carrera. So we cannot predict him well, while he seems incapable of not predicting us. Why? Because we are predictable. That, and because we are manipulable.*

*Or perhaps it is just something in the nature of war that a barbarian warrior understands instinctively, but which we cannot quite grasp.*

*I wish I felt better about all this. But I don't; I can't, because I cannot see or even guess at what the enemy is doing or has planned. All I know is that there will be something and we will not like it. Like the fucking "five minute bombs." The TU* really *didn't like those.*

The left side of the screen showed a much larger scale view of the *Mar Furioso*, the ocean off Balboa's northern coast. It was in large enough scale, and a small enough section of the screen, that the Zhong fleet was invisible but for computer-drawn circles around its ships, battlegroups, and amphibious and support flotillas.

One skimmer—reusable, stealthy recon drones used by the Peace Fleet—off of *Harmony* was engaged in following the Zhong fleet. Thus, Wallenstein could, at need, get a close up of the main fleet or, within a short span, any of its subordinates. Another, flown from the same source, kept a close watch on the island. That latter was a tougher job, since the Balboans had lofted to one thousand meters above ground some seventy-six quite large barrage balloons. There were on steel cables to make a pilot's life exciting and difficult; also—should said pilot come too low—short.

The Taurans had tried taking those down. It hadn't worked. Each was anchored at three widely separated spots. Get one anchor point and the severed cable trailed the ground until it was recovered, mended, had a new piece grafted on where needed, and was then dragged right back to its anchor point. They'd shot down several balloons, which was an easy trick. Then the Balboans had promptly carted another balloon to the apex junction, attached it, filled it, and lifted it. They seemed to have no real shortage, either. Some of the balloons seemed also to carry cameras. Khan the husband assured her that said cameras could not have given Balboa more than one hundred and thirteen kilometers of vision across the sea, except for the one atop Hill 287, which would give fifteen kilometers more than that. In fact, it was a little more than that, still, since the ships had height as well. In any case, as the intel chief said, "What can they do with the knowledge?"

*What indeed?* wondered the high admiral, with a knot in her stomach.

The risk came in not only from the cables, but from the antiaircraft mines that some of them carried, those that were not carrying cameras. These were light antiaircraft missiles, IR guided, that were mounted to boxes containing acoustic sensors. At least once, a Tauran fighter, going for a balloon, had had the bad luck of being tracked acoustically, which is to say passively, and then gotten an explosion not far behind, followed by a continuous rod ripping through one wing. The pilot hadn't survived, so far as was known, though she'd been seen to eject.

That, given that the Tauran Union had—amidst the enthusiastic popping of champagne corks and much hand-clapping—previously declared absolute air supremacy, twice, had proved most humiliating.

Eventually, in part to avoid further humiliation, they'd given up the antiballoon effort as a waste of time, money, and effort.

"Lead elements of the Zhong fleet coming close enough to show on the main screen, if we pan out, High Admiral," announced one of the Class Four petty officers manning the computer that controlled the main screen.

"No," said Wallenstein, "wait. The Zhong Fleet will do whatever they'll do. *I* want to keep a close watch on the island."

Marguerite was dozing sitting up when Khan nudged her. Placing a cup of coffee, sweet but black, in her hand, he bent down and whispered, "The Zhong are filling the landing boats now."

She gulped then, suddenly awake, half from the coffee and half from a mix of anticipation and fear, Marguerite spent a few seconds blinking away the residue of sleep. Then she looked at the left-hand screen where, yes, landing craft were beginning to form in moving circles and ovals, the circles and ovals themselves part of a larger pattern of formations. She saw that Xingzhen, the Zhong empress, was watching the proceedings intently.

At the push of a button by Khan, the left and center sections of the main screen joined, even as the island and fleet swam away. Now she could see the whole thing unfolding. Khan added in the graphics, turned over to the Taurans by the Zhong, that made a great deal more sense of the formations into which the Zhong were shaking themselves. They looked to be about thirty kilometers from land.

The normally secretive to the point of paranoid Zhong had given up the operational graphics only because they needed Tauran air support and didn't want a friendly fire incident with their allies of the moment.

While the Zhong didn't have much in the way of naval aviation, they did have a fair amount of naval gunfire to throw in in support of their landing force, including a decent light cruiser. No doubt other nations had sneered at them for decades for it, too, since naval gunfire just wasn't sexy like the missiles and carrier aircraft of other first rate nations' navies. In this particular case, though, NGS was just what the doctor ordered. Of the eighty-odd destroyers and frigates in the Zhong Navy, sixty were with the expedition. Of those, thirty-seven remained behind to screen the fleet against the nasty little submarines Balboa was known to have, while twenty-three steamed to within range of the shore defenses. Range, for the 100mm guns that were the almost universal standard for the Zhong Navy, was a theoretical seventeen kilometers, but a practical dozen.

This wasn't the first time the Zhong had used naval gunfire; they'd been intermittently pounding away for weeks. But this was the largest show to date, with fire blossoming over the azure sea from dozens of guns, and the target beaches being even more enveloped in smoke than they had been.

The Zhong, unbeknownst to Wallenstein and the Taurans, had seriously considered using chemical agents on the beaches. They'd given up the notion on the presumption that Balboa's elaborate fixed defenses would probably provide better defense than anything the Imperial Marines could carry on their backs, while the Balboans just might be able to retaliate. Chemicals were, after all, some of the easiest war materiels to produce.

The Taurans had dedicated three hundred sorties to a pre-landing preparation of the island. That was not small change, those roughly two thousand tons. But, it was generally agreed, the Taurans had to do their business and leave before the Zhong reached within two kilometers of the beaches. Otherwise, the world, fate, God, Murphy (who, it was well known, had emigrated to Terra Nova in the first wave), or the emperor Mong, whom the Zhong and Anglians both disowned, would fuck somebody.

With the ovals and circles at sea straightening now into deadly arrows, pointed not-quite-straight at the beaches, the Taurans half darkened the sky. They lashed down not only at the landing beaches, but at half a dozen others as heavily, and eleven more a bit more lightly, for the deception value. Known, or believed to be known, artillery positions got a special pasting.

Generally speaking, Wallenstein was surprised at the fury of the Tauran assault.

*My cousins have apparently got a few grudges from the Five Minute Bomber raids.*

The Zhong and Taurans had, if anything, been overly cautious about the use of the latter's airpower in proximity to the former's unarmored Marines. While the first wave of landing craft was eight hundred meters offshore, the last of the Tauran strikers was flying east toward their bases in Santa Josefina.

To smoke was now added a considerable cloud of dust raised by the bombs. Most of the island could not be seen with the naked eye or unaided camera.

"Switching to thermal imaging," Khan announced. The screen went blank, then red, then to a mix of stark black and red. It took a bit of time for both mind and eyes to adjust.

"Narrow focus on the island and the leading wave," Wallenstein commanded. "Order *Harmony* to bring the skimmer in lower, and have them prep another in case we lose this one."

"Aye, aye, High Admiral," said one of the communications boffins. Communication was nearly instantaneous, while the skimmer was close in any case. The focus of the crew and their commander narrowed considerably as the first waves of the Zhong Marines splashed ashore.

"What's that?" Wallenstein asked, as the skimmer approached a tilted triple turret.

"We've got lasing!" a petty officer announced. "Lasing from the whole northern coast. Lasing from the balloons. Lasing from Hill 287. Lasing . . ."

The room shook with an inarticulate cry of despair from the Zhong empress. She saw what Khan saw, and had divined the meaning just as quickly.

"It's a gun; I'd guess an eighteen-centimeter gun," Khan said, his voice heavy with defeat. "On a railway carriage. It came from one of the ammunition bunkers we didn't attack. I think . . . I think there are going to be a lot of them. And they're not lasing for its own sake." Tonelessly, hopelessly, he added, "Empress, you should tell the Zhong Fleet to retreat . . . High Admiral, tell her." Khan's chin sank onto his chest. "But, of course, it's too late for that, isn't it?"

# PART I

# CHAPTER ONE

Strike at the enemy with humane treatment as
effectively as with weapons.
—Alexander Suvarov

**The Tunnel, *Cerro Mina,* Balboa, Terra Nova**

There was still a smell of rifle smoke in the air, and broad bands of color in the skies. The latter came from buildings still burning in the city. Past the smoke and fire-lit, scattered clouds, the moon Hecate was in the constellation of the Leaping Maiden. With barely a glance at the familiar sight, Fernandez rolled his wheelchair through the widely agape, badly perforated steel doors leading down into the tunnel. Even with the power up again, and clean cooled air flowing, the place still reeked of smoke and, especially, of burnt human flesh. Still, there was hope that the fire had not penetrated the steel files and safes. Of course, that hope dimmed slightly as teams recovered the crisped bodies and brought them topside, to lay them out alongside the hundreds of other bodies atop this fortified hill overlooking *Ciudad* Balboa.

Fernandez's hope was dashed as one of his assistants pulled open a sliding file draw, revealing to him a mass of thermite-crisped ruin.

"They're all like this, Legate," said the underling. "Here and at Building Fifty-nine. Whatever else the Taurans fucked up, they made sure to burn their intel files and especially the files of their spies in our forces and country. We can't even tell which files are what, to see how big their organization was."

"Fuck," muttered Fernandez. He'd always had a few double agents and the mistress of the Tauran commander on his payroll, plus a couple of Tauran Union troops who were sympathetic to the Timocracy. And his organization had identified perhaps a score or so of spies.

*The problem, though, is that I know about maybe twenty, who are being rounded up even as I sit here, but I suspect hundreds. Damn, I needed those files. I can calculate to my heart's content, but it's all bullshit without something concrete to work with. And the fucking Taurans are good at this sort of thing; none of the people I know about are going to have a clue about any of the others. Shit! And I still haven't been able to get someone convincingly on the crew of Rocaberti, up in the Federated States. Paranoid motherfuckers.*

"Could be worse, Legate," the underling reminded. "We got their payrolls, after all, and the counterfeits are ready."

### Cristobal, Balboa, Terra Nova

It was a simple calculation really. Carrera needed X-many days to finish his preparations. There were Y-many Tauran prisoners to return. There were only Z-many that Carrera was willing to return, which was a number much less than Y. Parilla had promised the return of one hundred per day. Z over X, however, was less than one hundred per day. Even stretching it out by including Tauran noncombatants wasn't quite going to equal one hundred times the days needed.

"So fuck 'em," said Patricio Carrera, watching as the crew of an Anglian-flagged container ship, fitted out as a hospital ship, loaded the fifty-seven badly wounded Tauran POWs. The hospital ship claimed to be, and possibly even was, owned and run by a humanitarian nongovernmental organization. In the Tauran Union, however, what appeared to be and was billed as nongovernmental was often anything but.

"We'll give them however many we feel like," Carrera continued, "in order to stretch out the truce. And no more. Besides, we're just incompetent jungle rats, incapable of keeping to a schedule." He closed by repeating, "Fuck 'em."

The Anglian humanitarians doing the loading were enough that they didn't need any help from the legion. This was to the good as Carrera's troops, plus the numerous civilians who worked the port, were fully engaged on either side of the container ship unloading four Balboan-owned freighters that had docked in the last three days, bringing in over a hundred thousand tons of war materials between them.

Another nineteen ships were docked at the port of Balboa, disgorging the first of an eventual half-million tons—food, assemblies, fuel, building material, ammunition, personal items, major end items, medical supplies, replacement parts . . . basically everything needed for an army of four hundred thousand to fight a major war. Still other ships were being unloaded at other, smaller ports in the coastal interior of the country. One biggie and a couple of coasters were unloading their cargoes by the *Isla Real*. A couple of smallish ships, no more than five thousand tons displacement, sat idly by, doing nothing but spurring commentary.

Not that the Balboans paid no attention to the prisoners they were returning. Rather, legion medical personnel sufficient to provide care for the fifty-seven stayed with them right until the moment that the Taurans signed for them. The Tauran skipper, on the other hand, had orders to pick up one hundred. Infuriated at being shortchanged, he stormed up to Carrera demanding the rest.

"Fuck you," Carrera had replied, genially, setting the captain to sputtering, impotent fury. "You're in no position to make demands. You get what's here. If you annoy me, tomorrow there may be even fewer or none. Explain that to the bureaucratic swine you report to."

"It's not right to use wounded men like this, like bargaining chips," the Anglian insisted.

"It's not right to attack a country without a declaration of war, in the middle of the night," Carrera countered.

"Two wrongs don't make a right," the Anglian quoted.

"Who's interested in making a right," Carrera sneered. "I'm just telling you to fuck off and quit bothering me, and stop your silly moral preening, or I won't give you back anybody."

*I am, in any case, not giving you back a single uncrippled infantryman, artilleryman, engineer, or tanker. Nor are you getting back too many intelligence shits, lest they have seen and then reveal something I don't want revealed. Of course, I will give you back a couple who have seen things Fernandez has arranged for them to see.*

The weasel-faced Omar Fernandez was Carrera's intelligence chief, which meant he was also responsible for the propagation of certain disinformation. Though bound to a wheelchair by a would-be assassin's bullet, there remained nothing wrong with his brain. He was also amazingly ruthless, even more so than his boss.

### Parilla Line, South of *Ciudad* Balboa and south of the *Rio Gatun*, Balboa, Terra Nova

Eighty-odd Tauran POWs, under the command of their own, swung picks and shovels, or held open sandbags for the latter, in a broad ditch now approaching half a dozen feet deep, just north of a thin wire fence, itself north of a thick belt of concertina. The space between the two was alleged to be mined. None of the laboring POWs doubted that enough to test the theory. There were two other groups of POWs engaged in the same work.

Though under their own command, the Taurans were guarded by Balboan legionaries in their own pixelated jungle-striped uniforms and bearing the legion's own battle rifle. The Taurans had been allowed to keep their national uniforms, of which there were at least half a dozen on display in this group, alone.

Though it was still being worked on, the main line had been built years before. Centrally located, it was sheltered behind the swift-flowing, steep-banked river that fed the two lakes that fed the Transitway. To all appearances, it was oriented toward the north, with a presumption of an invasion from that direction having either taken or bypassed the capital of *Ciudad* Balboa. An invader coming from that direction would have run, first, into the stream. Moving farther south, presupposing he managed to cross that, there were some thick wire obstacles, currently being made thicker; broad, high-density minefields; and several layers of mutually supporting bunkers connected by tunnel and trench. Behind these came the *Cordillera* Central, the mountain range that ran like a spine down the length of Balboa's quarter-rotated S-shape. This had been partially hollowed out and tunneled through.

On the other slope, the reverse slope, there were a few positions and some entrenching to guard against an attack, probably airmobile, from the rear. From those bunkers and trenches still more trenches ran down to twenty-three very large, very solid bunkers, mostly of the cut-and-cover variety. Except for the degree to which man and nature had conspired to hide them, that, and the enormous size, they resembled nothing so much as Sachsen Christmas cakes, or *Stollen*, much as the *Legion del Cid* had used in a Sumeri valley between Multichucha Ridge and Hill 1647, over a decade before.

From the trees, older and newer, that covered the Parilla Line hung a fantastic number of metalicized strips. Some strips were older and, torn and tarnished, looked it. Others were brand new. Most were somewhere in between.

"What the hell are those things?" asked Anglian Captain Jan Campbell, of her chief NCO, Cimbrian Army Sergeant Major Kris Hendryksen. She was pointing with her finger at something down in the ditch. Her nose and chin pointed elsewhere.

She, heart-faced, blue-eyed, short, shapely—extravagantly shapely, as a matter of fact—and blond, was a late entry captain in the Anglian Army, once seconded to the Tauran Union Security Force-Balboa, which force was now extinct, prisoners where not dead. He, larger, of course, was a Viking, now letting his face go to beard. He was also, though some miracle of slave-capturing genetics on another planet entirely, tanning much better than she was, or indeed, than any of them but the couple of Tuscans in the group.

She and Hendryksen were lucky to be alive, having just managed to get away from the old Tauran headquarters at *Cerro Mina* before the Balboans troops had taken it. Ordinarily, they could just have surrendered. Hendryksen, being male, had figured out that was a bad idea, after the wounding and deaths of hundreds of Balboan female infantry on the hill's northern slope and the broad boulevard beyond. To Campbell, being female, it had simply not occurred that normal male soldiers would take any exceptionally dim view of the killing of female combatants. Hendryksen had understood his own sex better than she had. Plunging into an orgy of massacre and mutilation in revenge for the losses to *Tercio Amazona*, the legion's females-only infantry regiment, the legionaries had left hardly anything alive atop the hill, and burned alive or suffocated those who'd sheltered in the underground complex beneath it.

The metalicized strips lay on the ground as well. Hendryksen picked one up and, after checking the ends to make sure it was a whole strip, measured it by eye. He then checked another, determining that it was precisely half the length of the first.

"My guess," he said, "and it's only a guess, though an educated one, is that these are designed to screw with ground-penetrating radar. Maybe also the global-locating system, but I don't know enough about that. That they're a deliberate defensive measure, though, seems certain."

"Do the Balboans *do* anything that is not a 'deliberate defensive measure'?" Campbell asked, pointing with her nose at the menacing firing ports of the bunkers nearby and running up the slope. So far as she could tell, the bunkers were at least mostly empty, their nominal occupants currently guarding the detail of eighty or so Tauran POWs, digging a ha-ha under Campbell's command.

"They have us digging this ha-ha to keep the animals out of the minefields," Hendryksen said. "Naturally, that is its only purpose. It wouldn't do as an antitank ditch, or we would not be digging it, since we are not to be used in aiding the enemy's war effort."

Campbell shot him a dirty look. "You mean it's a ha-ha on the surface, so they don't feel compelled to shoot us for refusal to work on an antitank ditch?"

"See, that's why you're an officer and I'm just a—"

"Can it, Kris."

Smiling, satisfied with the jab, the sergeant major shut up. In the silence, Campbell continued studying what she could see of the defensive line.

"Formidable enough," was her judgment, a judgment in which Hendryksen largely concurred.

"Hard to flank, too," he said, "being anchored on the lake, I imagine, at one end and probably with a refused flank off in the jungle somewhere, at the other."

"Take it from behind?" she asked.

"Maybe, if in force, especially on the ground. I wouldn't count on the chances of an airmobile assault doing the job; the Balboans appear to be pretty much death on people who try to get fancy with them."

"They're not above getting 'fancy' themselves," she observed.

"True," Hendryksen agreed, "but they've definite limits."

"Why this?" Campbell asked. "When their major enemy, us, was bound to come from the Shimmering Sea side, why have this line facing the *Mar Furioso*?"

"It's still just an educated guess," he answered, "but my guess is port capacity."

"Huh?"

"There's essentially no way that an invasion coming from the Shimmering Sea side can get to the capital city until the port of Cristobal falls. Though they haven't let us see it, I'd bet a month's pay against yours that Cristobal can also be turned into a fortress, or is being turned into one, in short order. Thus, there *is* no real threat from the south. They think."

"We're no logistic slouches, ourselves," she said, "even if we won't commit the resources to it the Federated States will."

"Right," he agreed. "We probably could isolate Cristobal and supply over the shore a large enough force to besiege that city and take this line from behind. But I don't think they know that."

Jan was skeptical. "Why not?" she asked.

"Because Carrera's not a Marine nor, so far as we've ever been able to determine, has he ever done any major Logistics Over The Shore work."

"Oh." Though she was loathe to admit it, Jan had never done any LOTS work either.

"Wouldn't have to be just LOTS," said a nearby, tall and beefy, ruddy-faced Sachsen in a pause for breath between lifting shovelfuls of dirt to a sandbag. "There's a good port at *Puerto Lindo*, and one almost as good at Nicuesa to the west. Can't really use that last one, though."

"Why not?" Hendryksen asked.

"Add fifty miles to the supply line and need three divisions to guard the route," said the Sachsen. "I doubt the port could support more than two, with the increased need for trucking, so it would be a net loser. Even if the Tauran Union could muster the extra divisions, which it probably cannot. Worse, the road from Cristobal to Nicuesa is dirt, which is to say mud, most of the year. It may not be even theoretically possible to supply much of anyone from there without putting in an entirely new road.

"On the other hand, two brigades could probably secure the place to use as a supply dump, from which we could support a fair force further east by small boat and hovercraft."

"And you are?" asked Hendryksen. He already knew the Sachsen wasn't from his and Campbell's group. Since the Sachsen was also shirtless, he had no clue as to rank.

"Kapitänleutnant von Bernhard, at your service," said the Sachsen, dropping the sandbags and reaching out one hand to shake. "My friends call me 'Richard' or 'Rich.' My ship, the Z186, was in for a lengthy refit, so I was available and got volunteered by my service to work logistics for the TUSF-B. I hadn't been here six weeks before the war started, then I got caught up in the fall of the Transitway. I was almost halfway to the coast where I might have been able to steal a small boat when they caught me."

"Farther than we got," admitted Campbell. "They snagged us in a drainage ditch by the northern end of Brookings Field."

"And we were lucky, at that," said the Cimbrian, "that the group that caught us wasn't feeling bloody-minded."

The foot of Second Cohort, Second Tercio, struggled up the central *cordillera* laden like pack mules, bent over like old, old men. Appropriately, they sang an old song as they climbed:

> . . . *Si mi cuerpo se quedara roto,*
> *Formaría en la legión de honor,*
> *Montaría la guardia en los luceros,*
> *Formaría junto al mejor . . .*

Taking up the rear of his cohort's column, as it struggled over the ridge to the south, Sergeant Major Ricardo Cruz, Second Cohort, Second Tercio, wasn't at first sure he should believe his eyes. But there weren't too many blondes in his country, and none with quite the proportions of the woman he saw standing with a couple of other Taurans. One of whom was—

"Well, hell," Cruz said to Hendryksen, clapping the latter on the shoulder. "I am very pleased you made it." He turned then to Jan Campbell, remembered to salute, and said, warmly, "And you, too, ma'am."

"It was close," said the Cimbrian POW, a sentiment echoed by the Anglian woman.

"Were you on *Cerro Mina*?" Cruz asked in whisper. When they nodded, he said, "It was closer than you know."

"It's true then?" asked Campbell. "Your people killed everything living?"

Cruz shook his head. "No, ma'am, not quite everything. I was able to save a couple. And some of the others kept their heads. Still . . . still . . . it was pretty bad."

"But why?" Hendryksen asked. "Your people are death on the law of war."

"It was what happened to the women, the Amazons, who went in before us. You think you know a group of men . . . but you don't, not until you see them after they see 'their' women shot up. And before you ask, no, it's unlikely anybody is going to be court-martialed over it. Temporary insanity would be the plea, and no jury of ours would convict, while no jury of yours could be trusted."

Cruz turned around then, to see the tail of his column disappearing into the jungle. He dropped his pack, then pulled a can out. This he passed over to Hendryksen who shook it.

"Legionary rum? To what do—"

"Oh, just shut up and take it, you damned Viking!" said Cruz, slinging his heavy pack back across his back. "No promises, but if I get the chance I'll look you up again."

"Thank you, Centurion," answered Campbell warmly. *Why is it the really good ones are already taken?*


### Kaiserswerth, Sachsen, Tauran Union, Terra Nova

Khalid, Fernandez's chief assassin, maintained several homes in the parts of the Tauran Union that fell under his purview, as well as two safe houses, that were out of that purview. One of the safe houses was in Kaiserswerth.

*And will it remain safe after I do this?* wondered Khalid. "This" was something Khalid found truly, nay epically, bizarre, the preparation and placing into the mail of several hundred letters of condolence from the president of the Republic of Balboa, to the next of kin of

Sachsen and Gallic soldiers recently fallen in battle in Balboa, along with—*What the* fuck *are they thinking?*—checks in the same amount, six thousand Federated States Drachma converted into Tauran currency, as was given immediately to the families of Balboa's fallen to tide them over until the regular system of family support and insurance could catch up.

*No real question about how they came up with the information, though. They've got the bodies and they've got the records. Indeed, they know better than the nations of the Tauran Union . . . ohhhh . . . now I get it. Well, best get on with doing up the letters and having the computer sign the checks.*

Khalid, a man more than ordinarily religious in a nation and armed force themselves more than ordinarily religious, looked Heavenward and said, "Allah, I appreciate it that, being a bad man myself, I am, by Your grace, allowed to work for men even more wicked than I. It demonstrates that if there is hope for them then surely there must be hope for me." Then, laughing softly, he began churning out the letters of condolence.

Over the grinding of the printer could be heard, in Arabic, "Wicked, *wicked*, WICKED men!"

*On the plus side, at least they haven't forged letters on official stationary ordering widows out of their military housing . . . ummm . . . yet.*


**Port of Balboa, Balboa, Terra Nova**

Several ships tied up at dock had disgorged little and were not counted among the twenty that had brought in that half-million tons. Oh, they'd given up something, of course. The one labeled *Queenie* on her stern, for example, had vomited up a hundred thousand containerized sacks of rice, then had taken on several hundred other containers before sailing off to Yamato, there to link up with another, similar vessel, the *Quernmore*, where some cargo would be transshipped. Another, a substantial cruise ship that just happened to be in the area—where Carrera, who owned it, had ordered it to be—had been "commandeered," then filled to bursting with young children and a fair complement of adults and older boys to care for them. This ship, the *Emerald of Hibernia*, Balboan registry, was heading to a port in Valdivia, Saavedra, the narrow, mountainous country on the eastern coast of Colombia del Norte. This was partly for the children's safety, partly to reduce the logistic burden within Balboa should the war kick off again, as everyone really expected, partly to get a ship in position to bring back to Balboa the thousand superb mountain infantry Valdivia had offered to help defend Balboa against further Tauran aggression, plus another four national contingents that were of about the same size, equally elite, but less specialized. There was another reason for the trip, entirely, but that playing itself out would take some time.

Once that trip was complete, the *Emerald of Hibernia* was to make a trip down the other coast of Colombia del Norte, and through the Shimmering Sea, to pick up another six contingents, in size ranging from cohort to tercio.

With mothers weeping and rather more dry eyed, and often uniformed, fathers waving, that cruise ship began churning the waters behind it, backing up slowly to where tugs could take over and reorient it to make passage out of the port.

### Herrera International Airport, Balboa, Terra Nova

The bodies, of which there had been very many, were gone, at least. Yet the bloodstains of shattered cadets and fallen Gallic paratroopers remained in the carpets of the terminal. Idly, Carrera thought that, following the war, and assuming they won, those carpets should be collected, preserved, and put on wall display for the enlightenment of future generations. The message? *See here the courage of Balboa's children. Will the sons of her sons show less?*

If the bodies were gone, so were the windows. And with them gone, air conditioning was an exercise in futility. With that gone, the place became an oven and, worse, frankly reeked with the iron-coppery smell of a slaughterhouse.

*Screw this crap*, thought Carrera. Beckoning his sergeant major, Martinez, and his AdC, Santillana, he stomped out of the terminal to the tarmac to await the arrival of a very special contingent of volunteers. Over one shoulder, Martinez carried a case-covered silver eagle on a spiral-carved staff. The Balboans and Sumeris, especially *these* Sumeris, had a mutual admiration society going on and going back to the year 461.

The side of the first of the big airships read, "Republic of Sumer Airlines," in both English and Arabic script. Likewise did the next two. They were painted green, with the lettering white. The last two read differently, for Sumer had only the three airships of its own. They said, "*Aerolineas Balboenses,*" and didn't bother with any other language.

There were different kinds of airships in use across the planet of Terra Nova. Some required extensive ground support to make landing. Others, the most modern types, needed nothing but a flat surface. The two Balboan airships were of the former type. The three Sumeris, funded by lavish oil reserves, were of the latter.

Thus, while the Balboans dropped cables that were picked up by super-heavy vehicles, that dragged the airships to hollowed out docking bays, the Sumeri airships used maneuvering thrusters to come down more smoothly and neatly than perhaps any helicopter was capable of.

*Got to get us some of those . . . when we can afford it,* thought Carrera, admiringly. *Fortunately, Sada said I could hang onto these three until just before the shooting starts. And I do have some uses in mind.*

There was a small parade stand set up a hundred meters from the terminal. On either side of the stand, cameramen from *TeleVision Militar* stood by.

The stand had a sheltering awning and was on wheels so it could be pushed out of the way when not needed. It had already been used three times, to welcome in a cohort of Lempiran Mountaineers, another of Atlacatlan *Cazadores,* and the entire Atzlan Parachute Brigade.

The Lempirans and Atlacatlans thoroughly detested each other. Fortunately, the former, like the Valdivians, were most suitable for attachment to Balboa's Fifth Mountain Tercio while the latter could be sent, and had been sent, to Seventh Legion in Third Corps.

Onto the stand Carrera and his entourage stepped, with Martinez placing the staff of the eagle in a special holder built into the stand. Then they waited, but not for so very long. Nor had they expected to. Qabaash, the commander of this brigade—now this tercio—of the

Sumeri Presidential Guard Division, was an old friend, quite well regarded. If anyone could be counted on to have rehearsed his troops for a snappy exit from the airships and a snappy parade across the airfield, it was him.

Nor *did* the Sumeri disappoint. On cue—Carrera was certain it was on cue—every ramp on each of the five airships dropped, disgorging one or a few Sumeri guardsmen. Six of them bore colors and about thirty had guidons. He could see Qabaash emerge, too, followed by his immediate staff and his command's colors. Carrera's eyes were beginning to get old and difficult, and the heat shimmer off the tarmac didn't help a bit, but he was pretty sure he saw someone with a radio on his back, too.

*Well, just decent planning, that.*

Again on cue, and again from every exit, the rest of Qabaash's command surged, only this time it was like a mosque—or thirty of them—opening the doors following Friday services. A veritable wave of armed, uniformed Sumeris rolled across the airfield before beginning to separate out into the six major cohorts of the about to be formed Forty-third Tercio. It was all visually rather impressive. It was all also being recorded for later broadcast by Professor Ruiz's organization, which was broadly concerned with morale and propaganda, along with certain aspects of education.

Though the troops and organization certainly had extensive baggage still in the holds of their airships, little beyond packs and rifles was in evidence. That little included a bagpipe band, with some drums. At Qabaash's order, that band picked up a tune the Sumeris had learned from the *Legion del Cid*, in and around the town of Ninewah, "*Boinas Azules Cruzan la Frontera.*" Then, on a drum signal, the entire mass marched forward on line until Qabaash was within speaking range of Carrera.

Halting, Qabaash saluted, then quoted an old proverb, loud enough for all of his officers and most of his men to hear, "'If a pot is cooking, a friendship will stay warm.' Thank you for inviting us to the feast, *Duque*! First Brigade, Sumeri Presidential Guard, Forty-third Tercio, *Legion del Cid*, reports for duty!"

# CHAPTER TWO

The first principle of deception is to aim to strengthen an opponent's preconceptions.

—Anthony Clayton,
*Forearmed: A History of the Intelligence Corps*

### Tauran Defense Agency, Lumière, Gaul, Terra Nova

The air of mourning hadn't gone away yet. Janier wondered if it ever would. Officers and noncoms walked sullenly and silently through the marble corridors of the headquarters, heads down, and fearful as if they expected something like clawed arms to emerge from the walls and drag them off to perdition. Even the head of the agency, Elisabeth Ashworth, was making herself scarce, and she was universally believed to be far too ignorant to understand even the obvious aspects of the disaster.

Janier had, if anything, even more to mourn. His reputation was in ashes, true, but worse than that, his self-image was utterly cast down. He felt so low, so inadequate, so much the crux of an elaborate lie—*My whole life a lie!*—that not only had he not donned his reproduction uniform and baton of a marshal of Napoleonic France, he had, just this morning, burned both on a pyre outside his window. Even now, looking out the window, he could occasionally glimpse a swirling fragment of smoldering cloth or a bit of wood ash, spiraling up with the breeze.

Janier's much-abused aide de camp, Malcoeur, had actually shed tears as flames had begun to race across the gasoline-soaked blue cloth, with its elaborate embroidery of hundreds of gold oak leaves and wavelike piping. The jacket alone had cost Janier forty-six hundred Tauros. The baton, with its thirty-two fourteen karat gold eagles had cost more.

And then, wonder of wonders, after the fire had done its main work and a stiff and bitter Janier had left the scene, the AdC had gotten on hands and knees to recover the gold that had dropped down from uniform and baton. To keep? No. He placed the misshapen lumps in an old black lacquered box he'd apparently paid for himself, then left that on Janier's desk.

*Why would that toad, Malcoeur, care?* Janier wondered. *It's totally inexplicable and illogical. I treat him worse—much worse, as a matter of fact—than my dog. And he weeps for my pain? I do not understand it. Worse, if after all that, and all my failures, the toad still cares for me . . . then I am even more unworthy than I had thought. Shit.*

*Well . . . no . . . I can't deal with that concept. Let's just let it go with the notion that he's weeping for our defeat, not for my defeat. Otherwise, I'd start acting like a girl, too.*

While he still faced the window and the bitter ashes—literal ashes—of his defeat and humiliation, a knock came from behind. He spun his chair around with no great haste to see Malcoeur standing by the door, a thick wad of file folders under his left arm.

"What is it, Malcoeur?" the general asked, not ungently.

"Intel reports from the Old Earthers, *Mon General*," the aide replied. "Since we aren't allowed to . . ."

Janier, with the fatalism and pseudo-courage of the career-dead, supplied the rest, "Since our political masters, in fear of their political lives should the war kick off again, won't do a damned thing to so much as annoy the Balboans, the Peace Fleet is our only source of intelligence."

"Yes, sir. That."

"Well . . . set them down," Janier said. He had a sudden thought, one he voiced as, "No man ought to have to look at this crap completely sober, Malcoeur. Why don't you go down to the basement and tell the club to deliver to us a bottle of Adourgnac, along with two glasses."

## Bar *El Mono Loco*, Aserri, Santa Josefina, Terra Nova

A young woman named Maura screamed as her boyfriend drove the jagged edge of his broken bottle into the stomach of the Tauran and twisted, then ripped to the right. His victim, a Tuscan sapper, likewise screamed at first, as the glass made a hash of his innards. Then, in a state of shock, the sapper's scream turned to a groan. He turned ghastly white as his intestines, accompanied by a surge of blood, spilled out through his torn abdomen. The intestines unlooped themselves as they slid slowly to the floor, even as the Tuscan sank to his knees.

"Try to steal *my* girl, eh, motherfucker?" said the Santa Josefinan, releasing his ad hoc butcher's tool as he stepped back away from the spreading pool of gore and air of spilled shit and blood. Mouth gaping, the Tuscan looked up with eyes rapidly going blank. The Santa Josefinan lifted his foot from the ground, placed the bloody sole on the Tuscan's forehead, and pushed. The sapper went over backwards, ending up with his back on the bloody floor and the lower half of his legs folded under him.

"Come on, Manuel," said one of the Santa Josefinan's companions, Marco. "You gotta get outa here before the police come."

"Police?" asked Manuel.

"Yeah, dude, *police*. That Tauro motherfucker's dead or as good as dead. You sliced him bad, dude. You gotta get out of here and go into hiding."

"Yeah . . . but . . . but, *no*. Man . . . Marco, you *saw* he was hitting on Maura. He had no right . . ."

"Manuel, snap out of it. Don't matter about rights. The Tauros got the money, the guns, and own the government. You have got to get outa here."

"But where do I go?" asked Manuel.

"Balboa, man. Cross over the border tonight. But for now you have got to get out of here."

Under his friend Marco's prodding, Manuel let himself be led out of the bar and toward Marco's car, waiting in a nearby alley. Behind them, Maura still screamed. Unheard for all her screaming, the TV in the bar's main room was showing a program entitled, "Our Friends, the Tauran Union."

## High Admiral's Conference Room, UEPF *Spirit of Peace*, In Orbit over Terra Nova.

One of Khan the husband's underlings was droning on while standing in front of the big Kurosawa. Marguerite had mostly tuned him out, even as she wrestled with the implications of the disaster that had unfolded below. The scale of that disaster, so much worse even than she *could* have imagined, made concentration somewhere between difficult and impossible. For example, while one part of her mind knew and saw that the Kurosawa screen at one end of the conference room showed a map of Balboa, from Santander to Santa Josefina, it simply didn't register on the conscious part of her brain.

*Who's to blame?* she wondered. *Anyone that the Balboans haven't already stretched the neck of? Or worse? Do I fault Janier for going along with a plan I'd forced him to come up with, after the politicians made him execute it out of the blue? When nobody expected a war? I don't think I can. Do I believe the confessions the condemned made before they were hanged, blaming that nonentity, Endara-Rocaberti?*

*No, too self-serving. The Balboans wanted him blamed so it was probably someone else. Someone they'll take care of in their own way, I'm sure.*

*Or is it . . . or forget it, all the different twists and turns of the plotting down below have me so I don't have the first clue what to believe or what to expect.*

Marguerite had known all along that she didn't have the background, the training or experience, to run a war on the ground on her own. She had her doubts about her ability to run a war in space, for that matter, though she was probably better qualified than anyone on two worlds. Among those who knew her well, this humility—or realism—was likely her greatest strength.

That said, the skills that got one elevated to her level, in her culture, had little to do with tactical, operational, or strategic skill. Even administrative ability came in a distant second to willingness to prostitute oneself. And even that was usually less important than connections and political acumen. Marguerite sat in the chair she sat in primarily due to chance, a former willingness to whore herself out, and that same political acumen.

*And I'm long since done trading myself—my body—for advantage or, rather, at least not for my own advantage. Once a whore always a whore, I suppose, and if I had to put on the kneepads for my fleet or planet I could.*

*I'd thought chance would fall fairly evenly. And I counted on my political acumen and the things I had to trade getting me what I wanted and what my planet and civilization need.*

*Wrong. Wrong. Wro—*

"High Admiral?" asked the briefing officer, jerking Marguerite back to the present.

"What?"

"You looked distressed for a moment, High Admiral."

"No," she said, circling a hand to indicate that he should, "keep going."

"Yes, High Admiral. As I was saying, the Balboans seem to be playing a shell game. We know that twenty-six large freighters have docked and either begun or finished unloading. We know other ships have come in, picked up passengers, apparently noncombatants, mostly children, and left. We have seen at least one ship load up what we know to be allied troops to bring them to Balboa. We've got other ships hanging around that we don't have a clue about. They're just sitting there.

"Moreover, ma'am, the entire pattern of ocean shipping down below is in turmoil. It's like . . ."

"It's like kicking an ants' nest," Khan, the husband, supplied, from the chair next to Wallenstein. "And I can't tell if it's deliberate—the enemy playing a shell game—or an artifact of the half- or three-quarter-million tons of shipping the Balboans have removed from the stream of commerce for their own purposes. I've got no precedent for it that really suits."

"A couple of things we can be sure of," said the briefer. "The Balboans are digging in like madmen. They'd always had a lot of fixed fortifications, some they inherited from the Federated States and some they built on their own. Those were in four major groupings: Out on the *Isla Real* and the two largish islands near it, a coastal defense line along their *Mar Furioso* coast, most of which was a Federated States relic, the ring around the port of Cristobal, much of which also was a Federated States relic, and this line"—the briefer bent to push a button, which caused the area just south of the *Rio Gatun* to illuminate on the Kurosawa in red—"which they apparently call the 'Parilla Line' and which makes no sense to us. But beyond that they're doing an amazing amount of pick-and-shovel work. Fortification systems that were already powerful are becoming more so, right before our eyes."

"Something else, too, High Admiral," Khan, the husband, said. "While we can find all the old fortifications, we think, the new ones are being built under something that is scrambling our ability to see them. Their heat signature doesn't make them show up as too very different. And they're mostly under triple-canopy jungle, so the skimmers can't see much of anything. We've tried."

"Lidar?" she asked.

"Limited use," Khan answered. "Have to get really low for it to work against targets on the ground. And we'd have to fly around so much we're bound to lose skimmers."

"There is something, though," added the briefer, "that we can see and that's important."

"What's that?" asked Wallenstein,

The Kurosawa lit up a twenty-or-so-kilometer-wide area between the Parilla Line and *Ciudad* Balboa. "This we've taken to calling 'Logistics Base Alpha,' High Admiral."

"How do you know that's what it is?"

"Containers, ma'am. Thousands upon thousands of containers have been unloaded from ships, trucked or airlifted there, and dug in, in no particular pattern, though there have been some inexplicable gaps left."

"That lack of pattern," said Khan, "suggests to me more than anything that this was one area where the Balboans hadn't finished their planning. I think they're just dumping the containers and letting their logistic guys and gals figure out how to bring order from the chaos, which they don't seem to have the wherewithal to do."

"Why do you think so, Khan?" she asked.

"Couple of reasons, High Admiral," Khan answered, "but for one ... Close in on the log base," he told the briefer, "and then illuminate the known medical detachments."

Turning to Wallenstein, Khan explained, "While the Balboans are not above playing fast and loose with the laws of war even as *they* understand them, they take a fairly enlightened view of protecting at least their own wounded. Thus, they've marked all the field hospitals and aid stations they've set up clearly, over the trees, in such a way that the skimmers can see them and even the Taurans could if they ever resume overflights."

Wallenstein looked at the map again, which now showed so many red crosses for field medical facilities that . . . "What the fuck does it mean?"

"We haven't a clue," Khan admitted. "We've run triangulation of those with known Balboan organizational structure and none of it, *none* of it, makes the slightest sense. We've had our own medical people look at it to see if there's any conceivable pattern of casualty treatment and evacuation that fits that mish mash. Nothing quite does. We even ran a copy past the Tauran Defense Agency's C2 bureau. They're as clueless as we are but suggest very strongly that the Balboans are clueless there too, and did just what I said, dump supplies anywhere."

"Are there any indicators that they're trying to reorder those containers into some more sensible configuration?" the high admiral asked.

"Some," Khan said. "There are some standardized configurations showing up, here and there."

"Of what?" Wallenstein asked.

"Not a clue, High Admiral. We get only a tiny thermal signature, and that for no more than a few days before they get the containers insulated and buried. At least I think that's what they're doing. Sensing with radar has proven impossible over wide swaths."

"All right," Marguerite said. "I'll accept your analysis for the moment. What else?"

A circle appeared on the map, east of the capital. "We don't know what they're doing there, High Admiral. Or, rather, we know what but not why. The what is that they're setting up enough tentage to house maybe three hundred thousand people. Could be more. But why? It's completely outside what we think is their last-ditch defensive perimeter."

"Don't ask me," said Wallenstein. "Figuring that out is *your* job. Move on, but *do* figure that out."

"Yes, High Admiral," said the briefing officer, "moving on to, Santa Josefina. The Tauran Union people extracted a promise that Balboa would disband the two units—"

"Units?" she asked. "Define 'units.'"

"Tercios, High Admiral. Big regiments. In any case, the Balboans only went halfway. They took the suborganizations—'cohorts,' they call them, and 'maniples,' and sent them back to parent units, but they didn't reintegrate them down to individual levels. Those cohorts and maniples had reassembled in the vicinity of the city of Cervantes, in the eastern part of the country. I say 'had' because, while one Santa Josefinan regiment is still in that area, the other has disappeared. Oh, their tents are still there but the troops are gone."

"To where?"

"We believe they went home and are waiting for arms to be delivered. Possibly by the regiment that is still intact and in Balboa. Or maybe by sea. Or maybe across Santa Josefina's eastern border. Or maybe all three. Or maybe the arms are already there."

"That last," said Khan, "would not surprise me. The Balboans *do* seem to think ahead."

The understatement of that last set Wallenstein to laughing almost uncontrollably. When she'd recovered enough to speak, she said, "Oh, Commander Khan, I never knew you had such a gift for comedy."

Still wiping at her eyes, Marguerite said, "Esmeralda, honey, please set us up a trip to *Xing Zhong Guo* and Santa Josefina. The latter's president, their whole fucking government, needs a sharp lesson in the limits of disarmed neutrality.

"And see if you can't get General Janier to join us."

### *Casa Presidencial,* Aserri, Santa Josefina, Terra Nova

"They say that they're discharged, Mr. President," said *Teniente* Blanco of Santa Josefina's Public Force, a sort of combined police force, customs agency, coast guard, executive security service, and a few other things that an army, had the country had one, might have done. Blanco, an incongruous name, considering he was black, was both the chief of President Calderón's security detail as well as a kind of military aide. He was, in fact, a graduate of Atlacatl's well-respected military academy, though since then he'd seen nothing really resembling military service. Still, he was as close to a military expert as Calderón had available.

*Or is he? Hmmm.*

"Blanco, have you been keeping in touch with the Tauran force watching the Balboans?"

The lieutenant nodded, saying, "Yes, Mr. President."

"Make me, us, an appointment to talk with General Marciano."

"Here or there, Mr. President?"

"I'd prefer here." When Blanco said nothing, Calderón added, "You don't understand why?"

"No, Mr. President."

"Good," said the president, with some satisfaction.

Marciano really classified Santa Josefinans into two groups: those he detested and those he did not. The former group covered nearly everyone in the country, including the president, his entire party, the opposition party, the other opposition party, the party in opposition to the ruling party and both the other main opposition parties, the Tsarist-Marxists, the anarchists, the street sweepers, the banana harvesters, etc. The latter group included the police, to include Lieutenant Blanco, Marciano's personal housekeeping staff, the KPs in the mess halls, and the Santa Josefinan veterans of Balboa's *Legion del Cid*, which group he was pretty sure he was going to end up fighting, and soon.

Marciano's command, so far, hadn't seen any fighting, barring bar fights between his troops and the Santa Josefinans who resented their competition for the local women. There'd been quite a few of those, at least one of which had turned deadly.

"It's the lackanookie theory of ethnic disharmony," Marciano had judged, saying to his officers and senior noncoms: "This goes to the effect that two groups of men, in real or perceived competition for the same women, will automatically hate each other. I've often paused to wonder how much that's fed various guerilla movements over the ages."

During the Tauran Union's failed invasion, Marciano had gotten his orders to attack into the Balboan province of *Valle de las Lunas* late, almost as if he and his command were an afterthought. By the time he'd been able to get any combat power approaching the Balboan border, the battle had already been lost. At that point, discretion had seemed much the better part of valor. He'd pulled back to his defensive positions, hoping like hell that the Balboans hadn't noticed how close he'd come to invading them.

That was *not* cowardice, but sheer realism. If so much as one of his men had stepped foot, officially, across the border, Balboa would have been perfectly within its rights to turn its entire, *huge*, army against him and Santa Josefina, which had violated the core premise of neutrality, both.

*But,* thought the Tuscan commander, *of course we didn't violate Balboa's borders. We only almost did. And came close enough that they surely intend to get us out of here, too.*

"And that, Mr. President," said the Tuscan, "is why you are screwed. You brought us in, because you had no army of your own, and thought that there would be no consequences. But the Tauran Union had its own agenda, and that agenda has made you an enemy of Balboa."

"But you have ten thousand men or more," said Calderón. "There are, at most, four thousand former Balboan legionaries here."

"I have this," said Marciano, handing over a list of his forces in Santa Josefina. "It's less than eight thousand. It's a nice little package to hold off an open invasion until reinforcements can be flown in, but it's totally inadequate to defeat the guerilla campaign I anticipate. Against that guerilla campaign, reinforcement seems unlikely."

The president read off, "Four infantry battalions, two of them from Gaul, one Anglian, one Sachsen . . . a Tuscan engineer battalion . . . Haarlem artillery battalion with eighteen guns . . . a single tank company from Hordaland and a Cimbrian commando company . . . Götalander air defense . . . Sachsen military police . . . then a mix of everything in the Tauran Union in small packets of this and that . . . what's the problem, General? As far as we know the former legionaries here in Santa Josefina have no arms."

"No arms?" Marciano sneered. "I don't believe that. And even if true, arms are waiting just across the border."

"Then what should I do?" asked Calderón.

"Invent a time machine, then go back and talk yourself out of asking for us?" Marciano suggested. "Failing that, start your own army . . . indeed, you might consider Balboa's return of your sons to be an invitation to do just that, with them . . . and invite us to leave. I'm fairly sure I could talk the TU into giving you the arms we have here, too, if you did that."

"Politically and philosophically impossible!" huffed the president, in high dudgeon.

"Yes, I'm sure," agreed the Tuscan. "Well . . . failing that, expect the war here to kick off the minute the war in Balboa resumes. It may not take that long, either. You can assume it's going to be nasty, too. I have seen more than my share of guerilla wars and they are *always* nasty.

"Of course," added Marciano, "you and your family will be prime targets, so on behalf of the Tauran Union I'll extend an offer of sanctuary with my men . . . for your entire government and their families, for that matter. That will, also of course, mean the rapid collapse of your country and the ascension of the pro-Balboan guerillas to power. That, and again, 'of course,' will not mean peace since Santa Josefina will in that case become an enemy of a Tauran Union that will certainly be at war with the—"

"Are you all right, Mr. President?" the Tuscan asked of a Calderón who was rapidly turning pale with a slight tinge of green.

### Tauran Defense Agency, Lumière, Gaul, Terra Nova

Janier didn't have anything else to do, really, other than go home to his wife. *A fate surely best to be avoided*, he thought. Instead, with the half-bottle of brandy left over after he and his aide had put away a few, he continued pouring over the intel reports from Wallenstein. *Ah, now there's a woman I'd like to bed. Politically impossible, I suppose.* He sighed, thinking, *There is no justice.*

Janier read one of the files—it wasn't especially thick—concerning the big logistic base the Balboans were setting up

*Interesting that the lidar isn't too useful. Once you have lasers and computers it's not a big step to light ranging and detection. The big problem is processing power and consistency. I'm surprised that they don't have enough processing power to get more precise readings through the jungle canopy. We don't, of course, and wouldn't even if we were overflying Balboa. But I would have thought the UEPF could.*

Reluctantly, Janier closed the file and went to the next. This one covered the base, if it was a base, the Balboans were setting up east of the city. Whoever the UEPF intelligence officer who prepared the file was, he was plainly perplexed. Janier took one look at the map, glanced briefly at the figures for presumed future occupancy, then went to his own bookshelves for an unclassified estimate of the port capacity of all the minor *Mar Furioso* ports from *Valle de las Lunas* Province to Punta Gorgona, near the city.

He was an old-fashioned sort, in many ways. Instead of pulling up a computer spreadsheet and having it do the sums, he simply pencil drilled the total possible tonnage.

Then he pronounced his judgment, though his office was empty. "Minefield, not yet laid, with logistic black hole attached, and war crimes trials pending."

# CHAPTER THREE

"Good is better than evil because it's nicer."
—Mammy Yokum, in Al Capp's *Li'l Abner*

### Quarters Twenty, Fort Guerrero, Balboa, Terra Nova

The woman sat on the back porch to her quarters, staring out across the water to the space between barracks that showed the docks of the port of Balboa. She'd been here on the porch many times, yet never had she seen anything like the swirl of activity she had been seeing for the last couple of weeks.

*At least my Mike's alive,* thought Judy Tipton, living now under a kind of loose house arrest here in the former Tauran Union housing area on post, now designated as a guarded holding area for the families of prisoners of war and families of the dead. There had been a lot of dead, though rather less, as a percentage, for the regular Tauran forces in the Transitway Area than for the poor Anglian and Gallic paras who'd jumped en masse into the briar patches of *Lago Sombrero* and Herrera International.

She had to share her house now with another family, but since that consisted of one young lieutenant's widow and her three-year-old child, Judy thought she could put up with it. *Poor thing,* she thought of young Mrs. Lydia Gordon. *And, if she cries a lot? Well, I'd cry, too.*

Even there, the Balboans had tried to be civil about it. "We can only guard so many places," said the elderly warrant officer who'd come with the widow. "So we have to cram you all into where we can guard." He'd added, "It won't be long. As a widow, she's going to have priority for a flight out."

"It'll be fine," Judy had insisted, taking young Lydia under wing, more or less literally, and leading her to the spare bedroom. The warrant had carried in the woman's two bags and left them just inside the door.

It had been a couple of weeks since then and—however charitably inclined and sympathetic Judy may have been—Lydia's crying had started to wear. *But then, so have those Gallic tarts singing the* "Internationale" *under Balboan supervision.*

Then the Balboans had come and taken the widow to her old quarters to supervise packing up of her household baggage. When she returned, it was with travel orders cut by the legion's own travel section. The orders only took her as far as Asseri, Santa Josefina, though. From there, she'd be the responsibility of the Tauran Union.

*Decent of them, though,* thought Judy, *more decent by far than just putting us in tents behind barbed wire and feeding us gruel for however long it takes for things to resolve themselves.* She'd been around the Anglian Army enough to have heard that that was normal procedure in cases like this.

One of the chaplains occasionally came by, too, to check on them. This Judy found more than a little embarrassing, as the very same chaplain had once caught her in the middle of her living room, stark naked and shocked speechless, as a Balboan gun battery in the parade field lit up the night. *Oh, will I ever live that down?*

A knock from the stairs leading to to the porch caught her attention. The knock was followed by, "*Señora* Tiptón?" It was one of the guards. He hadn't quite gotten English pronunciation down yet, and might never.

"Yes, Legionary?" she asked.

"The car to take you and Mrs. Gordon to the *comisariata* is here," said the guard. "Comisariata" was not, strictly speaking, the right word, but it had entered Balboan currency a century prior and never quite been superseded.

"It's around the other side of the house."

"Ah. Thank you, Legionary. I'll get Lydia and be right out."

*And that was another point of decency,* she thought, *the Balboans giving us a credit—a limited credit, to be sure, but still a credit—to allow us to shop at the commissary. Of course, that means it's easier on them because they can feed us through our own efforts with food seized when they took the Transitway area, but even so . . .*

*At the very least, when I do get home and someone asks me how we were treated, I'll have to tell them, "Very well, indeed."*

## MV *Roger Casement* (Hibernian Registry), Port of Cristobal, Balboa, Terra Nova

The forty-foot container hung suspended by one of the ship's two cranes, a few dozen feet above its red-painted hull. The container swayed in the light tropical breeze coming off the Shimmering Sea to the south. About a hundred containers had already been loaded, and three hundred and twelve more were visible not far away, awaiting their turn.

It was a truism that no one really knew who owned any given merchant vessel. Between leases, lease backs, shadow corporations, dummy corporations, registrations under flags of convenience, and any of a hundred other tricks, merchant ships were essentially orphaned prostitutes. In the case of the *Roger Casement*, the owner was the Senate of Balboa, though even *years* of investigation were unlikely to prove that.

The *Roger Casement* had come in, bearing little but food and medical supplies, plus some building—which was to say, fortification—material. Its cargo discharged, orders had come from the corporation which at first glance might be said to own it, to pick up a load of Balboan fruit and coffee and deliver it to Jagelonia and Hordaland. The fruit, duly placed in refrigerated containers, was to be loaded where power could be supplied to those, for the most part aft of the ship's superstructure. The coffee was rather hardier, and would go aboard in normal containers.

All that was to go in later, though. The first cargo needed to go in first and low, where inspection would prove difficult.

If there was anything Balboa was not short of, in the current circumstances, it was weapons and ammunition of Tauran manufacture. The legion had, at last count, twenty-six thousand, four hundred and nineteen rifles of various types, from the Anglians' wretched things to the Gauls' and Sachsens' rather better ones. There were three thousand forty-eight light and general purpose machine guns, along with twelve hundred and fifty-three heavy machine guns of Federated States design. To go along with those were something on the order of fifty million rounds of ammunition. At least, that much had been inventoried so far. The process of inventory was still ongoing.

Additionally, there were one hundred and forty-one light mortars, as well as ninety-four mediums and seventeen serviceable heavies. Some others, adjudged unserviceable, were in the shop for evaluation and possible repair. For these, the legion had a bit over one hundred thousand rounds of ammunition of various types.

Of antitank weapons, both guided and unguided, light throwaways and heavier crew served, there were thousands. They were still coming in from wherever Tauran troops had lost them. Radios there were in plenty, along with night-vision devices, as well as plentiful batteries for both. Anti-vehicular mines, grenades, shoulder fired antiaircraft missiles? *We gots.* Signal devices and booby traps. *We gots.* Medical equipment and supplies? *We gots.*

Some of this largesse was currently being issued to the *Tercio Amazona* and some of the troops from the Fourteenth Cazador Tercio. Some was going to the Fifth Mountain and its Lempiran and Valdivian attachments, though they were mostly holding the materiel for others. A small portion was put aside for trophies for the various regiments. Some was intended for Taurus, for the Islamic groups created by, among others, Khalid the Assassin.

But roughly a third, by tonnage, was right here on the docks, intended for Santa Josefina as soon as the *Casement* had made its delivery of fruit and coffee and could turn around.

Interestingly, a small mule train, only forty-seven mules and a bell mare, carrying not more than eleven tons, in total, set off from the Balboan port of Capitano, on the Shimmering Sea near the Santa Josefinan border, at about the same time the *Casement* left Cristobal for Taurus.

**Off the *Isla Real,* to the southeast, North of *Ciudad* Balboa**

Ahead, a small boat, not much bigger than a largish yacht, and not nearly as fancy, reeled off two cables, one port, one starboard. The cables sported hydrophones. Translated from the Cyrillic, the cases from which the cables were drawn were labeled, "Archangel."

Behind the cable layer, and offset a few hundred meters, a coasting freighter slid a large-cylinder, steel-cased, explosive-filled, hence quite heavy, down a ramp erected to its stern. The mine rumbled down the ramp, dropped free, then hit the water, raising a great splash above the choppy waves.

The mid-sized coasting freighter was one of a pair. The cable layers were likewise matched. Both pairs were formed into two others, consisting of a cable layer and mine layer, each. Operating on opposite sides of the *Isla Real*, one mixed pair couldn't see the other. Neither could it be seen by the other. However, both were visible from much of the large massif, Hill 287, that dominated the island.

Anyone looking from that hill through a fair pair of binoculars would have seen the stern of the coaster, bearing the name, *Thetis*, as it made its way on a perfectly straight course toward Punta Gorgona, which course would take it just north of *Isla* Tatalao. They'd also have seen the mines rolling down the ramp into the sea. Were the binoculars good, they'd also have been able to see that the mines were of mixed types, that along with the cylinders were some equally large egg-shaped containers on wheeled cradles. The observer could have made out the rolling mines, as well as the splashes, but probably would have missed the reserve naval officer recording the grid where any given mine was released and the white cord that actually armed the mine, or, rather, began its timed arming sequence, once it was underwater and the *Thetis* reasonably out of the way. The cords were reused, once they'd pulled the safety out of the mines and been hauled in.

Recording the mine was possibly an exercise in near futility, since they almost never came to rest in a perfectly predictable way. Moreover, the Balboans were also dumping over the side some wedge-shaped gliding mines that could be guaranteed *not* to come to rest too very near the ship's path. Indeed, those gliders would end up roughly twice the distance from the ship as the depth of the water. The gliders were also on a long arming delay, a full week, to ensure that the job would be complete before they went active.

That said, it wasn't completely random; the ship's sonar scanned ahead and the mine chosen for dropping was selected based on the depth and nature of the spot ahead. Enough ready mines were held on deck to allow the crews to efficiently select the one to be used.

To add confusion to anyone trying to clear the mines, a mechanical device tossed false mines—mere flat plates—to port and starboard, even as a crane heaved some simulacra over the side.

The mines were of several types. Most of these were Volgan though Balboa had been able to get a small number of more sophisticated mines, some of which it had copied in slightly larger numbers. There was also a respectably large number of somewhat inferior Valdivian-made copies of an Anglo-Tuscan mine. The original was a device of great discretion and power. Even the copy was rather capable.

The most common mine laid was a fairly simple cylinder, filled with some six hundred kilograms of tritonal, and set off by magnetic signature, acoustic signature, or by water displacement. The mines weren't sophisticated enough to permit any combination of targeting parameters; the crews had to pick a fuse for one method and attach it just before rolling it down the ramp.

Less common were several versions of Volgan rising mines. These were generally placed deeper and, on receipt of sufficient signature, would begin to rise to the surface. This allowed the mines to be placed on the bottom, where they were hard to detect, hence hard to clear, and move closer to a target upon detection. That they were especially effective against submarines was an additional benefit.

Least common of the Volgan mines was the type once known on Old Earth as CAPTORs. In essence these were torpedoes, mated to sensor suites, that selected targets based on certain criteria and engaged them as if the mine were a submarine. The major difference between the Volgan torpedo mines and those of the Tauran Union and Federated States was that the Volgan versions could not self-emplace from a distance that some of the others could. Neither was really ideal for use against surface ships, being small with small warheads. They were best used against subs.

The Balboans were not being terribly sophisticated about all this. Instead, they were just putting down a *lot* of mines, enough mines to ensure that no channel could be cleared through them quickly. Still, since the *Isla Real, Isla* San Juan, *Isla* Santa Paloma, Punta Gorgona, *Isla* Tatalao, and the town of Chimaneca contained extensive direct and indirect fire capability, to say nothing of fixed torpedo launchers for some of them, clearing a path was likely to prove prohibitively costly until at least the main island was cleared. Then, too, the mix of mine types and the mix in their fusing made the mine barrage somewhat self-defending.

Nor was the intent to simply seal off the northern approaches to the Transitway. Balboa's life blood was trade and transportation. Cutting off the Transitway completely would be economic death. Instead, they were ensuring that the heavily defended *Isla Real* and its largish near neighbors couldn't be bypassed, hence that no invasion of the coast by the capital could succeed until the islands were taken. They were leaving unmined two gaps almost a kilometer wide to the main island's east and west. Thus, at their discretion, ships and trade could continue to flow until the legion elected to shut them down.

Three men stood on the northern slope of Hill 287, not far from the ground-laid portion of the chimney for the archipelago's solar power system. These were Carrera and Fosa, the chief of the naval arm, plus Legate Rigoberto Puercel, the chief of the corps responsible for the defense of Balboa's northern coast. Puercel commanded the Fifth Corps, built around the Eighth Training Legion, now the Eighth Infantry Legion, the School Brigade, and certain other units, some of which had been part of the "hidden reserve" but most of which were simply normal organizations, the members of which wore second hats. The Fifth Corps consisted of that same Eighth Infantry Legion, Eleventh Infantry Legion, which was newly constituted from preexisting tercios and allies come to help, Twelfth Coastal Defense Artillery Brigade, Twenty-fifth Combat Support Brigade, plus sundry other specialist and support organizations.

The Eighth Infantry Legion was more of a fortress legion. Moreover, since it was built around Puercel's previous command, the Eighth Training, and since his exec in that command was the legion commander, and since Puercel was absolutely going to stay on the island, in the real world command remained his.

Instead of the normal three maneuver regiments, the Eighth had four infantry tercios, two of which were foreign allied (both of which were on the way but had not yet arrived), and one regiment of disabled or handicapped static troops, the *Tercio Santa Cecilia*. These were also known by their unofficial motto, *Adios Patria*.

Instead of having an artillery tercio with three light or medium cannon cohorts, a heavier cannon cohort, and a multiple rocket launcher cohort, the Eighth had one cohort of man-portable (if barely) wheeled multiple rocket launchers, one of super heavy 240mm breech-loading mortars, and three of heavy 160mm mortars. Both types of mortars had more or less elaborate fixed positions, those for the 160mm guns being turreted with redundant, modified tank turrets. It also had a larger than normal complement of tanks, mostly hidden in fairly strong and well-camouflaged positions. The legion's service support tail, and its headquarters, generally, occupied some portion of one or another of the *Isla Real*'s thirteen deeply dug fortress complexes, arrayed mostly in an irregular ring about Hill 287. Two of the thirteen were dug in under lesser heights.

The different casernes and areas of the island were connected by two transportation systems, running in parallel. One of these was an asphalted two-lane highway, laid in a ring a couple of kilometers inland from the coast. The other was a 600mm rail system, open to the sky but dug in and protected by concrete revetments, a half a kilometer or so even farther inland.

The Twelfth Coastal Artillery Brigade was based on the island, though it had reduced strength cohorts of heavy artillery at both Punta Gorgona and Chimaneca. These were at reduced strength because they weren't expected to last very long, anyway, nor to do much good if they did. They existed, for the most part, for no higher purpose than to keep a potential enemy from wondering why the far ends of a future naval mine barrage were not covered by direct and indirect fire.

Similar were the sixteen former naval turrets, triple 152mm jobs, ringing the island. The Twelfth Brigade had a single maniple whose job it was to make those look active and threatening, even to the point of firing them on occasion. In fact, nobody in the know expected them to survive an attack for long nor much cared if they did. The turret's main function, like that of the understrength cohorts of heavy guns off on the mainland, was to keep people from asking the wrong, which is to say the right, questions.

Instead, the meat of Twelfth Brigade on the island was hidden. It consisted of four demi-cohorts of heavy guns, mounted on railway carriages, and four torpedo batteries, two to either side of the island. The torpedo batteries actually belonged to the *classis*, the Legion's naval arm, but were attached to the Twelfth.

Back on the mainland, the situation was considerably more dire than on the islands. For one thing, the Eleventh Legion was brand new, though most of its higher command and staff came from school brigade and were, individually, generally quite competent. The troops, however, had mostly not finished their initial entry training yet. They, still under their training cadres—in the Balboan system a rather lavish set of cadres, though—were grouped into new tercios, numbered Forty-sixth through Fifty-first Infantry, and Seventy-first Artillery, among others, The infantry were at roughly half to two-thirds strength in personnel, though the artillery was considerably stronger than a normal tercio.

Some of those men and women, indeed, had as little as two weeks in uniform. The bright dye of their uniforms said as much. Worse, many of them were still sitting on the island, working on defenses while awaiting transportation.

"Not for three more months, *Duque*," was Puercel's judgment. "I don't have the wire up or the mines laid. Christ; Cheatham's still got Balboa Foundation and Wall pouring concrete and building obstacles and nutcrackers along the beach. And the unmanned water-cooled MGs are taking a while to get out of storage and set up."

Nutcrackers were a kind of antilanding obstacle employing a wooden frame, a wooden lever, and a standard antitank mine to smash landing craft as they approached shore. The water-cooled machine guns were just that, except that, once someone started them firing, a curved and notched bar, to which a modified traversing and elevating mechanism was attached, caused them to fire continuously over a wide arc. The bar and T&E mechanism had been fairly easy to design and develop. Even the automatic cocking mechanism in case of a stoppage hadn't been all that tough. The twenty-four-thousand-round drum magazine had been a bitch.

"Plus," Puercel continued, "I don't have two of my five combat regiments yet. I don't have many of the half-trained trainees off the island yet. We are still bringing in food and ammunition from the mainland where it had to be offloaded since our port facilities are not up to handing large freighters. Two more months."

Carrera raised one eyebrow and pointed at first the *Thetis*, then the other coaster impressed into being a minelayer. The implication was, *This is on time. Why aren't you?*

"Because what he has to do," offered Roderigo Fosa, in defense of his comrade, "is a thousand times more complex than just loading some stockpiled mines and delivering them, with crews that have spent nearly ten years learning how to do just that.

"Can't we do something diplomatically," Fosa asked, "to keep the Zhong out of it? And yes, I know that would probably mean turning one of my people over to a ritual execution, but . . ."

*No*, thought Carrera, *because I need the Zhong to come into it. If they don't, the TU won't fight but will let this ceasefire drag on until we're bankrupt.*

"No, as a matter of principle," Carrera said. This was less than the truth but he couldn't reveal the truth. It was also not quite a lie, since he did consider protecting his people a matter of principle.

"How soon can you sail?" Carrera asked Fosa.

"Anytime," the latter replied. "But I thought you wanted me to intern my fleet in Santa Josefina just before hostilities recommenced."

"Correct. But what if you sail and put on a very defiant show for the Zhong?"

"They can kick my ass, which is to say, sink my fleet," the naval officer replied. "Remember, though, God be my witness, I asked for some modern VTOL fighters for the *Dos Lindas*"—the *Dos Lindas*, alleged to be named for the breasts of Carrera's late first wife, which were also alleged to be on demure display as part of the figurehead, was the legion's sole sailable aircraft carrier—"but 'no,' you said, 'too expensive,' you said, 'not our job . . .' "

"Never mind that," Carrera answered. "I was right then and I'm right now. And that's not the question, that they can sink your fleet even minus the carrier Warrant Officer Chu and the *Meg* took out. I know they can. The question is how much does it delay them, figuring out what we can and can't do, and then beefing up their fleet to be sure of success when faced with a fleet that looks ready and eager to fight."

"Oh . . . well . . . couple of weeks, I suppose," Fosa conceded. "A couple of weeks more, I mean."

"And how long to sail here from *Xing Zhong Guo?*"

"Month."

"Which gives me the time I need," said Carrera. "Put to sea, Fosa. Put on a good show. When the Zhong come, run for Santa Josefina and intern yourself. Denounce me if you think that will help, since we both know it will be fake."

*Like so very much of what we're doing and showing is fake.*

"By the way, Rod, have you finished loading the arms, ammunition, and equipment for an infantry cohort?"

### Arraijan Ordnance Works, Balboa, Terra Nova

The gliders—"Condors," they were called, though they differed from the manned versions—came in in containers, and left in containers, the containers holding also the tanks of hydrogen, frames, balloons and harnesses to lift the aircraft. Here in the Ordnance Works, they were pulled out, modified, then resealed and released. The modification for one type consisted of filling them with roughly three hundred to three hundred and twenty pounds of high explosive, seventy of incendiary material—magnesium—sixty of guidance and control package, and about twenty of speakers, battery, and digital player. In the process of mounting the speakers, sections of the polyurethane foam were cut away that, with the tiny convex-concave chips embedded within them, gave the condors their stealth capability. The frame around the speakers contained very small explosive charges to blow out the removed and replaced polyurethane panels to allow the speakers to be heard.

Another type carried an electromagnetic pulse generator. Still another carried a naval mine. And there was one made to dispense electrical wires to short out power systems. There were approximately as many types as human ingenuity could come up with, filtered by the demand of human depravity to do the most damage for the drachma.

Another particularly wicked type of modification was made to very few in number, only four in total. These were fitted with a cylinder containing a mix of various forms of counterfeit and real Tauran money, generally in fairly high denominations, especially the counterfeit. The cylinder, developed by *Obras Zorilleras*, the Balboan research and development organization, had sufficient explosive of a type no sniffer dog was likely to key on, to first disintegrate the condor that carried it then to cut itself into dozens of fragments, leaving the money to flutter to ground. The counterfeit came from the same mint that printed up Balboa's legionary drachma, which mint had been set up for Balboa by the Taurans. If one is going to do counterfeiting on a massive scale, it helps to have the engraving done by experts, and the paper and ink coming from the very people whose money you intend to counterfeit.

The guards on both types were very heavy indeed.

The guard force's problem was that the several hundred modified condors neither came in nor left in large groups. Instead, it was one here, one there, and a couple the other day. The most they'd ever managed to get out was thirty in a single day, and that was because the Balboans could cover the movement in the form of a massive distribution of ammunition to the *Isla Real*. The condors didn't go to the island of course; the move merely got them to the docks where they could be loaded on an about to depart ship.

Where they would go from there was anybody's guess.

### *Carretera* Balboa-Cristobal, Balboa, Terra Nova

Any given military veteran of the old, now liberated, Transitway Area would probably, if asked about the terrain, have answered to the effect of, "Miles and miles of fuck-all jungle, most of it not seen by a white man in a century."

For his area, and his time, that would have been approximately correct. The Transitway Area, barring the bases, towns, roads, dams, and such, was mostly jungle, and for a very good reason. Without trees to hold the soil in place the waters would have silted up in no time, while mudslides would probably have buried the place in the course of a couple of rainy seasons.

For much of the rest of the country, though, to include much of the country near the Transitway, the veteran would have been as wrong as could be. More than anything else, the noncity but populated parts of Balboa were farms. This was true also on either side and between the not quite parallel roads that ran from *Ciudad* Balboa, on the *Mar Furioso*, south to Cristobal, on the Shimmering Sea.

There were casernes, a few, and also a few legion-owned housing areas along the westernmost of those two roads, the one that avoided the old Transitway Area completely. These already contained the casing for some very large thermobaric bombs, said casings containing the bursting charges, the initiation flares, and the seismic fuse, so far unset. These only needed to be filled and have their fuses set to arm.

In addition, south of the Parilla Line, some others had been buried some time prior, though they did not extend into the old, formerly Tauran-controlled, Transitway Area. Teams were burying a few—three, no more—though none were to be filled yet. Getting them into position was proving a positive nightmare, since *here* the jungle *was* pristine . . . and thick.

Most of the rest, a total of ten, were going in under cover of defensive works preparation between and to either side of the twin roads. They, also, were not yet filled. Neither were their fuses set.

### *Isla Real*, Hovercraft Ramp C, Balboa, Terra Nova

Ordinarily the hovercraft had been used to ferry out new trainees and limited resupply, and to bring the cadres back to the mainland for rest and recreation, the island never having been set up for much in the way of the latter. There wasn't time for that now; the troops coming out were coming to fight; the ones going back were going back to finish their initial training and then, if things got bad, to fight. Supply was an ongoing crisis. Indeed, it had to be. Past a certain point of obvious preparedness and the Taurans would probably never have attacked, whatever the provocation.

Among the troops coming today, on this hovercraft load, were a mix of the Forty-first infantry, itself a mix of foreign allied cohorts, and a special crew, in more senses than one.

The Forty-fifth, the *Tercio Santa Cecelia*, was composed of the mentally retarded and the physically disabled, with only a minimal cadre of normal leadership, seconded from other units. The troops of the tercio might be assigned to anything, or attached over to another unit for anything. The core of them, however, formed the "*Adios Patria*" men and women, people who would man fixed positions from which there was relatively little hope of escape in the event of attack.

★★★

Sergeant Rafael de la Mesa had been a first class infantryman, once, a legionary on the fast track to centurion. Then an accident had intervened, breaking his back and leaving him paralyzed from the waist down. He tried to control his bitterness. He didn't always succeed. Sometimes it leaked through to fall in full acid fury upon his three charges, Julio, Juan, and Pablo. These were boys or young men, mentally retarded but not so badly that they couldn't understand the oath of enlistment or what it meant. Together, they and de la Mesa formed a fixed turret crew, though they didn't yet know which turret was theirs.

"De la Mesa?" asked a wheelchair-bound centurion, Robles by name.

"Here, Centurion," answered de la Mesa.

"Your crew is assigned to Turret 177. It's just south of the tadpole's tail, if you remember the island's layout."

De la Mesa mentally pulled up a map of the island, as best he could remember it. "I do," he said.

"Good," said Robles. Passing over a plastic folder, he said, "Here's your position data. I haven't looked at it, myself, but one of the attachments who can still walk said it's fine. You may have to get rid of some *antaniae*; there were droppings."

"Roger," said de la Mesa. "Juan?"

"Yes, Sergeant," answered a retarded boy, though one whose face said his Down's Syndrome was light.

"You have your basic load of ammunition?"

"Yes, Sergeant."

"You shall be killing *antaniae,* soon." Turning back to Robles, de la Mesa asked, "How do we get there?"

"Wait here," said the centurion. "A truck with a loading ramp will be along sometime in the next hour to carry you and your men to the turret. I'm afraid the road doesn't go close enough to your position to just let you off. They'll have to port you through a few hundred meters of jungle."

# CHAPTER FOUR

I have never managed to lose my old conviction
that travel narrows the mind.
— Gilbert Keith Chesterton,
*What I Saw in America*

### Admiral's Barge, over the *Mar Furioso*, Terra Nova

The UEPF *Spirit of Peace* was a bright, sunlit spark behind her. Ahead was Wallenstein's destination, *Xing Zhong Guo*, or New Middle Kingdom. This was the last significant state on the planet to officially adhere to a variant of Tsarist-Marxism. Of course, in true Han fashion they didn't call it that. Instead, they called it Enlightened Path to Perpetual Peace and Prosperity. Never mind that, as bloody-handed as Volga's Red Tsar had been, he was a piker compared to the Zhong's *Huangdi*, in terms of sheer volume of premature deaths by starvation or judicial murder. Never mind that, as far as prosperity went, the Zhong as individuals were among the poorest people on the planet.

*Whatever "enlightened" means*, thought the high admiral, *I don't think it means what the Zhong think it means.*

Fortunately, Marguerite would not be meeting the reigning *Huangdi*. The Han Chinese had lost none of their sense of aggrieved cultural superiority in coming to the new world. Thus, for those meeting the emperor—largely a figurehead now but a much revered figurehead—kowtowing was a minimum requirement. Since, as a practical matter, the UEPF had outranked the Zhong since the planet was founded, and since some of its past high admirals had insisted on proskynesis from the barbarians below . . .

*Well . . . better to just go along with what the diplomats worked out centuries ago, to just avoid the issue by keeping the two of us apart. Besides, if the SecGen of the Consensus, himself, rated neither proskynesis nor a blowjob from me, the local potentate sure as hell will not.*

Wallenstein had to be discreet whenever she travelled to the surface for anything that might trip the weapons grade paranoia of the Federated States. No matter the government in power, progressive or federalist, on one matter the massively overwhelming bulk of the *Federales* were united; they detested utterly the Peace Fleet that had nuked two of their cities to ash. This might not have been so bad, except that the Federated States had the ability to nuke the UEPF and its base on the island of Atlantis, both, to ash. And all that kept them from doing so was the belief, wrong, in fact, that the UEPF could visit like destruction on the Federated States.

The only other state down below that hated the Peace Fleet as much, and for approximately the same reason, was Yamato which, after suffering through the loss of two cities, and being on the verge of surrender, had been bucked up by the reprisal visited on the Federated States, and thought better of surrender. Had they actually been able to achieve a satisfactory peace with the FSC, they might have felt differently. As it was, the Federated States Army and Navy had imposed a blockade of the Yamatan Islands, engaging and destroying anyone trying to flee, letting no food in, and destroying every vestige of food transportation network and storage they could find.

In the end, over twenty million Yamatan civilians, mostly the very old and very young, had died of starvation and starvation-related causes. And *then* they'd surrendered, cursing to the depths of hell the Old Earthers whose actions had given them such deadly false hope.

*Fortunately* thought the high admiral, *the Yamatans can't hurt my fleet, so they can be safely ignored. Not so the FSC.*

The high admiral's travel plans were to visit the Zhong and entice their real government—to a man and woman selfish industrial feudalists masquerading as enlightened Tsarist-Marxists—to support the Tauran Union. Among those masqueraders, the alleged chief was the Zhong empress, herself. About her, beyond a name and a date of birth, which may have been falsified, there was amazingly little information available. Wallenstein wished desperately that she had more.

*I don't think it will be that hard, really. The high cadres probably don't care a fig for the loss of a few thousand children to a Balboan submarine, but they're quite annoyed at the loss of a major warship . . . an* expensive *major warship.*

*We'll see what we'll see though.*

On the other side of the passenger compartment, the high admiral's cabin girl, Esmeralda, slept with her head propped on a pillow set against the inside of the hull. In her one free hand was clasped a paperback Terra Novan novel she'd picked up back in Hotel Edward's Palace, on the Island of Teixeira, Lusitania, in the Tauran Union. Wallenstein smiled indulgently at her brown and, it had to be admitted, beautiful assistant.

*She used to turn so pale when she had to fly. Now it's no big thing. How she's grown since I was able to liberate her from the slavers at Razona Market. And if I hadn't? That doesn't bear thinking about. She jokes about becoming a big bowl of chili for Count Castro-Nyere's dinner . . . but it's not a joke. It could have happened. Imagine; my own system could have done that to the girl who is my child in everything but genetics. I could just . . .*

Marguerite pushed the thought away before she did, indeed, throw up. Even so, her rising gorge threatened to spill over.

*And wouldn't that* story *make the rounds? How the high admiral got space sick? No, that would never do. That . . .*

The shuttle began to shudder a bit as its extendable wings first bit into the thinly scattered hydrogen, helium, carbon dioxide, and atomic oxygen of the exosphere. The shuddering became somewhat more pronounced as it entered the thermosphere. Here the temperature of the atoms was on the order of forty-five hundred degrees, Fahrenheit. Despite this, and despite the speed of the barge, the external temperature remained quite cool. There simply weren't enough atoms and molecules to transfer much heat or generate much friction.

Through the mesosphere the barge plunged, then into the stratosphere. Here the pilot fought to get his command into a normal cruising altitude of about twelve thousand meters. At that height the barge would stay until it had approached rather close to the Zhong capital of Choukoutien.

## Choukoutien, *Xing Zhong Guo*, Terra Nova

Here, where secrecy was not so much needed, the admiral's barge could come to rest right in the middle of the capital's government complex. This was perhaps stylistically redolent of some of the Asian, and especially Chinese, architecture of Old Earth. Still, it was not much more than half the size of, for example, Beijing's Forbidden City, and not so well walled or moated.

*Secrecy's not critical*, thought Wallenstein, *but that's not to say it's pointless. The Zhong, so says Khan, the wife, are quite cozy with the Federated States, so I have to assume my presence here will be reported. That's not too important. What is important is that my words and intentions not be reported. And the only way I can think of to do that is by circumlocution and misdirection. On that, the Zhong are old hands. Elder gods, however many or few you be, I ask your help in this.*

With a scream of landing jets, the barge settled down onto the walled, cobblestoned courtyard that had been set aside since ages past for visits by the chief of the Old Earthers. This was the first time it had been used in over fifty years.

With a soft whine, Wallenstein's barge let down its side ramp and hatch. The barge shifted almost imperceptibly as the coming to rest of the loading ramp relieved the off-center weight on that side.

Li An Ming, whose name could arguably have been translated as, "Strong Proud Bright," met Wallenstein at the ramp to her barge. He wore *xuanduan,* or formal dress, consisting primarily of a dark blue, knee-length robe, over a red overlong kilt, with various ties, a white belt, a sash, and other accoutrements. The Zhong courtier was on his way into full kowtow when she stopped him, or tried to.

"There is no time for that," said Marguerite, "and it doesn't do a thing for me, anyway."

The Zhong, though she knew he spoke English, ignored her completely, dropping to his knees and then bending over to tap his head three times on the cobblestones of the ad hoc landing pad. Li An Ming arose from his kowtow smoothly, as from long practice.

He offered neither apology nor explanation, though the lack was an explanation of sorts: *I am Han. We have our ways. They suit us. We will not change.*

Mentally sighing, Marguerite thought, *Not my job to try to change a culture that hasn't changed all that much in about four or five thousand years.*

"The emperor is indisposed," said Li An Ming, "so you will be meeting with the empress."

Wallenstein nodded. This was a fiction of long standing. The emperor was most likely just fine, but it was possible for the Empress to kowtow to the chief of the UEPF, male or female, without it meaning subordination of the country.

"Lead on," she said.

Turning, Li An Ming began walking slowly toward a stone wall pierced by a red painted door, flanked by two life-sized stone statues, one bearing a battle axe and the other a mace. A bowing servant waited until Li An Ming had subtly maneuvered Wallenstein and the accompanying Esmeralda into their proper positions, then opened the door. After they had passed, the servant closed it behind them with exquisite delicacy.

The position Wallenstein was supposed to take, under current court etiquette, was well ahead of her escort. Since she didn't know the way, this was impossible. Thus, the only position both practical and at least minimally polite was for her to be a mere few inches ahead, where Li An Ming could guide her by subtle gestures.

Past the door, a long corridor opened up, with each side bearing nine weapons mounted in or hanging from racks. Some of these Wallenstein didn't recognize. Most, however, were not so different from their Old Earth, European counterparts. She recognized, for example, along the left wall, a saber, a straight sword, a battle-ax, a halberd, a trident, and a mace, but found three others more or less incomprehensible. The other wall was slightly stranger, with five weapons that had no obvious Old Earth, Euro equivalents.

*This was, I imagine, to impress my predecessors in command that the Zhong were perfectly willing to fight, with little more than their bare hands, if necessary, to prevent domination by the Class Ones of Old Earth.*

At the far end of the corridor, another servant opened another door, revealing only a stone wall on the far side. Li An Ming was there, however, to indicate by a sweep of his arm a piece of art that he wanted her to see, and which also indicated the proper direction.

"And over here, High Admiral, is a painting alleged to have been done by Ma Lin thirteen hundred years ago, and which my Divine Emperor's servant was able to acquire from your predecessor in command—how saddened we all were to hear of his death at the hands of the barbarians of Balboa!—at auction . . ."

Marguerite barely contained her smile at the memory of avenging herself on ex-High Admiral Robinson.


Xingzhen, empress of the Zhong had borne the emperor a son. This had not been the first child of the emperor, not nearly. Some discreet sabotage, an occasional poisoning, the odd duel; these had made her child eldest, and the future emperor.

*And, my child*, thought Xingzhen, *I shall certainly ensure that, when you wed, you do not get even one woman even remotely like me. I have ensured my lineage through you, but you must ensure my lineage through spreading your seed widely.*

Mentally, the empress reviewed the little she knew about the soon-arriving high admiral of the Old Earth fleet. It wasn't much. *Tall and blond . . . I like tall and blond. Pretty, say those who've seen or met her. That's good, too. Reasonably large breasted, as my playmates here never are. I like that, too.*

*Hmmm . . . I wonder if I would be so attracted to women if I hadn't been so much more of a man than the emperor proved to be?*


Li An Ming opened the final door himself, standing back then to allow Marguerite to enter. She took a step in, then almost gasped; the empress was *that* beautiful, from her not-quite-boyish coif to her perfect eyebrows to her eyes which seemed about three times the size of a normal Zhong's, to her pert nose to . . .

*Even her feet are beautiful.* Marguerite, who preferred boys to girls, if only slightly, practically swooned; the empress was *that* stunning.

The only thing that ruined it was the fact that the empress knelt and tapped her head on the polished wooden floor. Even there, though, Wallenstein could sense, in fact she could practically smell, *It's a show. This one is stronger than any man she knows. She is steel. She can make me . . . crap, how I need a break from being in charge.*

And when the empress arose from her kowtow, turning those three-times-too-large-to-resist eyes on the high admiral?

*It's not only her eyes that are three times bigger . . .*

"Esma, honey, could you wait outside with our escort? I really need to talk to the empress alone."

No doubt Wallenstein thought, at the moment, that she was being discreet. Esmeralda, however, thought, *She sounds just like Richard when I open my quarters door for him or go to his,* while Li An Ming thought, simply, *Perfect,* before gently closing the door.

"Would you care for something to eat, Miss?" Li An Ming asked, all smiles—they seemed genuine to the girl now, as they had not before—and politeness. "I think the empress and the high admiral will be *deep* in conversation for quite some time."

At that, Esma almost laughed. That the courtier did laugh suggested that the double entendre was not unwitting.

"We have a concept," said Li An Ming, "that is very difficult to translate into your tongue. This is *guanxi*, which is often translated to mean something like, 'relationship.' It is more than that, though, and is well illustrated by a saying, which I would translate as, 'Relationships are more important than rules.' Everyone in this part of our world understands this. Almost no one in certain other parts of the world does."

"We don't have the saying, as far as I know," said Esmeralda, "but my society back on Old Earth certainly understands the principle." She had to work to keep out of her words her hatred of the society whereof she spoke.

"As do all civilized folk," said the Zhong. "And right now, the high admiral and empress are cementing a relationship to the betterment of us all. Now, as I asked, would you care for something to eat?"

Esmeralda opened her mouth, closed it, opened it, closed it, then opened it again to say, "Please."

**Admiral's Barge, over the *Mar Furioso*, Terra Nova**

As it turned out, the Zhong empress, whose cheek rested against Wallenstein's shoulder and whose hand the high admiral held in her own, was not just the emperor's wife, nor even his chief wife. She ran the country, she and the hundred important families. The emperor was a figurehead, nothing more.

Nor was the empress quite as young as she appeared. Though much younger than Wallenstein, she was of a certain age and looked a certain half of that.

*And if ever I needed more evidence that what people want in bed is what they're denied in real life,* thought Marguerite, *what more than she and I could I ask for? I, who have to be so cold and commanding in public, wanting to be dominated in bed and made to perform; her, having to be so demure in public, needing to dominate in bed and make me perform . . . well, me for now, anyway. Though I would not mind making it long term.*

Unconsciously, Marguerite squeezed Xingzhen's hand, then twisted her own head to kiss the top of the empress's. Xingzhen, quite asleep, still managed to cuddle in closer.

Not entirely idly, Wallenstein wondered if she were in love. *Lust? Yes, clearly I'm in lust. And after so long without so much as a hint of sex I was more than ready. But love? In love? At my age? Why . . . it's been . . . let me think . . . ummm . . . a hundred and sixty-two years? About that. Surely I can't be in love. Surely . . .*

Even so, she reached up with her free hand to stroke the Zhong empress's silky-smooth, midnight black hair.

*Shit. Yes . . . maybe . . . in love. Shit. Oh, nonononono. It was bad enough the last time . . . and I have no reason whatsoever to think she feels anything like the same way. Oh, elder gods, that's slavery. A subbie I may be—at least in private—but I am not a slave. Shit.*

"Passing over the coast of Santa Josefina, High Admiral," announced the pilot of her barge, over a speaker in the passenger cabin. "Arrival in Aserri in about seventeen minutes."

Esmeralda sat on the opposite side of the cabin from Wallenstein, where she usually did. She sat alone, though Li An Ming was behind her, as were nine *very* competent-looking Zhong guards. She had reason to suspect that four of the oldest guards were much higher ranking than they pretended to be.

It had apparently been the empress's idea to call a peace conference in Aserri to which Santa Josefina, Balboa, the Federated States, the Tauran Union, and the Peace Fleet would be invited. Some Zhong diplomats were already en route, as were various functionaries for the FSC and TU. Wallenstein had tasked the Consensus's ambassador to Santa Josefina to set it up and run it.

The Balboans hadn't yet answered, a lack which had raised quite a broad grin on Xingzhen's angelic face.

"They can't come," she'd told the high admiral, before it became obvious that they would not come. "Or at least not without a lot of soul searching. They're just a regime of soldiers, comfortable and competent on a battlefield, yes, but quite uncomfortable off one, or on one that doesn't involve direct violence. And if they don't come, they can't make their case before the world. They'll be 'Warmongers who prefer fighting to talking peace.' Trust me, this is going to hurt them."

The high admiral had seen the truth of that. She'd also seen that the same logic applied in part to the Federated States. Hate the Peace Fleet as they might, they could not go on record as objecting to a conference that might lead to peace. Hence the open flight rather than the usual series of cutaways and deceptions.

Esmeralda closed her book and put it away in her bag. Of the five given to her by the Balboan agent, Khalid, she'd brought two with her. She was reading it not for the story, which she found deadly dull, and not for the illustrations, but to familiarize herself to places where she was more likely to find certain key words she would need to make the simple code Khalid had given her work.

*But I* can *contact them,* thought Esmeralda. *And it's just possible they might send someone to contact me.*

### Hotel *Cielo Dorado*, Aserri, Santa Josefina, Terra Nova

Things like major conferences for international peace or the end to specific national wars rarely happen instantly. This is especially true when those calling the conference don't really have an interest in working for peace nearly so great as they do in coordinating a war. Thus, while the Balboans were engaged in figuring out how to avoid the conference while maintaining the patina of aggrieved victim of Tauran imperialism, and while sundry TU diplomats and bureaucrats made their travel arrangements, for themselves, their wives, and their lovers . . . and sometimes all three . . . or four . . . while General Marciano arranged for a couple of companies of infantry and a company of military police for security, and while the Earthers' ambassador arranged contracts, the people who mattered, the de facto ruler of *Xing Zhong Guo*, the high admiral of the Peace Fleet, and—to his considerable surprise—the chief military officer of the Tauran Union Defense Agency, General Janier, met early.

"I really don't understand why they haven't removed me," said Janier, to Wallenstein, over dinner one night. "Did you . . . ?"

"No," Wallenstein admitted. "Oh, I would have put in a word if I'd thought of it, but I was in a blue funk until well after it became obvious that you weren't going anywhere."

"Then why? How? I don't—"

"They can't admit a mistake," said Xingzhen, more politically astute than either of her co-diners. "They can't allow anything but the appearance of perfection. If you are relieved they have to admit something bad happened. Oh, it obviously *did* happen, but as long as the reality is denied with a straight face then it didn't. Admit the truth? That would mean their perfect world, their perfect illusion of a perfect world, was a lie."

"Oh," said Marguerite.

"Makes sense, I suppose," admitted Janier. "At least as much as anything else in the fantasy of the Tauran Union makes sense."

*Clever bitch, this slant-eyed bit of perfection*, thought the Gaul.

"It's a fantasy world now," Marguerite agreed. "That's why you always needed, and still need, a successful war. There's no other way, pious platitudes aside, to make a real, rather than a fantasy, country."

Esmeralda hadn't been invited to dinner. She didn't want to be there anyway. Instead, she had first checked the e-mail address and password for the account Khalid had given her, then encoded a brief message using one of the books she'd brought. The hotel had had a business center, but it was too open and she was afraid she'd be seen. She asked the front desk for some help and, given whose party she was in company with, they'd found her a free computer at an empty desk in a small office. From there she'd logged in to the e-mail, opened the draft coded message from the Balboans, then typed in her own message, and signed out of the account.

## Legionary Recruiting Station, Cedral Multiplex Shopping Mall, Aserri, Santa Josefina, Terra Nova

Sergeant Morales, recruiter and transportation coordinator for the legion for the foreign city of Aserri, didn't quite know what to make of them, the five key members of the Tsarist-Marxist Party of Santa Josefina who had entered the recruiting station uninvited and without an appointment. On the other hand, he didn't, for the nonce, have anything better to do so, *why not? Just because we're opposed doesn't mean we can't speak together.*

Opposed? Yes. It wasn't that the Timocratic Republic of Balboa was without serious streaks of socialism; indeed, it was in some ways quite heavily socialized. But the socialism of Balboa was, at core, in opposition to the man-as-malleable ethos of socialism, all forms of leftism, really, as they'd developed on two planets. Balboa and the legion didn't try to change anybody, though they certainly fertilized some soil for people to change themselves if they wished, and to self-select if they wished.

Conversely, the five people standing in front of Morales's desk were convinced that, given enough training and education, enough propagandization and relentless bloody nagging, along with the power to remove the inequities and inequalities of all the rotten societies of the planet, they could, nearly anyone could, make of man exactly what they wished.

"May I help you gentlemen?" asked Sergeant Morales, though they struck him as young and scruffy. *University weasels, I imagine.* "Did you come to join up?"

"No," said the central and senior one of the five. He introduced himself as "Ernesto Gonzalo" and his companions as "The steering committee for the 'Popular Front for the Liberation of Santa Josefina.'"

*First I've heard of this crew,* thought Morales.

"And we won't be part of some perversion of socialism," Gonzalo announced. "We demand the real thing. But first we demand that the Taurans get the fuck out."

"And?" Morales queried, with an eyebrow raised. "What? Do you want us to invade?"

"No," said Gonzalo, obviously appalled at the thought. "But we could use some money and some ability to do some printing. And maybe a little advice."

"I'll get back with you," said the sergeant. *After all, how often does one find a band of scruffy, bearded, university students who are willing to ask for, and maybe even take, advice?*

# CHAPTER FIVE

A sincere diplomat is like dry water or wooden iron.
—Stalin

*Palacio de las* Trixies, *Ciudad* Balboa,
**Republic of Balboa, Terra Nova**

With so many men, and not a few women, called to the colors, the background sounds of the city were muted and, to a degree, warped. The street hawkers were mostly gone. Commercial traffic was at a minimum or, arguably, even less than a healthy minimum. Instead of the muffled sound of the limousine gliding through this wealthier part of the city, the walls reverberated with the sound of heavy diesel-engined trucks, barely muffled and doing nothing good to the cobblestones of the street as they crawled over them. At that, the diesels were a merciful cover for the sounds of weeping widows, still breaking forth with frightful regularity. There were occasional electronic wails as air raid sirens were mounted and tested. People wailed as well.

And even the wails of heartbroken women and children were to be preferred over the "spontaneous" patriotic demonstrations taking place several times a day under the guidance of the nation's minister of information, which was to say, of propaganda, Professor Ruiz. Carrera, leaning against a bookcase in the president's office, could, as *Dux Bellorum,* escape the torture. Parilla, however, was pretty much stuck.

*If,* thought Raul Parilla, president of the Republic of Balboa, *I hear the triumphal march from Verdi's* Aida, *one more time I swear I'll shoot myself.*

With the national symphony only three blocks away, the reappearance of Radamès remained a continuing threat.

*And the day is young.*

Of course, there were worse things than opera in the streets. *And bagpipes. Fucking bagpipes. All hours of the day and night. I used to like them but—Jesus!—there's a limit.*

The president, from whose office one could hit the sea with the well-tossed rock, kept all the windows closed now, against the noise. Otherwise, thought would have been difficult and conversation impossible. Still, light seeping in though the closed shutters reflected off the iridescent silverwood walls of the president's office.

"But what if they *are* sincere, Patricio?" asked Parilla. "Stranger things have happened."

"Really?" asked Carrera, either incredulous or sardonic; Parilla couldn't be sure. "When? Did the pope convert to Islam and me just miss it? These are a mix of diplomats and Old Earthers we're talking about, Raul. Sincerity just isn't in their repertoire."

*Sardonic it is,* Parilla decided.

"No, what they're sincere about is wanting back the people we hold and getting us to revert to the status quo, ante bellum. They want to get on the negotiating table what they lost on the battlefield. And that's all."

"*Now* you're showing your parochialism," said Parilla.

"Never said I knew the first fucking thing about politics or diplomacy," countered Carrera, with a dismissive shrug. "So teach me, O great launcher of coups d'état and elder statesman extraordinaire."

Parilla first gave Carrera one rendition of the tall finger of fellowship, then said, "Sit then, young one, and learn."

Carrera sat in one of the two chairs fronting the president's massive wooden desk. Parilla, getting on in years and walking stiffly now, ambled to the front of the desk, parking his posterior on the desk and folding his arms, in full lecture the young ones mode. Not that Carrera was precisely young anymore. He was, however, considerably younger than the president.

"No," conceded Parilla, "I don't think they're sincere . . . or rather, yes, they're totally sincere about wanting to go back to the status quo ante, but also realistic enough to know that it would take an extraordinary confluence of events to get us to accept that.

"One of the streams in that theoretical confluence would be to turn the Federated States from a slightly pro-Balboan neutrality to something like hostility. And, given that the *Federales* have elected a 'peace-loving,' which is to say Cosmopolitan Progressive, regime, I wouldn't want them to think we're not as peace-loving as they are."

"But the Tauran Union attacked us *first!*" objected Carrera.

Parilla gave his *Duque* a look that said, simply, *And so?*

Explaining the look, the president said, "The culture that thinks it's wrong for a small village in the middle of a war zone to ring itself in with mines to defend itself has little understanding of war. The culture that thinks it's wrong for a young boy to pick up a rifle to defend himself, his mother, and his sisters from enslavement and rape has lost all touch with morality.

"Trust me, Patricio, if the progressive voters of the FSC come to think we're not willing to roll over and grease our asses so that they don't have to be reminded of how the universe really works, they'll turn on us in a heartbeat.

"You came *from* them, old son. You *know* I speak the truth."

"All right," Carrera said, "even conceding all that, what the hell do we do? I can send Esterhazy but the fact remains, he has very little he *can* negotiate. We're not going to disarm. We're not giving back the Transitway. We're not nearly ready to give back the prisoners . . .'"

### Post Theater, Fort Williams, Balboa, Terra Nova

"So, the baron," said the captured Anglian sergeant, to an audience of hundreds, "the baron, full of his newly won skill at wit and repartee and ecstatic at the prospect of an end to twenty years of humiliation, rose from his seat, quelled the unruly peasants' laughter with a haughty glance around the audience, and leant forward slightly, looking at the Red-Nosed Clown. He paused and pointed his finger at the clown. An expectant hush fell. He frowned and said, firmly, 'Why don't you just FUCK OFF, you red-nosed CUNT.'"

As they did every morning, the Balboan guards watching over

the prisoners just rolled their eyes, thinking, *Anglian humor I will never get.*

Marqueli, the petite and perfect, shook her head. It wasn't so much that the joke wasn't funny. The first time she'd heard it, she'd laughed, too, though she'd hidden her laugh under a demure pair of hands. It was that the same sergeant told exactly the same joke in exactly the same way *every* morning before class. And almost the entire complement of her class, some nine hundred Anglian and Haarlemer noncoms, practically rolled in the aisles when he did.

"Which is, I suppose, why you keep telling the joke, Sergeant Dane," she said, from the theater's stage.

"Why, yes, ma'am," answered the sergeant, brightly. "The lads seem to enjoy it."

Resignedly, she nodded her head. "Take seats, please, gentlemen. Or, rather, wait.

"Who here intends to sleep through my lecture?" Like the sergeant's joke, this was part of the morning routine, too.

"Anybody? Anybody at all? Ah, good. Well, if you're embarrassed about identifying yourself and don't want to sit through the class, just stand up and go to the back. The rest of you fill in to the front. I'm little, after all, and can't fill this great big theater with my little lungs."

An Anglian sergeant major stood up and said, "Not so little as all that, ma'am."

That had become part of the routine, too. Whether he was referring to her or her lungs, which was to say, breasts, was left open.

"Thank you, Sergeant Major," Marqueli said. "Now if you would . . ."

The Balboans, for whom corporals were absolutely noncoms, had followed their own rules and lumped the corporals in with the sergeants and sergeants major. This was rather awkward for the Anglians and Haarlemers, for whom corporals were *mere*, and hardly worth counting.

"GENTLEMEN," bellowed the sergeant major, using a broad brush in the absence of a formed, legal, organization. "Fellow members of the mess. And you fucking lot. Siiittt . . . fuckckckinggg . . . DOWN!"

He shot Marqueli an apologetic look. *Sorry, ma'am, but when dealing with these bloody barely human corporals . . .*

Marqueli waited the roughly second and a quarter it took for the men to settle down, then began her presentation. "Today's lesson is about how you ended up here . . . here in Balboa . . . here in this theater . . . here listening to me."

"We fucking lost a battle," was the judgment of one of the Haarlemer corporals.

"Language, boy," said the sergeant major.

The Haarlemer hung his head. "Yes, sir. Sorry, sir." Looking up at the stage, he even managed to sound sincere as he said, "*Terribly* sorry, ma'am."

"You had a better general than us," said an Anglian sergeant major, not one of the more senior ones.

"The battle wasn't won by generalship," answered Marqueli. "It was won by brave boys of, for the most part, fifteen and sixteen and seventeen."

That was not actually her position, nor her husband's, nor that of the bulk of the legion. It *was*, however, the *official* position.

"Half true, ma'am," said *the* sergeant major. "If it wasn't won by great generalship, it was surely lost by bad generalship."

"Bloody frog bastard," said several dozen mixed Anglians and Haarlemers, simultaneously.

"There was an Anglian general in command on the ground, here," said the tiny Balboan woman.

"True, ma'am," said the sergeant major, "but the frogs were pulling the strings from back in Taurus. The key staff was nearly one hundred-percent frog. Our man—no great shakes, himself; I won't argue differently—was politically isolated. A limped-wristed, little-boy-bunging, incompetent politician-in-uniform Major General Solomon McQueeg-Gordon may have been, but the command wasn't really his."

Marqueli sighed. "Much as I might like to argue tactics and operations, Sergeant Major, I don't know the first thing about it. So— since I'm a girl and you and the boys are all gentlemen—you will just concede to me that generalship wasn't the big issue."

"Fair enough, ma'am. GENTLEMEN, you will concede to the lady that generalship wasn't the big issue."

"Thanks, Sergeant Major," said the teacher, bestowing on him a smile that, however innocent, was so brilliant that it made him wish he were twenty years younger and on her side. Or at least that he'd been there and in a position to give her away when she married.

"But what was?" she continued. "I'll give you my opinion. My opinion, my own little personal opinion, is that the root of the problem is the Tauran political class . . . one may as well say the bureaucratic class, since politics there *are* largely run and ruled by the hereditary bureaucrats, party flacks, an unaccountable propaganda ministry in the form of a brave press that's brave only when not pressed, the obscenely rich"—that got her a spontaneous round of applause from the troops—"ivory tower academics"—which got her a still more enthusiastic round of applause—"racial grievance mongers, corrupt chiefs of nongovernmental organizations, diplomats who drown in every little raindrop . . ."

### *Palacio de las* Trixies, *Ciudad* Balboa, Republic of Balboa, Terra Nova

"I suppose," said Carrera, "that we could stop the conference by starting the war there. After all, we've got a large tercio in Santa Josefina. They're scattered and almost entirely disarmed—no more than a maniple's worth of arms and ammunition between them, and almost nothing in the way of heavy weapons—but that's enough to storm the conference and kill a number of diplomats. The rest will scurry. Or we could get our people a couple of shoulder-fired surface to air missiles and take down . . . no, forget I said that."

"And let the blame fall on native Santa Josefinans?" Parilla asked, avoiding mention of that fact that his friend and subordinate had been about to suggest what amounted to a terrorist act.

"Well . . . yes."

"Problem is," said Parilla, shaking his head, doubtfully, "that no one really believes those troops are anything but ours. I don't think that works."

Carrera rocked his head from side to side for a few moments, before admitting, "Yeah . . . neither do I. So what *do* we do?"

"I think we're trapped. I think we send Esterhazy to the conference. But we'll send him with a team. Assembling that team, of course, could take some time."

Esterhazy, now as Balboan as anyone, was a former Sachsen field grade *Fallschirmstuermpioniere* who had also worked for SachsenBank. He'd signed on for the very first increment of the legion, way back before the campaign in Sumer. Since then he'd alternated between commanding engineer units, serving as the comptroller, and acting as a diplomat, the legion's messenger to those it wanted to help, or help from, and those it wanted intimidated. Most of the time he spent as comptroller.

"'Some time,'" Carrera echoed. "And maybe the horse will learn to sing?"

"Precisely. Moreover . . ."

Carrera's aide de camp, Tribune Santillana, stuck his head in the door. "Mr. President," said the tribune, "sir . . . Legate Fernandez is here with what he says is important enough news to justify interrupting you. Shall I show him in."

"Just send him, Tribune," said Parilla. "He knows the way well enough . . . Hmmm . . . well, no . . . follow and make sure he doesn't have a problem on the ramps."

"Yes, Mr. President."

Fernandez rolled into Parilla's office on the best power wheelchair the legion could buy. Even so, the damp climate wasn't good for the machine; it whined a bit as it climbed the thick rug.

"There are some intelligence decisions," Fernandez announced, "that really go so far past intelligence considerations that the wise intel mucky muck bucks them to higher. This is one of those."

Carrera made a give-forth gesture with his right hand.

"Some time ago," said Fernandez, "the cabin girl for the high admiral, herself, contacted one of our people, a recruiting sergeant in Santa Josefina. The girl's from TransIsthmia on Old Earth. That means Panama, our mother country. That means she's a cousin, however distant."

Carrera looked shocked. "Did you say Wallenstein's cabin girl?"

"Yes, sir. She's probably not all *that* distant a cousin of your late wife," he said to Carrera, "provided one tallies up multiple levels of cousinship."

"Holy shit."

"That's a way to put it.

"In any event," the intel chief continued, "there wasn't a lot of time. I was able to have one of my people get in contact with her. He, though this sort of thing is hardly his specialty, set her up with an e-mail account, a system of codes, and some minimal instructions, whatever he could come up with on short notice.

"She is now back on our planet, in Aserri, Santa Josefina. The question I cannot answer is, what do we do with her. Do we take her into our care, and wring her for whatever she can tell us about Old Earth, the UEPF, and Wallenstein? Or do we leave her where she is in the hope that she might get us something more specifically important? Or do we 'kidnap' her—which is to say have 'criminals and terrorists' kidnap her—so we can put her through a short training course before she is 'rescued,' to get more use out of her? Or what?"

"Skip the last one," said Parilla. "If we spirited her away, then let her be recovered, it's very unlikely that the high admiral would do anything but ground her someplace she couldn't do any harm. Certainly trust would be too much to expect after that."

"I agree, Mr. President," said Fernandez. "I tossed it out for completeness's sake."

"What are the odds," asked Carrera, "that she knows anything really important?"

Fernandez shrugged. "There's really no way to tell, *Duque.* You would think if she knew something important, we could just get it from a quick field interrogation. And, were she a trained agent, we could. But she's just a cabin girl, though my man's impression of her was that she was a bright and brave cabin girl. Still, she doesn't know what she knows that might be important. And she is very young."

"How far do you think she can be trusted?" asked Parilla. "Could she be bait for a trap?"

"It's possible," said Fernandez, adding with a smile, "and I haven't yet figured out how to do a background check on someone from Old Earth."

Fernandez so rarely smiled, let alone told a joke, that Carrera did a double take. "What do you suggest?" he asked.

"I'd suggest leaving her in place, but using the opportunity to get her some useful equipment, and maybe some weapons familiarization. There are indoor ranges open to the public in Aserri, at least some of which are holding arms for our tercio in Santa Josefina."

"Risks of doing that?" Parilla asked. "I don't mean just risks to us but also—since, as you say, she is a cousin—risks to her."

"No real risk to us, per se," said Fernandez. "All I've got in mind is giving her a ceramic knife with a plastic handle, a tool ring, a tiny cell phone with a few extra batteries since we don't know if she'd be able to recharge it up there, some poisons, a lipstick dagger. The usual. The risk to her, though, if she were caught, is immense."

"There's no way for her to communicate to us?" Carrera asked.

"No." Fernandez shook his head. "The only one up there communicating with anybody regularly down here is whoever or whatever the Yamatans have. And for all our pleading, they'll only give us information, not how they get it."

"What do you think it is," Carrera asked, "a whoever or a whatever?"

"Damned if I know, though I have my suspicions. It would be just like the Yamatans to have left behind on Old Earth a small organization or clan, dedicated to the perpetuation of the Imperial Way through intelligence work . . . even across five centuries. It could even be a criminal organization, or a part of one. They're a very strange people. If we couldn't interbreed, I'd wonder if we were the same species."

"Can you make a deal with them? They tell us how the word gets to them from the Peace Fleet and we let them share in whatever the girl can get for us. Did I say 'share'? Silly me, it will have to go through them, won't it?"

"I don't think they'd consider it a fair trade," Fernandez said. "Their asset, who—or whatever it is, has been working well for quite some time. The girl, on the other hand, is a wasting asset . . . an unproven wasting asset. And one that might be a threat to their source.

"So, no, I don't think so."

"I want to see this girl," said Carrera.

"I don't—" Fernandez began, before being cut off by Parilla's, "In Aserri? No, my friend, I expressly forbid you from going anyplace where you might be kidnapped or assassinated."

Carrera drew breath, as if intending to argue. He paused, then visibly deflated as he exhaled. "Good point. Okay, I'll concede the risks are high. So . . . you know Lourdes is a fine judge of character. And she can gribbitz eloquently as well. We'll send her with Esterhazy. There shouldn't be any problem with a false passport. Fernandez can brief her and prep her beforehand. And she can carry everything the girl needs in a diplomatic pouch."

"Why Lourdes?" asked Parilla. "She's your wife, after all. And, since Pigna's failed coup"—Lourdes had, in fact, been the one person most responsible for the defeat of that coup—"she's fairly well known both within and outside of Balboa."

"Precisely," Carrera agreed. "She's quite well known. She's well connected, obviously, so there'll be no doubt among the international community of the very, very caring and sensitive that we're taking the conference seriously. She's also the person whose judgment I most trust on this entire planet. If she meets the girl and tells me we can trust her, that she is capable . . . then I can act on that with confidence.

"She is also, to be sure, one of the most pigheaded women in the world on anything she's determined on—witness that Jimenez had to have her weapons hidden before she'd let anyone talk to me when I was . . . ill—so she won't be giving anything away."

"It *is* rather elegant," Parilla admitted. "Esterhazy to be his totally frightening Sachsen self . . . Lourdes to be a, still quite lovely, velvet glove with the mailed fist inside of it. The recipe I do not have . . . but the list of ingredients appeals."

Fernandez chewed at his lip for a bit, then said, "I'm going to assign Larry Triste to be the girl's control officer. For any asset with less potential, that would be beneath him. For this . . . he'll suit. And his judgment can supplement Lourdes's; we'll send him to Aserri to the peace conference. In fact, I'll send him early."

"This is all well and good," Parilla said, "but we should not lose sight of the fact that this peace conference has one aim: to disarm us and leave us vulnerable to our enemies."

"Raul," said Carrera, "I assure you that this is a fact I shall *never* lose sight of. And on that happy note, with your permission, Mr. President, I have to fly to Fort Williams, pick up my teenaged son and his—Jesus, have mercy!—even younger 'wife,' hopefully before the defiant bitch has managed to get herself knocked up . . ."

Parilla looked stunned. He knew the boy well and had met the girl. "You don't really think . . ."

"Has it been that long since you were a teenager, Raul?" Carrera asked, one eyebrow raised.

# CHAPTER SIX

A real diplomat is one who can cut his neighbor's throat
without having his neighbor notice it.

—Trygve Lie

### Hotel *Cielo Dorado*, Aserri, Santa Josefina, Terra Nova

Esmeralda woke up with company. Spooned up behind her, one arm
under her head and the other, the right one, wrapped around her, that
hand cupping her left breast, was her lover, Richard, earl of Care.
Richard, captain of the *Spirit of Peace*, still slept. Automatically, she
pushed back against him. It couldn't be said she enjoyed sex. She
expected that she never would. But she could enjoy Richard's
enjoyment and she could enjoy the warmth, if not the feeling.

Warmed by Richard, she thought, *He says he wishes he could take
off his skin and wrap me in it. I believe it, too.*

Richard had taken his pinnace down to Aserri the night before,
borrowed Esmeralda from the high admiral—an easy thing, that, with
Wallenstein so infatuated with her empress—and taken the girl to
dinner and then bed. There he'd done his best to show how much he'd
missed her on her too frequent official absences.

Before Richard, Esmeralda's only experience of sex had been the
rape of peasant girls to be expected from the sons and soldiers of
Count Castro-Nyere, the absolute ruler of her home province of
TransIsthmia, and the far more violent and even more violating rape
of the slave pens of Razona Market.

*How I might have felt about sex if the soldiers of Count Castro-Nyere and all the slavers at Razona Market hadn't fucked me until I bled, I can't say.*

For a moment, just a moment, the memories caused the girl to tighten like the skin of a drum. Then the warmth and the other memories—not least that Richard *was* serious about wrapping her in his skin, were it but possible—let her relax again.

Yet he, ever sensitive to her, at least, felt the tightening and startled awake immediately. "Are you all right?" he asked.

"Fine, love . . . I'm fine," she replied, softly. "Just a little nightmare." *The kind you have when you're wide awake.* "Go back to sleep."

With a gentle squeeze of her breast, and a light kiss against the cascading midnight of her hair, he did.

In the same wing of the hotel, on the same floor, but with a guard on the specific corridor, Marguerite Wallenstein and the empress, Xingzhen, lay wrapped in each other's arms so tightly that, but for size and color differences, it would have been near impossible to tell where one began and the other ended. As it was, Wallenstein, blond and tall, physically quite dominated the empress, while the empress held the whip hand emotionally, and also literally, when they thought they had enough privacy.

*Sadly, here we do not have enough privacy. But, my almond-eyed love, when this conference is over—which is to say when your generals and admirals and my General Janier and his people have worked out the details of continuing the war—you and I are going to Atlantis for a vacation. There's a nice* latifundia *there that goes with the office of high admiral. There, there'll be privacy enough for everything you want to do to me and everything you want me to do for you.*

The high admiral had always considered herself bisexual with a very slight preference for dominant men. What she was discovering was that she was bisexual with an absolute preference for Xingzhen.

*I never believed in love at first sight. The more fool I.*

**Headquarters, Tauran Union Security Force-Santa Josefina,
*Rio Clara*, Santa Josefina, Terra Nova**

An acetated and color-coded map, the colors and their intensity shaded for what was believed to be the density of Balboan-trained, -equipped, and -directed legionaries in various parts of the country. The map had been provided by the Santa Josefinan public force, though Marciano's own intelligence people thought it was pretty close to accurate. The map was accompanied by a police lieutenant Marciano introduced to his staff as "Lieutenant Blanco," who had brought with it a folder containing names and addresses for the *known* legionaries who had come back home.

Claudio Marciano was more than ordinarily torn. He hadn't yet been officially asked, less still ordered, to start rounding up the legionaries in Santa Josefina. But the orders would be coming along soon, he suspected. For that matter, it made a certain sense to start picking them up now, or at least soon, while they were scattered and—mostly, though he doubted entirely—disarmed. That would allow his people to use minimal force. Indeed, they might be able to arrange things so as to be seen as nothing more than backups for the Santa Josefinan Public Force. Minimal force would mean fewer civilians hurt or killed. With a little luck, perhaps no one would be hurt; none of his, none of theirs, no police, no civilians.

*And isn't that the ideal?* he asked himself. *To compel one's enemy to give up his purpose while suffering no harm oneself? Not that even Belisarius ever quite managed to do that.*

In any case, the lack of orders was no reason for him not to have his staff and subordinate commanders *planning* for the roundup. Neither was it reason not to be coordinating with the Public Force.

*Especially so since, once a roundup begins, the odds are really good that the other Santa Josefinan regiment will be across the border in no time. That will be fine—well, no, not exactly* fine, *but survivable—provided I can eliminate the internal threat before they pin us, and then get my command concentrated along their obvious axis of advance and main supply route. On the other hand, let me and my little pocket division have to split our efforts between a guerilla movement and a fixing force on the border or—worse!—having crossed the border and I'm screwed. Hard. No grease. And not kissed first. Ugly, in other words.*

The other alternative, hitting the well-armed, well-trained, and probably all too well led force around *Ciudad* Cervantes, he didn't even consider, and for the same reason he'd pulled back from the border once it became obvious that the battle within and for Balboa had been lost. There were simply too many of the bastards, they were too good—not perfect, certainly not supermen, but *too* good—and they were too ruthless and thorough.

*After all, it's not like the Santa Josefinans are the only troops there in their Valle de las Lunas. I've got it on pretty good authority that there's a five-cohort tercio of mountain troops there, too, straddling Hephaestus Mountain across the border. Eleven cohorts? Probably four or five battalions of decent artillery. Do not want to deal with that. Not, not, NOT.*

"Eleven cohorts?" he asked Lieutenant Blanco, currently serving as his *good authority.* "Eleven?"

"Including the three we are quite sure are already inside the country, yes," answered Blanco, "but not counting their Cazador maniples, or the engineers, or the light armor. Could be twelve; there may be four cohorts already in country. And there are rumors we have not been able to pin down that a very large cohort of women warriors is assembling close by, too, a cohort as big as any two others. Plus possibly another cohort, small but high quality, from their special operations regiment."

"And I am still troubled. What *is* your source?" asked Marciano, to which question Blanco only smiled in reply.

*My primary source,* thought Blanco, even as he kept his face perfectly neutral, *is probably Legate Fernandez. At least I think he's the one who's ordered me fed information by Sergeant Morales of the recruiting maniple here in Aserri. Is the information accurate? I don't have any reason to doubt the troop list he's been providing. It's just that I'm not sure of his reasons for providing it. Perhaps he just wants you to feel threatened into passivity. Perhaps his chief, the gringo named Carrera, remembers that you and he had fought side-by-side, against the same enemies, in Pashtia, and doesn't want you hurt.*

*For my part, I just want my country to be a real country again, independent, able to defend itself, not a beggar for help from big brother. I would prefer that we not become a part of another real country, either, for which Balboa is the likely candidate. We're similar, yes, but not so similar that I want us married to them. But there's no reason for us to end up annexed, since the Balboans have been kind enough to provide us a couple of regiments, already formed and ready.*

"Let's just say," said Blanco, with a sly smile, "that we have people on the other side." This had the virtue of being absolutely true and entirely misleading, both.

Though Marciano wasn't entirely misled. He retained, at least, some doubts about Blanco's true loyalty. Nor, if the police lieutenant was loyal to the idea of his country free of foreign troops and able to stand on its own feet, did Marciano consider that blameworthy.

*Dangerous to me and my men? Yes. Blameworthy? No.*

Marciano cast his attention back to the annotated and color-shaded threat map. "Funny that the ones inside Santa Josefina already are concentrated along the Shimmering Sea side of the country, with only a few here on the *Mar Furioso* side, near us. Or maybe not exactly funny . . . I've seen more humorous things."

"Why *did* they do that?" Blanco asked. His sojourn through the Atlacatlan Military Academy hadn't been designed for much more than to make him a decent platoon leader.

Marciano, who was as up on insurgency as anyone around, answered, "Putting the one regiment out away from us is probably to give them more time and warning to disperse if we move against them. The others probably belong to the regiment still in Balboa. My guess would be recon troops, or special operations troops. And their mission is probably to call for artillery to support and advance, and blow or secure bridges to keep us from either supplying or maneuvering, while letting them do both?"

"How both?" the policeman asked. "That makes no—"

"Different needs," the Tuscan replied. "The bridge we need gets blown. The bridge we're not watching gets seized and guarded. Different techniques. The enemy side of a bridge gets cut so they can fix it without too much interference from us while we have to expose ourselves to fix the bridge if they're on the other end. For example."

"Yeah, 'for example,'" the policeman agreed. "I think that means that the easier job, rounding up the ones near here, has to come first, but . . ."

"But that warns them to disperse on the Shimmering Sea side, which makes that job a lot tougher."

"Oh, well," said Marciano, softly, "I knew the other side back in Pashtia. They weren't stupid then, either."

### Hotel *Cielo Dorado,* Aserri, Santa Josefina, Terra Nova

The problem with bugging the hotel for real-time intelligence, something Fernandez's intelligence net in Santa Josefina was perfectly capable of, was that no one knew what the *UEPF* was capable of. Could they detect bugs? Could they detect the most sophisticated bugs? Fernandez had to assume so. At least he had to until someone could talk to the young cabin girl who said she wanted to help. If she said they couldn't, or wouldn't, or wouldn't bother, which were not quite the same things, and if the legate decided they could trust her on that, the only problem would be keeping all the various microphones from squealing out loud from feedback from each other.

Until then, Fernandez had ordered hands off or, rather, "No bugs."

Thus, although the high admiral, the empress, and Janier, plus their various staffs, all watched what they said, and tended to speak in circumlocutions, they didn't—at least for the nonce—really need to.

The only place they could speak freely was one conference room, and not a particularly large one, that was swept daily by Tauran, UEPF, and Zhong intelligence.

The conference room was on the hotel's third floor, separate from all other rooms, and reachable only by its own elevator. The walls were doubled, to prevent eavesdropping that way. And the place came with its own system for interfering with radio waves. It was nearly as secure as Wallenstein's own office, aboard the *Spirit of Peace,* and, though she didn't know it, much more secure than the main conference room on the ship, as well.

"We insist on control of the country, post conquest, east of the western border of the old Transitway Area and north of the central *cordillera,*" said the empress, "plus control of the *Isla Real* of the city, of the city of *Ciudad* Cervantes, of the city of Nata, of the Florida and Pablo Manuel locks, and of the military facilities in that sector.

"We further insist on the right of free immigration of our people to the entire country, without limit or quota, without let or hindrance.

"Lastly, we insist on receiving the war criminals Raul Parilla, Patricio Carrera, and Conrad Chu for trial in our courts followed by execution by us. Their crimes deserve no less."

"Preposterous," answered Janier. "The World League Mandate is ours, legally and by right. We could not give it up to you, nor give up half of it to you, under any circumstances.

"Though you are welcome to hang the criminals—"

"Nothing so quick and easy," said the empress, interrupting.

"Whatever. You can execute them any way you like, since we will not. But we cannot under any circumstances give you half the country."

"It's not more than a quarter," Xingzhen insisted.

"With right of unlimited immigration it is the entirety, within a generation," said Janier, with a sneer that only a Gaul could have produced. "By saying 'half' I was just averaging what you claim versus what you're trying to steal."

"Steal!" The empress's eyes flashed with outrage. "Steal! Let me tell you about theft, you Gallic pickpocket! Let's start with Zikawei, shall we. Stolen from us and then sold—Did I say pickpocket?" She hissed, "I meant *fence*!—to Yamato. The half of Liwan Island you extorted! Jilong!" she spat out, naming another former Gallic possession in *Xing Zhong Guo*, during less enlightened times. "Zhigu!"

*I should have expected*, thought Wallenstein, *a certain resentment toward the Gauls. I wonder why the subject never came up before. Maybe because talk is difficult when communicating by eating each other.*

Before Janier could make the answer he was clearly puffing himself up for, Wallenstein held up her hand to forestall his response, then said, simply, "The Federated States will not permit it, Empress. Taking Balboa will be difficult enough if the FSC stays out of it. It will be impossible if they join the Balboans. Their fleet dominates the planet in a way that even mine does not." *And, if they only knew it, they could dominate my fleet, too.*

"Then pay me in other coin," said Xingzhen to Janier, with a heat both angry and bitter. "You want my people to bear the major burden, to spend a cubic meter of blood for every liter of yours. Pay me to make it worth it."

"I will pay you, *bǎo bèi*," said Marguerite. *And I don't mean just in sex.*

The empress turned liquid eyes on the high admiral. "I know you will, *bǎo bǎo*," she said, gently, reaching up one delicate hand and then running one perfectly nailed finger down the high admiral's cheek. The gentle tone died then. "But I will not permit you to pay what this Gallic thief and his people owe me and mine. He and his *started* the fucking war that got my carrier sunk and my people killed."

Leaning in to rest her cheek against Marguerite's, the empress added, so softly Janier couldn't hear, "And I know you mean to give me immortality, so we can be together forever. I want that, too, *băo băo*. But that is for us, for you and I, alone . . . or, rather, together. My people must have their share, as well. They, after all, will be paying this Gallic fence's blood bill."

"We will pay the cost of the war," conceded Janier. "That is, the operational cost, pay, ammunition, fuel, rations, parts. If you lose major pieces of equipment, that is on you. We will not be funding you in rebuilding your navy."

"Not good enough," the empress insisted.

Janier sighed. "We will pay ten thousand drachma for any Zhong soldier killed, and five thousand for each one crippled."

"Still not enough."

"We will, as I already agreed, give you the chief miscreants if they can be taken alive. I can make no promise that they will be taken alive."

"More!"

Wallenstein had a sudden inspiration. "Would free access to Tauran military technology and a license to produce any of it be sufficient?"

Without hesitation, Xingzhen answered, "Yes. In advance."

"In principle," said Janier, "yes. It can be presented as aiding the common war effort. It will also annoy the Federated States, a selling point not to be underestimated with our politicians. But that is only in principle. The people who own the patents, the government agencies that have them classified, these are all difficult sells."

"Twenty years of rejuvenation to the primaries," said the high admiral.

Janier chewed knuckles for a few moments, then said, "I think that will be sufficient. Even so, we have a problem."

"Yes," said Wallenstein, "the peace conference might actually succeed in its stated aims, which will leave you out of Balboa, the Tauran Union shown as incompetent and weak—not even a real country, anyway—*Zhong Guo*'s losses unavenged, and the FSC still dominating the surface of the planet."

*And my planet without the five great powers set up, here, that will keep you all—all except for my beautiful empress, who is going to spend most of her life with me—at each other's throats forever, hence occupied here rather than going to the Earth.*

## Cedral Multiplex Shopping Mall, Aserri, Santa Josefina, Terra Nova

The mall was close enough to the hotel that Esmeralda could make it in a walk of no more than five brisk minutes. The walk was not only brisk, it was simply lovely. Cedral was its usual heavenly ideal of perfect weather—which explained the mall, as well as the rich who frequented it—and both resplendent with flowers and replete with their fragrance. The cars here were better tuned, burned better gasoline, and were fewer than in more populous parts. There were no stinking, fuming buses at this time of day; the service ran only in the early mornings and late evenings, and then only to bring in and take away the hired help.

The message she'd retrieved and decoded was that she should wear nice clothes, but nothing too noticeable, that she should go alone to the mall, that she should make sure she wasn't being tailed when she went, that at the mall she should go into the recruiting station and that there someone named Triste, a junior legate, would introduce himself.

It had a couple of suggestions on how to avoid being tailed.

Going alone was easier said than done, what with Richard on the surface. She'd had to wait two full days for his shore leave to end and he to return to the *Spirit of Peace*. Fortunately, crime in this part of Aserri was essentially unknown, so she didn't need an escort. Even so, Esmeralda hung back, heart pounding. It was treason, what she was planning and, even worse, treason against a man who loved her desperately and a woman who was almost a mother and who had saved her from a particularly shitty death.

*And though I can walk easily, now,* she thought, *back in the slave camp at Razona Market walking was always difficult when they*

*finished with me. That, I suppose is the difference between having to
and wanting to, or at least being willing to. That's the difference between
my own society at the high end, then, and now. And they still killed and
ate my sister.*

As usual, that memory, or series of them, was sufficient to buck
her up when her spirit wavered. She pushed on, walking through the
mall's wide glass doors and onto the gleaming tile. Just before passing
through the doors she saw a poster, color printed and crudely glued
to the wall, depicting what seemed to be a Tauran soldier with horns
growing out from the sides of his beret.

As per her instructions, she went to a restaurant. Just before she
reached it, on the same side of the mall, she noticed a realty office.
There she stopped, looking over the high-end property on offer in
Cedral. From there, she walked on to the restaurant, Tinto's, then sat
down facing in the direction from which she'd come.

She ordered a light snack, two small empanadas and a soft drink,
then watched for what seemed a long time to see if anyone was
following or watching her. From there she went into one of the three-
story department stores—she'd shopped there before, with Estefani
from the embassy—and went up two escalators, then down three.
From the bottom floor, she walked briskly in the other direction, then
took an elevator up to the floor she wanted. When it opened, she
stepped out, took a glance around, and walked into the recruiting
station.

Once she'd entered the station, Esmeralda looked for the recruiter
she'd spoken to before, Sergeant Riza-Rivera. He was there, but not,
like last time, at the desk labeled "Centurion Chavez." She thought the
sergeant went very pale indeed, once he saw her.

Riza-Rivera arose, walked to her, and announced, "Ah, Miss
Miranda. I've been expecting you. Your test is all prepared if you
would just follow me."

Riza-Rivera led her to a back office, one labeled, in fact,

"Testing.

Quiet Please."

He took Esmeralda through the door, closed it, and introduced
her to the light-skinned man sitting at one of the booths. Right behind

him was a tall, slender, really rather pretty woman, also in uniform. The man was mostly salt and pepper-haired. The woman was blond, what one could see of her hair with it pulled back into a bun.

"Legate Triste," the man said. Jerking his thumb at the woman he added, "She's Warrant Officer Aragon, Cass Aragon, and this is the last time she'll appear in Santa Josefina in uniform. I'm going to be your primary control, Miss Miranda, but she's your day-to-day contact while you're on planet, and your key out of here if things go to crap. She, after all, can go with you to places I cannot. Cass is taking a job at the realtor's here in the mall. Thus she'll be generally available."

"Now, miss, if you will have a seat."

# CHAPTER SEVEN

Being a mother is an attitude, not a biological relation.
—Robert A. Heinlein,
*Have Space Suit—Will Travel*

**Fort Williams, Balboa, Terra Nova**

Out on the parade field, a group of about a dozen Castilians was practicing carrying around a very heavy and large—huge, really—crucifix, the *Jesus Negro de Puerto Lindo*, on upraised arms. They'd borrowed it from the small town outside the Sergeant Juan Malvegui Military Academy for a victory parade through the city of Cristobal. They marched in a sort of truncated goosestep, singing the whole time.

> *"Nadie en el Tercio sabía*
> *Quien era aquel legionario*
> *Tan audaz y temerario*
> *Que a la Legión se alistó."*

★★★

If asked, Carrera couldn't have said why he was just now getting around to seeing his boy and his little one-girl crusade, Pililak. He'd been on this side before, watching the prisoner return and annoying the Kosmos, yet he'd never stopped by to see Hamilcar. He might, if asked, have rationalized it as, "Don't want the boy's relationship with the other cadets wrecked by connection to me," or even, "Oh, let the little bitch get fucked; she's earned it."

99

In point of fact, those two rationales might have played a part. Much the larger part, however, was, "How the hell do I deal with this? It is not a particular personal strength, dealing with runaway girls and sons that, by the grace of God, went to war and have come through whole."

Not that he was going to let his mind wander to those verities, however. Let the boy's mother sort that kind of thing out.

Nobody was working on repairing the damage from the fighting as Carrera's helicopter touched down on the pad, bouncing for a half a minute or so on its landing gear. That pad was not so far from the post pool, below Headquarters Hill with its four tile-roofed buildings, the flagpoles with their signal gun, and the club to the east of the flagpoles. They, at least, had survived the fighting unscathed; now two flags, Balboa's and Castile's, floated on the breeze.

The damage to the post and the buildings of its quad was severe. Even the quad's parade field was chewed up and cratered by artillery and mortar fire. It was a physical pain to Carrera to look out and see the damaged, scorched, soot-marked barracks, some with the tiles of their roofs showing gaping holes. He sighed, thinking, *If the place you were happiest in your life is home, then this was my home. I only hope it can be repaired, once the war is over.*

He heard them now, the Castilians bearing their huge cross, as they continued to sing:

> *"Más si alguno quien era le preguntaba*
> *Con dolor y rudeza le contestaba:"*

Carrera had any of several aircraft he could call on for transport, from a Cricket recon plane to a small helicopter to an IM-71 troop carrier, which was what he rode now. He'd really had to; none of the other things available would do for him, his son, and, *that defiant horny little bitch who escaped. Damn, love that girl. She'll produce some fine grandchildren, I'm sure. I'd just hoped it wouldn't be so soon. Rather, I hope it isn't too late.*

He was disabused of that notion as soon as his feet touched the ground. Having been advised in advance, the commander of the post and the Castilian cohort that had defended it, as well as Chapayev, the commander of Ham's cadet tercio, had made very sure to have the boy and his girl—*no, his* woman *now*, thought Chapayev and Muñoz-Infantes, both, independently—waiting at the pad. One look was all it took; Ham, rifle in one hand, with his other arm wrapped protectively around the—*My, isn't she pretty?*—girl; Pililak, "Ant," in her own language, uniformed but without insignia, leaning into the boy, her chin lifted defiantly.

> *"Soy un hombre a quien la suerte*
> *Hirió con zarpa de fiera;*
> *Soy un novio de la muerte*
> *Que va a unirse en lazo fuerte*
> *Con tal leal compañera."*

*You're too late, old man*, the girl's face seemed to say. *My lord is mine!*

Again, Carrera mentally sighed. Hamilcar had always been a bit distant from his dozen wives. *I see in your enfolding arm, my boy, every human male entrapped by the joys of a woman . . . or girl. Shit, what am I going to tell your mother?*

Face a mask of sternness, Carrera raised one arm, pointing into the helicopter. *To your seats, GO!* He left them there and, bent slightly, hat clasped tightly in his hand, walked to where Chapayev and Muñoz-Infantes waited. Those two smiled broadly.

Once past the arc of the rotors, Carrera and the other two, plus a couple of hangers-on, exchanged salutes. No words could be heard over the roar of the helicopter's engine, the whine of the transmission, and the *whopwhopwhop* of the air-churning blades. With a finger gesture, Carrera indicated they should walk up the hill toward the club east of the flagpoles, for a little chat.

> *"Cuando, al fin le recogieron,*
> *Entre su pecho encontraron*
> *Una carta y un retrato*
> *De una divina mujer."*

Ant could be defiant when her father-in-law was present and glaring. It was when he was not that the uncertainty crept in. In her seat—a rather better one, leather and upholstered, than the troops got—as Iskandr, whom most called Hamilcar, buckled her in, she began to tremble.

"Relax, Pili," said her lord. "I know you've only flown once before but . . ."

She gripped his arm with both hands, putting a temporary stop to his maneuvers with the seat and shoulder belts. "It's not the flight, my lord. While I am with you I fear for nothing. It's your father. My people have tales of the fathers of gods, wicked, bitter, cruel . . ."

"I am not a god, Pili, however much you and Alena the witch insist I am. I'm just a boy. And the old man . . . well, no, he's not going to be happy about you defying him. But he *is* going to be happy about . . ."

*Well, I hope he is.*

"If she's not pregnant," said Chapayev, "it's not for lack of trying."

"You could have stopped them," Carrera said accusingly, over his mug of beer.

"*Duque*," said Muñoz-Infantes, twirling a wine glass and smiling to show he was not entirely serious as he said, "if I could not stop my daughter from sleeping with this Volgan bastard prior to marrying him, and I could not, then nobody was going to keep your son out of that girl."

"She was very helpful with the wounded," offered Chapayev. "It's amazing the pain a young boy will endure with a smile if there's a pretty girl there to hold his hand."

"So?" asked Carrera, who wasn't really entirely in the mood to be mollified as regarded his self-willed daughter-in-law.

"So she did your line proud," said Chapayev who, truth be told, liked and admired the girl enormously. "So you should be proud. For God's sake, *Duque*, she's as brave and determined as any man in the legion. A not-yet-fifteen-year-old girl sets out on her own, across jungle like she's never seen before, crosses the fucking Transitway, nearly gets run down by a freighter, loses her food, her water, her map, her compass, loses enough blood to mosquitoes for an emergency room's need, and *still* finds the boy she loves? They write poems and songs about girls like that, they're so rare."

"Yeah, she did have big brass ones, didn't she?" Carrera smiled. "But if I don't terrorize the bitch there'll be no peace in the future. And, even then, Chappie, she's so *young*, too young for a baby."

"You wouldn't make her abort it?" asked Muñoz-Infantes, solid Catholic and scandalized as the very thought.

"I'm probably a bad Catholic and no kind of Christian at all," said Carrera, just as scandalized, "but I'm better than that."

"Good," said the Castilian defector. "I would hate to think my men and I fought for a monster."

"Still," said Carrera, "she's such an itty bitty thing, our Pililak. I'd hoped she'd grow a bit before he knocked her up."

"She's not so little as that," said Chapayev. "I think she'll be fine."

Carrera ignored his son and daughter-in-law on the flight back. He had the pilot take him over the artillery area south of the Parilla Line, then along the line itself. He looked carefully for the signs of "Volcano" fuel air explosive bombs being emplaced, but saw none.

*Let's hope they got them emplaced and then left them without anyone noticing.*

From the Parilla line they did a fly-by of the coastal defenses, especially the islands north of Fort Guerrero. There was little to be seen, of course, just some heavy mortars in pits at Batteries Wesley, Earl, and Eugene, all of which retained their old names from Federated States days. That, and some troops putting in barbed wire, though not much of it.

*Well,* mused Carrera, looking down through the bubble window, *the mortars were obsolete and cheap. Didn't even buy much ammunition for them, though I did for the cohort out on the island. And we got none of the guidance packages Kuralski wanted me to get. Not enough range to justify it. No, they'll hardly even be manned. Their highest and best use is as bomb magnets once they start pounding us from the air.*

*That, and there's always the chance they'll waste some special operations troops trying to take out harmless gun positions. It's happened before, after all.*

After circling the three islands off Fort Guerrero, Conure Island, Dancer Island, and Cella Island, some of which did have actual effective guns on railway carriages, hidden in tunnels, the helicopter turned east, beating its way along the coast to the *Casa* Linda and Hamilcar's mother.

### *Casa* **Linda,** *Carretera InterColombiana***, Balboa, Terra Nova**

Carrera stepped off the helicopter with trepidation; he could just picture Lourdes's reaction. He could see it now, the weeping, the wailing, the recriminations. He could imagine the devastation of suddenly feeling old on the part of a woman who could easily pass, and did, for being a dozen or more years younger than she was. He could hear it already, *"I'm too young to be a grandmother! Whaaaa!"*

*It's going to be horrible. It's going to be hell. I think maybe I need to go spend more time with the troops . . . like continuously until the war's over. I think . . .*

Lourdes took one look at Pililak, instantly divined her status, and ran over to the girl, feeling her stomach, pinching her cheek, and covering her head and face with maternal kisses. She asked a question, her mouth pressed close to Ant's ear. The girl responded with an enthusiastic set of head nods, her face split in a grin from ear to ear. This set Lourdes to a repeat performance, but with even more enthusiasm.

Meanwhile, Alena, with Ham's other wives and both his sisters—for the nonce ignored by their mother in this—led them through their ritual prostrations, adding something in her own language to Pililak that neither Carrera nor Lourdes understood. Then, at Alena's command, all the girls, and she herself, arose to their feet and gave a deep bow to Ant.

Lourdes assumed that, like herself, they'd been able to take one look at Pililak and see there was going to be a new baby. It was reasonable to think so, though it was wrong or, rather, only half-right.

"You're taking this rather well," said Carrera to Lourdes, once they were alone, seated in their own quarters. "I expected tears, fainting, wailing to the heavens."

"Well . . . she *is* awfully young," Lourdes admitted. "And not large, so a big baby may be a problem. But she's so mature, so tough, best of all so dedicated to our son . . . and besides, a *new baby in the house!* Nothing in life better than a new baby."

"Really?" he asked, head cocked and with an eyebrow raised.

"Well . . . almost nothing," she conceded. "Speaking of which, after talking with Alena, it seems Ham has a job to do . . . or rather, eleven of them."

It didn't take a lot of math. "Our house is become a bordello," Carrera fumed.

"Nonsense," Lourdes replied. "In the first place, no money is changing hands, and in the second place they're all married, but in the third place, it won't *be* in our house; I've set aside one of the guest quarters in the old staff building for them. After all, it's apt to get noisy. The girls will continue to sleep here except for one a night who goes to stay with Ham over there." She gave a deep laugh, adding, "You can smell it off them; the little tramps can hardly wait." She looked at her husband's doubtful expression and amended, "Trust me; you could smell it if you were a woman. Your sex are sight hounds, but we're bloodhounds."

Now it was Lourdes's turn for head cocking and eyebrow raising. "Ummm . . . speaking of which . . . I am . . . you know . . . going to Santa Josefina . . . in just a few days . . . might be gone for weeks or months . . . umm . . ."

"Shut up and get your clothes off, woman. You don't have much time and I'm not getting any younger."

Two days later, two of Ham's wives, Afiyat and Mehmood were smiling, broadly and continuously, while eight of the other nine were fidgeting like babies doing the pee-pee dance. Of those eight, the most fidgety was Jamrat, whose big day was tomorrow. The last—one might say the "Belle du Jour"—red-headed Sahiba, was nowhere to be seen, but was alleged to be spending the entire day under Alena's tutelage in preparation for her debutant night.

Ham, not inconsistent with that, was looking very worn out indeed. Past the *bohio* down by the beach, next to the long pier, on the family yacht where his father had escaped to do a little thinking and get some work done, the boy pleaded his case.

"Dad," he asked, "can I *please* go back to my tercio? *Please*? They're killing me."

"Under no circumstances," said Carrera, his smile wicked and malicious. "In the first place, it's not fair to the so-far-still-intact girls. In the second place, I have a different assignment for you, for which you will depart in a few weeks. In the third place, said-still-intact girls will, I am sure, make our lives here a living hell if they're deprived. And in the fourth place, no, because you deserve this after bagging Ant against my wishes and advice."

"But Daaaaddd!"

"Fuck off and do your duty, boy."

The boy's head hung. As he turned to go, his father spun the file he'd been looking at on the table in front of him, saying, "But I want you to look at this first and tell me how you would get troops ashore?"

### *Iglesia de Nuestra Señora, Ciudad* Balboa, Balboa, Terra Nova

Lourdes was already on her way to Santa Josefina and the peace conference. Triste had made the arrangements, both for security from electronic bugging, and from eavesdropping, as well as living arrangements on site for the twenty-two guards from the Fourteenth Cazador Tercio, who would provide security, the three clerks, the one en- and decryption specialist and the electronic security specialist from Fernandez's organization, and three cooks. In the interim, Lourdes's major domo could run the house perfectly well.

Eventually Carrera relented, if only in part, and gave his son a break. Yes, there was much wailing and gnashing of perfect white teeth, but the girls anxiously awaiting their semi-ritualistic defloration would just have to wait a little longer.

Carrera had to give a briefing to some troops. Since he hated saying the same thing twice, he brought Ham along to listen, as well as Alena to see to his care. The boy, though he didn't know it, was his father's continuity file. If everything went to crap and Carrera should be killed, or simply die, Xavier Jimenez could ask the boy what his father had planned.

The talk was to the survivors of the maniple of the *Tercio Amazona* which had stormed up *Cerro Mina* and been shot to bits for their trouble, the rest of the tercio, which hadn't seen action, and a few attachments. While waiting for the women and the few men to come in, Carrera spent the time praying. In his case, though, it was never so much about praying as just talking to God. What the boy was thinking as he knelt at the altar beside his father none but he knew.

Once the sounds behind him quieted to the point he was pretty sure all the *Amazonas* were seated, Carrera and the boy crossed themselves and stood. Carrera directed Hamilcar to go sit down in the front pew, next to Alena the green-eyed witch. As the boy turned, he tousled his hair. The Pashtun guards shifted position to where they could cover their god.

Carrera recognized a few of the female footsoldiers from a not-too-dissimilar talk he'd given some of the first graduating class at his own house, the *Casa* Linda. One, in particular, seemed familiar. He strained for a minute, seeking a name that would not, at first, come. When he remembered, he pointed at that woman, one he'd personally recruited, and mouthed, *Good to see you, Maria, very good.*

Carrera hated wasting time; that was part of his detestation of having to say the same thing twice. "We've won a battle. The war's not over. It won't be over until we are destroyed or the Tauran Union is a footnote.

"We're giving back their most useless prisoners to buy time, time to offload the equipment, time to dig in, time to assimilate our new volunteers and allies—bet you never guessed that the International Rifle Platoon Competition was intended to gather allies, did you?—time to get in position and ready for what's coming.

"It's going to be really bad, what's coming."

Carrera's finger pointed skyward. "Assume the United Earth Peace Fleet is against us, in spirit and, to the degree they can without drawing a violent reaction from the Federated States, materially, as well.

"The Zhong are coming in against us, though I can't really see them being able to move and support more than maybe two hundred to three hundred thousand men across the sea. Probably not even that many. The Tauran Union has already dispatched ships to help move them.

"The Taurans are fragmented. Indeed, some of them stand with us against their own bureaucracy. But we can expect anything up to a dozen modern divisions, equal to ours in manning, superior in equipment, with a tremendous air superiority. Assuming they can grab a port, of course.

"Bring out the map, please," Carrera shouted to somebody. He went silent then, while a large mounted map was wheeled out in front of the altar. On the map's mount was a laser pointer. This he picked up. He flicked it on and circled the *Isla Real* with the red marker, repeatedly.

"That's the strongest fortress in the world," he said. "Nothing else compares even remotely. In training, you saw your own little camps. You didn't see—or didn't see much of—the roughly one point one million cubic meters of concrete we poured, the hundreds upon hundreds of guns, the minefields waiting to be activated, the tunnels, the rails, the trenches. Trust me: One hundred and fifty thousand men couldn't take it if they had one hundred and fifty thousand years to try. And if they can't take it, no ships can sail past it. If ships can't sail past it, then no landing at or near the capital can succeed; they'd just starve to death. I'm not worried about the north."

The laser moved to the west, wriggling over the undeveloped jungles of La Palma. "They're not coming through here in any strength, though I'll put a few tercios down there—foreign volunteers, generally, plus the *Tercio de Indios*—to make sure they can't distract us or put the government into a panic. But there are no ports worthy of the name, no roads, only one airstrip that isn't muck most of the year, and that one's short. And, wearing loincloths or not, the Indians are good in *la jungla*."

Carrera flicked the red arrow over the port of Cristobal, at the southern end of the Transitway. "The Taurans will be coming here," he said, "though they're not going to limit themselves—not if they have two brain cells to rub together—to the old borders of the Transitway Mandate. And we'll meet them and beat them." He gave a little shrug and added, "You're going to have to take that on faith."

He stopped speaking for a moment while he physically wheeled the map board one hundred and eighty degrees around. On the other side, the women could see, was a better scale map of the eastern portions of the country.

"Here's where our danger comes from," he said. The red marker flicked from spot to spot to spot as Carrera called off the names of a dozen or more little ports dotting the northeastern coast of the country. "None of those, alone, could support an army of a size to matter. Taken together, however, and with the kinds of improvements a modern army, or one—like the Zhong's—with a lot of manpower, can create, they can support an army. Moreover"—the laser traced the long coastal highway—"from there they've got a highway into our vitals. And I don't have the force to meet it, not so long as the Zhong and the Taurans are attacking to the north and south.

"Worse,"—the red light settled on Capitano, a good-sized port to the southeast—"from here a full corps could come over the mountains, link with a force along the northern coast, and make that drive into our guts deadly.

"What is necessary is to buy time in the east until we have a decision, north and south. That's where you come in; you, Fifth Mountain Tercio, a chunk of Fourteenth Cazador Tercio, the mountain cohorts from Lempira and Valdivia, and a few others. And a few hundred thousand others besides that."

The Amazons stirred. They'd gotten used to the notion that the total armed force of the legion was larger than they'd believed. They didn't see where another few hundred thousand would be coming from.

Carrera answered their question. "I am going to half evacuate the city—we don't have bomb shelters for more than half, anyway—and move more than three hundred thousand civilians to a big 'refugee' area around and along that highway and some of the ports. The 'refugees' have a purpose of their own. While we, the legion, will feed them, and the more permanent residents of the area, as long as the enemy hasn't occupied their area, once they do come in—and they will—the food stops. Thereafter, the civilians will suck up as much as one thousand truckloads a day of enemy supply in food, medicine, etc. World opinion will *demand* that those people be fed and cared for. That will hurt them, my children. It might even make a western attack a logistic impossibility all on its own.

"However, I cannot be absolutely sure about that. Give the Tauran devils their due; they can move supplies.

"So the civilians aren't enough. I need that road kept closed. I need the ports kept closed or, at least, marginal. I need the feeder roads kept closed.

"Using the 'refugees' to hide among you, your forces and the others are going to close off invasion from the east. Of course, as in any partisan war, the regular forces could destroy you if they are willing and able to spread out in little packets to do so. Fifth Mountain is going up into the mountains as a regular organized force to threaten the enemy and keep him from spreading out enough to find, control, and annihilate you. Also to block the road from Capitano."

Smiling, Carrera continued, "Think about it. Hiding among those civilians you are going to be an intelligent, self-aware, self-replicating, mobile and undetectable minefield that the enemy won't be able to destroy in place, move, or clear permanent lanes through. To add insult to injury he's going to have to protect you, feed you, shelter you, clothe you, and provide medical care for you every moment you're not actively shooting at him.

Carrera gave a nasty laugh.

"And you are *perfect* for the job. You're women. You don't look like a threat, little 'helpless' things that you are. You'll be able to go places, see things, get information from the enemy's soldiers in a way nobody else could hope to. You'll be able to hide in plain sight; coming out only to fight."

"It won't last forever, of course. Eventually they'll catch on to you. Until they do, though, you'll have a field day. Even after they do . . . you'll still be able to fight them."

One of the Amazons, a big redheaded woman centurion—maybe a little less than perfectly feminine, especially along the jawline and with those broad shoulders, but still unquestionably attractive—raised her hand. "Uh . . . *Duque*, what about uniforms? Those'll give us away."

Carrera answered, "The Taurans claim to follow, and have in fact ratified, the Additional Protocol the Earthers inflicted on many of us some decades ago. So there's no need to wear uniforms except for immediate action, by the enemy's own rules.

"On the other hand, the Zhong don't follow the Protocol. If you get caught by them . . . well, you'll be subject to execution under the law of land warfare. On the other hand, before it becomes an issue we'll be holding some of *their* POWs. And we're holding a fair number of Taurans that we caught not only out of uniform but in our uniforms. They've already been court-martialed and sentenced to death. The enemy tries to do anything to any of you for being out of uniform, I'll hang those people . . . in a heartbeat. Anyway, if you don't want to do this, I'll understand. This is for volunteers only."

Carrera considered his audience for a moment, then spoke. "Show of hands," he demanded.

Every one of the women put up a hand. Carrera had known they would.

"Now there's one other problem," Carrera said. His eyes went up, toward the church ceiling and past that, to the skies and space. "The Earthpigs are going to be feeding the Taurans and the Zhong all the intelligence they can gather. We've got reason to believe they can pick up a lot . . . more than they used to be able to. We're still trying to figure out why the change happened.

"In any case, among the things they'll be able to see from space is electronics and especially anything electromagnetic. So all your neat do-dads, the night sights on your rifles, your Red Fang communications systems, your light-enhancing goggles, and global-locating systems, all have to be given up or stored deep against a rainy day. You'll be fighting primitive. So will the other units in and around your area and in *la Palma*.

"And, no, that's not true for the forces I'm keeping in the center and on the island. They'll be in so great a density that we couldn't hide them anyway. There's nothing to be learned by the enemy except that they're generally there. Each one will be like a lit match held against the sun. But an electronic thermal sight could pinpoint you girls for a rock from space or, at least, a bomb from a plane.

"I'll be able to give you some Yamato-made radios, a few, we don't think the Earthers can sense. And we've got a fair field telephone system you can get some limited use out of. Oh, and Legate Fernandez has had the Signal Tercio get some carrier pigeons trained. But that's about it."

Carrera shrugged, "Sorry."


### *Ciudad Capitano, El Toro,* Balboa, Terra Nova

There were enough Santa Josefinans in the legion to come up with two overstrength tercios, roughly eighty-five hundred men and a few women, and still leave a fair number in the rest of the force. In filtering them out from the other tercios, they'd been divided into those two tercios, based mostly on their home of origin. One tercio, *Tercio la*

*Virgen*—which most people found amusing, given Santa Josefina's thriving sex trade—came from Santa Josefinans from the capital region and the half of the country on the *Mar Furioso* side. The other tercio, *Tercio la Negrita,* was from the Shimmering Sea side of the country. There were color differences between the two tercios, though the title, *la Negrita,* didn't come from those.

The two regiments differed in other ways, too. *La Negrita,* for example, had no organic artillery component, just a single large battery of heavy mortars. Nor had they any armor, light or heavy. Instead, it went heavy on combat engineers and *cazadores,* and had four infantry cohorts, with extra strength light antiaircraft missile sections. *La Virgen,* conversely, had only three infantry cohorts, but an extra artillery battery and tank maniple, an extra air defense battery, plus an engineer bridging maniple, and an extra maniple of *Cazadores,* that last already in Santa Josefina. *La Virgen* also wore regular uniforms and used standard Balboan weaponry—except for some fairly intensive familiarization firing—while *la Negrita* was entirely in civilian clothes and had been issued Tauran arms for training. Other than those peculiarities, *la Virgen* retained, in the main, standard legionary tables of organization and equipment, while *la Negrita* had been organized around their home regions in Santa Josefina, which led to some wildly varying strengths at the maniple level.

The commanders of one of those maniples, Tribune Ignacio Macera, studied his map with his own tercio commander, Legate Salas, and *Duque* Carrera, tracing lines of march and attack with a twig, while arguing good naturedly about possibilities and impossibilities. All three wore civilian clothes. While Carrera had come in a staff car rather more beaten up than most, the two Santa Josefinans had come by boat. They'd come out from the Santa Josefinan port of Matama unarmed. They'd go back unarmed, too, since the not exactly ineffective Santa Josefinan Coast Guard seemed to be on the watch for infiltrators from Balboa within its purview.

The two Santa Josefinans were an interesting study in contrasts, the younger tribune being very black, tall, and thin, with tight black hair and an air of nervous energy, while the legate was mixed race, older, graying, balding, running to fat, and weary.

"It's a forty-day trip, *Duque,*" said Macera, the tribune, "from Capitano to Matama. Assuming you have them cut way north and then wind through the *Cordillera* Central. Mules can eat anything, but even the mules are going to need some high-quality feed on the way and to have a lot of fodder precut for them. That, or they'll take forever to get over the mountains and a lot of them will die on the way.

"My men can do that, buy and emplace the grain, make some piles of fodder out in the jungle. The problem is, though, that it risks the Taurans identifying what we're doing."

"So what do you suggest, Tribune?" Carrera asked.

"I've only got to seize the ship and hold the port until I can get it unloaded," said Macera. "There are fewer than two hundred cops in the area, some of whom will support us. Cut my ammunition and put a thousand pounds of feed on the mules. I'm tempted to say cut it to the bone and go for two thousand pounds, but I think I can get enough fodder out there along the trail that that won't be necessary."

Carrera considered and, finally, agreed, "Okay, cut a thousand pounds of ammunition. Now what about a diversion at Pelirojo to isolate you?"

Pelirojo was a small town, situated between and commanding two rivers and their bridges, halfway between Matama and the capital of Aserri.

"I really don't think so, *Duque*," replied Salas, one of the original Santa Josefinan volunteers for the war in Sumer. "I talked to Colonel Nguyen about it." Nguyen and his wife were Cochinese experts in guerilla warfare and terrorism, hired by the legion to train Balboans.

"Nguyen says the hardest thing in this kind of war is coordination and timing. He says that the enemy is almost always going to have better communications and faster transport than us. He also says the odds of tipping off the Taurans as to what we're up to are too great. But he also says there's no reason not to set up a little ambush just in case.

"And a nice demonstration by *Tercio la Virgen* wouldn't be to the bad either."

# CHAPTER EIGHT

"Fourth Estate . . . Fifth Column? What's the difference?"
—Richard E. Sampson, Accountant

## Julio Asunción Airport, Garabito, Santa Josefina, Terra Nova

There were two *ala* aircraft on the tarmac, one carried Lourdes and the bulk of the diplomatic party, the other carried refugees. The legion had planes capable of taking both in one lift. Instead, they'd used two smaller ones, NA-23s. Why? Because with what they expected the subtly screened Tauran women to say, Lourdes's presence would have undermined the anticipated message. She'd still stopped by to commiserate with the Taurans, back at Herrera International.

The widow Lydia Gordon, tugging her three-year-old by the hand, was first to step off the plane flown by the Legionary Air Wing, the *ala*. She and her child were followed by fifty-one other family members, some widowed or half-orphaned but most with spouses and fathers behind wire as POWs. To compensate for those fifty-three, only forty-seven mostly wounded prisoners were waiting at Cristobal's docks, back in Balboa, for transport. It was one of those rare days when Carrera decided to fulfill the letter of Parilla's promise to the Taurans.

It was also the first return of the family members. This wasn't through any ill will, nor even indifference. It was that the aircraft had been needed for other things prior. Though, it had to be said, there were advantages to letting the Taurans stew and fret over the civilian captives.

In any event, because this was the first load of civilian dependents, the press was waiting like a group of paparazzi privy to watching the crown princess of Anglia blowing the Household Cavalry . . . the horses, that is, not the troopers. The Balboan press was there, too, as were some less than honest or ethical . . . ah, but why be redundant . . . journalists, some of whom were on under-the-table legionary retainer.

Widow Gordon, when approached by the press, quite without being *openly* coached, had little good to say about the Tauran Union. "What? How do you *think* I feel about those pansies? I blame their incompetence for my husband's death more than I do any supposed Balboan strengths. What were they *thinking?* Silly question, I know. But those bureaucratic filth made me a widow in my twenties."

From there it got worse, running from the Tuscan woman who wept great snotty sobs on camera, then spit at the mention of the Tauran Union, to the Sachsen crew that stood together and sang, "Fuck the filthy Tauran Union," through all of its verses: "Asshats, bastards, cowards, dimwits, shit-feasting gallows bait . . ." And then there were the Gallic women, belting out the *Internationale* with feeling.

It was not known, and would not be known for a century when the pertinent files could be opened, whether the Balboans were somehow selecting people for return who were staunchly and especially anti-Tauran Union, or if they didn't have to because *all* of the dependent families—perhaps because of the common military outlook—were staunchly anti-Tauran Union.

And the images and words couldn't be suppressed, either, since several Balboan news teams were at the airport as well, feeding those words and images into the GlobalNet and through television across the hemisphere.

Perhaps the most annoying and frustrating thing to the Taurans was that they couldn't stop the return, either. The Balboans would take those women and their children to Aserri, whether the TU willed it or not. And, while there were substantial sections of the yellow press that could be directed away, that would only work if all the press could be directed to ignore the return. Since it couldn't, and since there was therefore no benefit to the cause by those otherwise cooperative elements of the media in shielding the Tauran Union, they wouldn't.

In effect, the conversation between press and Tauran Union defense and information ministries went something like this: *And fuck you; we have advertising to sell or we'll go under. Selling advertising requires we give, or at least appear to give, the whole news. Cutting things that displease you out, when someone else is giving the whole story, means people will go elsewhere. Then we won't be able to sell advertising, we go under, and then there'll be no more cooperation from any of us. Ever. So fuck you again.*

At least, that was the conversation reported between Zed Potter, the head of the Global News Network, and Monsieur Gaymard, the president *pro tem*, of the Tauran Union.

## Cristobal, Balboa, Terra Nova

The Balboans didn't give Jan Campbell a lot of warning. One moment she'd been supervising some mixed troops digging antianimal ditches, which—of course—could never be construed as antitank ditches, with von Bernhard's group the next over, while the next half-dozen guards, their rifles bayonetted, surrounded her and led her off. She could see plainly enough that Hendryksen was about to make a go at the guards no matter the odds.

"No, Kris," she insisted, one placating hand raised, "it'll be fine. Besides, them feeling they need this many guards for little me is quite the compliment."

Neither she nor the Cimbrian need have worried. The Balboans may have been playing loose with the laws of war—witness the ha-has that couldn't really be anything *but* antitank ditches—but they weren't interested in murdering prisoners once they actually *were* prisoners. Campbell was marched along the narrow jungle trail to a larger one, which larger one in turn led to a gravel road. At the road was a weasel-faced man in a wheelchair. Behind him were a four-wheel-drive vehicle, her guess being that it was captured from the Gauls, and a muddied van with a lowered platform resting on the gravel.

*Fernandez? What the fook does he want with me?*

"To let you go, Captain," the intel chief answered, quite without being asked. Well, it *was*, after all, an obvious question. "As to 'why?' which will be your next question, because my boss, who seems to have taken a liking to you, asked me to track down your whereabouts and see that you were well-taken care of: Properly buried, if dead, properly cared for, if wounded, and properly released, if a prisoner."

That was a total lie. Carrera might, just possibly, have directed that, had he remembered to. He hadn't had the time or occasion to think about it. However, Fernandez *did* have major responsibility for disinformation, and Campbell, it was judged, could play a useful part in that.

She, on the other hand, was pretty sure she'd charmed Carrera, to a degree, and thought it entirely possible he'd given such order. Even so, "It's not proper to release me ahead of . . ."

Fernandez lifted a palm, in unconscious echo of Campbell, with Hendryksen, a few moments before. "On the contrary, Captain, as we have learned from Tauran Union reactions to the murder of some meddlesome women, from our troops' *most* regrettable reaction to the quite legitimate killing of some of our female infantry, and from the eagerness everyone in the goddamned world is showing as regards returning the largely female population of widows and women whose men are behind barbed wire now, it is absolutely proper to get you off of our hands, you and every other Tauran or Zhong woman we hold.

"You wish to be equal and I approve of and admire that, Captain, I assure you. The world, however, laughs at our pretensions. Women are different, and the worlds of man insist they be treated differently.

"So, off you go, miss."

Fernandez indicated the four-wheel-drive vehicle, on closer inspection a Gallic Sochaux S4, with a new paint job, and said, "One of ours will drive and two guards will stay with you to protect you, not to keep you from escaping." He shook his head, wonderingly, saying, "I can't imagine any reason someone about to be released from captivity would escape. Please don't show me one."

"And take me where?" she asked.

"We don't want to muddy the water needlessly," Fernandez replied. "You'll go to Cristobal, to the place we've been using for the TU to pick up returnees and bring them home, by ship."

"My compatriots?"

"Since you don't share nationality with most of them, I am surprised to find you using the term. They stay here until released, exchanged, paroled, or we win or lose the war."

"So the war goes on?" she asked. "Slaughtering us and rubbing our noses in it wasn't enough?"

"That's up to your side," answered Fernandez. "You might suggest to them that peace is in their interests, too, and that they should pay, by rights, for all the damage they caused. Saying that, however, or promising to, is not a condition of your release."

Fernandez's face split in a wicked grin. "Speaking of what you should and should not say, however, we found the most interesting report from you in a file in Fort Muddville's Building 59. It seems you tried to dissuade the Tauran Union from attacking, or at least to convince them we would prove tougher than they imagined. It seems also that the Gauls overrode that report." Fernandez didn't for a moment think about telling Campbell about the burned files of Tauran spies within Balboa. That was a bit of information too much.

The memory of that report brought a scowl to Campbell's face. Given the results, it almost, not quite but almost, brought a tear to her eye.

"Yes, well, don't be too terribly surprised, Captain, if the Tauran Union sends you someplace totally incommunicado if you mention that report. Every government, to include Anglia's, is embarrassed to tears over the fiasco here. Some are perhaps teetering. I warn you, for your sake, not to say anything in public that might cause them to think you would be best used at a weather station, someplace unpopulated, cold, and forbidding."

Campbell rolled her eyes heavenward, thinking, *Yes, it's possible. It's also possible that the reason they're sending me home is so that I will mention my report, and embarrass my government further. My impression of Carrera is that he is not that devious. Fernandez, on the other hand . . . he just might be.*

Consulting his watch, Fernandez said, "Now, miss, I must run along. You, please, be a good girl and go with your guards to Cristobal, quietly. If any of them gives you the slightest trouble, drop me a line and I'll see to it that they get retrained for a mine-clearing maniple."

## Kaiserswerth, Sachsen, Tauran Union, Terra Nova

Khalid was on his third printer, still chirping away as it cranked out letter of condolence number eighteen hundred and eleven. The other two sat off the floor, against one wall, their lift tops open and in one case, graced with some boot marks. Those two had long since given up the ghost in printing off letters of condolence, or just of information, for the more than twenty thousand Taurans in legion hands, one way or the other. This didn't account for the printing of checks and envelopes.

Khalid had long since lost count of the number of ink cartridges used.

"Couldn't they have gotten somebody else to help?" he asked of nobody. "Anybody?"

Now he had them nearly ready, over twenty thousand stuffed envelopes. Of these, some contained checks. Of those, there were two groups: those the Tauran Union had been informed of the deaths of and those they had not. A third group consisted of those the various Tauran militaries had listed as dead, but who were, in fact, alive. The fourth were prisoners, and had been honestly reported as such. The fifth was to the Castilians, with whom the Balboans had been absolutely up front, since the Castilian dead had died on behalf of Balboa

*Ohhh, I shiver at the thought of those bureaucrats trying to get money back for insurance paid. Oh, wicked Fernandez!*

All the letters were packed in boxes stacked to the ceiling in his small apartment, but the groups with checks were kept separate, as were the ones for the "resurrected." Once these last hundred or so were done, all that waited was the word from Fernandez, which word had not yet been given.

*But when it is? Oh, the wailing and gnashing of teeth, the recriminations, the flush of embarrassment on Tauran bureaucratic faces. I surely hope someone records some of it, for posterity.*

The letter then sat in the printer's tray. Khalid picked it up and read it silently. It was been composed by some legionary psychologists, for a particular effect, at a particular time. The particular type number was "Fourteen C, Sachsen fallen, no details." It read:

Dear Mrs. Czauderna,

It is with deepest regret that the President, Senate, People, and armed forces of the Republic of Balboa inform you that your son, Moritz Czauderna, has fallen in battle with the forces of the Republic.

Regrettably, amidst the confusion intendant upon the Tauran Union's unprovoked attack, we have no details to give you. We recovered a body, a name tag, and nothing more. We have buried the body, with full military honors, among our own sacred dead. Your son was an enemy, perhaps, in life. In death he is our guest, an honored colleague and comrade.

After a final peace, of course, you may determine that you would prefer that Moritz's remains come home. Assuredly, we will give them up to you or your agent. If not, be assured he is welcome here and that, should you wish to visit his grave you shall do so as our guest for the duration of your stay.

It is our law that those who fight and fall in their country's service shall receive certain honors. This was originally a regulatory oversight, yet, as time has passed, we have come to see the wisdom of honoring even those who have fallen in battle against us. Thus, Moritz's gravestone shall be marked with the wound badge of the *Legion del Cid*, and the *Cruz de Coraje en Acero*.

We do not presume to make fine and meaningless distinctions among those who have given all they have to give. All who fall, friend or foe, without disgracing their countries, are so honored.

In addition, we know that bureaucracies can be slow and inefficient, or sometimes even negligent. Though we have made lists of the dead and captured available to the Tauran Union, it is possible that they have not yet been able to take care of you. Enclosed you will find a check in the same amount as we grant to the families of our own fallen, to tide them over until normal bureaucratic systems can come into play. Accept it, please, in the spirit in which it was given, a spirit that recognizes a common humanity, whatever causes may lead us to differ.

We weep for your loss as for our own. And we weep for our own very much. Perhaps together, joined in heart by our losses, we can achieve the peace that the bureaucratic elites have denied us.

God be with you.

Sincerely,

Raul Parilla
*Presidente de la Republica*

Khalid smiled, then began folding the letter to place it in an envelope. He wondered, *Did they deliberately misspell young Czauderna's name in the official report, so that the TU couldn't get to this woman in advance? Or did they leave his name off the list? And if they left some names off the lists, did they deliberately obfuscate others . . . all precisely so there would be an opportunity to show Balboa as gracious and merciful, and the TU, and even the national governments, as cold, heartless, inefficient, and contemptible.*

*Oh, wicked, wicked, WICKED, men.*

## Hotel *Cielo Dorado*, Aserri, Santa Josefina, Terra Nova

*So that's the bitch,* thought Lourdes, looking over Wallenstein, standing in the reception line, *that my husband, my president, and my country are at war with. Not bad looking, if a little pale.*

Wallenstein, on the other hand, took one look at Lourdes's magnificently large, brown-bordering-on-golden eyes, and thought, *He has much to fight for, my enemy.*

The reception was hosted by the embassy of United Earth. Hence it was Lourdes being presented to Wallenstein, followed by the ambassador from the Tauran Union, followed by Janier. Lourdes was polite to all three. Even so, when she got to Janier she hit him with a withering expression of sympathy.

Janier, being a Gaul, had an amazing capacity for arrogance, on the one hand, and gracious charm, on the other. He took her hand, kissed it lightly, the merest brush, then said, "My compliments to your husband, madam, not only for his battlefield victories but for his impeccable taste in choosing a wife."

*Hard not to like the bastard,* Lourdes thought. *Then again, Patricio said he found the frog likeable enough when they met on the boat to work out an attempt at peace, so . . .*

*Unfortunately, unlike my husband on the yacht, I am not here to create a peace but to sabotage one. The only question is whether it's better to do that by being sweet, by being a bitch, or by mixing and matching to suit. My instincts say, "mix and match." So it's politeness to the frog, for now.*

"Why thank you, General," she replied. "My husband has often said what a shame it was that the arrangements you and he worked out failed due to bureaucratic ignorance and cowardice. He's also said that, had you been in Balboa during the battles, the issue would have been more in doubt."

*Yeah, about three percent more in doubt. Maybe.*

*Oh, all right; maybe I have a wife's prejudice.*

Matthias Esterhazy was likewise in the line. He said little, even less than did Lourdes. Instead, he spent his energy on sizing up the opposition. He had considerable experience at that, some in his native Sachsen, more as Carrera's traveling envoy.

*UEPF? That twat Wallenstein wants the war to continue,* he thought, accurately enough. *But it's damned hard to think of her as an ally. Her ambassador, if in fact the cunt is her ambassador, has "earnest desire for peace" written all over. Never dealt with an Old Earth Kosmo before, but I suppose it's possible she's sincere. The Tauran ambassador—what was that eunuch's name? I'll get it later—is terrified of continuing the war, his organization being discredited and possibly disbanded, and his being out of a job. He reeks of it. He's got no faith in war as an instrument, let alone in war and the military as his instruments. Janier? Putting on a brave show, got to admire that. But he doesn't want the war to continue. He wants . . . if I had to guess, I'd say that he wants a peaceful retirement and a chance to write the memoirs that will lay all the blame for the loss of Balboa on the bureaucrats of the TU.*

Esterhazy looked around for the Zhong empress. He'd expected her in the receiving line and was terribly surprised she wasn't there. Then he did see her, pretending to be someone unimportant, standing by the bar. He finished passing the line and started to walk over. He stopped about halfway to the bar, thinking, *If she wants to pretend to be unimportant, who am I to blow her cover?*

Instead, the Sachsen went to the bar, got a drink, said no more than, "Good evening, madam," to Xingzhen, then went to a wall and parked himself, looking for the patterns of human interaction.

Matthias searched for those patterns, then found something he absolutely was not looking for. *Holy fuck!* He practically bounced from the wall. He had to keep himself from trotting over to Lourdes. When he reached her he leaned over her shoulder and whispered in her ear, "Do not let yourself be startled. But that portrait hanging on the wall over the fireplace in the *Casa* Linda? Well look at the short young brown woman hanging out near the high admiral."

Lourdes looked and whispered, though only to herself, "Holy fuck, they could have been sisters."

## Gym *Dorado,* Cedral Multiplex Shopping Mall, Aserri, Santa Josefina, Terra Nova

The embassy of United Earth had a gym, not too shabbily equipped, but that was inconvenient to get to from the hotel. The hotel had a gym, but it was nothing much as such things tend not to be. There was also, unsurprisingly, a gym at the mall. Better, it was down in the basement, and didn't have those plate glass windows to incite passersby into joining. Better still, there were multiple entrances. Best of all, it had, besides the usual machines and free weights, an angled track, pool, showers, locker rooms, and sauna. And it was close. Walking there, though, Esmeralda found several more of those posters with Taurans with horns growing from their berets.

"The important thing," said Esmeralda to Aragon, as they sat amidst the thick steam of the sauna, "is that my admiral definitely wants the war to continue."

"Why does she hate us so?" asked Aragon.

The cabin girl and sometimes lieutenant, junior grade shook her head emphatically. "She doesn't. She doesn't even dislike you. I might go so far as to say she admires you or, at least, your chief. But she has a problem and only sees one way to solve it long term.

"The problem is that . . . well . . . you would have to have lived there to understand. I'll try to paint you a picture. Old Earth is screwed. There are wide swaths fallen to our own, home-grown, barbarians. Where it's still civilized about a fifth of the area is under religious lunatics. They sacrifice *people*, Cass, to their old gods. Or they do it to terrorize the people they rule. They almost did it to me and they *did* do it to my sister. Killed her, cut her heart out on the Altar of Peace, and then ate her."

Esmeralda said it clinically. Cass Aragon could still feel the hate like an undercurrent, subtle but powerfully insistent. *I believe you, sweetie. And I'm sorry.*

"The highest castes," Esmeralda continued, "the Class Ones, do no work. They don't even supervise. They're on continuous vacation. And always, as befits their caste, first class.

"All the real work, all the work above obtaining raw materials and food, gets done by the Twos and Threes; the high admiral was a Two, though she was elevated to Class One before coming back here. I'm not sure why.

"A lot of the low-level work gets done by slaves. I haven't seen it, but I've heard the high admiral railing against the *latifundia* on Atlantis base, where it's almost all slave labor.

"The slaves are even below Class Sixes. They have no rights at all. Buy, sell, beat, kill . . . nobody cares. My family, until we ran afoul of the Castro-Nyeres, was at least free. Well, free unless some of the soldiers caught you, when they could do whatever they liked with you . . ."

"And you?" asked Aragon, meaning was Esmeralda ever caught by the soldiers.

"Oh, yeah," the girl answered. "Often enough. The first time I was only eleven. My father didn't find out until I was fourteen. He killed a couple of Count Castro-Nyere's soldiers. He was killed, in turn, then my mother, my sister, and I were taken as slaves. I don't know what happened to our mother. My sister I told you about. And me . . . I was saved by the high admiral."

"And you feel guilty that you're betraying her?" Aragon asked.

"Yes," Esmeralda answered, simply, staring down at the sauna's wooden floor.

"She's trying to change things there," the girl insisted. "She really is! She's trying to get in a position where she can change things there."

"At our expense?" asked Cass.

"At your expense," admitted Esmeralda.

"Go back to what you started to say before you started talking about United Earth. What are the high admiral's plans for Terra Nova?"

"She wants to set up what she calls 'a great power system,' where five roughly equal powers run the planet, but stymie each other. She says it has to be five or it won't work."

"I can probably guess," said Aragon, "but what are the five?"

"The Federated States," Esmeralda began, "the Tauran Union, the Volgan Empire, the Zhong Empire, and the Peace Fleet."

"Not Colombia Latina? Not Uhuru?"

"She doesn't believe in miracles."

"Not Yamato?"

"They're an appetizer for the Zhong and a way to break up the current Federated States-Zhong lovefest. Hmmm . . . speaking of the Zhong, the high admiral and the Zhong empress have a thing going on . . . which, come to think of it, suggests that the high admiral maybe *does* believe in miracles."

# CHAPTER NINE

Fight the enemy with the weapons he lacks.
—Alexander Suvarov

**Tauran Defense Agency, Lumière, Gaul, Terra Nova**

A yawning Jan still suffered from jet lag. This wouldn't have happened had she taken a two-day journey by airship from Balboa to the Tauran Union; then there'd have been enough time to get used to the time difference gently. It wouldn't have happened, but she'd not have been reporting in for another day and a half.

*Better this way.*

Instead of that, though, the TU used a smallish airship to transfer the wounded to Cienfuegos. From there they boarded regular jets to get them home as quickly as possible. One might well have doubted, and Jan Campbell certainly did doubt, that the bureaucrats who ran the TU really cared much about the welfare of the troops or their families. What they did care about, however, were the political implications, exacerbated by a press they considered largely rogue, if the troops were not returned soonest.

"So far as I am aware," Jan told the debriefing officer who'd met her at the airport and taken her to TDA Headquarters immediately, before she'd even had a chance to shower, "nobody who was in the Tunnel at *Cerro Mina* survived. Few people who were anywhere near the hill when the Balboans took it survived. I and my sergeant major only survived because we got off the hill as it was falling. So, no, I doubt your de Villepin survived."

The debriefing officer, a Gallic Gendarmerie captain named Fourier, seemed intent on what had happened to the largely Gallic staff that had been inside the Tunnel. He didn't seem to care much about the others.

*But then, to be fair,* thought Jan, *I hardly give a shit about the Gauls, either.*

There were a number of gendarmeries in the world, though not always called that. Gaul had one, as did Tuscany, Castile, Lusitania, Volga, Valdivia, and about fifty other states. Some were better; some were worse. Some were corrupt; others incorruptible. What they shared was that they were an armed military or quasi-military force, with training as both police and soldiers, with duties to enforce law among a civilian population, and a more military attitude to casualties, whether their own, of the civilians among whom they operated, of criminals, or armed foreign enemies.

Some were more military than others, of course, and some were so military they were formed into paratrooper and mechanized brigades. Carrera had once joked with a general of the Federated States Army about having "Low Altitude Riot Control Aircraft" and "Heavy Armored Community Relations Vehicles." Among some of Terra Nova's gendarmeries, that would not have been much, if anything, of a joke.

"Very sad, then," answered Fourier. "Well, his family will be taken care of, if they need it, which I doubt.

"Now what about this massacre I hear happened?" the gendarme asked.

"I didn't see it," Jan replied. "I heard rumors of it, then got some details from one of their senior noncoms. Their chief of intelligence also said something to me to suggest the rumors are true. As to the whys; the Balboan launched an attack with their female infantry unit, or a part of it, that attack was beaten off and destroyed, with heavy casualties, and when male Balboan infantry went in, with more support and after more time to prepare, and saw the dead and wounded women, they killed everything they could get their hands on. At least, that's what I heard."

"How," asked Fourier, "would anyone report that if the Balboans killed everybody?"

"The Balboans themselves," Jan said.

"Mmmm . . . well . . . maybe," the gendarme admitted. "I'd still wonder how it happened."

"It's not so hard to understand," Jan said, "Not for anybody who understands anything about men in battle. One soldier, or a couple, get out of hand; the reason hardly matters. Some people who might be inclined to surrender instead run. There being no obligation to let an enemy escape, some people fire at the ones fleeing. Regular soldiers, basically herd animals as almost all people are herd animals, then figure the herd had collectively decided on atrocity and they just go along."

Fourier spent a few minutes thinking that over, chin cupped in his left hand and fingers drumming his cheek. "I think," he said, "that you should not mention this, nor mention any rumors you heard. We are close enough to war already, a war that is in no way in the interests of the Tauran Union nor any of its member states to recommence. Why should we"—he shrugged—"add to the tensions?

"I agree with you, by the way, on how it typically happens. But besides that, the problem with war crimes charges and trials is that, outside of a few crimes that are indistinguishable from civil crimes—rape, murder, theft, and such—every other soldier who engages in a war crime has an almost pat insanity defense. Most of the rest have pat defenses of mistake. Or coercion. Though few or none of our idiot lawyers in the Cosmopolitan Criminal Court can see any of that.

"We lost so many intelligence personnel in Balboa," the gendarme continued, "that I find myself seconded back to the armed forces for intelligence work. This is what I did when I was in the regular armed force, so one can understand. In any case, here I find myself, debriefing you and any other of the returnees who might have something useful to say.

"I also must say that you are the first. The others can tell us something of Balboan fighting qualities, which are, so I gather, not contemptible . . ."

Jan went into a fit on laughter at that, before recovering and agreeing, "No, not contemptible."

"Well," Fournier continued, "they can tell us that and they can tell us something of Balboan medical practices, but that's all.

"Now tell me what *you* have seen, since you were not confined to a hospital.

"This will be better done with a map," Campbell said.

## Sachsen, Tauran Union, Terra Nova

Khalid hadn't chosen this particular post office box from a map, but because there were no surveillance cameras nearby; of that, he'd made very sure. Better, still, on half a dozen reconnaissance drives past it he had never once seen a policeman.

Security was important, but timing was everything. Khalid had the sequence of events down pat. *First, I mail the letters and checks to people we have good reason to believe the various Tauran governments have not informed of the death of a loved one, because they don't know, because we didn't tell them . . . or didn't tell them accurately. That's only a couple of dozen.*

After passing the post office box outside the *Ratskeller* of the town of *Nievenheim*, Khalid parked the rental van, stepped out, took a single box containing twenty-four stuffed envelopes, and then walked over and fed the contents into the post office box.

"Shot," he said, as the envelopes tumbled in.

*Now I drive to the campground north of Mogons, and wait overnight. Tomorrow, the letters to the families of the resurrected go out. Oh, wicked, wicked men.*

*And so much for that apartment. Fortunately, the rent's paid six months in advance.*

## Lenneberger Grosser Sand, south of Mogons, Sachsen, Tauran Union, Terra Nova

There was probably no greater proof of the Noahs' intent to create on Terra Nova a nature preserve *cum* animal and plant sanctuary than the Lenneberger Grosser Sand. Though there had never been, so far as could be determined, a glacial period in Terra Novan history, there had been plants on Earth, in the vicinity of the city of Mainz, which depended on the sandy environment created by the last of the glaciers. This environment, grass-covered sand dunes, basically, had been recreated here, south of what would eventually become Mogons,

Sachsen, and it had been done without any glaciation at all. It was at a campground fronting this area that Khalid had set up his tent.

The morning sun was at about forty-five degrees by the time Khalid roused himself. His sleep had been lousy, continuously interrupted by two gay guys, one apparently named "Stuart" or maybe "Slade"—it was hard to be sure, what with the slurred speech—and the other named or nicknamed "Thanas," buggering each other in a nearby tent until all hours of the night and early morning. Then, too, it was possible there were three or four rather than two. The only line he could be sure of was, "Oh, my, that's a big one."

Khalid, a Druze, was somewhat more tolerant of such activity than some. What he was not tolerant of was having his sleep interrupted. Only the fact that he had a more important mission kept the two, or four, buggerers alive. *Ah, well, joke 'em if they can't take a fuck.*

Still, it was in a foul mood that Khalid drove the few miles to the center of Mogons. He stopped at the first postal receptacle he came to, got out, and deposited the six score envelopes of the resurrected. Then he immediately got back into the rental and headed for Mauer, a university town on the River Nikros. There he simply parked and dozed, waiting for night.

*The Sachsen are efficient,* thought Khalid, *in their postal services as in everything else. The people in Target List One, should be getting their envelopes right about now.*


## Mettmann, Sachsen, Tauran Union, Terra Nova

Frau Lang, an older woman, heavyset, and gone to gray, opened the official-looking envelope, and read the first sentence. Immediately, she gave off an inarticulate cry and collapsed in a heap by her front door. The door was still open and the cry, if inarticulate, was still loud enough to be heard by the neighbors. If was mere minutes before the first of the neighbors arrived to investigate. By that time, the initial shock had lessened enough for her to begin to weep, to moan, and even to get out a few words.

"My son, my son, my son, he is fallen!"

"But how?" asked her nextdoor neighbor, Frau Muckenfuss. "The government told you he was safe and a prisoner."

Frau Lang drew in several deep breaths, finding in the effort a little moral strength, too.

"They *lied!*" hissed the stricken mother. "My David was killed. The enemy, or the enemy of the Tauran Union, told me as much."

"How can you believe the enemy?" asked Frau Muckenfuss.

"They have *no reason* to lie! Only our own people, the ones who brought this disaster upon us, upon me, have a reason."

Frau Muckenfuss took the letter from the other woman's hands. She read until . . . "Yes, yes, it does have the ring of truth to it . . ."

One of the other neighbors, Frau Pfannkuchen, picked up the envelope and looked inside. She drew a very official looking check from it. "I don't know anything about the letter, but this certainly looks real enough."

"The letter says they were sending a death gratuity," said Frau Muckenfuss. "I suppose it *is* real."

"I don't care about that," Frau Lang sniffed, "I want my son back."

"Maybe a mistake was made by somebody," said Frau Pfannkuchen, consolingly.

"If so, it was made by the idiot frogs running the Tauran Union," said Frau Muckenfuss, who had never been enthusiastic about the Tauran presence in Balboa. "I'm calling the *Tagesstern*," she added. "This kind of incompetence—no, it's not just that; it's also heartlessness—cannot be allowed to stand."

"Splash," said Khalid, watching the demonstration on the television, over a beer, in a guesthouse west of the city of Mauer. It gave fair promise of turning violent.

*Now I can dump everything into the system.*

### Tauran Defense Agency, Lumière, Gaul, Terra Nova

"Do you think they were putting on a show?" asked Fournier. The map was laid out on the desk, between himself and Campbell.

Jan blinked, in surprise. After so many hours of debriefing, and with the jet lag, she was nearing complete collapse. Even so, the question gave her a moment of alertness. And besides, she already had experience of the bloody Gauls torturing data to come up with the politically desired answer.

"Show?" she asked. "What kind of show?"

"Letting you see some heavy fortifications, to convince you that they were unconquerable?"

She was about to snap at the gendarme, but, exhausted or not, she had to admit the Balboans had shown some ability to date with disinformation. It was a fair question. She answered it fairly, too.

"I don't think so," she said. "For one thing, they were building the Parilla Line years ago. I can't say that any of the reports got sent here, but I read them when I was at Fort Muddville. The line was fairly heavy, if not as deep—in either sense—as it might have been. The mines I saw them laying were real enough, and the care they took in arming them seemed pretty real, too."

"But why does it face north when we, the obvious main enemy, would be coming from the south?"

Jan nodded. "I understand that. There was a Sachsen I spoke to, there where we were building 'antianimal ditches,' who thought that logistically, an attack from the south would be very difficult. He thought the Balboans thought it might be impossible. So that might explain why the fortifications face away from us.

"Then, too . . ."

"Yes?" prodded the Gaul.

"Maybe they're absurdly good at predicting events. We all know at this point they're no slouches, but maybe they're better than that, even."

"And?"

"We want peace now, yes?"

"Yes."

Sometimes extreme fatigue can induce confusion. Sometimes, though, it can induce clarity, and even insight. For the moment, at least, Campbell thought it was giving her an insight. "Well, as near as I could tell from the limited news I could see, the Zhong don't. All those fortifications could be aimed at wearing out a Zhong invasion. That would explain the layers, wouldn't it? First that uncrackable nut—or nearly so—of an island fortress out in the *Mar Furioso*. That bleeds the Zhong. Then the battle for the city. Then the Parilla Line. Then Fortress Cristobal. Even the Zhong might get sick of the butcher's bill before they won out."

Fournier shook his head doubtfully. "No . . . it's tempting, but no. I've had access to the views from space of the battle in Balboa. They did not predict us; they baited us. The bait was their existing military structure, the hidden hooks were the battalions of cadets they had been preparing for—well, you tell me; how long did they spend, how much effort, in advance, getting those hides for their cadets set up?"

"Years," Jan said.

"And they could do that because of the bait. But predicting the loss of a Zhong carrier on a humanitarian mission? Now, that requires weapons-grade crystal balls and batteries of Ouija boards. They may very well have based their fortifications on a presumption that invasion via the Shimmering Sea was logistically impossible, as your *boche* thought. But they didn't do it because of the Zhong.

"Now look at the map and show me where you think you were digging their 'antianimal ditch.'" He passed her a pointer.

Jan's pointer traced along the map. "Can't be sure, you know . . . they just came along and said 'dig from here to there' . . . but . . . I think . . . this section, from here to . . . here . . . about here, anyway."

Fournier tapped a spot with a pencil's point, a couple of thousand meters south of where she had indicated. "Did you see anything here?"

"No. Why?"

"There are some big concrete things, rounded lumps, more or less, we don't understand there."

"Sorry, never saw them."


## Karlesforst, Sachsen, Tauran Union, Terra Nova

Herr Kunth and his wife danced across their living room floor, with an old waltz keeping time. In an instant, with a single letter, their universe had gone from despair to boundless joy. After all, their only child, not so little *Hauptgefreiter* Kunth, was reborn, so to speak, resurrected from the dead. The letter from the Balboans said so.

Herr Kunth stopped the dance, took a couple of deep breaths, then released his wife with an affectionate pat. He then went to the front door and announced, at the top of his not inconsiderable lungs, "My son is *alive!* He's alive, I tell you! The stinking frogs didn't get him killed after all."

After making the announcement, though, Herr Kunth closed the door. The letter had a strong suggestion which, after just a moment's thought, he decided to take. It had also said that, in the interests of not adversely affecting his finances, the Government of Balboa would delay giving the true report of *Hauptgefreiter* Kunth's status until he'd had a chance to secure himself and his finances. Though they hadn't outright said so, the Balboans had strongly implied that any financial benefits their own government had given the Kunth family might just be withdrawn.

Going to the family computer, he dug up a gold dealer and began making arrangements to turn the tax-free three-hundred-thousand-Tauro insurance payment into gold and having that delivered to his work.

*Fuck 'em; they deserve to pay for the heartache they inflicted on myself and my wife.*

## Feydeau, Gaul, Tauran Union, Terra Nova

Monsieur Paul Hisson closed the door on his mother's apartment. Mama had been dead for many years, now, but her corpse had stopped stinking, at least, and still provided a nice little check monthly.

Not that he really needed Mama's retirement for the nonce. With his wife long since disappeared and the death gratuity for his late son, killed somewhere in Balboa, Hisson was fairly flush. Still, one never knew when the money would come in handy, so in her bed Mama's remains remained, as they would until Hisson himself passed on.

*I'd rather hoped Paul Junior would be able to collect on both Mama and myself until he was old and gray, but . . . c'est la vie. Pity, really.*

Hisson went to the front door, humming and subvocalizing a popular new song, *"Fuck the filthy Tauran Union."* The mail was due in a few moments and if the yellow bicycle didn't have Mama's check, the papers would hear of his indignation.

The bicycle-riding girl making the delivery was easy enough on the eyes that Monsieur Hisson wished for a moment he were twenty years younger. Still, the important thing was the check; with that he could pay for anything he might need in the way of feminine attention.

Scanning the half-dozen envelopes delivered by the charmingly feminine *cycliste*, he came to one that looked semi-official.

Hisson opened it and began to read. *"Désastre!"* he said, feeling mildly faint, followed by, *"Catastrophe! Calamite!"*

*Ah, well*, he thought, after beginning to take the problem philosophically, *at least young Paul will get the benefit of Mama's corpse. She'd have wanted it that way.*

### Bjorvika, Hordaland, Tauran Union, Terra Nova

While Khalid the Assassin had become a Balboan citizen in years now long past, and while Balboa's "military only" immigration policy had helped keep the legion topped off to strength, the numbers of former citizens of the states of the Tauran Union in the legion was not large. Moreover, of those there were, many had previous military training that made them more valuable in Balboa than they would have been supporting Balboa in their own countries. Still, there had been some who could have been used. It was Fernandez, himself, who had nixed that idea. "They'll be loyal enough in defense of their new home," he'd told Parilla and Carrera, "especially since we can watch them. We might be able to get a few into the intelligence-gathering business, that not being something that kills anyone *directly*. But to ask them to attack their old home, in their old home, while putting their former fellow citizens and soldiers at risk, or even killing them *directly* . . . I think that's asking a little bit too much. Of anyone. I'm not sure we should trust, or even permit to enlist, anyone who wouldn't be troubled by that."

Thus, direct action by former Taurans, against the Tauran Union, within the Tauran Union, was right out. Conversely, though, they had Sumeris, immigrants to various Tauran states who retained still their loyalty to their old country and its current ruler, Adnan Sada. They had some Xamaris they'd recruited directly. And, of course, there were a fair number of Volgans slurping at the legionary trough, which trough was on the TU's western border.

One small team of these, two Xamaris, who lived in Hordaland, and a single black Balboan who had come across the Scandza border and spoke the language, receipted for a single shipping container, delivered by truck and left at a small warehouse complex on the outskirts of Bjorvika.

The container had been marked "glider." It had come from Jagelonia, which had some reputation, internationally, for building and selling gliders, and, when the Hordalander customs folk had looked inside the container it had, after all, been a glider inside, albeit disassembled.

It had taken five trips in the back of a locally purchased and registered Gothenberg 3T to get all the parts out of the container and move them to the residence of the two Xamaris, a small tree farm (not that Xamaris knew a blessed thing about tree farming). There, in the shed, they'd put together the glider, the BLS, or balloon launch system, and installed the incomplete warhead. Since the warhead had had to pass through customs, it was completely devoid of anything smelling even slightly of explosives. Instead, it had a carbon black cartridge married to a liquid oxygen cartridge. This was more than adequate to the task.

After that, it was only a matter of waiting.


### Tauran Defense Agency, Lumière, Gaul, Terra Nova

Fourier wasn't alone this time, Jan was surprised to see. There was an older gentleman—*his suit* reeks *of Burlington Lines*, thought Jan—who seemed to speak French exceptionally well. Jan would have taken him for a Frog, until he turned his received pronunciation on her.

"Major Campbell—" the old gentleman began.

"Captain," she interrupted.

"Majors do not interrupt lieutenant generals, even retired ones," he said. "Neither do they correct them on matters of fact. I said 'major,' and I meant 'major,' I'll thank you."

"Yes, sir," answered Jan. "If you insist. Sir."

"I do. I am, by the way, Sidney Stuart-Mansfield, of Pimlico Hex, and I know all about you."

"Indeed?" Jan's head tilted to one side, a study in skepticism.

"Oh, yes, Major. I know things you do not even know yourself."

"For example, sir?"

"I know, for example, what you're going to be doing for the next several months."

"And what would that be? Sir?"

"You're going to be resurrecting our intelligence apparatus in the Republic of Balboa," said Stuart-Mansfield.

"Not possible," she answered. "The files are lost. We don't even know—"

"It is possible," said Fourier. "Intelligence operations in Balboa were a Gallic purview, almost entirely. We do not operate as you do. You would have lost the ability to contact agents with the loss of the local files and handlers. We have duplicate files here. We know still who was in our network and how to contact them."

"You know less than you think," Jan said. Before the Gaul could reply, she added, "You don't know who's still alive. You don't know who's been turned. You don't really know who was a double agent from the beginning. You don't know how many have been mobilized now, and cannot be reached by any practical means. You don't know—"

"But I know something, Major Campbell," said Stuart-Mansfield. "I know that you're going to take this in hand, and do your very best with it."

**PART II**

# CHAPTER TEN

Negotiation in the classic diplomatic sense assumes
parties are more anxious to agree than to disagree.
—Dean Acheson

**Hotel *Cielo Dorado*, Aserri, Santa Josefina, Terra Nova**

This first plenipotentiary meeting took place at the very civilized hour
of two PM, local. It was not impossible that some of the diplomats had
drunk to excess the night before, hence, tactfully, the meeting was
delayed until at least the worst of the hangovers might have dissipated.
This also explained why the cart-mounted television in the conference
room was plugged in and hooked up to a cable, but not turned on. It sat
at one end, past the tables laden with coffee and rolls, cheese and jam.

*And the really frightful damned thing,* thought Lourdes Carrera, *is
that three out of the five of us agree, the war must go on. At least,
unofficially we agree. I'd be happy enough with peace, after all, it's my
son and husband at risk. But when three-fifths agree on war, even if
they can't admit it, even to each other, war there is going to be.*

Only four of those five currently sat around the traditionally
doughnut-shaped table: Balboa, *Xing Zhong Guo*, the Federated States,
and the UEPF. And just getting the FSC to sit down at the same table
with the Earthers had been a frightful exercise. Three generations after
the blasting of Botulph and San Fernando, the Federated States of
Columbia *still* hated the United Earth Peace Fleet beyond words,
beyond even measure.

*Interesting problem, though,* thought Lourdes. *If the FSC knew the UEPF wanted war, as I know from our cabin girl defector—Jesus, what will Patricio do when he finds out who that girl looks like?—they would threaten war to force peace. Since they think the UEPF wants peace, they're slightly on the side of continuing the war. It's very strange.*

The missing party was the Tauran Union, their delegation being composed of the president pro tem, Gaymard, and General Janier.

*And Janier I cannot read more than a little,* thought Carrera's wife, who, like many women, took an entirely justifiable modicum of pride in her ability to read men. *This may be because he is not too sure any more of what he believes, himself.*

*Hmm . . . I wonder why they're late, the Taurans. Patricio sent something through Triste about some dirty trick we've pulled on the TU, but there weren't any details. I suppose there couldn't be.*

She'd wondered why it was a general here, representing half of what the Tauran Union could bring to the table, rather than the civilian chief. Triste had explained it: "Elisabeth Ashworth is a corrupt, deep-at-the-core Tsarist-Marxist, ennobled for political connections and loyalty rather than acumen. She speaks no languages but her own, and that not especially well. She is barely educated. She could not be elected dogcatcher of a dogless town, hence has relied on appointments to advance herself. She has never held a job in or out of government for which she was not totally out of her depth. She spreads ignorance and chaos wherever she goes. She has no idea about defense, and couldn't tell the difference between a pair of boots and an aircraft carrier. She would have been an embarrassment to the Tauran Union. Nobody understands why she is in the position she is in, least of all herself. And all of that is the opinion of those who like and support her. Her political enemies are much more negative."

"Oh."

"She is alleged, however, to be likeable and even charming."

"Oh."

"Though those who allege it may be prejudiced in favor of politically connected idiocy."

Lourdes was still musing on the unquestioned benefits of *not* having Countess Ashworth at the peace conference when the Tauran delegation, Gaymard and Janier burst in. The president pro tem wore a look of utter fury on his face. The soldier, however, struck her as having a very difficult time of it keeping a broad smile from appearing on his.

"One hesitates to insult a lady," said Gaymard, with a sneer, "so take this as an insult to your entire people, and not to you, specifically. You filthy, lying, treacherous, uncivilized, unprincipled, rude, ill-mannered, sorry excuse for a people. Barbarians! Uncultured! Un—"

"I think it was a very clever trick," said Janier, earning a fierce glare from his nominal president.

"What are you people talking about?" asked Wallenstein. At about that moment her communicator beeped. It was Richard, earl of Care, back aboard the *Spirit of Peace*.

"High Admiral," said the ship's captain, unheard by any but the high admiral, "I think you should check the news down there. In Gaul and Sachsen, especially."

As if on cue, Gaymard stomped over to the television, turning it on and setting the channel to the Global News Network. The scene shown was of burning automobiles and burning buildings, of policemen under glare-lit barrages of rocks. "This is your good faith," said Gaymard, accusingly, to Lourdes and Esterhazy. "This is your integrity. You lie to us about casualties then go directly to our people, pinning the blame for your lies on us."

"What in the name of God are you talking about?" Lourdes asked, in French at least as good as his. "You fool!" she added, since she'd imbibed a fair amount of the culture with the language.

While Gaymard sputtered, Janier explained the barrage of letters and the damage they'd done to sundry Tauran Kosmos, or cosmopolitan progressives. "It's not as openly bad in Sachsen," he added, pointing at the screen, "since they're a much more disciplined people than mine. But they have a history of boiling over when least expected.

"You really didn't know?"

"No," Lourdes insisted. "And if it were deliberate, I am sure my husband would have told me." *Unless, of course, he wanted me to be able to feign innocence. For that, he told me just enough.*

"All right," said Janier, though he didn't quite believe it. "Well, you, your husband, and Balboa have both acquired a raft of new enemies as well as new friends."

"And you?" she asked.

"Count me as a friendly enemy," Janier answered.

"Fair enough," she said, believing him.

"Come along, General," insisted Monsieur Gaymard, tugging on the general's sleeve. "I refuse to sit at the same table as this . . . woman."

And that, for the day, was that. At least in that conference room that was that.

In Marguerite's quarters, where the Zhong security types had escorted a twisted-armed Gaymard, Janier leaned against the wall, arms folded, enjoying the show. The empress carefully inspected her nails, pretending to ignore the show. Marguerite *was* the show.

Towering over Gaymard, she held the president pro tem by his necktie, shaking him like a terrier with a rat. As she shook she continuously berated him, "You stupid, insipid, miserable excuse for a man." The shaking and berating occasionally were interrupted for a brisk *slap!* or two . . . or three . . . or a full body smash, or a series of them, against the wall. So, thusly: "You stupid, insipid, miserable excuse for a man." *Slapslapslap.* "Who the fuck do you think you are, you elder-gods-damned ground bound fucking peasant?" *ThumpthumpTHUMP* against the wall. "I hold the fucking power of life and death over you and yours, you piece of shit!" *Slapslap. Thump. Slap. THUMP.* "Do you want to see yourself at age ninety, if you live that long?" *ThumpthumpTHUMP. Slap. Thump.* "And if you think your fucking whore of a wife is marginal now, give her a few decades." *Slap. Slap. Slapslapslapslapslap. Punch.* "Ooof." "Fuckhead! Imbecile! Moron! Walk"—*slap*—"out"—*thump*—"of"—*punch*—"ooof!"—"my"—*thumpthump*—"fucking peace conference"—*thumppunch*—"ooof" *slapslap*—"will you?"

At that point Janier was smiling more broadly than ever. Marguerite let the president pro tem out of her grasp. Tears slid down his face as the Gaul slid down the wall. But for his own tailored trousers, he'd have left a more obvious streak on the wall than the tears did on his face.

"Tomorrow," she ordered Gaymard, "you will be there and you will be polite to that woman. Is that clear? You will apologize! Now get out!"

Unable to speak, the Gaul merely sniffled and nodded. He started his progress to the door on hands and knees, rising only when he passed a chair against one wall.

"No," she said to Janier, who had begun to leave with Gaymard. "You stay."

"I am confused," said the general, after Gaymard had left. "I want peace, yes, since I have reason now—serious reason, you will agree—to doubt our ability to wage war successfully. But you want war, High Admiral; deny it though you may. How does flogging that bureaucratic nonentity get you closer to your goal?"

"His anger at Mrs. Carrera was professional before. It will be personal now, thoughtless now, consumed with rage now. That makes it more likely that the TU will say or do, or fail to say or do, whatever is needed for war."

"Ah. I see," said the Gaul. "But why won't that hate turn on you and the Peace Fleet?"

"Because I and it are everything he aspires to. He could no more turn on us than your current Black Pope could on the real pope.

"And besides, the weasel wants that rejuvenation more than anything. And I am the key to that. So he has to turn his hatred elsewhere, and the most convenient 'elsewhere' remains Balboa."

Janier said nothing about that, though he agreed she probably was right. He *did* say, after a moment's reflection, "I'd better go see to the weasel."

"Please do," said Marguerite.

Janier walked to the door. As he was pulling the door shut behind him he thought he heard the empress huskily saying, "You have been a *terribly* naughty girl. You must be punished . . ."

*Sometimes,* thought the general, as the door clicked shut, *sometimes I wonder if, if only one could get valid and true answers, sex wouldn't explain everything there is to know about people, both as a species and as individuals. Or perhaps it would only show that nothing is understandable at all.*

*Ah, no matter; whatever her personal predilections, I do like the high admiral.*

## Gym *Dorado*, Cedral Multiplex Shopping Mall,
## Aserri, Santa Josefina, Terra Nova

Esmeralda wiped the sweat from her forehead. "Can *I* ask a question?"

"You can ask," replied Aragon, "but I might not know the answer and, even if I do, I might not be able to tell you."

"Oh. Well, then, I'd better save it for a question I think you know the answer to and might be able to tell me."

Aragon sighed. "Don't be silly. It's not a rationing scheme. If you want to know something, ask. If I know and can tell you, I will."

"Is there any way for your country to get to Old Earth to liberate it?"

*Goooddd question,* thought Aragon. *But,* "No, I don't think so. At least I've never heard of any and can't imagine any way for us to."

"Could anybody on the planet?"

"The Federated States would if they could," Aragon replied. "And they probably could if they could get the Peace Fleet out of the way for a couple of years, without getting themselves nuked in the process. Right now, though, the FSC is stymied."

"No they're not," said Esmeralda.

"What?"

"They're not stymied. They're bluffed. So far as anyone knows, there is not a single, reliable nuclear weapon in the Peace Fleet or on Earth. The high admiral had demanded that some new ones be manufactured, or some old ones be refurbished, but when we left, the SecGen—that's the ruler, but he's not an absolute ruler—was still fighting over it with some of his supporters."

"Oh, my God." Cass Aragon went speechless for a few moments. Then she said, "Debriefing's over. I have to get this to my people. *Now.*"

## *Isla Real*, Balboa, Terra Nova

There was a rectangular indentation in the concrete over the entrance to the underground shelter. Eventually, it was supposed to carry the shelter's name. Since the shelter didn't yet *have* a name, however . . .

The faintest ghost of a smile lit Fernandez's face as his powered wheelchair rolled across the concrete between the heavy steel blast doors, followed by Warrant Officer Mahamda and some of Mahamda's men. Some of Mahamda's men carried some large beams. One had a hammer. Another had a pack on his back that clanged metallically as he walked.

The doors were big enough to accommodate a UEPF shuttle. Despite the lack of a name, Fernandez tended to think of the facility as Fortress Robinson. It was here that the former high admiral was housed under guard, he having been captured in Pashtia in the course of trying to deliver non-Earth-built nuclear weapons to the Salafi *Ikhwan*, the now-defunct terrorist group. It was here that he and the former inspector general and marchioness of Amnesty, Interplanetary, Lucretia Arbeit, had trained several Balboans to pilot the legion's deepest secret—deeper even than their small nuclear arsenal—that they had a UEPF shuttle and that it worked.

Making it work had been problematic. It had, in the first place, been badly shot up where it had been sheltered, in a cave in Pashtia. What damage the bullets hadn't done, had been done when infantrymen and combat engineers, none too skilled, had been put to taking it apart and carting it off in pieces. Worst of all, seemingly insuperable, had been that the control box had been utterly toasted, ruined beyond redemption.

*I imagine,* thought Fernandez, *though I can't prove it, that the reason the Earthpigs never mentioned the shuttle is that they know the control box was ruined—last minute "I am under attack" squawk maybe—and know it can't be flown without it.*

The innate conservatism and lack of innovation of Old Earth, which lack was driven by the need for stability, had saved the shuttle. Five centuries before, in the course of winning his colony's independence from Earth's United Nations, Carrera's multi-great grandfather-in-law, Belisario Carrera, had taken a shuttle.

Finding that had taken recourse to Belisario's personal diaries—a Carrera clan treasure—plus thousands of man hours hunting through old probate records, before the control box for that old shuttle had been found, stashed away in the bowels of a museum, under the care of its curator, Professor Alfredo Figueredo. The museum really had no clue of the importance of what they'd had and mostly forgotten they'd even had it. Only Figueredo had been able to remember where the damned black box was hidden.

And, to Fernandez's near surprise, the old control box had fit, fit perfectly. Better, it had still worked. Matched to the shuttle, and the latter powered up in its Faraday-Cage-writ-large of a hangar, and suddenly Balboa had become not only a nuclear power, but, in whatever tiny a sense, a space power.

And, within a few years, the legion even had pilots trained by no less a personage than the captive former high admiral and inspector general of the Peace Fleet.

*Which children of whores*, fumed Fernandez, *neglected to mention to us that the fucking Peace Fleet had* no *nukes.*

Fernandez's wheelchair stopped. Four of Mahamda's men continued on, into the depths of the shelter, while the rest dumped their loads to the concrete floor of the top deck. The stuffed pack clanged even more metallically when tossed to the concrete. Under Mahamda's supervision, the remaining men began assembling the wooden beams into two large crosses.

The last trace of the ghostly smile had flitted away by the time Robinson and Arbeit were dragged to the top deck. They were tossed to their knees on the concrete at Fernandez's feet, their hands bound. Head inclined, Fernandez stared first at Robinson, then at Arbeit.

"Refresh my memory," he said. "When I spared your lives rather than leaving you aboard the *Hildegard von Mises* as it sunk, it was on the condition that you would cooperate actively and eagerly with us, was it not? That you would withhold nothing, would volunteer everything?"

"Yyyeesssss . . ." Both of the Old Earthers hissed their answers out together.

"Ah, good," said the intel chief. "And so I want to know the complete status of the fucking Peace Fleet's nuclear arsenal."

"No one really knows," said Arbeit, licking her lips nervously as her eyes flitted from Fernandez's feet to the twin crosses, "least of all, since we haven't been aboard ship in years, us. But he can tell you more than I can."

The former high admiral gulped, then said, "I *told* you, sir, why I had to borrow nukes from Kashmir and other places to give to the Salafi *Ikhwan*. Because I couldn't be sure."

"So if someone said that the Peace Fleet has not a single, functioning nuke aboard any of its ships?" Fernandez asked.

"Legate Fernandez," Robinson continued, "please believe me. *Please*. I don't know if there are no functioning nuclear weapons in the fleet. I only know that the ones we had were questionable. I told you about why I obtained the Volgan, Kashmiri, and Hangkuk bombs."

"Is it plausible," asked Fernandez, "that every last one of them is defunct? Think carefully on your answer, because if I don't believe you, if I think you're trying to withhold information, if I think you've broken your word to us . . . to me . . . then you and this psychotic bitch of an ex-marchioness are going up on crosses. In two days we'll start asking questions again. If then you've answered everything in exactly the same way, even though you'll be hanging separately, then on the third day I'll let you down. If you have not, you stay there another day, and your legs get broken."

"No nails?" asked Mahamda innocently.

"Oh, no," replied Fernandez, "we'll just tie them up. It hurts more that way, you know."

"Yes, sir . . . but what about tradition?"

"Trust me, it's traditional. Robinson?"

"You have another source somewhere aboard the fleet, don't you?" asked the ex-high admiral. He was trying his best to remain calm and helpful, but Fernandez was pretty sure he was inches from gibbering.

"Yes," Fernandez agreed. "The cabin girl to High Admiral Wallenstein, your replacement."

Mention of Wallenstein's name converted some of Robinson's terror into hate in an instant. He was a lot easier to deal with that way.

"Okay," Robinson said, " . . . what we're talking about is, to a degree, semantic. You said 'cabin girl,' so probably a lower caste girl, not well educated and unlikely to pick up fine nuances. But consider, Legate, that a nuke that cannot be relied on is *not*, in fact, useable. Try to use one on, say, the Federated States, or even one of its allies, and let them discover that the bombs don't work, and the Peace Fleet becomes radioactive debris in orbit. *Fast!* That would be true even if that were the only defective one and all the others were good.

"When I was in command, I had hundreds of nukes. Statistically, based on records of old testing, over a hundred should have worked. In practice, I could not tell which ones would and which would not. I couldn't even rely on the test sets to tell me, since they were older than even the fleet was."

"So how many," asked Fernandez, "could be expected to work now?"

### *Estado Mayor*, Balboa, Terra Nova

"He doesn't know," said Fernandez to Carrera. "He says he doesn't and I am inclined to believe him.

"That said . . . I am not entirely sure I trust what I believe," Fernandez admitted. "The way I went about it was nonstandard . . . and a mistake in procedure. It may be, sir, that you need to replace me."

"Fuck off and die," answered Carrera, "but not until the war's over."

"Yes, sir."

"What about the cabin girl?" Carrera asked. "You said she'd seemed positive."

"Robinson had a good point there; the girl is unlikely to know the difference between unserviceable and unusable."

"Any chance she's a double agent?" Carrera asked. "Any chance she's feeding us a series of lines that the high admiral wants us to swallow?"

Fernandez nodded slowly, not in agreement but in recognition of the question. "I've asked myself that, *Duque*, then rejected it. There's no possible benefit to the UEPF in us believing their nuclear teeth are just dentures. Less still if, believing it, we went running to the Federated States and got *them* to believe it.

"So . . . much as it pains me, I've got to go with the common denominator of what the cabin girl and the ex-high admiral have told us. There are nukes up there. Some work. Some don't. And they're not useable because the Earthpigs don't know which ones work and which ones don't. But . . . what's it do to our plans?"

"I'm not sure," Carrera answered. "It will take some thought. There are a couple of things I'm sure of, though."

"What are those, sir?"

"I am sure that we and the UEPF have a common interest in keeping the status of their nuclear weapons secret. And I am sure the Yamatans or their 'special source' are not being forthright, or we'd have heard more about this."

Fernandez considered those for a moment, then said, "I'm sure enough about the first one, but the second? Well . . . maybe not. The Yamatans seem to just shut down whenever the subject of nukes comes up. They can be so detached and logical about everything else, even when they're being loons they're logical loons, consistent with their preconceptions and assumptions. But with nukes the subject seems to drop a hundred points of their national average IQ."

"What did you end up doing with Robinson and Arbeit?" Carrera asked.

"Well, you said you needed him for the project. So I just told them I'd do some checking on my own, then get back to them about the crosses. I had the assembled crosses left outside of their cells, to spur their memories in case there's anything they forgot to tell us."

"*You*, Legate, are a wicked man."

"Somewhat," Fernandez admitted. "But, sir, when the time comes, I want to try that evil cunt Arbeit for murder of a slave, then nail her up."

"Have to be an *in camera* trial," Carrera said. "But . . . maybe."

"That said, though Robinson owes me in proportion for five or maybe six lives, depending on how much truth may be in a nightmare, I am sure my Linda would have wanted me to keep my word. So as long as he cooperates, he lives."

"There's something else," Fernandez said, "something you need to know about."

"And that would be?"

The legate shook his head, not in negation but in puzzlement. "The Taurans are trying to reactivate their network of spies and informers here. At least to some extent they are."

"How do you know?"

"Double agent. Female. They contacted her via her cell and she reported to us via the old drop we had set up, pre-war.

"Problem is," said Fernandez, "that I never had a good handle on their network. I could estimate that there were X or so spies, of which

I had turned Y, knew about Z, and had no clue about W. But it wasn't more than a guess."

"What did you do with the Zs?"

Fernandez gave one his rare grins. "The ones I did know about? Didn't round them up for questioning, followed by execution, which was my first instinct. Mostly I took a couple of hostages from each, wives, children, lovers, and left them in place but watched. There was also a small number—precisely three—who, once they saw which way the wind was blowing, after we booted the TU out, came over to us, giving up whatever they knew. Since the Taurans hadn't, at that time, had a chance to try to reestablish their network, those I just took into custody. They're still alive and healthy, and have all their organs and fingernails. None of those were in the legion, by the way, or I would have nailed them up, no matter what."

"Who were they?" Carrera asked.

"One professor at the university, one student—no, they didn't know about each other—and the wife of one of our tribunes. Seemed she was having an affair with one of the Tauran officers. All she wanted was immunity from prosecution and not to tell her husband."

"Did you give your word?" Carrera asked.

With a sigh, Fernandez said, "I did."

"Pity," said Carrera. "I'd love to let the husband have first crack at the bitch."

"Oh, yeah."

"How are you planning on fighting this?" Carrera asked.

"It's tough, really," Fernandez replied. "If I'd gotten to their files before they burned, we'd be sitting pretty. As is, I've got to treat the ones we know about as bait to try to get at whoever they introduce into the country to reestablish their net. In the long run, though, they will reestablish that net."

"Give me six months of Tauran, Zhong, and UEPF ignorance and I'll be happy."

"I'll surely try, *Duque*."

# CHAPTER ELEVEN

You and I were born in a period of troubles and have
grown up at a time when the Fatherland is in danger.
—Tran Hung Dao,
Fourteenth-Century Vietnamese General,
"Proclamation to the Officers"

**BdL *Dos Lindas*, at sea, *Mar Furioso*,
one hundred and thirty-seven kilometers north of *Isla Real***

There was only a double handful of nations on Terra Nova that
maintained aircraft carriers at all. The Federated States had a dozen
huge ones, plus another ten amphibious carriers that would do in a
pinch. Yamato had four that collectively were not as large as any single
version of the smaller Federated States amphibious jobs. Volga had
one that couldn't put to sea. Bharat had two old ones they'd bought
from elsewhere and was building a new one of their own. *Xing Zhong
Guo* had two small ones, though they once, recently, had had a third,
larger one. Gaul and Anglia maintained a couple each, mid-sized.
Tuscany had two that were more in the nature of helicopter carriers.
The few others were old, or small, or not fit for sea, or some
combination of those.

And then there was Balboa, which had, in theory, two. One of
these, the *Dos Lindas*, was old and not particularly large, seaworthy
but not fit for duty in line of battle against any threat greater than a
megalodon . . . the fish, not the submarine. She had done good service

in the campaigns against the Xamari and Nicobar pirates, though she'd come far too close to destruction in the latter. *Dos Lindas* remained useful against minor threats—or what would once have been called, on different seas on a different planet, "teaching the wogs a lesson"—and it had fair antisubmarine capability.

The other Balboan carrier was more than a hulk, but not all that much more. It didn't even have a name, but only a code: BdEL1 (*Barco del Entrenamiento Legionario Numero Uno*). It rode at anchor in the bay formed by the tadpole's tail on the northern point of the *Isla Real*. It couldn't move. It had only one elevator, the other having been taken for repairs to the *Dos Lindas*. Instead of three lasers for air and missile defense, it had only one, and that for training gunners and maintenance crewmen.

Its chief virtues were that it cost almost nothing to keep anchored and in use as the *classis's*—the legion's naval arm's—chief training facility. Aboard the BdEL1, everything having to do with the surface fleet, from carrier take-offs and landings, to servicing aircraft aboard, to antiaircraft gunnery, to cooking in narrow rolling spaces, to damage control could be trained on the cheap and well.

Thus, if nothing else, the *Dos Lindas* had a well-trained crew. And, while obsolete compared to any carrier of any other navy, that didn't mean it was useless, even in the current contretemps. It served as a command control platform for the fleet, currently strung out on picket duty from near the border with Santa Josefina to near the border with Santander. It was a fair antisubmarine platform, especially against Zhong Guo's more primitive and noisier subs. And its aircraft served well as scouts further out to sea for the more potent land-based aircraft of the *alae*—wings—of the Sixteenth Aviation Legion.

*But we're so old,* lamented the admiral of the *classis* and former captain of the *Dos Lindas*, Legate Roderigo Fosa, *and the old girl's so weary. Time for her to become a museum ship or something, and for us to buy a new carrier.*

What caused that train of thought in Fosa was his maintenance officer going down the list of problems—new problems, not old ones on deferred maintenance—cropping up.

"In short, Legate," said the maintenance chief, in unconscious imitation of his commander's thoughts, "the old girl needs a long rest. Or retirement."

**Kiaochow, *Xing Zhong Guo*, Terra Nova**

Major Wu Zixu, *Xing Zhong Guo* Imperial Marine Corps, tugged his wife around a warehouse corner by her dainty hand. He was large, for a Zhong, and besides, she was willing. It was an easy job to get themselves hidden. And it wouldn't do to let the troops lining the deck of the LPD, *Qin Shan*, and the dock to which it was tied, to see them kissing.

His wife, Jiao, lived up to her name, Dainty and Lovely. A tiny little thing, except for her swollen abdomen, Wu's family had paid a bride price for Jiao that had nearly beggared them, the family being military and the military being rather underpaid and, unlike some, scrupulously honest.

Not all arranged marriages worked. Some, however, worked so well that one had to wonder why anyone tried the other way. This one had worked very well. Husband lived for lovely wife; wife for heroic husband; and both for the child whom the wife bore in her belly.

Jiao sniffled, tried to control it, failed, and lay her head on her husband's chest, weeping openly. "I am so afraid," she said, through her tears. "I am so afraid you will never return."

Wu turned his head and bent his neck to rest his cheek atop the woman's shining, blue-black hair. He rubbed the cheek back and forth, while keeping one arm around Jiao's expanded waist, with the hand of the other stroking her hair as well. It was an impending agony to leave her, the two having grown so close since their arranged marriage.

"Don't be silly, wife. Of course I'll come back. That is, I will if the cooks don't poison me." At that, he sighed. "I shall miss your cooking, woman." *I shall miss a lot more than that.*

"I will not be able to write every day," said Wu. "I may not be able to write at all, depending on what Admiral Wanyan orders. But do not doubt, do not doubt for a minute, that you will never be far from my thoughts."

She couldn't answer the sentiment in words. If she'd tried she'd have broken down completely. Instead, Jiao held her departing husband tightly, nodding into his chest.

Wu heard a loudspeaker blaring from the ship, calling all the tardy to board. At that, Jiao did break down completely, her enveloping arms crushing him to her.

"Careful," he said, "or you'll be expelling the baby before it's ready."

That earned him a small laugh and a somewhat larger decrease in the flow of tears.

"You *must* come back to me," said Jiao. "Promise!"

"I . . . I can't promise. Except to try."

Kiaochow was one of four major bases of the Zhong fleet. It was also the most centrally located of three of the four. The fourth, Liaoxi, which was more centrally located, was completely unsuitable for the assembly of a fleet, since it largely consisted of submarine pens, carved out of a mountain overlooking the port.

As the most centrally located of the three suitable bases, Kiaochow now saw the assemblage of the greatest Mandarin-speaking fleet since the eunuch admiral, Cheng Ho, on Old Earth, had returned from his last voyage to India in 1433 AD. Kiaochow was also the port from which the aircraft carrier *Anshan* had sailed on its final, humanitarian mission to Balboa, from which mission, of course, it had not returned. *Anshan*'s old berth remained empty. Indeed, the Celestial Throne had decreed it would remain empty in perpetuity. Like other imperial promises, that really depended on the will of future emperors.

Conversely, the promise of the fleet assembling was immense.

Originally, the Zhong Navy had intended to send half of its frigates and destroyers, and both of its light carriers, to the coming war against the Balboans. This plan had presupposed the Balboan fleet, such as it was, would split itself between *Mar Furioso* and Shimmering Sea. In the event, the Balboans—apparently, and insultingly, believing they could do nothing against the Tauran fleets, but could at least hurt the Zhong—had simply abandoned forward defense in the Shimmering Sea, concentrating their meager fleet against *Xing Zhong Guo*.

The fleet already assembling would surely have been adequate to simply brush aside half of the Balboan *classis*. It was clearly adequate to defeat the entire *classis*. But mere victory was not enough for the Celestial Throne, which is to say Empress Xingzhen. It had to be an awe-inspiring victory, a stomping of the Balboans as if they were mice, to suit not only her ego, but the majesty and honor of the empire she (unofficially) commanded.

That necessitated delay while another quarter of the Zhong surface combatant arsenal, and more submarines, assembled. It also necessitated confusion and discomfort, as two divisions of Imperial Marines and another half-dozen of infantry, plus support, waited in their miserable, cramped, smelly holds. Some of those holds were officially and thoroughly naval, four Landing Platform Docks, twenty-nine Landing Ship Tanks, forty-eight serviceable Landing Ship Mediums, which really weren't suitable for carrying their normal combat loads of troops on long voyages, nearly four hundred landing craft, scattered among the ships, and thirty-three large freighters, commandeered and converted for the war.

All the troops were miserable, but none so miserable as the ones in the civilian freighters. Those holds weren't just miserable, cramped and smelly. Oh, no, they were also noisy, as crews welded helicopter platforms and pairs of heavy-duty davits, above, and loaded critical cargoes on deck and below.

Why such a huge force for landing? For much the same reason as the huge number of surface combatants. The Zhong intended to brush aside resistance contemptuously.

**Liaoxi, *Xing Zhong Guo*, Terra Nova**

The Zhong Navy's submarine force had a number of components, of wildly differing capabilities. There were, for example, half a dozen nuclear-powered ballistic missile carrying submarines, and a few cruise missile carrying submarines, for deterrence. These were far too few and far too precious to risk on Balboa, or anywhere near Balboa. Nor would they have added much to combat capabilities. Of course, they carried torpedoes and tubes but, as with other navies' strategic submarines, their captains were chosen, if not for timidity, than certainly for absence of temerity. The things were just too important to risk on anything less than the existential.

There was also a large number of diesel-powered coastal defense submarine, none of which had range to reach Balboan waters on their own, across the vast expanse of the *Mar Furioso*. Oh, they could range, some of them, if barely, and they carried enough consumables for the trip, but only that. Still, there wasn't a lot of sense in sending them to confront Balboa, only to have them have surface to beg for food. Still, some—quite a few, actually—would be used, but they would be used in company with the main fleet, and would feed off of the same service support that would be fueling, feeding, and arming the surface fleet.

The final significant component of the Zhong submarine force was made up of the eleven nuclear attack submarines. Six of these were required as escorts for the strategic subs. One was in dry-dock and wouldn't be out any time soon. The remaining four were ordered out early, to take position to dominate Balboan waters, should the call to battle be sounded.

Noisy machinery and the stench of diesel overrode the sound and smell of the sea that reached into the man-made cavern. Green safety nets, normally stretched out over the gap between platform and water, were pulled up, out of the way. Normally, set on moveable frames in the horizontal plane, they prevented crew and loading personnel from falling down where the boats could pin them between hull and rock, crushing the life from their fragile and weak bodies. Behind the now vertical nets, hundreds of well-wishing shore monkeys waved goodbye as the Dynasty-class hunter-killer submarine, *Mao Zedong*, cast off from the dock.

Captain Liu, standing in little open compartment, atop the sail, that went by the name of "bridge," watched carefully as his boat pulled out of the underground pen. The captain was remarkably white skinned, a result of spending so much time not merely at sea, but under it. He waved back at the shore monkeys until the bridge passed the western edge of the pen and entered the long tunnel. *Why not? I expect to return someday and will need them then as I have since taking command.*

The speed of exit was a bare crawl, and, thought Liu, could perhaps have been better done by towing machines—perhaps on rails—than by the sub's own power. In any case, the bare and rough rock walls sliding by at less than a slow walking pace were a necessary frustration; it was a dangerously tight fit.

Looking ahead, Liu saw the hint of a wider area, though still not very wide. This was where the half water-filled-tunnels that led to four other pens joined up to form the main exit—the only exit for submarines—to the sea.

Maneuvering through that bend in the otherwise straight tunnel system took some finesse. Again, Liu mused on the possibility of using some kind of automated system, perhaps if they ever got the alternate entrance and exit tunnel carved out. At thought of that, the captain scowled. Supposedly that alternate exit would be dug; the beginnings of it already had been. Liu would believe it when he could take his sub out through it. As it was, it appeared to be yet another boondoggle, full of sound and fury, and being dug . . . or not . . . by a well-known idiot with impeccable connections to the imperial palace.

*Corruption will be the ruin of us,* the skipper thought. *Already our trade is being crippled by the foul and contaminated, sometimes murderously contaminated, products put into the stream of commerce by those pirates masquerading as the guardians of the people. "To each according to his ability to steal, from each according to his inability to get at decent goods."*

*What has become of the revolution my ancestors thought they were fighting for?*

Liu, who loved his work, was always careful to keep such thoughts purely private.

In the deep interior, the lights above the sub had been quite bright fluorescents, bright enough not to be able to see the small guide lights along each side of the tunnel. As it neared the exit, the tunnel's bright overheads gave way to diffuse normal daylight from the tunnel's mouth and the minor red guide lights. For a nighttime exit, it would be all on the little guide lights, those, and night vision devices, to get the sub to sea.

At the point where the guide lights took over and the fluorescent lights ended, an antitorpedo fence—because, yes, some of the Zhong Empire's enemies could guide a torpedo or mine right into the underground base—was pulled into the walls to permit the sub to leave.

The guide lights were each a single bulb, with parallel quad slit openings, designed to let the viewer gauge his rough distance by the tendency to blend into one when processed by the eye and brain. Too far away and all four slits would present one light. Too close and the viewer would see all four. Only if two were seen was the distance just right.

The lights were protected by rubber guards, which also served to protect the boat and its anechoic tiles from the rock. Liu didn't have an excess of faith in those; his was a seven-*thousand*-ton displacement vessel. He thought the odds were poor of the rubber stopping his boat before it did damage to itself, or the lights, or even the walls, even at the current snail's pace.

As the sub lined itself up in that wider, hangarlike section where the tunnel bent, Liu saw two more subs behind his, awaiting their turn. There was another, he knew, that had already passed out of the base and made its way to sea.

*I wonder why the daytime exit? To intimidate the Balboans? It might be. Let's hope they're easier to intimidate that the bloody Cochinese.* Nothing *intimidates them, the ungrateful shits.*

Ahead the rough semi-circle of light widened and grew. Soon enough, in this easy and straight final passage, the sub's bow was graced with sunlight. The line of natural illumination passed down the sub's forward length, over the sail, and then down the stern to where the asymmetric screw lightly frothed the water. From there buoys marked the safe passage out. Liu followed that marked path for several hours, on a zigzag course, threading his way around the numerous peninsulas and islands that jutted out into and up from the Sea of Zhili. At last with that inlet from the *Mar Furioso* behind him, he ordered his command down into the dark depths of the *Mar Furioso*. From there, the course was generally west-sothwest, to Balboan waters.

## IYN *Akizuki,* Sea of Hangkuk, Terra Nova

*Xing Zhong Guo*'s Dynasty class of nuclear submarines outweighed Yamato's largest submarines, of which class *Akizuki* was a member, by a factor of more than two. The Zhong had greater range. They carried more weapons. In an underwater knife fight between any Zhong Dynasty class and *Akizuki* or any of her sisters, the smart money would still have been on the Yamatans.

The Yamatan Navy wasn't out for a fight at the moment, though they wouldn't have ducked one, either. They simply took a keen interest in everything the Zhong did, anywhere near Yamato, the Zhong being, at the moment, the only real threat Yamato faced. In this particular case, with a major invasion fleet obviously assembling, and the cutting edge of the Zhong submarine fleet at sea, Yamato's interest in Zhong goings about was extremely high. It would remain so until that invasion fleet went elsewhere, as expected.

Where it was going? Well, everyone in the know already knew. It was going to Balboa to punish those arrogant upstarts for sinking an, in fact innocent, Zhong aircraft carrier.

What was Yamato going to do about it? That had been a matter for considerable debate in the secretive bowels of Yamatan government. Some, albeit not many, were persuaded to help Balboa, openly or clandestinely, because of the Balboans creditable performance in opening up the oil routes between Yithrab and Yamato. Others, not unreasonably, said, "Screw them; they were well paid for their efforts." Still another party thought, "Screw the Balboans, indeed; but wouldn't it be in our interest to put a couple of torpedoes up the asses of the Zhong submarine fleet, letting the Balboans take the blame?"

Unfortunately for all but the first group, the emperor had the final say. That boiled down to, "We wish the Balboans well. Indeed, we wish them so well we are going to share any intelligence we have with them. But we've had enough of wars that do nothing good for us; the Balboans will have to be content with our well wishes and our good intelligence."

Which explained why a Yamatan submarine was waiting as, ultimately, four of *Xing Zhong Guo*'s Dynasty-class nuclear submarines departed their base, passed through the Yellow Sea, and began the long trek across the *Mar Furioso* to Balboa's coast. It didn't explain why a Yamatan submarine named *Akizuki* stopped off at a Federated States naval base on an atoll in the middle of the ocean to replenish fuel and stores, then departed without another word. It didn't explain why that same boat surfaced with some regularity to send encrypted data back home. And it certainly didn't explain why that same data was then forwarded to Fernandez in Balboa.

But then, while the emperor had said "share intelligence," he hadn't said, "but don't actively gather it."

## Hotel *Cielo Dorado*, Aserri, Santa Josefina, Terra Nova

Though there was, by definition, no head or foot to the round conference table, there are still certain grouping and axes, not always apparent except to the participants. Starting at what one arbitrarily might call "twelve o'clock" was the UEPF, Wallenstein at the center flanked by one of the two Khans and the local ambassador to Santa Josefina. To her left was the Tauran Union, Monsieur Gaymard, who still seethed with obvious hate, General Janier, and General Marciano, who got along surprisingly well. Moving further clockwise was the Zhong delegation, the empress and one or two of her military advisors, whoever could be spared from planning the invasion with those Taurans of Janier's staff who weren't at the table. Then came the Federated States, an ambassador and four flunkies. On the other side of the FSC contingent were the Santa Josefinans, usually Calderón and a civilian advisor from the diplomatic office. There might have been a military advisor, but Blanco was as senior and experienced as those got in the country and he was too laughably junior and inexperienced. Then came a small delegation from La Plata, followed by Esterhazy, Lourdes Carrera, and Triste. On the other side of those were three from Atzlan. The last two were not technically at war but, since they had already loaned Carrera their two most capable and fanatical brigades, it could be said that they were in a conditional state of war with the Tauran Union, and quite possibly with the Zhong.

There were also sundry newsmen present, by common agreement, though no cameras were permitted. There was also a mixed group of security guards provided by Balboa and Marciano's command.

Lourdes glanced right, at Esterhazy, and nodded. He stood up and said, "Copies of what I am about to say will be provided to the press as well as to all parties to the conference.

"The Republic of Balboa is aware of the massive invasion fleet now assembling in the ports of *Xing Zhong Guo*. Indeed, it was in part due to the threat presented by that fleet that we agreed to attend this conference. A peace conference, however, is supposed to be about peace, not a cover for renewed war. Moreover, while a fleet is port in not so great a threat, a fleet that has begun to sail *is* a threat."

Wallenstein, who knew every important detail of that fleet from her royal lover, cast her eyes Zhongward. The empress shrugged, *I have no idea what these barbarians are talking about.*

"Six days ago," Esterhazy continued, "four Zhong hunter-killer"— that was bound to upset the generally ignorant press more than the simple "attack" might have—"submarines set sail from Liaoxi. Those submarines are now within two weeks of entering Balboan waters.

"Given the generally uncivilized intransigence of the Zhong delegation, here"—which got a sputter of indignant outrage from the empress—"and their obviously imperialist designs upon Balboa, the Republic of Balboa makes the following demand and the following announcements.

"First, the demands." Esterhazy glared straight at the empress, a violation of protocol sufficient to have cost him his head in her own country. "Stop those submarines and turn them around. If they reach our waters they will be engaged without warning."

The next point was one they'd argued about for over a day. Ultimately, knowing her mission, Lourdes had agreed to Esterhazy saying, with a sneer, "After all, given the losses your fleet has suffered *so far*, it isn't like you can afford to lose much more."

That had the desired effect. The empress stood up and threw a book, which Esterhazy ducked, while one of her underlings drew a wicked-looking knife. The latter, in turn, went back under cover when, magnetlike, it drew a dozen rifle muzzles.

"My second demand is to the Tauran Union. You and the Zhong are here together, and cooperating, because you are effectively allies in the persecution of the Balboan people. We will return no more prisoners until those Zhong submarines turn around and until you remove the threat your forces here in Santa Josefina pose to the Republic."

*That* set both the Taurans and Calderón to steaming fury.

"Our third demand concerns a subject near and dear to Tauran hearts, and the hearts of cosmopolitan progressives, everywhere. As various nations within the Tauran Union have asserted universal jurisdiction over sundry crimes against humanity, so the Timocratic Republic of Balboa takes this precedent to heart and asserts universal jurisdiction against anyone corrupting the international legal system by launching politically motivated prosecutions. Thus, we demand the extradition to Balboa, to face *capital* charges, of the Chief Prosecutor of the Cosmopolitan Criminal Court, Ms. Fatima Gamble, of the corrupt judges Isabelle Mussolini, Chile Mmassasisi, and Anita Kraul, as well as various other members of the ruling *junta* in the Tauran Union, whose names shall be made public at a later time.

"And finally, that is all we have to say. The Republic of Balboa withdraws from this conference until its just demands are met." Then, ostentatiously, Lourdes, Triste, Esterhazy, and their party closed their files, stood, where needed, and stormed out together.

## MV *Roger Casement* (Hibernian Registry), Matama, Santa Josefina, Terra Nova

Matama was hardly a huge port. Indeed, it only had two berths with sufficiently deep water for a container ship of the *Casement*'s displacement. That saved confusion; the soon-to-be rebels knew exactly where to go.

The mule train from the Balboan port of Capitano had arrived the week prior, having made not a lot more than five miles a day, and often rather less, going cross country over the mountains. Not all the mules had made it, either. Starting with forty-seven mules, plus the largely unladen bell mare, and not quite five tons of arms and equipment, high-quality feed for the animals, and dry rations for the half-dozen men of the column, only the men, forty-one mules and the bell mare had made it. This hadn't meant much of a loss of cargo, since the fodder was consumed regularly, and the arms and ammunition could be reloaded. That said, one hundred and twenty rounds of mortar ammunition had been a complete loss, when the mules carrying it plunged over a cliff and into a broad stream below. That was about a third of all the mortar ammunition carried, so it was not a light blow.

Still, they did manage to bring to the outskirts of Matama three light mortars, with two hundred and forty rounds of mixed ammunition, plus a dozen general-purpose machine guns, with tripods and nearly twenty thousand belted rounds. There were one hundred and twenty rifles, as well, along with twenty-two submachine guns, and thirty-six thousand rounds of ammunition. Of antitank weapons there were only a few of heavier versions, with a mere twenty rounds, plus three dozen light weapons. Twenty night-vision devices with batteries were there, as well as ten radios, with *their* batteries, just to keep to nice round numbers so beloved of quartermasters the worlds over. There were also several cases of grenades and pyrotechnic signals, three first-rate Sachsen sniper rifles, with match-grade ammunition, a truncated demolition kit, and four shoulder fired antiaircraft missiles, without which no guerrilla movement can feel properly dressed.

They could have carried more but, what with the rains, the dunnage to protect the ammunition really *was* needed. They brought no uniforms, armor—neither of heads nor for torsos—individual load-carrying equipment . . . none of it.

It was, in any case, enough for the roughly one maniple of Santa Josefinan legionaries, all in mufti, assembled within thirty miles of Matama. For the rest of the overstrength tercio in Santa Josefina, the *Casement*, with a little luck and some planning, would provide.

# CHAPTER TWELVE

A nation without defense cannot exist; a people
without a military cannot be secure.
—Naval Recruitment Poster,
commonly seen on walls in the city of Choukoutien,
*Xing Zhong Guo*

**Outside Matama, Santa Josefina, Terra Nova**

By and large the pattern in Santa Josefina followed that of Colombia
Central, generally; most of the population was with the healthier
climate and better weather of the *Mar Furioso* coast or central
*cordillera*, while the Shimmering Sea sides had a single not-too-large
port most suitable for the export of fruit, with a single road leading to
it. Ordinarily, this lack of a transportation net would be heaven for a
guerilla force. In this case, however, since the guerillas were pretty
much disarmed, since almost all their arms were coming on a single
ship, and since getting those arms issued required a better
transportation net than existed, it was highly problematic. It was made
more problematic by the dispersal of Legate Salas's tercio across a
quarter or more of the country. The legate himself, with a few guards,
radio operators, cooks, half of his staff, and a single Santa Josefinan
officer of police, on leave, stood in a bunker about five miles from the
port of Matama, waiting for the word that his unit's sister tercio, *la
Negrita*, had begun its demonstration along the border with Balboa. At
a greater distance, Macera's overstrength maniple of infantry, now

freshly armed by the recently arrived mule train, waited in bunkers for the word to move into town.

*Would have been nice,* thought the legate, *if I'd been able to bring all forty-five hundred of them here. Then we'd just have them line up and issue the arms. But, go figure, adding eight percent to the population, essentially all male, almost all strangers, to the town, overnight, would be bound to raise a few eyebrows.*

One of the radio operators turned up the volume on the civilian radio he was manning. "It's the signal, sir," he told Salas.

Salas listened for a few moments as Radio Balboa went into a scathing denouncement of the provocative and—so far as anyone knew, who was actually in a position to know, nonexistent—Tauran maneuvers along the border, then read off a statement from *Presidente* Parilla claiming that he had ordered some unspecified forces to defensive positions.

*Which will,* mused Salas, *of course, look remarkably like offensive positions, to anyone but the ignorant press. I can see it now; we control the press in Balboa, so nobody's going to see our preparations there. Poor Claudio Marciano, constrained by the international community of the very, very caring and sensitive, is going to have to ostentatiously scramble to meet our threat. The uncontrolled press here will see that, won't see that the initial operational provocation was ours, because we won't let them see that, and will blame him.*

### Headquarters, Tauran Union Security Force-Santa Josefina, Rio Clara, Santa Josefina, Terra Nova

Claudio didn't have time for the press, what with the task of getting his troops off their asses, out of their billets, and into their defensive positions. Besides, he had a public affairs officer for that kind of thing. The PAO was a Castilian, that being one of the very few positions Castile felt it could fill so long as one of their battalions was aligned with the other side.

"Take care of them," Marciano told Castilian Major Serrano, on his way out the door, heading to one of the outlying battalion camps. "But remember, while you and I may not like the fucking press, the press sure likes fucking us." With that little tidbit of advice, Marciano jumped into his vehicle and told the driver, "Take me to the combat support battalion camp."

"Yes, sir," said the driver, his general's tone telling him, *and don't spare the horses.* The four-wheel-drive vehicle bounced away over one of Santa Josefina's cracked and potholed roads.

There was a town about three quarters of the way to the combat support camp. A river ran through it, with the town's main drag passing through the center, and over a bridge. Marciano's driver was approaching the bridge at a bone-jarring clip when, suddenly, a Hordalander tank appeared, pivot steering in a widened spot in the road and then lunging for the bridge. Marciano's driver had to jerk his vehicle off the road at the last minute to avoid running into the tank.

The driver noticed that the bridge bore some of those devil-horned posters demanding the Taurans get out of Santa Josefina. *Ungrateful shits*, he thought.

After that one Hordalander tank, came another, then another. Marciano thought, *Well, since they obviously don't need me to get them moving, may as well turn it into a pass in review.* Accordingly, he stood up in his own vehicle, and saluted the next tank passing. That tank commander, a senior sergeant, the Tuscan general thought, returned the salute formally, then twisted a little key on his helmet and said something into the boom mike that ran from the helmet to a point in front of his mouth. Thereafter, as the Hordalander heavy armor passed the vehicle, commanders beat Marciano to the draw, salute-wise.

From a position well inside the window of the shady house, Corporal Moran, of the Second Cazador Maniple, *Tercio la Virgen*, tracked Claudio through the scope of his rifle. The precision marked crosshairs floated for a moment in a loose spiral around the Tuscan's head before settling on the bridge of his nose. *I couldn't miss this one*, thought Moran, *if Araya's little sister were blowing me. Again.*

The rifle wasn't a legion-issued sniper rifle, but an old-fashioned, percussion-primed, brass-case-firing, large-caliber hunting rifle, with a scope, such as any reasonably prosperous Santa Josefinan might own. He'd bought it with legion money, to be sure, and it remained legion property.

Moran and his spotter, Private Araya, were in a light green painted room in Araya's family's house in the town.

"Go ahead," Moran told his underling, "ask for permission. Make sure they understand I have the Tauran in my sights and it is a guaranteed kill if they hurry." Moran rather hoped he'd be turned down. He'd never met the Tuscan but knew, from those who'd served in Pashtia, that Marciano had been a good ally and comrade. He hoped he'd be turned down, but was willing enough to do the job if not.

Araya, wearing headphones connected to a radio, tapped his corporal on the shoulder and said, "No, Legate Villalobos says hold fire. No explanation."

"Okay," agreed the corporal, though he continued to keep his crosshairs on the bridge of the Tuscan's nose.

Marciano heard the steady *wopwopwop* of his helicopter force, assembling on the Gallic infantry battalion currently in reserve. He wasn't remotely stupid. He'd seen the way Carrera operated before, in Pashtia, and had acquired a fair measure of the man.

*If the son of the bitch is making an "uproar in the east," odds are not bad that he plans to "strike" . . . somewhere . . . "in the west."*

*Thing is, do I launch on my own authority? Do I wait for the president to authorize it? Do I wait for him to ask the Tauran Union to order me? I've tried to get answers, in advance, but . . . well . . . a person who's never dealt with one can understand just how immobile and stupid a powerful bureaucracy can be.*

It wasn't hopeless, of course. After all, the president pro tem of the Tauran Union was in country. *And getting a straight answer out of that weasel . . . no, fuck it. I'll send in the troops as soon as I figure out where to send them. The shitbirds of the TU can court-martial me later, if they want.*

### Esquisito, *Valle de las Lunas*, Balboa, Terra Nova

The border between the two countries was for the most part artificial, the result of an initial United Nations Interplanetary Settlement and Boundary Committee land grant to MERCOSUR, followed by some bungling judgments on the part of MERCOSUR, followed by the final result of Belisario Carrera's war of liberation against the UN, followed by a number of minor wars and border skirmishes between Balboa and Santa Josefina, all further muddied by any amount of ignorant arbitration of the part of, mostly, Santander and the Federated States.

The net result of that was that at no point did the boundary between the two countries have any recognizable natural boundary. In every case where such boundaries could have existed, they had been bypassed or ignored. Thus, what might have served as the natural boundary, the multichannel *Rio Naranja* in fact wandered back and forth across the border, but was mostly on the Balboan side. Thus, Balboa had the crossings, Balboa had had the opportunity to lay mines east of the river, Balboa knew where the lanes through the minefields were, and Balboa had the opportunity to fortify behind a not insignificant natural obstacle.

On the plus side, from the Tauran point of view, the TU had most of the high ground overlooking the river, at the likely crossing points. That said, their view was at greater than practical direct fire range, even with the tanks.

There were other areas where the terrain was seemingly more favorable for Tauran offensive action; *Puerto Armados,* for example, was rather exposed. Even there, though, the limited road net didn't really favor offensive action by anyone.

Legate Villalobos, in any case, wasn't interested in offensive action. His job was to frighten the Tauran forces in Santa Josefina into settling down for a long session of glaring at each other over the mines, and keeping them frightened enough to stay there no matter what else might be going on in the interior of the country. So far as he could tell, from the maniple of *Cazadores* already infiltrated in the Tauran occupied area, from the remotely piloted vehicles keeping track of the Taurans from the air, and from his own eyes, as he watched them pull into defensive positions a couple or three kilometers away, the first part of that program, at least, seemed to be working.

The only things that really had Villalobos concerned were the Tauran attack aircraft, circling like vultures overhead. He had, of course, his double-strength air-defense artillery complement. That, knowing the rough capabilities of the typical Tauran combat plane, was little comfort.

## MV *Roger Casement*, Matama, Santa Josefina, Terra Nova

Captain Saldañas of the *Casement* was also Tribune Saldañas of the *classis*. It really wouldn't have done to have someone not committed to the legion in command of such a key mission. Indeed, all the noncooking sailors of the *Casement* were also members of the *classis*. It made it much easier to cover up things like, oh, say, a couple thousand rounds of belted machine gun ammunition, spilled from the steel door swinging open, at the front of a poorly sealed container, as it was being moved to a higher perch on the ship.

*I swear to God,* thought Saldañas, *I will track down whoever left that fucking container unsecure and shoot him. Unless, of course, it turns out to be a member of my own crew in which case keel hauling seems in order.*

*On the plus side, at least, the customs folks weren't here to see it. Though they'd probably not have said anything, considering what we've already unloaded. On the other plus side, young Macera here seemed about to blow a gasket when the shit spilled out, and watching groundpounders like my brother go into apoplexy is one of life's truly incomparable pleasures.*

The *Casement*'s radio room was just under the bridge. Since it had pretty much everything imaginable in terms of communications equipment, to include some things rarely found on a merchant vessel, and since *Casement* was probably not going anywhere significant again until the war was over, Saldañas had turned it over to Macera. Soon, Legate Salas would be coming aboard to make it *his* communications center. That's when some of the more esoteric communications equipment—notably the complete audio-visual studio in one of the containers—would come into its own, though by then it would be offloaded.

The first formed troops Saldañas saw came trotting in a mass, heading south along Ninth Street. They seemed to split up, with half of them moving west-southwest, down First Avenue where it was met by Fifth Street. The latter group he saw only through a short gap in the warehouses fronting the coast. It wasn't long between catching sight of them and hearing the first outbreak of small arms fire coming from inside the town. About thirty men also began to race for the Coast Guard barracks and docks, not all that far from the *Casement*.

"Dammit," said Macera, "I'd hoped our cop could talk the rest of the cops into surrendering without a fight. I *really* hope it doesn't spill over to their houses."

Saldañas pointed to several customs police coming out of their little office just off the main wharf, unarmed and hands clasped behind their heads. They surrendered to several pistol-wielding legionaries who'd come in with Macera. "That's a good sign, isn't it, Tribune?"

"Could be worse," Macera agreed. His radio crackled to life, then gave the couple of beeps and the rushing sound that indicated secure, encrypted communications.

"Boss," said the radio operator, Centurion Lopez. "That wasn't the police station; that was the jail. They figured we were an attempted jail break and . . . well . . . they seen their duty and they done it. Two dead, both of them theirs, plus three prisoners dead. We've got one wounded. Private Vargas may or may not make it. I've got a stretcher team taking him to the hospital about a kilometer to your south, Hospital Antonio Fidel. God knows, they've got enough experience with gunshot wounds."

"Roger, Centurion," said Macera. "Keep me posted on Vargas. Out." The next post had Macera drawing a circle on his map around the town of Pelirojo. Then the tribune turned to Saldañas, saying, "Captain, I think we should begin unloading the arms and equipment now."

Saldañas gave a sardonic grin. "I started three days ago with a little of the ammunition and some of the less offensive-looking supplies. Had the manifest and container labels marked for 'Delivery, Tauran Union Security Force-Santa Josefina.' Customs didn't give it a second thought. The arms, on the other hand, are still waiting." He gave the orders for that, then listened as Macera's radio reported the cutting of the landlines and deactivation of the cell phone tower in the town, plus surrenders among the police, key intersections and bridges secured, and even some criminals killed.

*Which is all to the good*, thought the captain.

## Headquarters, Tauran Union Security Force-Santa Josefina, *Rio Clara*, Santa Josefina, Terra Nova

Marciano, half-resting against a desk, took one look at the message handed him by a runner and went into a stream of profound invective, largely in Italian, that was both lengthy and, insofar as it made full use of various concepts, terms, and phrases not found in Italian but common in French, German, and English, really quite original.

It was three days before Marciano got word of the uprising in the south. He still didn't know about the arms being landed, or the place of the *Casement* in it, because, by the time he got an overflight, the *Casement* had been almost entirely unloaded.

He might not have found out even then but for the events of months before. The mechanism of the discovery went back to the Tauran Union's loss of the Balboa Transitway. Prior to that, most of whatever supplies couldn't be purchased locally, and barring a trivial amount flown in by air, had come through *Puerto Bruselas*, on the *Mar Furioso*. Once the Transitway was gone, however, and ships had to sail the long way to Santa Josefina, the Tauran Defense Agency had *eventually* determined that there was a Tauro to be saved by changing the chief supply port to Matama, and trucking the goods over the central mountain range.

There'd been no real hurry about it, though. Most food and fuel were locally purchased. Little ammunition was being used. Replacement troops came in via airship, for the most part. Some parts were needed, of course, and things like military-specific batteries, of which there was a vast number of completely incompatible types, for equipment that could almost never use civilian batteries. Even there, the minimum requirements could be brought in, more or less space available, on the airships or occasional planes. And there'd been sufficient stockpiles that switching simply hadn't been a priority.

But with the advent of the overstrength tercio massing on the border, switching ports had moved up quite a bit in prioritization. Marciano had given the necessary orders. Contracts for civilian trucking had been negotiated, and the advance party had moved out for Matama.

They had not, however, quite made it there. By the time the column—no more than a score of vehicles and under a hundred men—had reached the road intersection in the town of Pelirojo, the town was under Legate Salas's control. In the ensuing ambush, soldiers from such diverse states as Lusitania, Mannerheim, and Anglia, plus medical personnel from Castilla, had been almost utterly annihilated, either killed or captured. Only a lone vehicle, a Gaul-provided, Mannerheim-driven, Sochaux S4, had managed to escape to bring the word.

Those shots, historians would later agree, constituted the first shots in the broader war between Balboa and its allies, on the one hand, and the UEPF, Tauran Union, and *Xing Zhong Guo*, on the other.

"They could have fucking told me," Marciano said, as his contempt for Santa Josefina climbed upward a notch. He crumpled the note and tossed it on the desk.

"They probably didn't know," answered his exec, *Oberst* Rall, of the Sachsen Army. "Infrastructure here is poor, without a lot of redundancy. I'd be surprised if the landlines didn't wash out, or the cell towers didn't have their power cut, regularly."

"Don't try mollifying me, Rall. I have my heart set on sneering at Santa Josefina and its moral welfare and I don't want anything interfering with that."

Marciano was grinning as he spoke. With an answering grin, Rall, agreed, "*Jawohl, Herr General. Zu befehl.* And I couldn't agree more. Even so, what are we going to do? They've engaged our men and killed a number of them. We can't just take it." Rall pulled out a map and laid it across the desk.

When Marciano remained uncommunicative, but for a scowl, the Sachsen continued. "If we try to contain it, there are two avenues of approach to the capital. That takes a minimum of two battalions to outpost, and we don't have them. On the other hand, if we take the town where our men were ambushed, Pelirojo, that is where the road branches. We can hold it with one battalion, I think."

"And our reserve, Rall? And how we handle attacks there and across the border?"

The Sachsen gave that an apparent half-a-minute's worth of thought, more for show than anything. He'd already decided to recommend that, "We can outfit a small mobile force, say the Hordalander *Panzers* and a company of Sachsen infantry on trucks. But the bulk of our reserve striking power ought to be in the air."

"Still leaves us the problem of taking the town back," said Marciano.

"I've taken the liberty already of getting the Cimbrian commandos on the road," said Rall. "We don't even know what's there yet. They'll recon the town, and we can build our force around what they find. For the nonce, I think we start assembling a counterattack force at Cerveza.

"The enemy can't be in great shape," Rall said. "We knew they were scattered all over and are probably still assembling. For now, from Cerveza we can cut them off if they try to take the southern road to the capital. If they try to go after Cerveza . . . well . . . we're regulars, better trained and better armed. We'll just stomp them."

Marciano tugged at an ear. "They thought that in Balboa, too, you know, Rall."

"Different circumstances," said the Sachsen. "We walked into an ambush they'd been laying for ten years. Here, we're the ones who've been on station for a while.

"And, yes, yes, sir, I know they know their own ground better. But they know their own ground in the places they grew up, or worked or lived in. How many, do you suppose, grew up right in Cerveza?"

"All right," said the Tuscan. "Get things in motion. But restrictive rules of engagement for now. The mere fact that the enemy shot first is probably not enough to get the Tauran Union to authorize offensive action. That, too, is one of the side effects of the defeat in Balboa. The bureaucrats weren't keen on war to begin with. Now they're positively gun-shy.

"Yes, sir. I concur, for what they may be worth. But the Cimbrians, at least, have to be able to fire in self-defense, yes?"

"Yes," the Tuscan agreed. "And if we can get the artillery in position to support them if they need it, we'll go for third party self-defense, too."

"Speaking of self-defense . . ."

Marciano rolled his eyes. Rall's tone alone said, "Serious problem."

"Okay, what is it?" the Tuscan asked.

"You remember that bar where Corporal Martinelli, of the sappers, was eviscerated?"

Marciano gave it a moment's thought, then answered, "*El Mono Loco*, in Aserri? I remember."

"Well, seems there's been another incident. We didn't lose anybody, but two dozen Tuscans broke up the place last night, killed three of the locals, including one girl. She was probably an accident, but the two men were definitely *not* accidents, since the sappers carved 'This is for Martinelli' on their faces before cutting their throats."

Marciano put his head in his hands, asking, "Do we know who did it?"

"They're all in custody, sir, yes. On the other hand, they're nearly a platoon of engineers and it's not clear we can spare them all indefinitely. And none of them will admit to anything or testify against anyone."

"There are times, Rall, when I wish I were Carrera, or could operate under his rules."

"Why?" asked the Sachsen. "What would he do?"

"Either ignore the murders or line up the sappers and shoot every tenth one."

# CHAPTER THIRTEEN

Insurrection by means of guerrilla bands is the true method of warfare for all nations desirous of emancipating themselves from a foreign yoke. It is invincible, indestructible.
—Giuseppe Mazzini

**Pelirojo, Santa Josefina, Terra Nova**

The town had streams on three sides of it, two of them, east and west, rather large and the third, to the north, narrow but swift. The rivers tended to channelize movement naturally, and had dictated the placement of roads and bridges.

Anywhere near the main road, one could still smell the burnt rubber and overdone human meat, heavily overlaid with the stink of diesel. All along the main street running through the town, from where Highway Twenty-three crossed the bridge over the river to the west to both branches that split off from it in the center, were the wrecked vehicles of what, upon interrogation, turned out to be a slice of service support troops.

*Which half-explains,* thought Salas, *why they were such easy meat. The other half of the explanation, of course, is that they didn't know we were here, or that we were weapons-free.*

The bodies, at least, had been taken away for a Christian burial. Still, when men burn in vehicles, parts of the men always remain behind.

*Hence that clinging, long pig aroma.*

179

There were also fifty-three prisoners. Ideally, so had Colonel Nguyen advised, the prisoners would be placed somewhere where Tauran fire was sure to kill them. Salas could see the logic of that, could see the intensely demoralizing effect and also the enraging effect.

*But I'm not a barbarian. My duty is to safeguard the prisoners, not use them to score a propaganda point. And Carrera himself can kiss my ass if he thinks I'll violate the customs of war for such a trivial advantage.*

*'Course, if he were here he'd be less likely to be kissing my ass than having me shot for disobeying orders. Well . . . before I commit an avoidable war crime I'd rather be shot.*

Legate Salas had known happier days. *Not a lot of satisfaction in machine gunning people who don't know there's a war on*, he thought. *Not a lot of joy in knowing what's going to happen once they—their side—figures out that there is a war on.*

He'd had reports on that, too, from scouts his cohort in Pelirojo had sent out up Highway One, to the north, that the Taurans were unlikely to be ambushed again. He'd also had scattered reports of enemy scouts actually *behind* the town. If true, the defenders, once it came time to defend, wouldn't be able to count on any mortar fire five minutes after the Tauran attack started.

*Thing is, this isn't key terrain to me. Or, at least, it won't be once we've finished dispersing the arms and other supplies to the units. I need to hold this only until then. Well . . . and until the cohorts are fully into the jungle.*

*The other thing, though, is that if they hit me right this minute . . .*

Salas looked around. There wasn't much to see, but he could hear the sounds of preparation. He could also hear the sounds of argument, as civilians told his troops to fuck off, *their* houses weren't there to be turned into battle positions. Not for the first time, he contemplated the old saw, "When you've got 'em, by the balls their hearts and minds will follow."

*But . . . nah. The downsides, at least for now, are too great. We need them on our side, not harboring grievances. And the whole idea of a native Santa Josefinan military is just too strange to them. Besides, when the Taurans level this place, even though we didn't take any but public buildings, it'll be a big shot in the arm for our recruiting efforts.*

*But what worries me is that my troops are not the "First Infantry*

Tercio, *Liberation Army of Santa Josefina.*" They're an amalgam of *different maniples and platoons, squads and some individuals, scraped out of every* tercio *in the legion with a Santa Josefinan to spare. Technically and tactically, they're about as good as any in the legion. Maybe not quite as good, because we have fewer officers and centurions, but still . . .*

*But still, the really worrisome thing is that they aren't a real regiment, they're just a collection of disparate parts, and we never had the chance to fully turn them into a regiment.*

*And, sure, the Tauros are a bunch of disparate cohorts, but at least at that level they're cohesive.*

*And, now, I suppose, it's time to make my speech.*

With a shout, Salas summoned his driver and his commandeered economy-class sedan. They drove off, taking Highway Twenty-three in the direction of Matama. Several miles outside of town the driver pulled off the road then turned right to follow a narrow trail to where the radio container waited, with generators humming in the background.

"You ready?" Salas asked his chief of propaganda.

"As we'll ever be, sir. Your speech is sitting there. You probably should rehearse it a few times before you go live."

Silently, Salas nodded. He was perhaps a little thankful for the delay offered by the chance at rehearsal.

## Irazú, Santa Josefina, Terra Nova

The Hordalander tank had the name, *Thanatos,* or death, painted on the barrel. The tank crew had been in country long enough for three things: to have acquired a taste for the local women—except for the tank commander, who generally referred to *himself* as "Thanatos" and who preferred boys; to have picked up enough of the language to have some chance with the local women (or, in the case of the TC, boys); and to have acquired a certain appreciation for the music. Thus, they had a civilian radio going just atop the tank's turret, while they relaxed there, and over the glacis, catching a few rays. Yes, yes, it was normally bad practice, but it wasn't as if the enemy was likely to throw an airstrike at them.

The tank company, minus one platoon that was still up supporting the troops by the border, was currently not even in artillery range of any enemy. Instead they were sitting in a public park, the objects of *intense* curiosity from the locals. They expected to stay there at least through the end of the day, then move by night to the assembly area by Cerveza.

In any event, the radio was on and, if no one was dancing, still the music had the most gratifying tendency to put a little spring in the step of the Santa *Josefineñas*, which spring put a lovely bounce in Santa *Josefineña* bosoms.

Rather, it did right up until the music cut off with a protesting squawk, to be replaced by one of those annoying "We interrupt this broadcast" messages.

The best Spanish linguist on the tank was the driver, Corporal Arthur Kjelstrup. He translated for the rest.

"People of Santa Josefina, I am Ricardo Salas . . . of the Liberation Army of Santa Josefinan . . . the Lord God and the dead generations laid in our soil since the founding . . . call the children of Santa Josefina to her flag . . . to strike for freedom . . . and to resume her old place as an honored member of the nations of this world by becoming . . . once again . . . a *real* nation in this world.

"The guiding spirit of our country . . . having sent her sons and daughters away to learn the arts that our corrupt national elites have denied them . . . summons them to her colors and her cause again. . . . Relying, in the first place, upon those newly trained sons, but confident also . . . in the second place, of the unstinting support . . . of our brothers and cousins across Colombia Latina . . . and in total and complete confidence in the dear God who is . . . the wellspring of liberty . . . Santa Josefina rises now to strike for her freedom from foreign occupation.

"Our country is ours alone. . . . It is not Tauran. . . . It does not belong to Old Earth. . . . Less still is it the country . . . of the government and president . . . who called the foreigners in to occupy us. . . . The Taurans could be here for one thousand years; *still* would this land be *ours*. . . . They could leave tomorrow; *still* would the traitor . . . and licker of foreign boots, Calderón, have relinquished his right to call himself a citizen.

"Santa Josefina . . . sacred and holy . . . calls upon all her true children . . . to rise in arms against the foreign occupation . . . to drive them out . . . to take back what was ours . . ."

Though the speaker was still talking, Corporal Kjelstrup stopped translating. The tank crew exchanged nervous looks among themselves until the gunner, Sergeant Qvist, said, simply, "Oh, shit."

### *Rio Clara,* Santa Josefina, Terra Nova

Corporal Moran shook his head in disbelief. "They said *what?*"

Araya shrugged. "I don't understand it either, Corporal. But maniple headquarters says, 'no,' 'don't call us; we'll call you,' and, 'go talk to the locals and see if you can't drum up a little demonstration to block the roads.' They also said they were trying to get a riot going in Irazú."

"Okay," said Moran though, of course, neither his agreement nor Araya's was precisely necessary. "Well . . . you go see about getting a group together. I'm going to go check on the road and the bridge. Maybe we can take it out if we get the order. At least I might see something worth reporting."

"Jeez, Corp," said Araya, "I don't know anything about explosives . . . if we had any, which we don't."

"I don't know much," admitted Moran. "How to use them, safely for limited purposes. And I know nothing about making them. Maybe we could steal some."

"Maybe. Though we might be better off trying to buy some."

"Yeah, maybe. Anyway, you run along."

Once Araya was out of the way, Corporal Moran walked the few paces down the hallway to the next room, Jaquelina Araya's. She gave him a big smile once the door opened.

### Irazú, Santa Josefina, Terra Nova

It was shocking really, not least to the tank commander of tank *Thanatos* who, safe behind his armor, had never really imagined a serious threat coming from the locals. But then a veritable hurricane of Molotov cocktails had engulfed the tank ahead of him, as the company tried to escape from the town in a long, clanking column. The Molotovs didn't initially set the tank alight. Rather, they cut off oxygen to the engine and stalled the thing temporarily.

Modern tanks were designed generally to prevent gasoline from firebombs leaking down into the engine compartment. Despite this, and probably because of the sheer amount of fluid, coupled with the many different angles from which it came, some of the burning fuel from those must have dripped down to torch off some of the plastic over the wires or the rubberized pieces, or the fabric gaskets of the engine, for black smoke began to pour out from the engine grate behind the turret. That, in turn, caused the crew to pop hatches and try to escape, before being driven back in by something the tank following could not see. And then a single firebomb had smashed against the inside of the partially open commander's hatch, letting burning fuel pour down upon the TC. His scream, followed by those of his crew as the flames spread, were heard by every man of the company. Why the fire suppression system failed to activate, as it should have, would remain a mystery.

The driver, alone, managed to escape, as he was separated from the fighting compartment of the tank. But as soon as he'd crawled across to glacis and down to the ground, choking and heaving from smoke inhalation, a small mob of Santa Josefinan men, bearing clubs, surrounded him and began kicking with their feet and pounding with their clubs.

It was then that the tank, *Thanatos*, opened fire on the crowd, sweeping across the mob with its coaxial machine gun.

"What the fuck?" screamed the gunner. "What the fuck are you doing you goddamned maniac?"

"Back up, back up," screamed the tank commander, still wildly flailing with his coax at the scattering crowd. He ignored the gunner, or perhaps his span of attention had narrowed to where he couldn't hear. Too afraid to stick his head up, as a proper tank commander would have, he tried to direct the driver by viewing through the narrow and inadequate periscopic vision port on the rear of his cupola. The tank ended up backing into a relatively narrow side street, preparatory to turning around and running like hell.

The vision blocks were perfectly acceptable for some purposes, but really made it difficult to see fine details like the fifteen-year-old

Santa Josefinan with the sister five months pregnant by the Gallic legionary . . . the fifteen-year-old with the Molotov cocktail . . . and the lit match.

Ignorant, the boy had aimed his fire bomb uselessly at the turret. Inexperienced, he'd missed that and landed it across the engine grate. It wasn't enough to stop the tank immediately. The next one to try to throw did even worse; he set his own hands alight, then, panicking, dropped the Molotov at his feet, making a large flambé of himself. His screams could be heard over the roar of flames, though not inside the tank he'd intended to target.

The third and fourth fuel bombs, however, possibly following the fifteen-year-old's unwitting lead, landed across the rear deck and bursted into fireballs. Those *did* cause the tank to stall temporarily. They did not stop the turret.

What did stop the turret was a combination of things. First was that the narrow side street meant the tank's main gun bumped against something solid, and was no longer able to traverse in that direction. Second, however, and more important, was that the tank commander, seeing the flames and being something of a coward, panicked. Ripping off his combat vehicle crewman's helmet, he undogged the hatch and practically flew up.

Sadly, Molotov cocktails five and six landed on the turret roof at about that time, catching him in their fireballs, melting his eyes, setting hair alight, and making him scream like a terrified little girl, until the inhalation burn running down his throat caused the tissue there to swell, cutting off his breath.

And then the tank commander of tank *Thanatos* got to experience the very Platonic essence of a shitty death, more than one deadly effect, racing at a snail's pace, to see which one would kill you. In his case it was even more than usual as the flames set his subcutaneous fat alight, too. For a while, no more firebombs flew as the mob stopped for a moment to enjoy the arrogant Tauran's death.

While the TC burned alive, above, the gunner, who did not panic, managed to get the hatch shut again. Some burning fuel got in but the automatic fire suppression system did for that, even as it half-suffocated the crew. Still, after a few minutes, they were able to breathe again *and* get the engine started again. Ignoring the possibility of running over civilians, the driver then took off like the proverbial infernal bat, crushing cars, knocking over streetlights, but moving so fast that no more Molotovs hit his tank.

### Headquarters, Tauran Union Security Force-Santa Josefina, *Rio Clara*, Santa Josefina, Terra Nova

"I'm a Sachsen," said Rall, with perfect seriousness, and perfect hate. "My recommendation is that we go into Irazú, round up five hundred men, one hundred for each of ours, heard them into a public building and burn them alive. Not that I expect you to do that."

"And I'm, at heart, a Roman," said Marciano. "I'd instinctively crucify that same five hundred. The problem is that that wouldn't solve our problem."

"A thousand then?" Rall suggested, hopefully. "A nice round number, one thousand."

"No," said Marciano, definitively. He explained, "The problem with a reprisal, young Colonel, is that the people you're reprising against have to believe you can keep it up. If we reprised for the death of our troops, we'd be pulled out of here within hours, the Santa Josefinans would know that reprisal was not a Tauran policy, and we—rather, our replacements—would never have a moment's peace.

"Besides, we're here to *protect* their poor little pacifist delusions.

"So no, no point. But there *is* a point to clearing a way through the town. And that, tsk, tsk, will cause a certain amount of damage. Which—who knows?—may be sufficient to dissuade the townsfolk from *fucking with our goddamned columns again!*"

"I'll see to it, sir," offered the Sachsen.

"Please do."

### Cerveza, Santa Josefina, Terra Nova

It had been an overstrength company, with twenty Sachsen-built *Smilodon* tanks. Of those, six had been left facing the Balboan border while fourteen had been sent to the attack force assembling at Cerveza. Of those fourteen, the Taurans were down to thirteen now, with one—

the one ruined in Irazú; still sitting there, as a matter of fact—needing something close to a depot-level rebuild. Additionally, two more had broken down on the road, though those had been recovered and moved forward to the assembly area at Cerveza.

In that assembly area, the crew of the tank formerly known as *Thanatos* were busy scraping their old nickname off. They hadn't yet decided whether to rename their tank *Pederast* or *Pussyboy*, in memory of their late commander's efforts to abandon them.

Not that he'd ever entirely succeeded, of course. Why some remnants of burnt flesh and melted fat still stuck to the turret roof, though the loader was scraping at those, and tossing the scrapings contemptuously over the side, even while the gunner and driver took turns obliterating the name.

"How did we end up with a weasel like that for a tank commander, anyway, Sarge?" asked the loader, from atop the turret.

"Recruiter may have had a bad day," answered the new tank commander, "or been behind in his quota for the month."

"What's going to happen to us over him opening up with the coax on the crowd?" asked the driver.

"Well . . . nothing to you, for sure," answered the former gunner. "There's no objective way for higher to tell it wasn't me doing the shooting . . ."

"I can tell them," said the loader. "I saw the panicky piece of shit override you."

"Yeah . . . well . . . your testimony might not be so persuasive. Same crew and all. Still, don't sweat it yet. We might manage to get killed before they can convene a court-martial on me."

On that note, the remaining crew laughed. The laughter cut off when the first truck of the Tuscan artillery battalion rolled past, dragging its 105mm gun smoothly behind it.

"Yeah," agreed the loader. "Yeah, we just might."

### Outside Pelirojo, Santa Josefina, Terra Nova

There were only two companies of *Jaegers* in the Cimbrian Army's *Jaegerkorpset*. At any given time one of those, in rotation, was assigned to the Tauran Union Security Force for Santa Josefina. Considering they were from a small and not very populous country, without a huge military tradition in modern times, and frankly fairly pacifistic, the *Jaegers* were actually quite competent. Across the world of Terra Nova they were generally considered about as good as anyone's Tier II special operations forces—Federated States Rangers, for example, or Zioni *Sayaret*—and probably somewhat better than most such. Being, as individuals, way too big and way too blond, mostly, they'd stand out like a sore thumb trying to blend in with nearly any local population. But out in the jungle—once they got used to the jungle, which always took a bit of time—they were just fine.

The town was off to the east, busy and noisy with preparations.

To the west of the town of Pelirojo, Lieutenant Carsten Christian Clausen—"C-Three," to his friends—was grease-painted dark enough to blend into pretty much anything but daylight. He'd even dyed his hair black, not trusting fully to the Anglian-issue bush hat cap he'd scrounged to keep the rain off and the mosquito net that critical extra half an inch from his face. And, since his own army's camouflage pattern was carefully designed to blend in with local conditions approximately as well as a slag heap at the north pole, he and his men wore battle dress they'd had made, at personal expense, by local tailors, from a locally produced camouflage material.

The downside to that, more or less unknown to C-Three and the rest of the Cimbrians, was that the factory that made the camouflage material in their uniforms was a subcontractor to the *Legion del Cid*. In short, an argument could be made that the Cimbrians were wearing enemy uniforms, or would be, if the war were officially on and the guerillas wearing uniforms.

This was an agricultural area, for the most part. What jungle there was consisted of secondary growth, with scattered patches of true rainforest here and there, the latter having exceptionally dense fringes. It was in one of those dense fringes that C-Three lay, narrowly slitted eyes watching as the crews of four mortars dug up and moved entire plants to provide camouflage.

"A platoon," C-Three wrote in his notebook, without looking down, adding the location and time and, "160mm, Zioni model, on wheels."

Satisfied, finally, that no more of the enemy were coming, C-Three scuttled back, snakelike, to rejoin the other six men of his patrol, picked up his pack, and, scanning continuously, moved out for his next reconnaissance objective.

## Hamilton, Federated States of Columbia, Terra Nova

As the GaulAir jet touched down on the airstrip beside the river, newly minted Major Jan Campbell wasn't at all sure how it came to pass that Belisario Endara-Rocaberti was still alive, let alone living in comfort mainly at Federated States' expense in one of the city's better suburbs, and under continuous guard.

*Certainly the Balboans' request for extradition should have had the fucker nailed up by now on* Cerro Mina. *Hmmm . . . can I use that? Maybe . . . maybe if he thinks the asylum the FSC's given him won't last. Conversely, maybe if I threaten to have him extradited to the TU. Or what if I offer him asylum, new identity, all that? Hmmm . . . can I offer the swine asylum? The crimes of which Balboa accuses him were crimes initially against us.*

Jan took one look at the olive-skinned flunky sent by Rocaberti to the airport to meet her and surmised, *cop.* She travelled in mufti, totally unofficially, and on a tourist visa. The drive from the airport was made in silence. Whether that was because the flunky knew no English or simply because he'd been instructed not to speak to her, she had no clue. Neither did she much care, however. She'd been to the FSC before, on a short exchange program, but never to the Hamilton area. She enjoyed both the sights of the old city and the pristine countryside beyond.

The driver finally pulled into a tree-lined private driveway, then parked the car by the front door. He held the door open for Jan, then raced to open the front door to the house for her. She entered into a hallway that reminded her, to an extent, of some of the publically accessible stately homes of the Kingdom of Anglia, with a fine slate floor, ornately plastered ceiling, and some fairly decent art—not a whit of it Balboan—hanging from brass rods set into the walls.

The driver led her through the hall, then through a door, down a narrower hall, and finally to an office. After knocking, he announced her, in Spanish. "The Anglian woman is here, sir."

*What a creepy little butterball this one is*, she thought, as Belisario Endara-Rocaberti arose to greet her, holding out a plump hand.

"My dear Major," said Rocaberti, "what a pleasure to meet you."

Seated, Jan didn't waste a lot of time. "I need people who can pass as Balboan because they *are* Balboan, who can travel freely, observe carefully, and make contact discreetly. There are a fair number of Spanish speakers I could use, but this—your little group of exiles—strikes me as much more suitable and more motivated."

Rocaberti began by starting to list a series a of demands, the first of which was reestablishment of his clan as the paramount clan of the country. He'd gotten to the word "rightful—" when Jan lifted one hand, palm out.

"Get that out of your mind," she said. "The very *most* you will ever have, under the very most favorable circumstances, in your native country, would be the right to continue breathing. If war comes again the current regime will be extirpated, true. But there'll be no pseudo democracy covering for a corrupt oligarchy. The place will be divided up and occupied. There will be no local government."

The butterball visibly deflated, she saw. "But if you are smart," she said, "you won't even try to go back. There are simply too many people who hate your guts. No, I don't know whether you were behind the murders of those women that led to the last invasion. But enough of your compatriots will think so that your life in Balboa would be measured in hours. You need a better plan."

"Like what?"

Said she, smiling, "It's very nice along the northern coast of Gaul this time of year."

*Well*, thought Jan, on the drive back to the airport, *wasn't that economical? Of course, the weasel needed a kickback "to support the families of those freedom-loving souls who have gathered around me." Blah-blah-blah.*

*And so now I have my sacrificial lambs, nine of them, who will get a minimum of training, some disinformation, and will be sent to Balboa, half to identify the shards of the old organization and half to be caught by Fernandez. They'll spill their guts, of course; who would not? And that's fine. Fernandez already has reason to believe the TU is the essence of incompetence. That will fit well with his preconceptions. And having caught and ruined the "organization" from Rocaberti's crew, he'll be a lot less inclined to think there's another one, one that matters.*

*Time to start tracking down people worth spending some effort on. First stop, Gaul, then Tuscany, then Volga. If necessary I can return here, too.*

*Also, note to self, check with the Sachsens and see if they have some good ins in* Volgoboronexport. *It might help to know what the Balboans have bought overseas.*

# CHAPTER FOURTEEN

Man is not what he thinks he is; he is what he hides.
—André Malraux

**Log Base Alpha (so called), Balboa, Terra Nova**

A twenty-foot container sat on its side on rollers, big logs chosen for regularity, just to the north of Tribune Ramirez, who stood in a wide and fairly shallow ditch the direction of which he had set out with a compass. Thick ropes led from the container, southward, framing the tribune on either side. A couple of dozen legionaries, stripped to the waist against the heat and humidity, stood by the ropes. There was a large pile of dirt just eastward, though the pile slowly shrank as legionaries turned the loose spoil into hard packed sandbags. A single tiny female, Cochinese, with almond eyes, stood just out of the ditch, watching.

Troops stood around, some with picks, others with mattocks, most with shovels. They looked down expectantly into the ditch as Tribune Ramirez measured the bottom of the excavated hole carefully.

The common thought was along the lines of *let us hope the motherfucker is happy this time.*

There were rollers there in the ditch, too, though only a few. Finally, Ramirez stood up. He'd decided, *Yep, twelve degrees, close enough and a bit over, which is fine.*

"Move her in," Ramirez ordered. His first centurion gave a series of commands. Immediately, the two gangs of soldiers began tugging on the ropes. Slowly at first, then with speed increasing to a slow walking pace, the container rumbled to the south until it reached its tipping point. At that point the southernmost side began rotating downward, very slowly.

"Halt," the centurion ordered, once the container had started to tip.

A sergeant and a couple of men eased it down into the ditch, where it came to rest on a roller.

"Pull!" shouted the centurion, calling off a work chant, setting the men to dragging the thing the last couple of meters forward. It came to rest with its northernmost end about five feet into the earth and the southern end about a foot or a bit less.

"Perfect," said the tribune. "Cover up the sides and then open her up. Make sure to leave the open space to the sides open, just like the rollers caused below."

He didn't feel like explaining that the open space was to allow dirt to displace from a near miss with a bomb or shell.

After a series of sandbags were used to cover the gap, most of the men with the mattocks, picks, and shovels turned to shoveling the spoil around the sides of the container, taking special care to make a smooth, flat support at the northern end.

"Anything else we need to know, Mrs. Siegel?" Ramirez asked.

"No," the tiny woman answered, "or at least I can't think of anything. We took a lot of care when we packed these to have everything you and your men might need, to include a field kitchen, with fuel, and dry rations for a month or so.

"Well . . . on second thought, if any or your men are as butterfingered as the Cochinese political prisoners who did the physical packing, I'd have a senior NCO or centurion supervising so they don't set off anything that's explosive.

"Otherwise, you should be fine. What number is this one supposed to be?"

Ramirez consulted a spreadsheet, then answered, "12543."

"Okay," she said. "I'd make sure that's the right one, Tribune, but other than that you should be fine. You'll find a lot of crude lumber inside, which ought to be useful for making your battery a little more comfortable."

## Near Concepción, *Carretera InterColombiana*, Balboa, Terra Nova

Sergeant Ponce, female, large, and strong, saw the maniple commander, redheaded Tribune Cristina Zamora, point at a hill and heard her say, "It's perfect. Not only is it perfect, but they'll be here." Ponce was a squad leader of combat engineers, who, in this instance, were *all* female, and all unusually large, and strong.

The hill at which the statuesque redhead pointed was surrounded on three sides by water. It sat, the very edge of it, right at five hundred meters from a three-way intersection of the main coastal highway, the less well-developed road to a small port to the north, and another dirt and gravel road that led inward to a town up in the hills to the south. Overlooked by the hill, a steel bridge crossed the river that surrounded it on three sides.

The centurion for the reinforced platoon agreed, "It looks like a likely spot to me, too."

*Well, duh*, thought Ponce.

The centurion, Maria Fuentes, short and cute, said, "I'll bury a mortar and—what do you think, one hundred and sixty rounds?—about three kilometers that way"—she pointed generally to the tree-clad southwest hills—"and put some caches in about five hundred meters behind us, enough to support a platoon raid on whoever occupies that hill."

*Way optimistic*, thought Ponce. *Way.*

Zamora answered, "No, not a hundred and sixty rounds of mortar. They'd never get a chance to fire it before the counterbattery came in and turned them to paste. Sixty rounds is enough. They can fire that and still get the hell out of the area before the artillery hits them. Though you might bury the other hundred not too far away."

Ponce thought, *Got some digging to do, I suppose.*

"All right, sixty," the centurion agreed. "And two more caches of fifty nearby."

Ponce went over to the platoon optio, Marta Bugatti. She didn't say anything, but just stood there until Marta said, "Go get me three of your people and the truck and mount them up. Then we'll go do some excavating."

In a less than two minutes the truck sped off bearing three of the sappers and Bugatti.

"Where else have you identified?" Zamora asked.

Ponce stood behind the centurion when she pulled out a map and pointed to four more caches.

"What about mines?" asked Zamora.

Fuentes scratched at her ear and said, "I had an idea. You might not like it. Then again, you might."

*Pretty sure it was my idea,* thought Ponce, *but if you want to take the blame . . .*

"What's that?" Zamora asked.

"Mines, particularly antiarmor mines, are big, bulky, and noticeable, right?"

"Sure."

"Detonators aren't. I'm putting in plastic AT mines, pretty much everywhere, and recording the locations."

Ponce kept her face blank. *Just* who *is putting in mines? Oh, all right, that's not entirely fair of me; your grunts are helping.*

Fuentes continued, "When we want to arm one, we send out one or two girls in civvies and just uncover the mine, insert and arm the detonator, then cover it again and camouflage it. Nothing's a mine unless we want it to be. Everything is mined where and when we want it to be."

Zamora patted Fuentes's shoulder, and, with a broad smile, said, "See, and I *knew* there was a reason you're in charge of a platoon."

"I'll pass that trick on to the others."

"There is one thing that bugs me, though," the centurion said. "Where did all these mines come from? I mean, we *did* sign that treaty after all."

Not sure if Zamora knew the background, Ponce answered, "It seems that whoever drafted the silly document hadn't bothered to ask about what a land mine really was. So . . .while we couldn't stockpile the mines in advance, legally, instead, Carrera stockpiled *millions* of empty metal and plastic casings, more millions of pounds of explosive that just happened to be cast in chunks the exact shapes and sizes of those casings. Oh . . . and detonators and bouncing charges, of course. They were all stored separately so they weren't mines until we put the parts together . . ."

Zamora asked, "Cynical or realistic?"

It wasn't clear to Ponce who she was asking. In any case, the sapper continued, "The process of assembly takes about thirty seconds or so, each, and can be, and is being, done by little old ladies in tennis shoes in a couple of warehouses near Arraijan. It actually takes longer to record where we put the mines than it does to put them together."

Sneering, the sapper asked, rhetorically, "Kind of makes you wonder about the minds of people who try to ban certain types of weapons because of aesthetics, doesn't it? I guess their delicate sensibilities make it just too, too distasteful for them to really try to understand the weapons themselves. So they fail."

"Yes," Zamora replied, "and a good thing for us, too."

Fuentes added, "We're not just setting them up for harassment and road and area denial. Sergeant Ponce's putting in some fairly dense fields between places we think we'll want to attack and places where we can hide. There'll be paths through; paths we'll know and the enemy won't. We hit them; we run; we run right through the mines. If they follow, they'll regret it."

"You do that a couple of times," Zamora commented, "and they'll probably stop trying to follow."

"That's what we thought," Ponce said. "There are also some other places where we're putting down just a few mines, along with a bunch of metal fragments or tiny magnets—"

"I know about the 'Dianas,'" Zamora said. "It'll make clearing those few a real chore, since it's effectively impossible for a magnetic mine detector to tell the difference between a 'Diana' and a real mine.

"Okay, I'm satisfied, Maria. I'm going to go check out First Platoon. The Nguyens will be staying with you for a week or two. Treat them nice. They've got experience in this area and a whole *bag* of tricks."

## BdL *Dos Lindas, Mar Furioso,* Terra Nova

Up on the flight deck, one of the carrier's navalized Turbo-finch attack aircraft touched down, bounced, bounced and hooked, then came to a bone-wrenching stop. The 'Finches were little more than upgraded crop dusters, with a fair payload and a lot of endurance. Though the takeoffs and landings were riskier than with the ship's Yakamov helicopters, the maintenance load from using them was so much less that they were preferred for anything where they would serve.

There were several sonar-listening stations out on the *Isla Real*. There was also now a twin set of underwater microphones stretching east and west from the island, listening. Volgan surplus, the system was called "Archangel." Sadly, these were something less than state of the art.

Additionally, the *classis* had dropped three lines of sonabuoys, all passive, out in the *Mar Furioso*. So far, neither the fixed stations nor the sonabuoys had picked up a sign of the four Zhong subs. Neither had they picked up a sign of the presumptively much quieter Imperial Yamatan Navy sub tailing the Zhong. They did get occasional messages via Yamato on the location of the Zhong. That was why Fosa was reasonably certain that they were being provided by a Yamatan submarine trailing the Zhong.

One thing that bugged Fosa, because he didn't really understand it, was that the Zhong were moving slower than their theoretical capability for effectively silent sailing. Did they know about a Yamatan trailing? Was there some timetable they were supposed to meet but not exceed?

*I haven't a fucking clue. And our little flotilla of coastal defense subs, and their skippers, really don't understand the capabilities and limitations of a nuke boat.*

*And the positioning intel from Yamato? How long is it taking to get to us? I'm pretty sure they've got a sub trailing the Zhong. But that sub's not contacting us directly. Whatever they've got they're sending home. Then it's going by secure line to their embassy here—that's what Fernandez says—then to us. How much massaging is the information getting before I get it? If we're talking two days then I need to go into full run-away mode when they tell me the Zhong are three days out. But what if it's taking three? Or four? Or less than one?*

*This is our only carrier. Patricio's told me he's going to need it for the end game. I can't risk it to the Zhong.*

## Zhong Submarine *Mao Zedong, Mar Furioso,* Terra Nova

Some two thousand miles to Fosa's east, Captain Liu of the Zhong Navy submarine fretted. He could have, though of course would never have, told Fosa the reason for his tardiness. It was the bloody Archangel system the Zhong knew the Balboans had bought from the Volgans. Most Zhong weapons systems were derivative of Volgan systems. Some were outright copies. In few cases had the Zhong actually been able to improve on Volgan performance. In no case had they ever been able to reach claimed Volgan performance.

Thus, when the salesmen in the cheap suits had come peddling Archangel to the Zhong, they'd made some very extravagant claims for it. Whether the Zhong believed those claims entirely or not, they had to take them into their calculations. This was why Captain Liu's *Mao Zedong* and the other three subs of the Dynasty class on their way to Balboa were taking their sweet time about it. They believed if they rushed, they'd be found and engaged.

### Vicinity, Town of Concepción, Balboa, Terra Nova

Mrs. Nguyen—"Madame"—spoke fair Spanish. Her husband, Colonel Nguyen, did not. They both spoke excellent French. Since Maria had high school French, a couple of years' worth, they got by.

"Recruited girl . . . name 'Han,'" Mr. Nguyen said, in the Spanish he was still working on. "She marry one you people . . . or maybe white round eye. Not sure. She recruit bunch us. We help."

Colonel and Madame looked to be somewhere between seventy and one hundred, though they acted healthier and fitter than that. Gradually, in mixed French and broken Spanish, it was revealed that they had something like a century's worth of fighting as guerillas between them. They were a great help, much more than one would expect from hired guns. Sergeant Ponce thought it was mostly a case of loving their work.

"You got sleep," the colonel said. "You got eat. You got . . . stand down . . . plan . . . prepare . . . rehearse. Enemy use that. Come in when sleeping . . . quick-quick . . . helicopter . . . no warning."

"We could mine all the open areas," Fuentes offered. Sergeant Ponce just shook her head. After a bit, the centurion came to the same conclusion as Ponce had. "No, no we couldn't. We have a lot of mines, not an infinity."

"Got better trick anyway," he said. "Need little air legion . . . you call, '*ala*,' yes? Anyway, need little help from thems peoples."

Ponce's sapper girls had dug a rather large hole about two feet by twelve and chest deep the night before. While they'd been digging, Ponce and one other had constructed a cage around a one-ton, unfused bomb, then had run a current through the cage. Now, cursing, straining, and groaning, they rolled that Tauran aerial bomb, provided courtesy of the Tauran Ammunition Supply Point at Arnold Air Base, up to the hole.

The hole—more of a slit trench really—was centered in an open area about three hundred meters on a side. Off to one side was the spoil. On the other they'd laid out some fast-growing progressivine cuttings they intended to transplant to help camouflage along. In Balboa's soil and sun, and with Balboa's rain, the progressivines could reasonably be expected to cover the thing entirely within a week.

With a final curse, Ponce exhorted her girls to a last push. The bomb rolled into the hole and stayed there, swaying a bit as it rocked on its side. A bright gray and green trixie leapt from a tree at the edge of the wood line and flew across the open space, cawing in indignation at being disturbed.

While Ponce and the sapper girls busted their butts, the Cochinese advisor worked on educating their leader.

"Trick with Zhong," Mr. Nguyen said, "is threaten face."

Fuentes shook her head. "Like . . . threatening to punch them?"

Nguyen, frustrated with the difficulties in communication, shook his head. He answered, "No . . . no . . . threaten . . ." Then he stopped for lack of the right word and concept. "What you call what show to world? Appearance?"

"Like . . . honor?" Fuentes asked.

The colonel nodded enthusiastically. "That it. You call 'honor.' With us—Zhong, Yamato, all us—we call word translate 'face.' With Zhong, must be able to make commander lose face."

"What's that have to do with putting a bomb in a field?"

"Big shame," Nguyen said. "Okay lose helicopter once, maybe. Maybe twice. After that, commander enemy look stupid if lose a third. Won't take risk."

"Ohhh."

"Yes, make lose face. Helicopter come . . . wind bend tree . . . tree has wire . . . wire runs bomb. Bomb go boom. Helo go boom. Do once. Do twice. Enemy lose face. After that, you sleep sound. Plan easy. Secure."

"Ohhh."

"You good girl," Nguyen said, reaching up to pat her on the cheek. "Remind me own daughter."

"How is your daughter?" Maria asked, quite sure that the daughter was a grandmother herself by now.

Nguyen looked very sad for a moment. "She dead," he said. "Killed young . . . planting bomb." Then he added, his chin lifting with pride, "In war against Zhong."

The hut had had most of the furniture removed and replaced by long planks atop stumps and milk crates. On the planks sat two of Fuentes' squads, plus a couple of the cooks and artillery types temporarily reclassified as infantry. There were some covered cages along one wall, as well as some plates filled with a red powder. At one end, facing the girls across a makeshift lectern, Madame spoke.

"Since your enemy," Madame said, "has so very kindly given you so many, *many* bombs—*such* generosity!—during and after their last invasion, surely someone ought to get some use from them."

"Among other uses . . ."

"Okay," said Madame, "ten-minute break." The break was perhaps a few minutes early, but Madame had noticed the female leader of the group, the one called "Centurion Fuentes," waiting in the back of the classroom.

The women shuffled out, most of them, as they reached the door, lighting up one of the canned cigarettes that came with the rations. Centurion Fuentes didn't entirely approve, but the cigarettes were made from tobacco infected in ages past with a virus that removed most of the harmful effects.

Fuentes had been paying attention, but had come in late. Moreover, she wasn't able to attend every session. Still, Madame never ridiculed an honest question and seemed to have some idea of the thousand different directions the centurion was being pulled in.

"Madame Nguyen," asked Fuentes, "what about magnetism from the bombs? Won't they be found? What about radar from the air?"

"Well, naturally, child, you should de-gauss them, if you can."

Fuentes hadn't heard the term before. "Degauss?"

"Ah . . . eliminate the magnetic signature. I've shown your Sergeant Ponce how to do it. And bury the bombs with a radar-scattering shroud over them to keep the enemy from finding out which landing zones were so trapped and which weren't.

"Then too, some places, you can put the bombs in underground but don't wire them to the saplings. Just like you are doing with some of the antipersonnel mines. That way, so you see, the enemy gets accustomed to using a particular landing zone, or trail, or road until some night you ladies pay a visit to the place and the next day—or the next, doesn't matter really—it goes boom right in their overconfident faces. On the other hand, all you must do is get to the area and assemble the mines. You need not even carry detonators with you. Just bury them nearby. Then even a strip search would reveal nothing."

Fuentes nodded, then smiled, tentatively, as if she were long out of practice in smiling. "I've got to ask, and I hope you won't think I'm prying, but where did you and your husband come from, that you know all this?"

Madame sighed, "The colonel and I?"

"The *colonel*?" Maria asked.

"Yes, he was a colonel. You would say a 'legate.' We're from Cochin. For the last couple of years we've been teaching the Revolutionary Warfare course for about-to-be-discharged veterans.

"He's more a regular who knows how to operate like a guerrilla than an actual guerrilla himself. I was a real guerilla, though some might say a terrorist.

"We fought for our country, between us, for over a century. Then we discovered that Tsarist-Marxism wasn't compatible with patriotism. Things got bad for us. We were recruited and came here.

"Listen to the colonel," Madame warned. "I know a lot of techniques, but he understands things like intelligence, communications, and coordination, and the consummate importance of *never* letting the enemy think he's doing well."

Madame checked her watch and announced, "Break's over, girls, back to class." The women began shuffling in from outside.

"Let me show you some of the difference, a trick," Madame said, and beckoned them to follow her out of the hut and into a concrete house. Inside that house, on one wall was a picture, painted by a perhaps not terribly, talented local artist. It was hanging askew.

"What's wrong with that?" Madame asked.

"It's crooked," one of the very new Amazons answered. "So?"

Madame wagged her finger. "Only a fairly senior officer of the enemy is likely to be bothered by a picture askew. Idiocy and focus on mere appearances often increases with rank. So you booby trap the thing so the bomb goes off—so an electrical connection is made—when the picture is righted."

The young Amazon's eyes lit up. "Ohhh."

Madame went to the wall and pulled the cover off of one of the cages. An *antania* hissed, threateningly. *Antaniae* were winged reptiles with septic mouths. They were noted mostly for cowardice and attacks on the feeble-minded and young.

"Now these," Madame continued, "are a different sort of trap. They can chew through mere rope, so they must be chained. They're at their best in tunnels, where you know they're they but the enemy does not . . ."

Madame bent to pick up a plate containing a reddish-brown powder. "This," she announced, "is made from the seeds of Satan Triumphant, dried and ground . . ."

# CHAPTER FIFTEEN

The conventional army loses if it does not win.
The guerrilla wins if he does not lose.
                                —Henry A. Kissinger

**Log Base Alpha (so called), Balboa, Terra Nova**

One of the gunners sat atop his gun's container, dipping his chorley bread in a hot sauce composed of somewhat diluted Joan of Arc pepper. These were one of the milder peppers found on Terra Nova, though not especially mild, in objective terms. Joan of Arcs were a poor relative of their distant cousin, the Satan Triumphant pepper. The chorley was made from the seed of a plant that might have been a native, or genengineered, or imported from some other planet besides Old Earth or Terra Nova. The plant, which looked like nothing so much as a low-growing orange sunflower, produced seeds that resembled tiny kernels of corn and produced a bread high in gluten and tasting somewhat naturally buttery.

Tribune Ramirez leapt atop that containers and stood over the eating gunner. He scanned his area with satisfaction. There were sixteen containers there now. Eight of those were laid on their sides, buried and sandbagged, with the southernmost edges elevated at ten or twelve degrees above the horizontal. From each of the eight, a narrow trench zigzagged back to where a wider trench ran generally east west, connected all the others. That wider trench was sandbag-

and stake-revetted, and of octagonal trace. In spots that main trench became a tunnel, as the troops had covered it with logs and sandbags over long stretches.

At each end of the main trench was another container, though these were dug in and buried flat. More zigzag trench ran northward from the main trench, leading to Ramirez's command post, the aid station, the cooks' shelter, and three more, fairly close together, for the supply section. In a couple of other spots there were holes dug for the unit's scanty supply of vehicles, two light four-wheel-drive command vehicles and three medium trucks. The unit owned more vehicles, but they were held elsewhere.

Around the perimeter, in little knots that were sometimes connected to each other by slit trenches and sometimes not, with those slit trenches being sometimes connected to the main trenches and sometimes not, forty or so fighting positions had been dug. Some were of odd shapes. There were still parties of men working on those, especially on the entrenching, and so it was reasonable to suppose that eventually all the fighting positions would be connected by trench.

There had been a pile of premade concertina, single-strand barbed wire, and stakes, once all the barrier material had been removed from the containers. Sadly, an engineer officer had shown up, waved something official looking in Ramirez's face, and then carted all the material off.

On the plus side, the engineer had left a two-man chainsaw team behind for a while, and these had cut a very impressive amount of logs for overhead cover and reinforcement. When they'd been called away, another, somewhat larger team of engineer demolitions types had shown up. They hadn't blown anything up, but they had wired a number of branches and entire trees for demolition to the south of Ramirez's position.

Overhead, his men were adding an extra layer to the triple canopy of the jungle, in the form of radar-scattering camouflage screens, or nets. He had his doubts about the usefulness of the screens, since anyone overhead would have had weeks to search through the foliage, assuming they could get through it at all.

*But what do I know? Maybe they'll be of some help against the planes once the bombing starts.*

### Concepción, Balboa, Terra Nova

Madame showed them how to pack a bicycle with explosives and a timer, and how to scrounge or make their own munitions when the materiel they'd been supplied ran out as it would if the war lasted long enough.

Madame Nguyen also spoke to them at length about maintaining political control and what needed be done with enemy prisoners of war. None of the Amazons cared much for what she said on those subjects, which didn't mean she was wrong or that they wouldn't do it.

Supplies rolled in almost daily. Keeping track of them, receiving, accounting for, and transmitting them, was the job of the platoon optio, Marta Bugatti. One day, each platoon in the maniple received at least one "secret" weapon. It came in an electronics-proof case. When opened, the case revealed a remote-controlled miniature tank with just enough armor to protect it from small-arms fire and about a quarter of a ton of explosive. The little robots were wire guided and each carried a closed-circuit lowlight TV for the operator to see where it was going. There was also a loudspeaker on each one so the operator could make announcements to the enemy.

"What the fuck?" Bugatti asked when she saw it.

"I read about the idea in Franco's class," her centurion told her, "in the single science fiction book we read. 'I am a thirty-second bomb. I am a thirty-second bomb. Twenty-nine. Twenty-eight . . . '"

"Oh, *funny!*"

"How many did we get?" Fuentes asked.

"Three of the little terrors," Bugatti replied. "They're called"—she consulted the hand receipt—"'Davids.'"

"Okay," Maria said. Pulling up an image of the area to her mind, she said, "Send them to cache areas one . . . three . . . and four. And have one girl per squad trained to drive them."

"Wilco, Centurion," Marta answered.

*It was a good thing*, thought Pastora, watching the Amazons dig in one day, *that Carrera didn't skimp on the engineer tools. We are, all of us, moving mountains.*

Centurion Cesar Pastora, Fourteenth Cazador Tercio, was, with his small command, a part of the Amazons' cover. Mixed in among the women, they were expected to buy a little time, simply by being men and thus by being the more probable perceived font of violence. Eventually, they'd be dead or captured—there just weren't that many of them—but in the interim they'd serve as cover.

Pastora's small platoon and Fuentes's much larger one got along famously, except insofar as the individuals tried to keep just how well they were getting along a secret.

*The amazing thing*, thought Pastora, *is that we get any work done at all, what with every one of my boys having to service three or four of Fuentes's chicas. 'Course, to be fair, the girls are more into emotional support than just sex, and they manage to get three or four times more work out of the boys than I've ever been able to.*

Better, Pastora *liked* the *Amazonas*. And as more than just women. They were tough and smart and eager to please, as soldiers. It also didn't hurt that . . .

"My sister's a squad leader in your regiment," Pastora told Optio Bugatti. "Let's say that that gives me a certain perspective on the *Tercio Amazona* that some others may lack."

*And she was a tough bitch, even as a baby.*

Pastora added, "There may be some other things that we lack, too. Have you noticed, Optio Bugatti, that your women are actually quite a bit better at camouflaging things than my men are? No joke."

"Could be," Bugatti agreed. "Maybe all those years we'd been learning to coordinate colors and patterns had some indirect payoff. Don't know."

"Could I ask for some of your troops to assist mine?"

"Make it worth my while," the optio said.

"I'll cook dinner—which is to say, warm up our canned rations— for both of us tomorrow . . ."

"Tempting," Marta answered, "but . . ."

". . . and I'll have my platoon dig a dozen bunkers for yours."

"Done."

The evening sky was unusually clear, with two moons, Eris and Bellona, visible, along with any number of constellations. Of the latter, the most easily discerned were the Smilodon, the Leaping Maiden, and the Pentagram.

As promised, dinner was canned, most of the cans still snuggled against the coals, keeping warm. It wasn't bad, and Pastora had, so Bugatti thought, done something with it to make it better than merely and barely edible. Then again, he'd been with the legion for better than ten years; he ought to have learned a few tricks.

"The enemy's going to be coming in ignorant," Pastora said, over what passed for dinner. "But he's not stupid. You ladies will be able to live openly but discreetly among the refugees, coming out to fight in secret and only occasionally. But only for a while. Eventually you're going to end up going underground."

From one can, one kept far from the fire, and which had only had a couple of thin perforations made in the top, Pastora poured ration-issue rum. The rum went into another can containing water and a couple of the little fruit drink packets.

"We know they'll catch on," Bugatti agreed. "We've made some camps in inaccessible places for the long haul."

"Want me to look them over?" Pastora asked. "I'm sure, based on everything I've seen, that they're fine, but what's a second opinion hurt?"

He held out the can of fruit juice and rum, saying, "You can drink this safely; *nothing* can live in the presence of legion-issue rum."

Pastora refrained from laughing when Bugatti sipped, and made an oh-Jesus-what-is-that-shit face. Pastora mixed his a little stronger than she was used to. Moreover, uncut, the rum was strong enough to use as a fire starter.

"Yeah, sure, Cesar," Marta said, passing the can back.

"How's the charcoal production coming?" Pastora asked.

The charcoal was for underground cooking in the messes they'd dug here and there. Under the Nguyens' tutelage, they'd run plastic, while it lasted, and then bamboo pipes a good distance from where the food would be cooked. That was to draw off the smoke, if any, and give the heat a chance to dissipate below the level that thermal imagers could find it.

Bugatti answered, "We've enough—rather, we'll *have* enough—for a couple of months, if we're frugal." She took the can back from Pastora and sipped again, the fiery rum racing to her toes.

"You'll have more than that," Pastora said.

"No, not for all of us," Marta disagreed.

"Dear Optio," Pastora said, shaking his head, "it's not going to be 'all of us.'"

Marta shook her own head. "I don't understand. Sure, we'll take losses but—"

"You'll take losses. We're going to be destroyed." Pastora laughed as if it were actually funny; though that was the rum laughing. "You know what they say: 'On your feet or dead; never on your knees.' When the enemy comes, we're going out to fight him. When we're crushed, he'll think for a while that he owns this area. Then you girls have your turn.

"I remember you, you know," Pastora said. "From the *classis,* off the coast of Xamar. You have a very distinctive . . . ummm . . . profile."

Marta Bugatti was suddenly horribly ashamed. She'd been hired as a sea whore, originally. Covering her face, she stood to go. Pastora stood, as well, put his hands on her shoulders to stop her, and said, "No. I'm *proud* of you, Marta. One woman in a thousand, if that many, can do what you've done, rise as you've risen. I don't think any less of you."

Marta sat again and took a much longer drink from the rum mix. She shook her head.

*I really* like *this one,* she thought.

She put the can down, stood herself up again, and repeated back to Pastora, "'On your feet or dead; never on your knees?' Come on, I'm not that doctrinaire about it."

*And besides,* she thought, *the enemy will be here soon enough.*

### Combat Information Center, BdL *Dos Lindas,* *Mar Furioso,* Terra Nova

Both Intelligence and Communications were waiting as Fosa entered CIC.

"They're here," said Fosa's communications officer. "Archangel has picked up two definites and three more probables, about two days' sailing away. Three days, if they slow down."

"I expect them to slow," said Intel.

"Show me," Fosa said, walking to the plexiglass plotting board. An enlisted sailor was already inscribing the known locations, heading, speed, and depth in solid red and the probable in dotted red. They weren't in any kind of formation that made sense to Fosa but, *Then again, why should they be. And why should what makes sense to them make sense to me? I'm a surface swabbie, after all, and my three dimensions are mostly above the water, more fragile, and moving way faster.*

*Thing is, that last one. If he's the Yamatan we've been expecting all along . . .*

"Get me Fernandez on the secure line. Route it through to my day cabin.

"Oh, and did the two newsies come aboard?"

"Yes, sir," said Comms. "The exec's arranged to bed them down in officer country and is currently taking them on the 'no you can't go here unescorted' tour. He said he's going to show them the films of the pressies the ground pounders hanged in Pashtia and shot in Pumbadeta, just so they get the point."

"Good."

The phone line hissed, beeped three times, then hissed again.

"Omar? Rod," said Fosa. "I've got the plots on the subs. And I'm going to ask Patricio for permission to try to take one out . . . two, if possible. But which one's the Yamatan? Be damned ungrateful for us to sink the sub that's been trying to spy for us."

*Hisss . . . beepbeepbeep. . . . hisss.* "I can probably get the Yamatans to pull their man back," answered Fernandez, "but I can't say how quickly."

"Twenty-four hours?" asked Fosa.

"Maybe, maybe not."

"Damn! If I wait more than that much time, I'm risking them getting close enough to the *Dos Lindas* for a shot at her."

"Then you're going to have to play it by ear," said Fernandez. "It's not like getting the sub—or even two of them—really helps us all that much."

"It does for Patricio's end game," Fosa reminded. "Especially since I am unenthusiastic about drowning."

"End game . . ." mused Fernandez . . . "end game. Yeah, you have a good point. Look, Rod, I can't promise anything, but whatever can be done to get that Yamatan sub either out of the way or clearly identified, I'll do it. The big problem is that they've never admitted that they're feeding us intel that way."

"You can tell them that we know there are five out there, and that the Zhong sortied only four. If they have another explanation . . ."

"There is one, you know," Fernandez said. "The Federated States, even under the Progressive Party, still takes a keen interest in undersea doings in this hemisphere."

*Hisss . . . beepbeepbeep. . . . hisss.*

"Oh, shit," said Fosa. "Now that you mention it, if there's one thing we absolutely don't want to do, it's piss off the FSC about now. What do I do if a sixth sub pops up on screen?"

"Run," answered Fernandez. "Or get sunk. But in any case, remember that drowning's less painful than anything Patricio's likely to do if you bring the FSC into the war against us."

## Roughly four miles south of Concepción, Balboa, Terra Nova

Pastora was out there with his men, with logs weighing in excess of a couple of hundred pounds perched on shoulders, as the *Cazadores* ferried the logs from a woodcutting area to an area being bunkered in.

"I am glad we are not alone in all this," Bugatti said, as she and Centurion Fuentes watched the sweating and straining group of *Cazadores* shouldering loads that none of the women could have hoped to. Well, none but the engineer, Sergeant Ponce, who took up some of the less stout logs. Then again, Ponce was a fireplug with tits.

"You're glad?" said Fuentes. "I am ecstatic that I am not entirely in charge. Speaking of which, how are you and Centurion Pastora getting along?"

"We get along pretty well, actually," the optio said, smiling broadly.

"I know. And that surprises me. I thought you preferred . . ."

"I'm not doctrinaire about it," Marta answered, primly. "Besides, it's not like I'm the only one who's gotten all gooey."

Fuentes nodded. She thought, sadly, *Half my girls will cry themselves to sleep when the men march out. And don't march back.*

★★★

Doctrine and sound judgment were as one in this: Everything was to be used to resist an occupation. Besides the *Amazonas* and *Cazadores,* and below them in the military scheme of things, were the refugees, not all of whom were helpless. There were one hundred and eighty-three people in Fuentes's platoon's area whose credentials were pretty much impeccable: Retired soldiers, veterans discharged into the Home Guard, children of soldiers and the widows of soldiers who had been given jobs in legion-owned factories.

The *Amazonas* and *Cazadores* trained those as and when they could. Where there was no time or opportunity to train them, those impeccably credentialed civilians were a source of labor. The others, those not so trustworthy, could be used, too, but not for some of the more secret projects.

It was expected they would become a useful source of intelligence. The credentialed ones were also a means of controlling the others whom the soldiers didn't know and had no real basis for trusting. Ultimately, they might be a source of recruits.

Until that day came, though, all the rest, the nearly fifteen thousand otherwise useless mouths without credentials, worked on open projects: Communal bomb shelters, sharpening wooden stakes to use for foot traps, making charcoal, drayage and storage.

Some, those with agricultural backgrounds, were put to growing food. Though it would be a while, even in Balboa's growth-inducing clime, before anything could be harvested. And there was always the chance they'd have to destroy it to keep the enemy from subsisting off of it.

### Pelirojo, Santa Josefina, Terra Nova

The sun had *just* given its first hint of day, a thin red glow on the eastern horizon.

The town was pretty well fortified, by now, at least in terms of bunker preparation and preparation of the few buildings Salas had taken over. The defenses had some mines out, but there was a serious shortage of barbed wire. For whatever reason, the *Roger Casement* hadn't had any concertina at all, and only a limited amount of single-strand barbed wire. Salas's subordinate commanders were cutting and emplacing wood and bamboo stakes, to make up the difference, but it wasn't as good for most purposes. Off in the distance one could hear them chopping, then hammering, then chopping some more to add points.

There'd been a small meeting engagement. One of the Cimbrian patrols had run into a platoon from Salas's tercio of Santa Josefinans. The frightening thing about that was that the engagement had taken place southwest of the town, behind it, in effect.

Salas looked down at four bodies, stretched out bloody and lifeless in the village square, all dressed in something that looked remarkably like legionary camouflage. They weren't legionaries, though, or at least not legionaries from the *Legion del Cid*. A couple of his intel people were searching the bodies; a small pile of various items was growing on the concrete where the loot was tossed.

*Is this a war crime, wearing our camouflage pattern? What about when we're not wearing it? When the equipment's different enough to put us on notice that they're not our pals? I don't think it is. And I think that I'm better off not treating it like it is. Though I'd better get the word out to be very suspicious of anyone who looks like he's in legionary uniform.*

Salas bent down and began to go through the pile himself, even before his people had a chance to sort it. He opened a wallet, then scanned through the pictures.

*Pretty wife,* Salas thought. *And the girls seem to favor her, but not the boy.* He looked at one of the bodies, decided that was not the owner, and settled on another. *Sorry, old man. In another life, we might have spent a fine evening remembering our youth "with advantages."*

He replaced the wallet in the pile, not least because it struck him as innately dirty to be going through a dead man's personal things.

"Map, sir," announced one of the searchers, holding it up, an acetated, folded, inch-thick map, with drawings and diagrams done apparently in alcohol pen.

Salas grabbed the map and unfolded it. *Doesn't tell me much. I can assume, from the route they drew, that there is probably no other patrol on that particular route. Doesn't tell me a lot about where they are though.*

"No radio?" the legate asked.

The section chief shook his head. "No, sir. There were seven of them in the patrol. Three, as far as we know, got away. And one of those was humping the radio."

"Where were they from?" Salas asked.

"Cimbria," was the answer. "Don't let the black dyed hair fool you, sir. Check the roots. Every one of these guys is blond as the high admiral's cunt . . . so I hear."

Salas nodded, then said, "I need a prisoner, or, better, two."

"Yes, sir, and the platoon that made contact is chasing them. But these guys are their equivalent of *Cazadores*. Not much chance of catching them."

"No, I suppose not. Any word from our own scouts?"

"Yes, sir. We know where the enemy is: Cerveza. Looks like a tank company, an infantry battalion, maybe half a battalion of engineers, and a battalion of artillery, though we haven't found all the gunners, we think.

"All out of range, sir."

"Yeah . . . close call whether to risk a . . ." Salas suddenly stiffened. It was something in the air, a change in pressure perhaps. Some old vets insisted it was precognition. Whatever it was, it told him to throw himself to the ground, shouting, "Incoming!"

# CHAPTER SIXTEEN

You can't describe the moral lift,
When in the fight your spirits weary
Hears above the hostile fire,
Your own artillery.
—Aleksandr Tvardovsky,
*Vasily Tyorkin*

**Cerveza, Santa Josefina, Terra Nova**

There was only one battery of guns visible from the road, and that, in the bare hint of presunrise light, not much. The other battery, for one had been left behind facing their Balboan border, was hidden over a rise and down a dirt road.

Standing close by that visible battery, was the commander of the Haarlemer *Korps Licht Rijdende Artillerie*, the Corps of Light Horse Artillery. A broad smile beaming from Lieutenant Colonel van Heutsz's florid face, with drama in his every muscle twitch, the Haarlemer slowly raised his right arm, palm forward and over his head. His left hand, with watch facing inward from his wrist, was held in front of him.

Thought van Heutsz, *Oh, this is going to be so good.* Van Heutsz liked ceremony. And why not? It had been decades since the Haarlemer red legs had gotten in a shot in anger.

Hidden in the jungle, the Hordalander tank company began revving engines. They were soon joined by trucks, both nearby and

217

farther away. A second group of tanks, smaller, but with the same distinctive diesels, kicked in on the other side of the battalion. A section of bridge layers from the Tuscan engineer battalion kicked in with their contribution, followed by a pioneer company from the same group.

Van Heutsz counted the seconds down . . . *five . . . four . . . three . . . two . . . one . . .*

He dropped his hand like a saber stroke. "Fire!" A half-dozen 105mm cannons belched flame. Their first target was the battery of heavy mortars spotted on the other side of the town of Pelirojo. A fraction of a second later, the second battery joined in on a different target.


### Southwest of Pelirojo, Santa Josefina, Terra Nova

It wasn't actually a battery; a full battery of heavy mortars ran, in the legion, to twelve guns. But it *was* a third of a battery, four guns. Given that six was usually the number of guns in a battery anywhere in the Tauran Union, the Cimbrians could be forgiven for reporting it as a battery, just as Marciano's intelligence section could be forgiven for accepting that report. That the other two-thirds of the battery hadn't been found—for the excellent reason that it was nowhere in the area—supported the assumption.

The guns were pretty well dug in, in pits about a meter and a half deep. They had no overhead cover, of course, unlike some of the 160s in fixed positions inside Balboa. They did have a certain amount of protection from the trees between themselves and the Tauran guns, since they fired a higher angle than field guns ordinarily would. And, while the guns were open, the troops, the ammunition, and the all-important fire-direction center had solid cover over them.

The first Tauran salvoes came in at such an angle to the thick canopy of the tree that the wood and leaves may as well have been solid. All six shells exploded at a distance from the target well outside their effective burst radius. Still, some hot, sharp shards of metal made their way to the gun positions, enough to kick up dirt and set the troops to scurrying for cover.

The next salvo, following on the first by mere seconds, did better.

True, two of the shells went off either in the remaining canopy—such as the first salvo hadn't cleared away—or hit one of the trees, but four passed by all that, hitting the general area of the gun position. The third salvo actually did worse, random chance putting three of the shells into the trees. The fourth, however, saw all six rounds pass safely through the canopy and the splintered wood, to fall with fair precision on and about the gun line. One mortar was wrecked beyond redemption when a high-explosive shell struck it on the left buffer tube, between the elevation crank and the barrel. The crank was blown off, while the baseplate was split and the barrel ripped from the base plug. The two soldiers manning the mortar became for the most part so much strawberry paste.

The centurion in charge of the platoon was knocked half-silly by the blast. The concussion might have done more serious damage, except that the mortar pit, itself, tended to direct the blast up, while its walls soaked up the fragments. When the centurion looked up to see a head fly one way, while three-quarters of an arm went the other, he ordered, "Into the bunkers! Leave the guns alone for now; there's nothing we can do without a target we can range to!"

Still, the shelling continued.


## Pelirojo, Santa Josefina, Terra Nova

Salas was probably saved by the Cimbrian bodies. At least, the first salvo landed on the far side, with the bodies between him and it. One of the shells was sufficiently close to shred the body, and throw another one right next to Salas, where it formed a sort of low and leaky berm.

Those first rounds were it, though, for that part of the town. The second battery then shifted their fires to a position identified by the Cimbrian *Jaegers* as a key antiarmor battle position.

As soon as Salas sensed that the fire had lifted from him, he stood and scanned around for his driver. *Where is that no good . . .*

The legate was shocked by the sound of a horn, coming from right behind him. Turning, he saw his driver in his commandeered vehicle, the driver's face split by a broad grin. "You rang, sir?"

"Yeah," said the legate, jumping in on the passenger side, "take me to the cohort commander. Fast."

## Cerveza, Santa Josefina, Terra Nova

The Hordalander company commander had reorganized his truncated company, thirteen tanks, into a more normal configuration: three platoons of four, with his exec taking the third platoon.

The area they had to pass through was typical, some remnants of old tropical rain forest, with exceedingly thickly grown fringes, a lot of open farmland, the occasional *hacienda*, and some streams. The ground was rugged enough to be "interesting," but little of it, on its own, was impassable to tanks. "Interesting," is this case, meant something like, "We tankers are very interested in getting home alive, so you Sachsen ground pounders and Tuscan ditch diggers, get out of your bloody trucks and clear that wood line."

Since that *was* the infantrymen's job—engineers, too, to a point— the Sachsen battalion commander, *Oberstleutnant* Barkhorn, actually agreed with this approach.

First contact came about three kilometers northeast of Pelirojo, along an east-west-running escarpment through which Highway One ran at near right angles. Pretty plainly intended to be an antiarmor ambush, the Sachsens tripped it well before the tanks entered the planned kill zone. Dismounting, themselves, well out of range, the Sachsen company formed up, then moved west toward the escarpment.

The guerillas waited until the better part of a platoon of Sachsens was in the river between the escarpment and the road before opening up. Some of their fire went high, some low, but enough was on target to set nine of the Taurans floating, mostly face down, down the river.

By that time, though, the Sachsen battalion's own 120mm mortars were set up, in range, and ready. They dropped a deluge of shells on the Santa Josefinans, long enough and heavy enough for the rest of the Sachsen company to get across the stream. The Santa Josefinans pulled out in good order, but had to leave several bodies behind.

Just past the escarpment, and partially, at least, because of the availability of water from the river, the first houses began. These were nothing much, mostly the scrap wood shacks of the very poor, occasionally interspersed with better houses, of concrete block or adobe. These, Salas's tercio had entirely left alone. Even so, at the first sound of firing the Santa Josefinan civilians head streamed off, east and west, into the fields and forests. Their houses, poor and pathetic things, were left abandoned.

There had been however, one concrete block-built government building that Salas's men had taken over and fortified.

Barkhorn found considerable comfort in the sound of shells flying overhead, not least because he knew they were keeping the guerilla's heavy mortars pretty much out of play.

In range and accuracy, his own task force's 105s beat the heavy mortars six ways from Sunday, as the phrase went. But, and it was a big "but," once in range, the 160mm mortars the Cimbrians had identified outclassed the 105s in weight of shell, in effectiveness of shell—by a factor of three or four or so—and in rate of fire. In particular, were the mortars' shells nasty. Since the stresses of being fired at low velocity inside the smoothbore tube were not nearly as bad as those from being fired at high velocity from a rifled gun, the mortar shells could be made of iron, which fragmented better than steel did. Since they tended to come down almost vertically, they spread those fragments better. And they simply packed a lot more explosive. Being on the receiving end of a barrage from 160s was an experience no one wanted twice.

*Still, so far, so good,* thought Barkhorn. Then he heard an explosion that did *not* sound like either the Hordalander tanks' cannon, the 105s, the 120 mortars, or anything much but a mine. The radio calls for medevac confirmed it; one Hordalander tank had taken a mine right through the driver's seat. He was dead, said the radio, and the three in the turret in poor shape.

Barkhorn was in the process of ordering, "Evacuate them by ground to a covered position, don't risk—" when there came several more blasts, these ones doubled.

"Fuck!" exclaimed the radio, in the voice of the Hordalander tank company commander, speaking German. "They're dug into one of the bigger buildings. Recoilless rifles or those Volgan things that might as well be. Get me some infantry here; I lost another tank! And a fucking ambulance!"

★★★

A Santa Josefinan sergeant lay beside one of the Volgan heavy smoothbore rocket launchers that had come in on the *Casement*. These were effectively recoilless muskets, since the rockets burned out completely before the round left the tube. Effective to a range of five hundred meters, more with an exceptional gunner in windless conditions, they had a tandem warhead. The major charge could penetrate as much as thirty inches of steel, plus there was a smaller charge on a prod, to defeat reactive armor.

The sergeant—he went by "Segura"—told the gunner to hold fire as the Tauran tank eased into the thin minefield between the building and the highway. He was about to give up on the mines and order the gunner to fire when suddenly the ground erupted under the tank, and an armless and legless body was propelled upward through the driver's hatch. The tank commander had been standing in his hatch, but shortly after the explosion he sank down into the tank.

A smaller armored vehicle followed the tracks engraved by the tank in the dirt. "Track that one," said Sergeant Segura. The gunner wordlessly nodded. "Fire when you have a clear shot," the sergeant amended, then crawled off to the other rocket launcher. By the time he got there, another Tauran tank had shown up and had taken up an overwatching position, out of the minefield.

The sergeant felt the first rocket launcher fire, then saw through the loophole of the second as the small armored personnel carrier stopped and burst into flame. The overwatching tank turned its turret, slightly, then fired at the building. It wasn't entirely clear the tank had seen where the rocket had come from, since it missed at a range it should not have missed at. Even so, a chunk came off of the building. The turret turned just a bit . . . just enough . . . just . . .

"Fire!" ordered Segura.

The government building into which the Santa Josefinans were dug started coming apart as the hurricane of 120mm tank shells rained down upon it. Eventually, the wooden and plastic and cloth parts caught fire, the heat and smoke driving the defenders to try to escape to the next building. The tanks, though, saw through the smoke and dust easily. One of them, machine gun chattering, swept across the group of scuttling Santa Josefinan guerillas, knocking down several and driving the rest back to the burning building.

With fire racing along the beams holding up the tile roof, the defenders' options narrowed drastically. They tried sticking white flags out the windows but these simply drew fire. The problem was that ambulance. They hadn't intended to destroy an ambulance but, what with all the smoke, fire, sound, and confusion, it had just sort of gotten in the way. They still didn't even know that they *had* taken out an ambulance.

Conversely, the Taurans did know, and were most annoyed by it. Briefly, Barkhorn considered telling him men to let the guerillas surrender then decided, *Fuck 'em. You don't get to shoot up an ambulance and then surrender all nice and sweet. Instead, you just die.*

"What the fuck, Sarge?" asked one of the younger legionaries of his squad leader, Sergeant Segura. They'd both been driven back, back where the heat and smoke weren't so bad. Still, the troop was gasping from a combination of exertion, fear, and smoke. "Why won't they take a surrender?"

"Dunno, Private," answered the sergeant. "But we need to get word out that they're not taking prisoners."

"How?"

"Fucked if I know, son."

It was a damned good thing that the Santa Josefinan civilians had scampered off, given the approach being taken by the Taurans to buildings, now that they'd lost some of their own to defenders inside them. That approach was simple; concrete and adobe homes were smashed from a distance with cannon fire. Wooden ones were set alight with tracers from the machine guns. In cases of doubt, Tuscan sappers with demolition charges disintegrated still others.

In the space of half an hour, the one government building and fifty-odd personal homes lining both sides of the highway were either smashed to dust or burning merrily.

At the far end of that little linear monument to free fire zones, the Tauran task force stopped briefly, to reorganize for the assault on the town and to spread out across the rivers that had channeled them into what could have been a disastrously tight kill zone. While they were doing so, the first couple of sorties of air support came in. These weren't directed at the town of Pelirojo, nor at the troops immediately defending it. Instead, the flight of eight Anglian-flown. Tauravia-built, Hurricane fighter-bombers split up, with four circling like vultures overhead, while four more split off and went for the 160mm mortar position, now clearly marked by smoke and dust.

Salas watched from a distance as the four enemy aircraft swooped low over the one platoon of 160s he'd put out. He was not so far away that he couldn't see the eight silvery canisters come tumbling off the planes. And the mixed orange, red, and black fireballs that arose from those left him in no doubt about the fate of his platoon.

*Shit. I thought that by taking a disadvantageous position or a less advantageous one, anyway, I'd be able to preserve the guns until they could be of use. Didn't count on how good the enemy's recon would be. Damn me to hell. What's it going to do to the cause when we lose this battle? Because we are going to lose it. Shit.*

*Ah, well; the Nguyens said that the battle doesn't matter; the* war *is what matters.*

### Pelirojo, Santa Josefina, Terra Nova

There was a minefield east of the town, anchored on two of the three rivers. So much the Cimbrian *Jaegers* had reported. *Oberstleutnant* Barkhorn had intended that the Tuscan sappers would clear lanes through the minefield under cover of the artillery, while he swung the bulk of his force south, across the broader river, to take the town in flank.

As it turned out, that river was a bit too deep for wading. Nor did the Tuscan sappers have the ability to bridge it. They could, so they reported, bridge the faster flowing but much narrower stream to the north.

"Do it," Barkhorn ordered through his Tuscan translator. Then, leaving one of his infantry companies to support the Tuscans at the minefield, Barkhorn led the other two across the scissor bridge erected by the Tuscans across the northern stream, the *Rio Pelirojo.*

"You want us to follow?" the Hordalander commander had asked.

"Yes, but not yet," Barkhorn responded calmly. "While the enemy is watching the minefield, my infantry will get an assault position for a drive into the town. You mill about and make it look like you're going to burst through the lanes the Tuscans cut in the minefield. When I'm ready, I'll call you. Then load up the engineer company that's clearing the lanes and come running."

"Wilco," replied the Hordalander.

Legionaries Herrera and Madrigal, on observation post north of the town, were just possibly a little too junior for the decision that faced them. It would have been better for them if they'd had a radio to report to maniple headquarters about the several hundred enemy infantry practically racing through the woods toward the town. But radios were in somewhat short supply and besides, they had a field telephone. Legionary Madrigal was currently squeezing the little black rubber-covered button that should have made someone on the other end answer, and so far had failed—pardon the expression—*signally.*

Madrigal let the phone drop from his hand. "*Mierde,* Herrera, nothing. No motherfucking answer."

"Shit," agreed Herrera, "what the fuck are we going to do, Mad? What the hell happened?"

"My guess would be artillery cut the wire . . . yes, even though we buried it. Shit happens. As to what we're going to do . . . how long you been in?"

"Two years and about a month," Herrera answered. "Why?"

"Because that makes me senior. That means I get to cover you. You keep low but get back as fast as you can and tell the tribune that we got company, a lot of company, coming from the north."

"Man . . . Mad . . . I can't leave you here alone."

"Just go before I change my mind, Herrera. This sucks enough without being reminded of how much." Madrigal jerked a thumb rearwards. "Now GO!"

Herrera froze for a couple of seconds, no more, then, with a nod, turned and crawled out the scrape hole he'd shared with Madrigal. He crawled another fifty feet or so, at which point he was in a low draw. Instead of standing upright, the legionary got to his feet but stayed bent over. In that position, he began to trudge for the town.

Madrigal looked at his rifle with distaste. A Tauran bullpup design, captured in Balboa, he'd never so much as fired one. Supposedly the things were zeroed, but he had his doubts.

*Oh, well,* he thought, moving the stock to his shoulder, *I'm probably more likely to hit with an unzeroed unfamiliar rifle than I am with a zeroed one.* He took aim at someone talking on a radio, a few hundred meters to his front—*at least the sights are simple*—then began slowly squeezing the trigger.

*Oberstleutnant* Barkhorn was moving forward quickly, approximately at the juncture of the two companies he had with him. He'd already had his own battalion's 120mm mortars cease fire, to let the tubes cool for when he'd really need them. He could hear and feel the Haarlemer artillery flying overhead and pounding the guerillas that were supposed to be keeping the minefield from being breached. He'd had a report from his intel officer, back at Cerveza, that the enemy were, in fact, moving toward the northeast and the minefield. With a little luck, he'd charge into a vacuum, and route them out of the town at a single go.

Satisfied with progress, Barkhorn turned to give the handset back to his radio bearer, when that young soldier's head disappeared in a spray of blood, brains, and fragments of bone.

"*Scheisse!*"

# CHAPTER SEVENTEEN

Engage people with what they expect; it is what they are able to discern and confirms their projections. It settles them into predictable patterns of response, occupying their minds while you wait for the extraordinary moment—that which they cannot anticipate.

—Sun Tzu, *The Art of War*

**Pelirojo, Santa Josefina, Terra Nova**

Herrera's careful jaunt turned into a dead run for the town once the firing commenced behind him. Bullets sang by, knocking off bark from the trees or impacting more solidly upon them with deadened *thunks*.

*Whatever Madrigal did,* Herrera thought, *it must have been something impressive to get himself that much attention. Hope he makes it; got my doubts.*

Shouting the running password, past the last of the trees the legionary ran, across the open field of recently planted corn, then past the first couple of buildings and toward the school building that maniple had picked for its headquarters. Only to find . . .

"Jesus, where the fuck is everybody?" Herrera asked of the company clerk, currently bundling up some files into a cloth bag.

"They all headed east," said the clerk. "Cohort commander's orders. Why?"

"Why? WHY? Because the fucking Taurans are coming from the north, that's WHY! I saw them, hundreds of them, myself."

The clerk turned white. Reaching for a field telephone he held it towards Herrera. "Tell cohort. They won't believe me. *Tell them!*"

Salas was watching as the cohort commander, Legate Rodriguez's, eyes widened and his skin turned pale. The cohort commander was facing west, more or less instinctively. That was where the enemy sappers were reported to be chewing through the minefield. It was also where the bulk of his artillery was landing, albeit at a slow rate of fire. Rodriguez listened for a few moments, said, "Buy me whatever time you can," then dropped the field phone and reached for the radio handset offered him by one of the headquarters RTOs.

Announcing himself to the mid-ranked tribune on the other end, Rodriguez announced, "The move on the minefield's a feint. Back to your positions on the north of the town . . ." Before he could finish the sentence, from the left came a tremendous volume of musketry, punctuated by large-caliber cannon fire.

Barkhorn fought down the urge to throw up as his radio bearer's body sank to the earth. Kneeling down beside it, he stripped off the radio, then threaded his own left arm into the carrying strap on that side. Holding the handset to his face, even as he was putting his arm through the shoulder strap, he ordered the artillery to shift one battery to the center of the town, to keep the enemy from redeploying back to the town's northern edge and for both batteries to, "Expend ammunition like it was water." Then he told the Hordalander tank company commander to pick up the sappers and come running. Lastly, and by this time he had the radio under his full control, he ordered his two infantry companies, present, to, "Jink it for the town. Get me the first row or two of buildings!"

"Forget it, Rodriguez," said Legate Salas, once the cannon fire kicked in. "They've suckered us out of position. This town is lost. Save your command."

Rodriguez opened his mouth as if to argue, then closed it again. He nodded slowly, a couple of times, then agreed, "Yes, sir."

Rodriguez hesitated. "Sir?"

"Yes, Legate?"

"You *have* to get out of here. *You* made the announcement of the revolt against the government and the Taurans. If they get you, the people . . ."

"Don't you think I know that?"

At the southwestern most edge of the town, where a residential area jutted out from the town center, Salas raised one hand to stop his driver. Both were afoot; a moving vehicle, even if commandeered civilian and looking the part, was just too obvious.

Behind, the pair could hear the sounds of the battle raging through the town. Overhead, the Tauran Hurricanes still circled like vultures. What concerned Salas, though, was a fairly steady *wopwopwop* coming from the south, ahead.

As Salas faced, from his right a single missile, an Anglian Shooting Star—like almost all the tercio's arms, captured in Balboa—shot up toward the circling Hurricanes. The thing was fast, but not so fast that the Tauran fliers couldn't drop countermeasures and split up. Still, the helicopter that Salas and the driver had heard ahead of them popped up over the wood line from the stream over which it had been sheltering, then moved briskly for the location from which the missile had been launched. At this range, and with its fixed wheels brushing treetops and grass, depending, the helicopter—a Tuscan-built Z921 gunship—was safe from even the best shoulder-fired missiles.

What it was not safe from was the twin-barreled antiaircraft gun—Volgan, by way of Balboa but so common around the planet as to be essentially sterile—that opened up from off to the helicopter's flank.

From where Salas stood, it wasn't clear if the helicopter had taken one of the 23mm shells or if the pilot had been panicked. It didn't make a lot of difference; the chopper dropped in altitude, smacked hard into the ground, rolled with its main rotor splintering and disintegrating, and then blew up in a great ball of black smoke and orange fire.

"Come on," Salas ordered the RTO. "That's our cue to run."

Barkhorn had the Teuton's built-in distaste for *Francs-tireurs*. Thus, the youth of the civilian-clad corpses unceremoniously tossed against the wall of the school to make room for the command post moved him not a bit. Had they surrendered, he'd have shot them out of hand.

*But, then, they* didn't *try to surrender, did they?* thought the Sachsen. *That would be a concern if they were riflemen, but one of them was obviously a clerk of some kind. When clerks fight to the death, it's time to start worrying.*

He spared a moment to examine the rifles the two guerillas had been wielding. *Gallic*, he thought. *Captured, I have no doubt, in Balboa not so very long ago. Ammunition is compatible with ours, so we won't be able to afford losing an engagement or, if we do, we'll be supplying our enemy.*

A tank parked next to the building thundered, the muzzle blast making Barkhorn wince. He'd already received some complaints over the radio that the Hordalanders were endangering his own men. It might be time to rein them in before somebody got hurt.

*The only thing one can be sure of hitting when there's a friendly-fire incident,* thought Barkhorn, *is the front page of the* Altstadter Allgemeine Zeitung. *The treasonous swine.*

Barkhorn's operations officer leaned against a desk. He had a radio handset tucked in between his ear and his shoulder. With his left hand he held a map, while annotating the map with an alcohol pen with his right. Barkhorn took a few steps and looked over the major's shoulder at the map.

*Yes, well go figure that they'd be running away to the south; it's the only route open.* With his own radio, Barkhorn summoned up the Tuscan aviation battalion, the gunships of which were attached to his command. Whoever answered didn't sound familiar and either didn't speak German or didn't want to.

"Anyone here speak Italian?" asked Barkhorn. Unfortunately, no one in the tiny headquarters seemed to.

"Nearest translator is with the sappers, sir" said the operations officer. "Want me to try to work through him?"

"Never mind," said Barkhorn. "Do what you're doing. I'll get the translator with the sappers."

That took some time. The translator with the sappers had all the pertinent codes and frequency-hopping patterns, of course. What he didn't have was them set on his own radio.

"The German speaker with the gunships," so the translator told Barkhorn, "went down. Baited ambush they say. They strongly recommend not using them without some better way to communicate so they don't lose any more. Sir, my recommendation would be don't push it."

*Man, I fucking detest coalition warfare.*

"Right," Barkhorn agreed, though the tone of his voice said he most certainly did *not* agree. "Will the fuckers take a position along the Pelirojo River, facing west, and prevent anyone from escaping?"

After a few moments, the translator came back, answering, "Yes, sir, they'll do that, but it won't do much good."

"Why is that?"

"They say some of the guerillas running away are leaving their arms behind—"

"Yeah, that's the truth," Barkhorn again agreed.

"They say they can't tell the difference between a guerilla and an unarmed civilian and they don't want to be tried for murder if they—"

"Just stop there," said Barkhorn. "I know the rest of this fairy tale."

Barkhorn's operations officer piped in. "It's true though, sir. Tuscany's signed the most restrictive provisions of the Kosmo"—cosmopolitan progressive—"treaty regime. We've got it tough but they are unbelievably tied up."

"Fuck!"

"Fuck or fucked," said Operations, "but speaking of the latter, maybe we should lay off and let them go, sir."

Barkhorn's glare was withering, but his operations officer was loyal enough even to go against his commander. "I'm serious, sir. If there are any civilians mixed in, or anybody the press can claim were civilians, and we kill any of them, the press back home will crucify you. And, for all General Marciano's as good a commander as can be found anywhere in the Tauran Union, he can't protect you. He's a Tuscan and you, and maybe me, too, will not be tried by Tuscany. No, sir; we will be dragged back to Sachsen for our court-martials."

"Shit!" exclaimed Barkhorn. "Oh, all fucking right. Get me the artillery."

### South of Pelirojo, Santa Josefina, Terra Nova

Legate Salas really didn't understand it. Indeed, he'd been halfway to safety before he even noticed it. But the enemy weren't pursuing, not even by fire, not even with aircraft.

*How fucking stupid can they be? Have they never heard of the tenth principle of war, annihilation. If they let us go, we'll be back.*

He thought about that first question and, being a fundamentally fair man, had to concede, *Oh, all right; not so stupid that they didn't run me and mine right out of town. And maybe they never did hear of the tenth principle. Or maybe they just aren't allowed to follow it. I confess, I don't understand it but the Taurans are, by all reports, quite odd when it comes to their militaries.*

Salas and his driver had found it easier walking in the trees that abounded on both sides of the narrow, swift-flowing, south-running river. To both sides he saw ragged knots of his own men, dejected with defeat, slinking away with heads sunk on chests. *Going to be tough to buck the boys up from this one, or at least to restore moral in this cohort. Going to take some thought, and some very careful treading.*

To Salas's left there was a brace of twin 23mm guns, with their crews looking determined as they scanned for Tauran aircraft in range. One of these was certainly the same crew that had taken down the helicopter gunship.

*On the other hand, for some it won't be hard at all.*

*Of course, while the big problem is morale and confidence, those aren't the only problems. We put a lot of mines into the defense of Pelirojo. Those are lost to us now. And, while I have more, I don't have huge numbers. I need to get an organization set up for making mines.*

*I've lost weapons, too, and ammunition. Not least the irreplaceable heavy mortars. I could try to get some dragged in from Balboa, or maybe sailed in.*

*I've got more small arms, mostly cached in the jungle. But those were for expansion, once we had enough prestige to recruit reliably. We've lost a lot of prestige, and we weren't starting with all that much.*

*And, while it's not as bad as the loss of what little prestige we had, we lost position. With Pelirojo in Tauran hands, they can seal off that flank with one battalion, rather than the two they'd have needed with us holding it. That means they're still too strong for the* Tercio la Virgen *to cross over.*

*It could be worse, I guess, but I'm not sure how.*


## Pelirojo, Santa Josefina, Terra Nova

*Could be worse,* thought Barkhorn, sipping a not-too-very-cold beer in the smoking ruins on Pelirojo. *I'm not sure how it could be worse, but my ops officer insists it could.*

The town still smoked in odd places. They'd managed to collect most of the bodies for decent burial, too. Unfortunately, the press had shown up before they could be buried. Between the smashed houses, the scorched public buildings, the bodies, and the civilian clothes on the bodies, the press quickly became convinced that a massacre had taken place. That Tauran casualties had been so low, under thirty dead, only added to that conviction.

It hadn't helped any that—go figure—some genuine civilians had been caught up in the fighting. What really made it awful, though, was when some of the Tuscans sappers and Sachsen infantry had been caught by the press planting firearms on the civilians.

For now, Barkhorn was still in command, despite all the whining from the press for his relief and court-martial. When asked how he expected it to go, the battalion commander had answered, perhaps optimistically, "Fifty-fifty. No better than that."

And then trying to explain to the idiot press that, "No, almost all the rifles captured were Gallic. We are Sachsens, Hordalanders, and Tuscans, and we use different rifles. Moreover, the serial number of every rifle we've captured can be traced to those lost in Balboa, during the recent unpleasantness there."

*And no, you moronic twats, we didn't put the*—oh, ever-so-naughtyevilbadwickedbadbadbad *landmines out*—they *did.* Barkhorn didn't even try to explain that one to the pressies, any more than he bothered to correct them when they included the wrecked medical ambulance, basically an armored personnel carrier, a "tank," in order to drive up the losses they could report. What, after all, would have been the use?

*An atrocity against us gets turned into a victory for those perpetrating the atrocity? Against stupidity, the gods themselves . . .*


### Hotel *Cielo Dorado*, Aserri, Santa Josefina, Terra Nova

A single sheet of paper fluttering in her hands, Lourdes paced frantically from one side of the room to the other. Nominally a bedroom, the hotel had been kind enough—which is to say, well-paid enough—to remove the bed and put in a small conference table.

The doors were closed and guarded by the detachment sent from Fourteenth *Cazadores*. The flanking rooms were occupied by other Balboans of the diplomatic party. Triste had swept the place for bugs, and set up some odd little box he had brought for interfering with electronic devices. He turned on the TV to make sure it was working. When the TV produced a "picture" that looked like nothing so much as a bad LSD trip, he pronounced it safe. At that, Lourdes temporarily stopped her frantic pacing while Esterhazy leaned back in his chair.

"Are Raul and Patricio being stupid?" Lourdes asked of Esterhazy and Triste. "Or am I? The Taurans beat the crap out of our . . . mmm . . . unofficial ambassadors to that *mariposa* Calderón and we go back to the bargaining table? Makes no sense to me, none at all."

"I sense more Parilla than your husband, Lourdes," said Esterhazy. "This smacks of subtlety. Whatever Patricio Carrera is, subtle he is *not*."

"That's not entirely true, Matt," objected Triste. "He can be subtle, when everything else has failed."

"Precisely," Lourdes confirmed. "His preference is never subtlety, any more than it is tact. Not his thing. Sneaky, yes. Subtle?" She shook her head emphatically. "No. And I'm talking here the deepest-seated instincts and emotions you can imagine."

"It may not be that subtle, you know, Lourdes," said Triste. "The Taurans dealt us a pretty bad blow over in Pelirojo. Maybe he just wants to buy time for them to recover."

"That's possible, but I somehow don't think that's it."

"Well, what else could it be?" Esterhazy asked, adding, "I *am* asking because it befuddles me, too."

Lourdes gave him one of those, *Oh, stop being a dumb shit* looks, then realized that she had no grounds for that, since she was just as clueless. Shamefacedly, she hung her head.

"Can I see the message?" asked Esterhazy.

"Oh . . . sure . . . sorry." Lourdes passed the message over, explaining, "It came by courier this morning."

Esterhazy read aloud for Triste's benefit.

"'Dear Lourdes . . . in light of the recent setbacks by our freedom-fighting allies'—*heh, so he's still maintaining the fiction that the* Tercio la Negrita *is something besides an arm of the legion*—'in Santa Josefina, and the strain on our economy here, the president has directed that you and your party return to the negotiating table. You are authorized to offer the Tauran Union an accelerated return of prisoners of war and detained persons, to the tune of twelve per day over the one hundred we have already agreed to and have generally provided, as able. This does not mean we will offer to return those held while talks were in abeyance who would otherwise have been returned. However, as a gesture of grace and mercy, we will return several hundred dependents'—*Hah! That means he has several hundred suitably brainwashed to undermine the TU*—'immediately, even though it will mean allowing the Tauran Union to land aircraft at Herrera International.'"

Esterhazy laid the paper down on the conference table. "Nope, I don't get it either, Lourdes. It's not like it's in our interest to encourage the Taurans to be hard asses, which this is going . . . ummm."

Triste looked up and said, "Oh." Lourdes said, "Oh." Then Esterhazy said, "Oh."

Janier shook his head doubtfully.

"Oh, elder gods, General," said Marguerite, "you've gotten to where you doubt even your doubts."

"*Et dona ferrentes,*" said the Gaul. "I've been led by the nose into a trap before."

"'Et dona ferrentes'?" asked the Zhong empress, Xingzhen. "I've never . . ."

"It's from Virgil's *Aeneid,* dearest," answered Wallenstein. "A shortened version of '*quidquid id est, timeo Danaos et dona ferrentes.*' 'Whatever it is, I fear the Greeks even when bearing gifts.'"

"Never heard of it," answered the empress, though she was lying. Her education as a girl intended to rule the emperor had been most thorough. At Marguerite's arched eyebrow she half-admitted, "Well, I *might* have heard it somewhere."

"I'm serious, Janier," Wallenstein said. "They've got you so hornswoggled you really don't seem to have *any* self-confidence left."

Janier shrugged, sadly. "With them? Probably not, or none that I can find inside myself, anyway. It's a hard thing, you know, High

Admiral, to have every self-delusion stripped away so suddenly . . . and so violently."

"General," asked Xingzhen, "are you an educated man?"

"I confess," said Janier, "my education has been somewhat narrowly focused."

"Well . . . back on old Earth, way in the dim mists of time, there was a king named, 'Alfred,' in the place the Anglians came from. Alfred wasn't even really supposed to *be* the king, but he ended up as king anyway.

"He was in a war with the people from whom this planet's Cimbrians derived. And poor Alfred"—the empress shook her head, pityingly—"kept losing.

"Sometimes, as with you, his enemies defeated or stymied him when he was not there. Sometimes, also as with you, they did the same when he was present. He began, one suspects, to count ties as victories . . . or even to count losses that were less than total as victories."

"I fail to see—"

"Never interrupt an empress," Xingzhen cut him off. "The point is that with each defeat, Alfred learned something. With each frustration, he found out something new about his enemies. The day finally came, after all those defeats, when he turned the tables. He had learned. After that he could not be beaten on land or even at sea, even though his enemies were a great seafaring people.

"And Alfred also became the first and only king among his people to be called, 'the Great.'

"The short version of which, General, is snap out of it. You have a job to do."

# CHAPTER EIGHTEEN

> Do you have the patience to wait until your mud
> settles and the water is clear?
> —Lao Tzu, *Tao Te Ching*

**Combat Information Center, BdL *Dos Lindas*,
*Mar Furioso*, Terra Nova**

This far down, Fosa could barely feel aircraft taking off and leaving, and that only sometimes. He could not, of course, see them. CIC was the second most well-protected part of the *Dos Lindas,* after sick bay. He found he spent more time down here now than up in the island. His chief of the air wing could handle air operations well enough. He needed to be down here when the threat was finally revealed.

Archangel, the Volgan submarine tracking system, had, like its Federated States counterpart, been designed for an earlier day and noisier submarines. The Zhong subs, being nuclear, were inherently noisier than diesel electric boats or air independent boats. But they weren't all that noisy, hence the continuing inability of the passive system to confirm the presence and exact location of more than two at any given time, which two disappeared regularly amidst the clutter on the ocean floor. Oh, Archangel could pick up more hints than that, but whether those were real, echoes, shadows, or big, bloody carnivorous fish . . . well, without something extra, who could say?

They did have something extra though. Among the other things the legion had done in preparing their defenses, they'd used a variant on an old technique for fortress artillery, the acoustical survey. By this method, through setting off explosions at sea, they'd managed to map the ocean floor to a considerable degree of accuracy. Since they had it so accurately mapped, they were also able to employ an old technique, "SOFAR," Sound Fixing And Ranging. This was also a double entendre. The short version of all that was that, by this point, they could set off a couple of booms of a given size at a couple of known points and have some chance of finding any new anomalies off shore. It was an imperfect system, given the vagaries of wind and wave, especially under littoral conditions. It was also fairly unlikely to spot a sub in any number of places along the ocean floor.

On the other hand, given the limited number of targets out there, the system at least gave Fosa some idea of where to look. Though, even with the training wing aboard the other "carrier," the stationary BdEL1, he really didn't have enough aircraft for the search mission. This was so, even in the near and constricted waters.

That said, if he happened to find one of the Zhong subs, he had enough to rain death upon it. In total, Fosa's aviation assets ran to forty Yakamov YA-72 helicopters, ten of them equipped for antisubmarine work, the rest perfectly capable of carrying light torpedoes, plus another sixty fixed-wing aircraft, twenty-four for attack and thirty-six for recon, though not all of those were available at any given time. Indeed, the number of aircraft available had been dropping slowly but steadily for a while now. It was beginning to worry him, too.

The attack birds—Turbo-finches—could also carry torpedoes. The ones they did carry were light ones—strictly for antisubmarine work, basically depth charges with attitude—because Balboa didn't have anything really except for fairly heavy antiship torpedoes and rather light, antisubmarine ones. Still, if medium had existed, something under two tons, say, in the Balboan inventory, they could have been carried. The 'Finches could also carry substantial depth charges both in number and power. A few of them were on standby with mine pods slung underneath. There was a large number of concrete training "bombs" lined up, too, more or less as an afterthought, since one never really knew what might work . . . and because they were available in plenty. Meanwhile the recon aircraft, modified Crickets, were kept pretty busy keeping sonar buoys out there, for the ASW Yakamovs to track.

Sometimes, Fosa thought he knew where as many as four of the five submarines were. Unfortunately, since one of those was a de facto hidden ally, the Yamatan, he couldn't do a damned thing with the knowledge since he couldn't tell who was who.

"Get me Fernandez on the secure link again," he said. "I'll take it in my day cabin."

"Yes, Rod," said Fernandez, before Fosa even had a chance to ask. "The Yamatans agreed—you know how they are; without ever admitting anything—to remove their sub, and, by the way, we're 'very welcome.' But their sub, which, of course, is a figment of our imaginations, is on a fixed schedule to check in, and the time's not up yet. Or wouldn't be up, if, in fact, there were a Yamatan submarine off our coast, which, of course, there is not."

Fosa sighed. Yeah, he knew the Yamatans. Not for the first time he felt a wave of grief wash over him for his mentor in naval warfare, Tadeo Kurita, whose mortal remains—an outline of a small man waving a sword—had been flash burned into the hull of his ship. The sword, his family's ancient heirloom, from Old Earth, itself, was welded to the hull. Both were protected by a frame of steel and thick sheets of polycarbonate. Barring a direct hit on them with something substantial, the ship would go down before the shadow or the sword were lost.

It was the holiest place on a ship all the crew considered holy. It was the final stop on every new shipmate's tour of the vessel.

Before Fosa quite managed to formulate an answer, there was a knock on the hatch to his day cabin.

"Come in," he ordered.

"Sir, message from Archangel." The rating handed the sheet over.

Fosa read and said, "Crap!"

"What is it, Rod?" asked Fernandez.

"There are," answered Fosa, "apparently six subs out there now."

Fernandez coughed in surprise. "Unless the Yamatans have two on station—and I'm sure they have made a point to deny there were two when I suggested one—there's really only one other good probability of just who that sixth sub is."

"Yeah, I know," said Fosa. "May as well tell the Yamatans to stick around; the Federated States Navy is here. And, unless they're forthcoming as to why very quickly, I am starting the *classis* to Santa Josefina."

"Nah, Rod, let's get rid of our problems as we can. And turning tail is premature. I'll have the foreign service folks ask the FSC's ambassador," said Fernandez, "but you can't count on the FSN keeping their diplomats informed when subs are at issue."

"All right, I'll hang on a bit longer. But I can't wait forever."

"You could try spooking the Zhong, you know," suggested Fernandez. "The key, though, especially if the FSC is observing, is to get the Zhong to fire first. Never mind if they fire because we've put them in an impossible position; the ruling Progressive Party, down south, will only care about who shot first."

"Yes, Omar; now go teach your mother to suck eggs. I *know* that's the intention. Getting them to do it is the tricky part."

## Zhong Submarine *Mao Zedong, Mar Furioso,* north of the *Isla Real,* Terra Nova

About forty-three miles north of the *Isla Real* there was an east-west-running underwater ridge. Just south of that was a not inconsiderable trench. South of the trench rose an escarpment beyond which the ocean floor leveled off. It was there, over the ridge, that Captain Liu turned to port, or east, and brought his boat above its lowest and quietest speed. He proceeded ahead some twenty-eight thousand yards, then stopped. He let his passive sonar and nav people figure out precisely where he was. Then he took on a bit of ballast and let his boat sink, using the planes to glide to the northern side of the ridge. He trimmed his tanks for as near-to-perfect neutral buoyancy as could be obtained, then waited there, stationary and as quiet as a nuke boat could be, for a full six hours, just to see if anyone would show up to play. When no one did, Liu executed a supremely slow one-eighty until his boat was aimed due west. He moved west then, still as slowly as possible, for eighteen thousand yards, then turned south and came to a complete stop. There, he took on a little ballast—just a tad—and let his boat sink very gently almost to the sea floor.

Liu could hear the enemy fleet, roughly halfway between the escarpment and the big island that was Objective One for the invasion fleet, when it arrived. It was hard not to hear them. Apparently they'd been listening to someone who'd told them that the days of purely passive sonar were over, because at least one of their ships was pinging like mad. He could only hope that if they'd tracked his approach, he'd lost them when he dropped below the ridge.

Despite the active pinging, the Balboans apparently hadn't quite given up on passive means. Over the course of the next three hours, a double row of sonar buoys was laid over the trench. Their distinctive *plonks* were plotted on the chart in the con, along with estimates of their endurance.

"Do they know we're here, Captain?" Liu's chief of boat had asked.

The captain shook his head and answered, "I don't think so. We don't make much nose, albeit more than a diesel electric or AIP. We're behind the ridge. We're under the layer." He shook his head more emphatically. "No, I don't think so."

The chief of boat was skeptical. "Then why put out that double row of passive sonar buoys, sir?"

"It's just a logical place *to* put them."

"Skipper," said Sonar, "we've got an unidentified submarine, I make it a Yamatan Teruzuki class, exiting the area at very high speed."

"Show me a plot," Liu ordered. The presumptively Yamatan sub, its course, depth, and speed, appeared on the plotting table.

"Why did they leave so quickly?" asked Liu.

His exec had the answer. "They were near the surface . . . near enough for communications back to home. They were probably ordered out of the area. As to why . . . ?"

"Yamato and Balboa are thick as thieves," said Liu. "Have been for years. If they've been tracking us—and that's the way to bet it—they've been doing so on Balboa's behalf. If they left in a hurry . . . it's likely because the Balboans wanted them out of the area so they could go hot on our asses."

**FSS *Oliver Rogers*, *Mar Furioso*, Terra Nova**

That there was both a Federates States Navy submarine and a Balboan coastal defense artillery battery both named for the same man was a source of considerable amusement to those who were aware of it.

"No question, sir, that was Akizuki, turning tail in decidedly *un*Yamatan fashion."

The *Rogers* had been tracking the Zhong undersea flotilla since they'd left the Sea of Hangkuk. The Yamatan was harder; indeed, they hadn't known about it until it stopped off at an FSN base in the *Mar Furioso* for replenishment. Since then, they'd been tracking it, too. Though they hadn't been privy to the conversations, they'd seen every time the *Akizuki* had come up to communicate with home, every time it had voided waste, and every change in course.

"Why?" asked *Oliver*'s skipper, Meredith.

"Best, guess, Skipper," offered Intel, "is that they've been warned the Balboans are about to engage and to get the hell out of the area. You just don't see Yamatans turn tail and run unless someone tells them to.

"Ummm . . . Skipper," added Intel, "maybe we should assume they know something we don't and follow their example."

"Awfully tempting," said the captain, "but doesn't fit our orders. Any chance that home didn't note that Yamatan leaving the area?"

"None, Captain. Looks like they deliberately gave it away."

"Okay, base can make the decision about what to do then. For us, we sit here, observe, and report."


**Kurita Memorial, BdL *Dos Lindas*, *Mar Furioso*, Terra Nova**

The gun deck had been repaired. Rather, the old one had been cut away, except for a lip to provide a decent weld. The replacement had been obtained by removing a twin 40mm, mount, and platform from the BdEL1 and welding the latter to the lip. No one, of course, touched the steel that was Tadeo Kurita.

Fosa sometimes came here to think . . . or just to reminisce. For the nonce, he sat in the trainer's seat, to the right side of the gun, nearest Kurita's shadow, with his arms folded over the trainer's handwheel and his chin resting on his arms. Fosa thought long and hard about the next step; how to get the bloody Zhong to fire the first shot, without at the same time also firing the last shots at sea, with his fleet somewhere under the sea when the smoke cleared.

*I've got eight of the thirteen Meg boats available, the other five being scattered at various spots along the Shimmering Sea. When number fourteen finishes its shakedown I get that one, too. Though it won't really be any good that quickly. Of the ones I have, they've limited endurance and are hard as hell on the crews, so at any given time I've got four or five available: One replenishing, sometimes two, one in transit, coming, and one in transit, going. I could push them harder but that will leave them weak when I really have to push them harder.*

*I could send the Megs north and have them sweep the escarpment, trench, and ridge. They're the quietest things around, at least in glide mode. And they're unusually resistant to detection with active sonar, too, what with the smooth plastic hulls and the cones and pyramids that connect the inner hull with the outer.*

*Okay, so let's suppose I can do that and that the Megs can find the Zhong hunter-killer boats; does that get me much? Probably not. At the first sign we're on them the Zhong take off and the Megs have neither the speed nor the endurance to keep up. Then, too, there's no way for me to really control them, and they can't tell me what they've found or not found. They can't even do a maneuver to let me know since I can't detect them for beans, either.*

*I fucking told Patricio we needed something that can track subs from above, without risking a major combatant . . . something like those drone boats the FSN has. But would he listen? Nooo!*

*Odds of a Meg being able to take on a Zhong Dynasty class? Not good. Our successes so far were against, on the one hand, a Gaul who probably had no idea the things were even armed, and, on the other, a warship that had no clue it might be engaged. Most modern Zhong subs around? Megs having sonar taken off Volgan boats of the old generation? No surprise? No fucking way. Or, at least, no certain fucking way.*

*Well . . . we want them to shoot first or, at least, for it to appear that they've shot first. What if I send the Megs out to hunt, and put one or two really fast surface ships, one or two of the Lycosa class corvettes, to search along the ridge and escarpment in as threatening a manner as possible. If the Zhong open fire the Lycosas have a fair chance of outrunning a torpedo or diverting it or simply outmaneuvering it.*

*What if they don't fire?*

Fosa grappled with that for no little time until he had a truly wicked idea. *If one of the Megs can find even one of the Zhongs, the Meg can fire at the Lycosa from very close to the Zhong. To the FSC, that will look like the Zhong shot first.*

*Ah, no . . . the problem there is that the FSN, the state-of-the-art as far as navies go, might see the Meg, despite gliding and despite the plastic, the cones, and the pyramids.*

*Or maybe . . . and then, too, a little distraction might help.*

Fosa stood up and grabbed the sound-powered phone affixed to the hull behind the gun. "Get me the following people, in CIC, in four hours, for orders . . . yes, yes . . . use the Gertrude to get all the Meg skippers up. And connect me to Carrera."

*Because this requires authorization higher than my own.*

### *Submarino de la Legion 1, Megalodon, Mar Furioso,* Terra Nova

They'd worked most of the night; the crew were half exhausted. Even so, it was the most experienced crew the *classis* had.

*Would have been worse,* thought the skipper, Captain Chu, *except that both the other boats on rest and replenish back at the pens kicked in to help. Well, they could afford to; they don't do a damned thing, hardly, until we accomplish our mission or fail to. They've got their boats tied up to the docks inside the big island's south coast, and, no doubt, themselves racked out in bunks.*

Chu's mission was to find the sixth submarine, or, rather, the fifth, now that the Yamatan had taken off. But it wasn't enough just to find it. They had to find it without being spotted themselves, and they had to do it in such a way as to be absolutely *sure* the gringos hadn't seen them. Moreover, they had to do all that in such an obvious way that the FSN *would* see them if they were at all detectable.

He and his crew had been trained by Volgans and Yamatans, good men, good submariners, all with that requisite touch of the pirate, to boot. But one thing he'd taken away from his training was a vast respect for the FSN, generally, and its own submariners, in particular. The Volgans and Yamatans made no bones about it; they were the class of this world.

"I don't think they're better men than we are," a Volgan had once told Chu, "but they are very damned good men in boats we can only sigh with envy at, with technology in those boats we don't even know enough about to sigh over."

The Yamatans, who worked with the FSN on very friendly terms, were at least as profound in their praises.

There were deep mine barrages laid east and west of the island. A small area had been left, between the *Isla Real* and the *Isla San Juan*, which was unmined. Sure, an enemy ship could pass through the same gap. And be engaged by rifles, machine guns, tank cannon, mortars, heavy artillery, torpedoes . . . no, the gap wasn't a weakness in the defense, any more than any fortress with a sally port considered that sally port a weakness.

Chu's boat, the *Meg*, passed through the gap on the surface by night, with the Leaping Maiden smiling down on it and the faint glow from the moon, Hecate, in its final quarter glowing above. There were plenty of fixed lights to guide them through. Once past the *Isla Real-Isla San Juan* gap, the *Meg* had continued almost due north, with its clicker going at normal speed.

The clicker was a trick developed by OZ, *Obras Zorilleras*, the legion's research and development arm. The idea was that as long as an enemy thought they could track a Meg class easily, they wouldn't try looking for better ways to track one. The clicker—each one in each boat, each just a little different—simulated a badly cut gear, giving off, as such gears would, a steady *clickclickclick* that varied with the speed of the boat. The very latest boat, the one not yet ready for service, had three clickers on it, to simulate several badly cut gears, as one might expect under wartimes pressures.

In practice, the clicker was used to let an enemy know exactly where a Meg was. Then, when it was cut off and the boat moved off under its rather quiet jet pump, or by gliding, none but the crew would be any the wiser.

On the other hand, the clicker had been used twice already. It was possible that either the FSN or Zhong Navy, or both, were familiar with it and would not be fooled.

With the islands behind them, Chu gave the orders to dive, descending down into the pressure hull himself after dogging the hatch behind him. Coolant surged through tubes running through the rubbers inside the ballast tanks, chilling the ammonia inside the rubbers.

The *Meg* had an odd—really a unique—method of flooding and

evacuating its ballast tanks. Like the pressure hull, these were cylindrical. Basically, the boat took advantage of the very low boiling temperature of ammonia. The ammonia was kept inside flexible tubing made of fluorocarbon elastomer with a seven-hundred-and-fifty-angstrom thick layer of sputtered aluminum, followed by a five hundred angstrom layer of silicon monoxide with an aerogel insulation layer. Heating elements inside the tubes—called "rubbers" by the sailors and designers, both—heated the ammonia into a gas, which expanded the "rubbers" and forced out the water. To dive, the ammonia was allowed to chill to a liquid rather than heated to a gas. Chilling was really only a factor when quite near the surface, and then only if the water was warm. It was, of course, warm here and now, hence the provision of refrigerant.

It was slightly quieter to dive than to rise, since the boiling of the ammonia made more sound than its condensing.

As originally conceived, the Meg-class SSKs were intended to carry up to five, but more typically three, Volgan supercavitating torpedoes, each. They'd gotten kills against the Gallic Navy using those. But, on reflection, the *classis* had come to the sober, and sobering, conclusion that those kills had been flukes, that the Gauls had just panicked at finding subs that weren't even supposed to be armed, armed with something approaching state of the art, or what was believed to be state-of-the-art.

The key to getting rid of most of the supercavitators had been the Gallic captain, the skipper of The Gallic Navy's Destroyer 466, the *Portzmoguer*. He was the Gaul who had not been surprised and had not panicked. And he had survived as, reasonably, one would expect any skipper to survive who was neither surprised nor panicked.

The problems with the supercavitators were probably not surmountable short of mounting nuclear weapons on them. They operated in a very noisy, self-created bubble. This ruled out sonar while travelling, and did nothing good for wake homing. They moved very quickly, spewing hot gasses out their rear. This meant there could be no wire or fiber-optic guidance. The noise they created lasted for a longish period even after they stopped to reacquire a target. This screwed with their on-board sonar. Electromagnetic sensing from a torpedo was too short ranged to be useful.

The one good thing that could be said of them was that some of the potential targets may not have worked out the proper solution to them, or may have believed Volgan (or Sachsen) marketing propaganda about them. This wasn't enough of a chance to base one's fighting load around. Thus, the supercavitators, all but one per sub, had come out and been replaced by Volgan super-heavy sixty-five-centimeter torpedoes. The bulk of the load remained the twenty-one inchers, with a smattering of twelve-and-three-quarter-inch defensive, which is to say, antitorpedo, torpedoes, developed by a consortium composed of *Obras Zorilleras,* Yamato Celestial Armaments, and a Volgan concern that was effectively an arm of their government.

"Skipper," announced Nav, "past phase line Zulu."

"Kill the clicker," ordered Chu. "Bring us down to seventy-five meters."

# CHAPTER NINETEEN

The most complete and happy victory is this, to compel one's enemy to give up his purpose while suffering no harm oneself.

—Belisarius

### Combat Information Center, BdL *Dos Lindas,* *Mar Furioso,* Terra Nova

A rating set a cup of coffee down in the slot on Fosa's command chair, then backed away hastily and scurried for safer pastures. The commander of the *classis* was in a vile mood and nobody really seemed to know why.

Aboard the carrier, they'd worked out a trick of sorts between Chu's *Megalodon,* the two corvettes, the *Jaquelina Gonzalez* (ship's motto, "A whore, yes, but *our* whore."), the recently christened *Inez Trujillo* (ship's motto, "Follow me, you cunts."), and Archangel.

It was supposed to work like this: Archangel—which had, at best, only poor plots for the submarines, given the escarpment, trench, and ridge, plus the fact that they weren't moving much—would give best-guess center of mass coordinates to the two corvettes. These would move toward those coordinates, actively pinging, then turn around and take a back azimuth, then repeat. *Megalodon,* with its towed array behind it, would take those azimuths and draw out where they intersected. Those intersections would be the center of mass of

249

possible submarine activity. *Meg* with its clicker turned off, would then move there, and measure, and listen, and determine if there was a Zhong or FSN submarine there.

The direction program was to start in the east and work west. Moreover, after each set of azimuths had been "broadcast," the corvettes would go to a set point and enter a period of at least twenty-five minutes' physical inactivity, this being a sort of period, a punctuation mark, added to the statement, "they might be there." It would also give the *Meg* two sources from which it could triangulate its own position without having to surface, as a backup for their inertial navigation which was, at best, second rate.

The nice thing about it was that no surface ship or submarine had to use its underwater telephone, or Gertrude. This was expected to serve to keep both FSN and Zhong in the dark about *Meg*'s activities. The bad part was that other than the simple information already arranged, nothing else could be sent by those methods. On the other hand, for real emergencies, the Gertrude was still there.

In addition, the Yakamov YA-72s would continue laying passive sonar buoys and actively dipping. There was also to be a special trick for the Zhong and FSN, both, a kind of deception and distraction operation. 'Finches were lined up on the airfield on the island for just that trick.

The real problem for Fosa, then, was half intellectual and half emotional. When Chu turned off his clicker, *Meg* went invisible. One second it was there, happily clicking away, and easily loud enough for Archangel to pick it up with precision. The next the pump jets were cut to next to nothing, the ammonia had silently condensed, and the thing was gliding along with just enough push from the pumps to keep from stalling.

Maybe if there'd still been something to do besides wait, but, no, after air, ship, and base crews had worked all night, everything was pretty much ready.

Fosa sipped at the coffee, fuming inside, *I can't see a goddamned thing or say a goddamned useful word to influence this any more than I have. I'm powerless and I fucking hate it.*

*Ah, screw it. I'm going topside to do a little leadership by walking around.*

★★★

Fosa stopped at deck level and went out onto the flight deck through an oval hatchway. He stopped for a moment and watched a Cricket, a light recon plane with an extraordinarily short take off run, bounce twice down the deck, and seemingly leap into the air. There were two men inside the Cricket, one to drop lightweight mini-Athaliah sonar buoys over the side.

For now, as far as Fosa could see, the forward parts of the flight deck were the domain of the Crickets. He turned aft to where nine of his dozen Turbo-finches were lined up, two-two-three-two. Deck crews worked on jacking up ordnance, all practice, onto each of the 'Finch's thirteen hard points. The square elevator whined behind him. Fosa turned to see a tenth Turbo-finch emerge from the hangar deck. A dozen men, including the pilot, physically manhandled the plane over and around to make the first row go from two to three.

Between the domain of the Crickets and the domain of the attack aircraft, there was a space given over to the comings and goings of the YA-72s. For the most part these—maintenance hogs, every one—were struck below. Still, the ASW versions were getting a steady workout, while some of the maintenance crew were reconfiguring the non-ASW Yakamovs for ASW work.


## UEPF *Spirit of Peace*, in orbit over Terra Nova

There were any number of ways to detect, albeit imperfectly, submarines from space. More of those ways were available to the Federated States and Tauran Union than were available to the United Earth Peace Fleet. What the UEPF had were repurposed whale, shark, and school of fish detection systems, dating back to the days when Old Earth had been concerned with Terra Nova's ecology more than with the barbarians from Terra Nova breaking free and changing Earth's domestic political arrangements. To say nothing of looting the place and burning it to a cinder.

Thus, for example, Commander Khan, the husband, was able to track *Meg* nicely on a feed sent from UEPF *Spirit of Harmony*, in orbit over Balboa . . . right up until the *Meg* slid below fifty meters, at which point it didn't give off enough heat nor, being on the small end for subs, create enough disturbance to be noticeable, especially given jet pumps and gliding. Nor was synthetic aperture radar worth a damn at that range and to those depths. And using lasers was likely to garner unwanted attention from the Federated States, something devoutly to be avoided.

The primary method of submarine detection below, acoustic, was completely outside of the UEPF's capability, barring only a limited capability on Atlantis Base.

Khan didn't worry about it overmuch, anyway. The Balboan submarines were reputed to be very noisy. Surely the Zhong could keep track of the one that had, like a ghost, just faded away and disappeared off of *Peace*'s screens.

Still, he sent what he had to the Tauran Union and Zhong navies. Maybe one of those could get some use of it.

In fact, the TU's sailors would have gotten nothing from the information. But the Zhong submarines could have, if the information had gotten to them in a timely fashion. This was, of course, impossible, as it was impossible for the FSN's *Oliver Rogers,* albeit for different reasons. But a key piece of information, there to be seen from the time stamps, was that the *Meg* continued to move *after* the clicking stopped, and still at a speed greater than the gliding alone could quite account for.

### *Submarino de la Legion 1, Megalodon, Mar Furioso,* Terra Nova

The submarine had gone about two hundred and fifty meters north of the escarpment when Chu ordered, "Make your depth one hundred and twenty meters."

"Aye, Captain," answered Junior Warrant Huerta, a new submariner, still under instruction. "One twenty—one two zero—meters."

The sailor at the diving station responded, "Make my depth one hundred and twenty meters, aye, sir." The one beside him checked his panel and announced, "Rubbers are collapsed; no chilling needed, ready to apply minimal heat to maintain neutral buoyancy." A third along the same bank said, "Helm, fifteen degrees down angle on planes. Making my depth one hundred and twenty meters."

The exec said, without facing Chu, "Forward group admitting ballast, Captain . . . aft group admitting ballast."

The boat nosed over and slid silently into the trench until it reached the ordered depth. At that point Chu ordered a heading change to sweep the north side of the escarpment all the way to where it ended, with the towed array deployed and the magnetic anomaly detector searching for the enemy, as well as for the neutral FSN boat. Speed was fairly slow, though not as slow as they'd adopt when the intersection of *Trujillo*'s and *Gonzalez*'s sonar runs said a sub was probably near. Still this was probably going to take a couple of days.

Huerto turned around and bent his head slightly. "Skipper, if I may ask . . . ?"

"Go ahead."

"Why here?"

"I'm giving the Zhong the benefit of the doubt, assuming that they'll take advantage of the . . . of the ground, so to speak . . . and take cover behind the escarpment."

"And they won't hear us?"

"Doubt they have their towed arrays out, or that they'll deploy them until they hear a clicker making for open water. And, yes, Huerta, before you ask, it's a risk."

"Okay, Skipper. Just curious. . . . Skipper, why just us? We could do it in half the time if there'd been two of us, one to sweep east, one west."

"Friendly-fire issues," answered Chu, "those, and paranoia on the part of the enemy issues, coupled with it was just too much of a pain in the ass to try to coordinate the corvettes' directional runs. We thought about it, yes."

"Oh."

"And one other thing, just to put your mind at ease, Huerta."

"Yes, Skipper."

"The air wing's going to start distracting them here real soon now. And when it comes time for the major show, there'll be two out here. But they won't, as we've had to, be going in blind because we'll have pathfindered the way for them."

**Zhong Submarine *Mao Zedong, Mar Furioso,* north of the *Isla Real,*
Terra Nova**

Captain Liu leaned back in his chair, calmly reading the *Analects*. It
was one among a number of traditional works that enjoyed special
status in Zhong society. A seaman showed up at the captain's open
door, bowed as deeply as the cramped space would permit, and said,
"Sir, sonar has something weird. The watch officer requests your
presence on . . ."

The seaman never quite finished, as Liu had the book closed on
"weird," and was pushing past the seaman on "presence."

The watch officer was an up-and-comer, well-connected at the
imperial palace. Somewhat to Captain Liu's surprise, Senior
Lieutenant Kuang had actually proven to be—if a little too elegant for
comfort—also intelligent, competent, and diligent.

*Who would have expected this from the bowels of the imperial
hierarchy?* The captain had wondered. *Is nothing sacred? Is there
nothing we can depend on?*

"Captain," said Kuang, pointing to the plotting table, "we've had
three . . . *plonks.* Not quite overhead. Here, here, and here, sir."

Liu refrained from asking if there were any ships nearby to account
for the plonks. The plotting table showed there were not.

"Aerially dropped somethings, of course," judged Liu, "but what?"

"They hit the water like bombs, Captain," Sonar said. "But . . . no
booms? If they were bombs, there should have been a sea-shaking
kaboom."

"Mines?" asked Liu.

"It's possible, of course, sir," said Kuang. "But one expects a
pattern with mines or destructors. There was no pattern here."

"No pattern *yet*," Liu corrected.

"Yes, of course you are right, sir. Not *yet*. Should we change
position?"

Liu looked as the chart again, noted again that *Mao Zedong* was in
a cut in the escarpment, as good a position as one might hope for, then
answered, "No. I think that's what they're trying, to spook us out of

our position. But this is too good a spot to give up lightly. No . . . we stay here for now."

"Yes, sir," said Kuang, doubtfully.

### FSS *Oliver Rogers, Mar Furioso,* Terra Nova

The *Rogers* had three huge advantages over the Zhong Dynasty-class boats. One was the sheer sophistication and power of its sonar. Nothing else could match it. Another was its own quietness, which allowed it to take full advantage of its sonar. The third was a crew, to include the sonarmen, of exceptional experience and ability.

"It was a big fucking rock, Skipper," said Sonarman Lester. "Or concrete. Rather they all were. And all were inert, in any case."

Meredith asked, "How can you tell?"

"Combination of things, sir. One, the sound it made entering the water. Streamlined, yes, but not quite like a bomb or mine or destructor. Metal is different from rock is different from metal with explosive inside. Another, density, which affected the speed at which it fell. It fell with the speed of a rock. Third, the sound it made when it hit bottom. Not sure how to explain it except as being 'dead,' sir. Like a rock. But, since nobody is likely to go to the trouble of carving a rock to sound like a bomb, I'm going with cast concrete."

"Trying to scare off the Zhong then," the captain said.

"Intel analysis and estimates are above my rating, Skipper. I can say it wasn't anything live. And I can say they're not getting close enough to the Zhong to really scare off anybody."

"Certain?" asked the captain, with his left eyebrow raised.

"Oh, c'mon, sir; you know nothing's a hundred percent in this. But I'm pretty sure."

"We'll go with it then. Log it in as Balboa trying to tell the Zhong to leave its waters, *nonviolently.*"

### Combat Information Center, BdL *Dos Lindas, Mar Furioso,* Terra Nova

Once again, the ship shuddered slightly as a concrete practice bomb-laden Turbo-finch lifted off from the flight deck, followed by another, similarly "armed." Between them they carried twenty-six fake bombs, which ought at the bare minimum catch and keep the Zhong's attention.

Fosa was in tune enough with his ship to feel the take offs, slightly, though it wasn't necessary that he do so; the intercom system announced it, after all.

Not for the first time, Fosa was wracked with doubts. They were dropping the practice dummies on a fixed schedule. Would *Meg* be able to keep to the schedule? Would it matter if not? Was it better if they could and did or better if they couldn't and didn't?

*The only thing I can be reasonably certain of is that* Meg's *still alive.*

### Submarino de la Legion 1, Megalodon, Mar Furioso

The offset dummy bombing also served to help *Meg* navigate to where it was believed the Zhong subs lay. It was preplanned, each probable position—some behind the escarpment, others behind the ridge— would be dummy bombed with an offset of one thousand yards, though the direction of offset varied so as not to look too obvious. Chu had the table of variances.

This close, and with enough water under the keel to permit it, Chu cut the engines to almost nothing, allowed more of the ammonia in the rubbers to liquefy, and glided past the first probable location. And . . .

"MAD says she's there, sir. About eight thousand tons. Probably was degaussed before leaving port but picked up a charge on the voyage over. Nuke boat, but not of the newest or the best. I make her as a Zhong Dynasty class."

"Note it," Chu ordered. "Get the position. Put it in the burst message we'll send when done."

Thought the captain, *God, I love being in a plastic submarine, with air independent propulsion, and nearly no moving parts.*

While there were a few bunks in a separate compartment, the sub really wasn't designed around them. The crew, except for the black gang, stayed up in a common compartment in chairs that had cost, as far as Carrera and the Senate were concerned, way too much. These folded back to allow the crew to sleep at their stations. Some of the stations, on the other hand, were paired so that one man could watch over two functions.

Chu alternated watches with Huerta. The others stood, or, rather, sat, their watches. When neither on duty nor asleep, they interspersed the long periods of boredom with food—nothing special there, just normal legionary rations—video games, with the sound effects fed to headphones, or reading. The games and the library were both accessible from digital readers every man had. Some just stared at the main screen where the computer did its best to estimate the watery terrain ahead.

At each probable or possible contact point, PROBSUB or POSSUB, in the vernacular, the entire crew went to battle stations, as the *Meg* began its gentle roller-coastering, on planes and ballast tanks, with minimal shove from the jet pumps. Sometimes they left a Zhong behind with the classification, CERTSUB. More often, they had to call it a NONSUB. They never did find all four expected Zhong boats. One of them was simply not there along the escarpment. Neither was it in the trench or behind the ridge.

All those other subs were important, but for what the *classis* needed to do the key piece of information remained, could a presumptively top-notch submarine from the Federated States Navy spot a Meg class.

Trailing its towed array, *Meg* searched east and west, north and south.

"Nada!" cursed Chu. "Bring us around again. Nav, are we over that last plot?"

"The two corvettes are still marking this as the spot, yes, Captain."

Auletti, the sonarman, cocked his head slightly, then pressed his headphones tight to his head. He took one hand off the headphones to turn a couple of dials and punch a few commands into his console.

"Well, I'll be fucked. Captain? Ummm . . . Skipper?"

"What is it, Auletti?"

"We've been looking in the wrong direction." The sailor pointed straight up. "We're under them. Eight thousand tons and *no* magnetic signature to speak of. Quiet nuke. That's the FSN."

Chu smiled. "And they didn't see us. Excellent."

"Assume heading, due north," ordered Chu, and the sub duly swung around and moved off, leaving escarpment, trench, and ridge behind. At a point about two hundred statute miles north of *Ciudad Balboa*, Chu brought the *Meg* up to just below surface level, let up an antenna buoy, and sent a very brief, encrypted radio message.

### Combat Information Center, BdL *Dos Lindas*, *Mar Furioso*, Terra Nova

*Now* Fosa had some work to do. From aboard the *Dos Lindas*, to the flight deck of the *Barco del Entrenamiento Legionario Numero Uno*, to the airfields at the tadpole's tail of the *Isla Real*, to the sub pens on the south side of the island, to the SSKs already under the *classis*, and the corvettes on picket duty, sailors sprang into action.

First to set off were the two Megalodon-class submarines that had been refitting in the sub pens. They followed much the same route as had Captain Chu, out the "sally port" between the islands, north to the escarpment, down into the trench, and then east or west to take up positions *right* behind two of the Zhong subs that had been positively identified. That took the better part of a day.

When the day was up, *Jaquelina Gonzalez* and *Inez Trujillo*, both of which had been playing navigation aid, took a far more aggressive posture. They *knew* where the Zhong were and, even if they couldn't pick them up well amidst the clutter, the fact that they pressed close would likely make the Zhong think they could.

And they *did* press close with their active sonar. Close enough to drive the Zhong beneath them half-mad with nervous anxiety. Then they'd switch off and go for a different one. Then back again . . . and reverse again . . . and, finally, pull back toward the island.

That was when SdL Nine, *Esox*, floating behind and rather below the Zhong Submarine, *Mao Zedong*, fired one torpedo . . . at the Lycosa-class corvette, *Jaquelina Gonzalez*.

# CHAPTER TWENTY

There is a touch of the pirate about every man who
wears the dolphin's badge.
—Commander Jeff Tall, Royal Navy

### SdL 9, *Esox*, *Mar Furioso*, Terra Nova

Even though it was in the Zhong's blind spot, the sub had maintained
its position, once arrived, entirely by manipulating the heat in the
rubbers. Then the captain had let the clock tick down until . . .

"Fire control. Firing solution is ready. Torpedoes are ready."

"Shoot!"

"Unit One away. Running straight and normal. Good wire."

Upon firing, *Esox* killed the juice to the rubbers, which killed the
heat, letting the gas condense. Whatever tiny noise the liquefaction
might have made was covered by the almost immediate movement of
the Zhong sub. While that one took off to the east, *Esox* sank directly
down.

*Esox* also kept control of the fifty-three-centimeter torpedo it had
fired via a pair of wires that trailed out behind the torpedo. It just
wouldn't do to actually *hit* the *Jaquelina Gonzalez.* There would be, the
captain was certain, all kinds of paperwork from something like that.

"But we do have to make it look good," the skipper told his torpedo
man.

"Skipper, what about the Zhong? We can put one right up his ass,
right this minute, and nobody the wiser."

The captain shook his head. "No. Nice thought but no. In the first place, someone—the FSN, notably—*will* be the wiser. But in the second place, we'll ruin the joke."

### FSS *Oliver Rogers, Mar Furioso*, Terra Nova

"Sonar, what the *fuck* was that?" demanded the captain.

"Sir, one of the Zhong—had to be the Zhong—has fired at the Balboans. The torpedo model is Volgan, but all the Zhong torpedoes started as Volgan. And . . . there's another one. Sir, a second Zhong Dynasty class has fired. The Balboans are running. What? Forty-two fucking knots? Jesus, I didn't know one of those corvettes could do forty-two knots. I'm *impressed*."

"The Balboans ran," said the captain. "I've never heard of that before. *I'm* impressed."

"Helm?"

"Aye, Captain."

"Things are about to get really unpleasant around here. Get us away. Heading one nine zero. Slow."

"How do I log that, Captain?"

Meredith answered, "As the Zhong having fired the first shot."

### Zhong Submarine *Mao Zedong, Mar Furioso*, north of the *Isla Real*, Terra Nova

The sound penetrated the hull. When it reached him, Captain Liu's face went instantly from porcelain pale to ghastly white. His eyes darted back and forth. *I gave no order. What the . . . ?* In the initial shock he almost asked if his own boat had fired, but no, he would have felt that right through the deck.

"Behind us, sir," Kuang announced. "But there's nothing there." The imperial cousin hesitated, then added, "And now we know about those plonks. Torpedoes . . . mines . . . and the one we apparently set off just missed us." The possibility of there being a submarine right behind the *Mao* didn't occur to either Liu or his crew. After all, if there'd been a sub there, it would have fired to hit, not to miss.

"Captain, that was a hostile act!"

"Bring her about, due north," ordered Liu, snapping out of his state of shock. "No, belay that. Heading is zero nine zero. Slow. Make your depth three hundred meters."

"Sir," reported Sonar to the captain. "I make our sister ship, *Wu Zetian*, turning about at flank speed."

*Hmmmph*, thought Liu. *Panicking. The one cunt dynasty is—like its namesake—going to have a short life expectancy.*

That sister submarine had been named after Old Earth's sole Chinese female empress regnant. It was believed in naval circles that the choice of name had been made by the current empress, Xingzhen, possibly as a means of testing the waters. The Zhong, like their ancestor Han, were fully cognizant that more than one empress had ruled through the reigning emperor. They were reasonably accepting of that, provided the forms were maintained and she took a back seat in public. They were, however, less than thrilled with the thought of genuine female rulers, who made it plain they were such.

Even if she were testing the waters, the current empress, though ruling in everything but name, was wise enough to rule through the emperor.

Sonar reported, "Captain, dipping sonar, active and passive, all around and ahead of the *Wu Zetian*. And . . . *plonk* . . . and . . . *plonk* . . . and . . . *plonkplonkplonk*. I make those as light torpedoes . . . Volgan Model Thirty-fives. *Wu Zetian* is effectively boxed in, Captain. She is going deep."

## Aircraft Trixie 53, *Punta Cocoli* Airfield, *Isla Real*, Balboa, Terra Nova

As with all the legion's combat pilots, Rafael Montoya was a graduate of Cazador School. He wasn't by any means the best graduate of the school, skin of his teeth being the usual descriptor. As such, though he was bright and tough and brave, Montoya was just not considered either officer or centurion material.

Still, no armed force ever has quite enough of smart or tough or brave. He'd been shunted to pilot training where his talents could be put to good use without having to suffer through his decrements. As a pilot, he'd fairly shone, learning to fly everything but the jets the legion had taken on in fair numbers over the last several years. He was in the line for that school, too, though.

Montoya, sad to say, knew too much. As such, in any armed force with a solid intelligence bureaucracy, he would probably not be risked on anything with even the slightest, remotest, most ridiculously unlikely chance of capture. Or, at least, not yet, he wouldn't. Indeed, Fernandez, who had such a bureaucracy at his command, considered locking him away more than once.

What did Montoya know? He knew the legion had stealthy gliders, so stealthy, in fact, that the Federated States Air Force couldn't pick them up at fairly close range from their Airborne Command and Control Ship. But, all things considered, it wouldn't have been disastrous if the FSAF had discovered that fact. No, Montoya also knew that the UEPF's base on Atlantis couldn't see a Condor glider, inbound, outbound, or hanging around overhead, scouting. *That* was a deep secret, or, rather, two of them, because the second secret, that Balboa was scouting out the Earthpigs, was an advertisement that the legion intended to attack Atlantis base at some point in time.

Still, Fernandez wasn't heartless about it. He'd let the boy fly some missions, so long as the chance of capture was very low. In this case, it was essentially nil, submarines not being noted for either their ability or intent to take prisoners.

Thus, Rafael Montoya, *Cazador* not too very extraordinaire, and pilot fairly extraordinary, zipped down the thirteen-hundred-meter runway of the airstrip at *Punta Cocoli*, his plane laden with one Volgan lightweight torpedo and four smallish depth charges, each set for a different depth.

As soon as he was airborne he reported in to the YA-72 helicopter controlling the attack on the Zhong submarines. He reported in as, "Trixie Five Three." Someone there, whose voice he didn't recognize, ordered him to take a position at such and such altitude, circling and such and such direction, and wait. "Don't call us, we'll call you."

"Story of my life," answered Montoya, as he pulled back on his stick to climb to the ordered altitude, *especially where women are concerned.*

That last was simply untrue. Montoya's success with women was nearly legendary. But, as he often moped, *The ones I really want don't want me, and Caridad Cruz and Marqueli Mendoza are married . . . to friends.* Montoya was, sadly, on the down slope, which is to say the post-breakup misery, of his last affair, so such thoughts were only to be expected.

"Trixie Five Three?" sounded in his flight helmet.

"Yo?" Montoya answered. He could almost feel the man on the other end of the radio link wanting to reach through and strangle him for violation of standard radio procedures.

"We want your depth charges dropped at . . ." and the controller read off an eight-digit grid. There was no question of setting the depth on the depth charges; the computer could have handled it but the depth charges themselves could not. Their settings had been made back on the island.

"Roger," answered Montoya, punching the grid into his on-board fire-control computer, then pushing his stick left and forward. The Turbo-finch dropped altitude until he pulled up about a hundred meters above the ocean surface.

*Do not, notnotnot, want to be too close to one of these fucking things if it goes boom on hitting the water.*

The computer did most of the heavy lifting for this. Montoya just lined his plane up along the path the screen showed, then followed it until the computer announced, "Dropping." The four large splashes below didn't reach the aircraft.

"Dropped," reported Montoya.

"Come around again and drop your torpedo."

"Roger."


## Lightweight Torpedo 35-RSAPEJSCDOTTMCJSC-1097, *Mar Furioso*, Terra Nova

The brain that could profitably be fit into a lightweight—in this case about half a ton—torpedo that was, in essence, a throwaway, was fairly stupid. Similarly the on-board sonar was not of the best. The target selection capability was limited. Still, torpedo 35-RSAPEJSCDOTTMCJSC-1097 had been just thrilled when they'd loaded it under the portside wing of a Turbo-finch, then spun it up to semi-active. Rather, it *would* have been thrilled . . . if it had been capable of anything beyond counting fast on its figurative fingers. As things were, though, the torpedo merely noted that it was alive, totally

missing that *also sprach Zarathustra* moment, and began reporting
its state pretty much continuously to the pilot in the cockpit. Not that
it knew anything about either, of course.

But from somewhere the torpedo could not, in its metallic
ignorance, know anything about, data came back. A smarter torpedo
might have marveled at the continuous updates, the passage of the
waters below. A Yamatan torpedo might, all unheard, of course, have
begun composing *haiku* in praise of the glimmering waves.

This torpedo, however, was not Yamatan. It was Volgan:
businesslike, unimaginative, competent but not brilliant. Like other
things Volgan, it was intended for use in mass, without a lot of
extraneous computing or communicating capability for one torpedo
to coordinate with another, and completely without a care for
fratricide. The data it cared about was highly limited; things like:
*What's my target? How deep? How soon, so I can save power by not
spinning up until necessary?*

Torpedo 35-RSAPEJSCDOTTMCJSC-1097 did have something
like a thought, as it was released from under the wing of the Turbo-
finch. It was something like, or at least had the sense of, *Oh, goody.*

### Zhong Submarine *Wu Zetian, Mar Furioso,* Terra Nova

There were two known lightweight torpedoes underwater and
searching for the *Wu.* They were known because they were actively
pinging. But there had been other impacts of heavy objects upon salt
water heard. What those were was anyone's guess. The boat's exec
certainly tried to guess. *More dummy bombs? Mines . . . well . . .
probably not mines, not all of them, not unless the Balboan monsters
were witless, which they do not seem to be, since those had impacted
closer to the coast. Torpedoes passively listening?*

"Captain," announced *Wu*'s sonar operator, "I've got four *plonks*
above us . . . falling without propulsion."

*Wu*'s exec—in contrast to the *Mao*'s, a clever commoner saddled
with an aristocratic captain—thought, *Well of course. After you
panicked, their Archangel had no problem tracking us. And since we've
stopped they still know where we are. So those are either more torpedoes
or, if the Balboans think this way, depth charges, Nobody much uses*

*those anymore, of course, but it is said they think cheap, wherever possible, so maybe. Either way . . .*

The captain's eyes darted back and forth across the plotting table. He saw no good way out. The captain stood there in perfect indecision while the clock ticked away and the recent enemy donations fell through the sea.

The exec didn't start tracking time until almost a quarter of a minute after the latest *plonks*, from above. So it was only his best guess when he said, "Now," some ninety seconds after the *plonks*. His guess was fair, though; there was an explosion above the *Wu*, which reached her in the form of a shockwave, the bang, and then the sound of the explosion, the boom. This was followed by another, then another, and then a third, each about five seconds apart, or slightly less. Each blast came a little worse than the last one, because they were closer to *Wu*'s depth. The risk was greater, too, as the hull was already stressed because of the great water pressure. The final boom was close enough to jar the *Wu Zetian*, though the hull kept its integrity.

This could not be said for the captain, who ran off for his cabin without a word.

*At least the weasel didn't piss his pants*, thought the exec.

"Sir," said Sonar, "another *plonk*. This one was a torpedo, I think. And, sir . . . ?"

"Yes?"

"What if it got a bounce back from our hull from the blasts?"

The exec almost ordered, "Ahead full!" He didn't give the order but thought, ruefully, *That shitheel of a captain's contaminated me.* "Hard port rudder. Ahead one-third."

"The torpedo was pinging, sir . . . hmmmph . . . it's stopped, sir."

*Oh, I dislike the sound of that.*

"Oops, it's started again . . ."

## Lightweight Torpedo 35-RSAPEJSCDOTTMCJSC-1097, *Mar Furioso*, Terra Nova

The torpedo, competent but not brilliant, sliced through the waves at the aircraft's normally slow speed, plus a little, then quickly sank to a depth of eighty-three meters. Thereupon, its control surfaces deployed and it began a long, slow, spiraling glide, listening. The listening was enhanced by the fact that the torpedo's own engine, an underwater rocket, was not active.

When 35-RSAPEJSCDOTTMCJSC-1097—or -1097, to its friends— was at about one hundred and thirty meters, there was a series of rather loud bangs far below it. Its brain was competent enough to classify those as, "depth charges, neither friendly nor enemy, and not to be targeted, however . . ."

The "however" referred to a few hundred lines of programming that said, in effect, "wait for the echo."

Naturally, several echoes came, not just from the first four blasts but from bounces off of bounces off of bounces. It was all very confusing, especially to a brain that, while competent, was not brilliant. So -1097 oriented its nose toward the most likely of the echoes and then narrowed things down somewhat with just a bit of pinging. Once -1097 had a fairly definite plot for the probable target, the pinging cut out, and its control surfaces aimed it for the Zhong submarine. This latter was making enough noise, if barely, for the torpedo to follow its swing westward.

The *Wu* moved west at five meters a second. The -1097 sank at a rate several times that. And with each meter sunk, the acoustic signal from the submarine grew louder and more distinct. It was not long until the, once again, not brilliant but competent, brain in the computer decided, "They're fucked."

At that point the rocket motor in the torpedo fired, launching it down at many times the *Wu*'s speed. The one-hundred-and-sixty pound warhead detonated right against the hull, right over the captain's quarters. Hull breech followed, initially with a deluge of water that killed the captain instantly. A crewman, facing generally astern, saw the water burst out of the door to the captain's cabin, which was only for privacy, hence neither watertight nor strong, anyway. The crewman survived his captain by not much over a second as the combination of water and sudden rise in the air pressure, hence in heat, raced with simple crushing to see which killed him.

## Zhong Submarine *Wu Zetian, Mar Furioso,* Terra Nova

There are occasions where slow and deliberate reason is indispensable.

There are also occasions when panic works best. This was one of the latter. While some quick-thinking crewman slammed hatches and spun wheels to lock them, and while there was still a modicum of control, *Wu*'s exec didn't bother thinking; he simply shouted, "Surface! Emergency Blow!"

The ballast tanks were almost immediately emptied of water by high-pressure air. Another few seconds' delay and the water pressure would have been too great for that. Then the sub would have continued on down until the hull collapsed in a sudden cataclysm. That, or, had it somehow survived the pressure, the crew would have died one by one, on the bottom, in the dark . . . slowly and miserably.

Under the twin forces of displacement and the push of the screw, *Wu* picked up speed as she ascended. Moreover, with the planes and rudder in the stern providing more resistance than the smoothly ovoid bow, she took on a definite nose upward posture aggravated by the planes on the sail being turned leading edge upward, too.

When she breached . . .

### Aircraft Trixie 53, *Mar Furioso*, Terra Nova

"Holy fucking shit!" exclaimed Warrant Officer Montoya as the water below and to his starboard suddenly boiled, then exploded, the explosion being followed by a good fifty meters of submarine, topped by a sail, shooting out of the water. The forward portion of the sub slowed and reached a tipping point before crashing back down and disappearing. For a moment, its screw and rudder appeared before they, too, sank out of sight. A second or two later, like a cork, it bobbed back to the surface, more or less in parallel to the water. The screw was still turning, but slowly.

Hatches opened. From them, with what struck Montoya as commendable discipline, little manlike shapes emerged, one man helping another out and, in a couple of cases, teams of two aiding the injured. The shapes wore different colored uniforms, the colors generally standing out brightly against the black of the hull. He tried to count them then gave that up; there were too many, coming too quick, and without enough of a pattern. He guessed he saw maybe eighty-five or ninety men emerge.

Brightly colored life rafts blossomed on the ocean surface. The pilot didn't see where they came from, only that they were suddenly there. They were not, however, all that close to the sub. A few teams of men jumped into the water to retrieve them, swimming them in where the injured could be more easily loaded.

*Yeah, good discipline . . . good teamwork.*

Montoya reported in the event, then was told, "Thanks for being the fifty-second person to call us with this information. We do, of course, appreciate it. Now fuck off and quit bothering us."

"You're going to save them, right?" asked Montoya. He didn't get an answer, but he saw a couple of Yakamovs vectoring in and dropping lines, with maybe half a dozen more off in the distance but closing.

"Go and circle them," said control. "See if you can spot any sharks too close to the surface . . . ummm . . . you *do* have loaded machine guns, don't you?"

This time it was Montoya who didn't answer. *Arrogant pricks. Yes, of course I do.* Even so, he took up a position fair for spotting a shark.

One of the nice things about the Turbo-finch, being derived, as it was, from a crop duster, was that it could turn on a dime. At least, when it wasn't carrying a huge load of ordnance it could. At the moment, Trixie 53 was carrying almost nothing besides Montoya. It easily kept to a tight pattern over the life rafts and the few Zhong sailors still in the water. The only touchy part was keeping out of the way of the YA-72s as they came in to pull Zhong submariners out of the drink.

While circling, Montoya formed the impression that the Zhong had all abandoned ship. Then one lone sailor appeared at the bridge, atop the sail. That sailor shook his head ruefully, then climbed over the side of the sail and began to descend by the ladder welded to its side. He turned about once his feet had settled, then rendered a really smart salute to the ship before stripping off his upper garment, dropping off his shoes, and diving in.

However calm he'd seemed to Montoya as he'd gotten out, there was nothing especially relaxed about his swimming. He made it like a torpedo—*Oh, all* right; *he's a little slow for a torpedo*—straight for the nearest yellow life raft.

He'd made it rather less than halfway when the whole eight-thousand-ton boat shuddered, some huge bubbles appeared to either side, and it began rapidly to sink. The swimmer disappeared, pulled under with the downward tow of the *Wu Zetian*.

"Shit," said Montoya to himself. "A man that calm and purposeful needs to live." He nosed his 'Finch over and swooped low just a bit off from the spot the swimmer had disappeared. With one wing almost touching the churned-up sea, Montoya looked to his left. *Crap, he's there! But*—he leveled out and looked at the nearest life raft—*no, they don't see him.*

Montoya pulled back on his stick, tossing his plane into a loop. This was a dangerous maneuver, this close to the water. No matter. Leveling off again he found the swimmer once again by eye. The nearest life raft didn't get it.

*Oh, I can fix that.* Montoya pulled up, swooped down, and fired his machine guns at a spot about twenty meters from the life raft. All the raft's passengers shuddered and looked up.

Coming back around, Montoya wagged his wings then cut throttle to just above a stall. Twenty pairs of eyes, all wide with terror, followed him. The warrant pointed ahead, frantically. He was rewarded with one of the Zhong suddenly standing, stripping off his shirt, and diving into the sea, swimming in the direction Montoya had pointed. Taking his eyes off the sea for a moment, Montoya gazed around at other aircraft, dozens of them, winging it trippingly in other directions.

*Well . . . yeah . . . we thought, after all, that there were four Zhong subs. Why settle for one?*


**Corvette *Jaquelina Gonzalez*, Mar Furioso, Terra Nova**

It was never really much of a contest. The torpedoes fired at the *Jaquelina Gonzalez* weren't even set for particularly high speed, as compared to the corvette's own forty-two knots. They were being guided by submarines that had precisely zero interest in actually hitting the ship. And they were fired in conditions where the ship had land to hide behind.

Nonetheless, to make the show look good, *Esox* and her sister let the torpedoes almost run out their wire before having them self-destruct.

It made a nice couple of splashes.

### BdL *Dos Lindas, Mar Furioso,* Terra Nova.

"Thanks, Patricio," Fosa said over the secure line, then replaced the phone on its gray-painted receiver.

*Tell the boys 'well done,' he says. Like that makes up for the rest. Sure, I'll tell the boys . . . but 'it's time to go' . . . they won't be happy over it. I'm not happy over it. But . . . well . . . no sense in wasting lives.*

### Coto, Santa Josefina, Terra Nova

In the little border town, half in Balboa, half in Santa Josefina, a long line of civilian-clad and disarmed legionaries waited, with their passports out, for permission to cross the border and return home. There were seven or eight hundred of them, thought the immigration agent on duty.

*No fucking way we can deal with this ourselves, just me and a half dozen other agents,* he thought, too, as he frantically dialed the number for headquarters, some distance away.

Unknown to the border control agent, a scant two hundred meters away a Tauran soldier was also calling his headquarters, just as frantically. To each, the answers were similar. The Tauran was told, "We have no authority to arrest anybody here, and the press and the human rights lawyers will be all over us if we try." The border control officer was told, "What the fuck do you want us to do? Yes, we can send a half-dozen men down to help you clear them through, to search baggage, and such. But they're citizens. They've broken no laws here. They have the right to come home. And the president asked them to a while ago. So fuck off."

Corporal Sanchez, Second Cohort, *Tercio la Virgen,* had no idea why he was ordered to turn in his rifle and equipment, put on civilian clothes, and go home. At first, he'd balked, too. After all, the order wasn't coming from the tercio commander. His sergeant though, had set him straight. "Don't give the border police a fucking reason, except that you're homesick. As for why, can you think of a better way to get through an enemy to where you can attack his vitals? And don't bother asking where we get reissued arms. I'd be really surprised if that becomes an issue. Now shut up and change clothes. Oh, and remember to show up at the *Bar la Cascada* at the end of the month to collect your pay."

# CHAPTER TWENTY-ONE

If, notwithstanding the notification of the neutral Power, a belligerent ship of war does not leave a port where it is not entitled to remain, the neutral Power is entitled to take such measures as it considers necessary to render the ship incapable of taking the sea during the war, and the commanding officer of the ship must facilitate the execution of such measures.

When a belligerent ship is detained by a neutral Power, the officers and crew are likewise detained.

The officers and crew thus detained may be left in the ship or kept either on another vessel or on land, and may be subjected to the measures of restriction which it may appear necessary to impose upon them. A sufficient number of men for looking after the vessel must, however, be always left on board.

The officers may be left at liberty on giving their word not to quit the neutral territory without permission.
—Second Hague Convention, Article Twenty-four

**Hotel *Cielo Dorado*, Aserri, Santa Josefina, Terra Nova**

Empress Xingzhen's agonized and outraged scream shook the walls of the hotel. "Those bastards!" she cursed. "Those fucking evil little brown pigs! Those filthy..." Tears began to course down her ethereal face, as she rocked back and forth, her own arms clutched about her, on the bed she generally shared with the high admiral.

Wallenstein came out of one of the two bathrooms that came with the suite. "What . . . ?" She didn't ask more; it was enough to see her lover in pain. She raced, long legs eating up the short distance to the bed, threw herself upon it, and wrapped the empress in a tight hug with one arm, wiping her tears with the hand of the other, and covering the grief-stricken woman's face with kisses.

Xingzhen started to break away, then collapsed into the high admiral's ample bosom. Shuddering, still sobbing, shaking with unrelieved hate and lust for vengeance, the empress managed to get out, "They . . . they . . . my boat . . . my ship . . . it was *mine* . . . named by me . . . *mine* . . . aiaiaiaiaiai . . . they *sank* it . . . aiaiaiaiai . . ."

One hand pressing the empress's head tightly to her chest, Wallenstein looked around until she saw a formal-looking sheet of paper, lying on the bed. She picked it up with the other hand, then began to read it. She got through the first paragraph then thought, *Oh, shit.*

"I'm going to nuke them out of existence," the empress hissed. "Their grandchildren will have nightmares. They will . . ."

"Hush, love," said Wallenstein. When not engaged in making love she was the senior of the partnership. "You're not going to do anything of the kind."

"What? I will . . ."

"Shut up," said the high admiral, more gently than the bare words would usually permit. "If you try to, the Federated States will obliterate you. You have what, two hundred warheads, most of them tactical?" Wallenstein neglected to mention that she wasn't sure she had even a single functional nuclear weapon.

"About that," said Xingzhen.

"Twenty missiles that can range?"

"Twenty-five," said the empress, who, calming somewhat, then admitted, "though their reliability is low."

"Right . . . let me tell you a little secret, my very dearest; Balboa will kill many more of yours than you will of them. That's right, they have at least seventeen nuclear weapons, ten of those, or more, being city busters. And that's not even counting the FSC, which will not permit nukes going off in their hemisphere."

"Now what happened," Wallenstein demanded, "the short version?"

"We had four of our newest and best nuclear submarines move to a position to cover our invasion fleet. You knew that; I told you that. We had to, to protect the invasion fleet from a sortie by the Balboan carrier."

"Yes, I knew," Wallenstein said, "and I approved. Please continue."

"Well," said Xingzhen, with a small sniffle, "the stories conflict. We had four out there, but two of them apparently were sunk. Of the two surviving, one says we fired first—under vast provocation—and the other says they don't know what happened but that they did *not* fire, that a torpedo passed them from behind."

"The captain of the second one trying to cover his ass against a future inquest?" Wallenstein suggested.

"I don't know," said the empress. "I suppose it's possible. But I don't *care*. They sank my ship! *Mine!* Do you know how hard it will be to convince my people to accept a female ruler when the ship named for another female empress sank? They're a silly, old-fashioned, narrow-minded, and superstitious lot. The Balboans have deprived me of my due. They must *pay!*"

"Easy say, hard do," said the high admiral. She thought for a couple of seconds and added, "For you. Impossible for me.

"Get dressed and call in your girl to do up your face, my love. Then let's go talk to Janier.

"By the way, where are the two surviving subs now?"

"Out at sea several hundred miles; maybe even five or six hundred. Once they managed to break off from the Balboans, they didn't stop until they were safe enough to come up close to the surface to get a message out."

**BdL *Dos Lindas*, Mar Furioso, Terra Nova**

The *classis* moved as a single unit, with two Volgan-built frigates in the lead, zigzagging across the line of travel, pinging mercilessly for submarines. Mercilessly? The number of cetaceans damaged or killed by the sonar argued for a certain lack of mercy, yes.

Two corvettes worked the sea closer in shore, while three more, among them the *Inez Trujillo* and the *Jaquelina Gonzalez*, under the control of another frigate, swept the sea to starboard. The ring was closed by several more ships, grouped behind, while within the ring, the *Tadeo Kurita*, the *Dos Lindas*, and a few nondescript replenishment ships sheltered. Below several Meg-class SSKs patrolled, among them the *Meg*, herself, and the *Esox*. Two of *Dos Lindas'* ASW helicopters, along with some of those carried by the frigates, took turns in dipping their sonar into the sea or laying passive sonar buoys to the northern flank. Overhead, a half-dozen Turbofinches fluttered, their normal ordnance replaced by a half-dozen air-to-air missiles, each. Nobody, least of all the pilots, really expected the 'Finches to do any real good if attacked by modern aircraft.

The radar down in CIC, and on the bridge, too, showed at least a hundred non-naval aircraft. Given their speed they were unlikely to be anything but Mosaic-Ds. Besides, Fosa wasn't exceptionally worried about the air threat.

*And besides*, he thought, looking glumly at his fleet from *Dos Lindas's* bridge, as the entire crew sailed towards the Santa Josefinan port of *Puerto Bruselas*, currently the main port for supplying the Tauran Union in the country, *it's not like we have huge ambitions.*

Fosa felt a sudden pressure, then felt a wave of sound as a brace of Mosaics buzzed the flight deck at no very great altitude.

Fosa nodded. "As expected and just about right on time." Turning to his air boss he ordered, "Call the 'Finches back to the ship. And radio those fuckers in the fighters and tell them if they buzz my ship again I'll have their balls tacked to the figurehead's pretty little bronze hands.

"Oh, and get the correspondents from the *First Landing Times* and Global News Network up here, with their cameramen. I want them to start broadcasting soonest."

### Headquarters, Tauran Union Security Force-Santa Josefina, *Rio Clara*, Santa Josefina, Terra Nova

Marciano ran from his quarters, his boots untied and him still tucking his shirt in. The panic in his AdC's voice moved him just as fast as the emergency warranted. The Balboan fleet had sortied and seemed intent on coming to and smashing the TU's remaining major port. Without that? Well, it was eventual defeat by the guerillas, no matter the success Marciano had had so far.

When he arrived in the headquarter hut, the staff was in full-fledged panic mode, such as his AdC's demeanor had only hinted at. Only *Oberst* Rall, the Sachsen, seemed to have his head about him.

"What's going on, Rall?"

"Damned if I know, Herr General," answered the Sachsen. "Suddenly, with no advance warning, we get reports of a mass of Balboan fighters swarming by the border and out to sea. The regiment of—we are pretty sure—Santa Josefinans on the border, less one battalion, starts marshaling for what looks like an assault across the border. But worst of all, their fleet sank a couple of Zhong subs and sortied toward *our* port. Sir, we're screwed if they destroy the port.

"The only good thing is the guerillas to the south are quiescent.

"I've sent for the—speak of the devil."

The Anglian commander of the fighter-bomber squadron, Squadron Commander Halpence, looked ghastly pale. He wasted no time, but simply reported, "Sir, we're on the ass end of nowhere for parts. Of my dozen Hurricanes, three are down for maintenance or in for service and, to some degree or another, bloody disassembled. I can keep maybe two or three aircraft up continuously for the next couple of days. After that, I make no promises."

"Can you attack a fleet?" asked Marciano.

"Not that one," said Halpence. "Not with any real hope of success. They've got three immensely powerful lasers mounted fore, aft, and in the tower. I understand they have no qualms about using them on aircraft. My men would be blinded before we got in range." The Anglian seemed to relent slightly. "Well . . . we would if we went straight in at them. The terrain here's complex, so maybe there's a place we can get a shot in before they know we're there. I confess I don't know where that place might be."

"Fine," said Marciano, "find it. Find one. The Balboan fleet is sailing for *Puerto Bruselas*. If they wreck that, we can probably forget keeping any aircraft up for long." When the Anglian didn't move immediately, Marciano grew unusually harsh. "What the hell are you waiting for, Squadron Commander? Move."

The Anglian dismissed, Marciano returned his attention to Rall. "What about the carriers in the Shimmering Sea?"

The Sachsen half-snarled, "They're still cowering either on the south side of Cienfuegos or in the port of Caimanera."

"Why *still?*"

"The Balboan submarines. They know the Balboans took out a Zhong carrier recently and, a few years back, one of the Frogs' subs, plus a destroyer. They don't know how and it has them . . . a little timid, shall we say?"

Marciano rolled his eyes. "What is it about we military types that we invest in our enemies superhuman powers if they beat us once or twice? Are we so arrogant as to believe we could only be beaten by supermen?

"I *know* the Balboan legion. I *know* their commander and, under different circumstances, would count him a comrade. I *still* count him a friend. But a superman, he is not."

"He's pretty good though," said the Sachsen, with a wry grin.

"Well . . . yes," agreed the Tuscan, with a complimentary shrug. "Good, that is. But a superman? No."

"Kingdom of the blind," said Rall. "Makes him look better than he is. Makes his troops look better than they really could be, too. Almost like Zion and Yithrab."

"We need more aircraft," said Marciano, "and the only place to get them in a hurry is from the fleets."

Rall inhaled deeply, held it for a moment, then exhaled. Getting the navies to cooperate? *Tough, very tough. Even so,* "I'll get to work beating the navies into submission to get in position to support us here."

"Don't hesitate to ask for help, *Oberst,*" Marciano said.

"I won't. Oh, and one other thing, General."

"Yes?" asked Marciano.

"We still have a modest HUMINT capability on the other side of the border," said Rall. "It seems one of the Santa Josefinan infantry battalion—cohorts, if you prefer—has turned in its arms and come home. Just walked across the border in civilian clothes, last night. Showed their passports and sauntered across, a whole battalion of them. Do you suppose the junta down in Balboa is losing its grip?"

"I wouldn't count on it," said Marciano. He raised the inevitable quizzical eyebrow. "And we didn't arrest them because . . . ?"

"Because our status of forces agreement gives us no domestic powers of arrest, and because the office of the president of Santa Josefina thought it was just ducky that her wandering sons were coming home."

"And the arms for this battalion," asked Marciano, "when do we expect those to arrive? So they can attack us from behind, I mean."

"We're working on that one, sir."

"I need a helicopter," said Marciano.

"Already standing by at the pad," answered the very efficient Rall. "And if you hurry you can see their fleet rounding the Burica Peninsula."

"How did you . . . ah, never mind." Turning to a troop who seemed underemployed at the moment, or perhaps simply a bit more calm than most of the rest, Marciano ordered, "You! Yes, *you*. Map, pen, notebook, field uniform. Come with me."

On the way to the pad, Marciano noticed, *Goddamned progressivines growing back around the perimeter. Note to self, get the engineers to work cutting them back.*

The Octaviana 602B helicopter, a four-seat job intended primarily for scouting and command and control, made it to Sour Gulf, one of two major gulfs on the *Mar Furioso* side of Santa Josefina, in about twelve minutes. It flew well above the surface of the planet, straight and level. Then Marciano's stomach heaved as, without warning, it dropped down to maybe ten meters above the waters of the gulf, moving generally northwest and keeping close to the coast for camouflage. Popping up over the trees of the Burica Peninsula, it turned north, shielding behind the peninsula's central range of hills, then dropped down almost to the beach fronting the *Mar Furioso*. There, still blending into the tree behind it and high enough to avoid raising a cloud of sand, the Octaviana hovered, giving Marciano an excellent view of the passing fleet, a bit over twenty kilometers out to sea.

Marciano counted aloud, "Twenty-four jets in the air for cover. Pilot?"

"Concur, sir, though it's not clear how many are staying and how many are relieving. Or who by whom."

"Good point, but if I order the fighters in, twenty-four appears to be a likely—or at least possible—number of opponents."

"Good point, sir," the Tuscan pilot agreed. "But that doesn't account for the other ones the Balboans might send in."

"Tell me something I don't know," snarled Marciano. "We can

take some pounding on the ground, if full-fledged war breaks out. We can't survive if they smash the port. Speaking of which . . ."

Marciano continued calling off the ships as he identified them. Some he was questionable about. Were the Lycosa-class corvettes better classified as large patrol boats? There were enough small ones, after all. Why was a forty-four-hundred-ton frigate a frigate while a thirty-eight-hundred-ton destroyer was a destroyer? *Makes not a bit of sense to me.*

About two ships he had absolutely no doubt; the seventeen-thousand-ton *Tadeo Kurita*, with its dozen six-inch guns, was a cruiser by anyone's standards, while no one could mistake the *Dos Lindas* as being anything but a carrier.

He remembered reading an after-action report of some of the mayhem inflicted by *Kurita* on the Nicobar pirates. *They're so going to trash my supply port,* fretted Marciano, *And outside of some pretty good but badly outnumbered aircraft I have not a thing to stop them with. If I had my artillery battalion overlooking the port but, no, the 152mm guns outrange the hell out of my 105s. And the 100mm guns the cruiser mounts are almost as bad, and fire faster.*

*So . . . no, the artillery wouldn't do me much good, even if I pulled it out of supporting the troops along the border and the ones at and around Pelirojo. I wonder if that's what Brother Patricio had in mind; sortie his fleet to pull my artillery out of position so his guerillas—and no one but the stinking press believes the guerillas on the Shimmering Sea side are anything but his—can attack.*

*And they'll be in range of the port in nine hours, give or take. Well . . . that little bit of grace is something, at least.*

"I've seen enough," said the Tuscan. "Take us back to *Rio Clara.*"

### FSS *Oliver Rogers,* Mar Furioso, Terra Nova

The skipper was, everyone agreed, cutting it a little fine. He'd already reported in to Hamilton, the capital of the Federated States, that the shooting had started at sea and the Zhong had started it. This had started something of a row between the Navy and War departments, on the one hand, and, on the other, the Department of State, which loved the Zhong Empire with a deep and abiding adoration, and wanted the Federated States to come into the war on the side of the TU, which they loved even more than they did the Zhong.

The boat's captain wasn't privy to any of that, in any detail; it was easy enough to guess at, though. The loathing between the military and the diplomatic corps was as abiding as was the diplomats' love for all things elitist.

The tougher problem—"and one way above my pay grade," as Meredith had said, while waltzing the one-eyed widow—was that the Federated States had made a tacit pledge to Santa Josefina to allow them to continue with their experiment in moral welfare and to defend them while they did so from all foreign threats.

From the FSC's point of view this made perfect sense. The average army of *Colombia Latina* was, and had been for over a century, just a junta on the hoof, awaiting only the moment and the opportunity to kick out the latest bunch of Tsarist-Marxists, Anarchists, Socialists, Fascists, or corrupt oligarchs, and at the same time creating civil wars that the FSC wasn't always able to stay completely out of. As far as the FSC was concerned, since they had to maintain a navy able to dominate two oceans and engage a star fleet, overhead, anyway, it was cheaper by far to promise to defend *Colombia del Norte* from anyone else than to have to continually get involved in the petty domestic squabbles their own armies typically caused. And this didn't even address the poverty that maintenance of large military forces in the area tended to exacerbate, which poverty led to or magnified all the other problems the *Colombianos* faced.

What that meant, however, was that with a potentially hostile fleet bearing down on one of Santa Josefina's principle ports, the *Oliver Rogers* just might have to get involved directly in stopping that fleet lest the country remilitarize, with all the predictable problems that would entail for both Santa Josefina and the Federated States.

*Rogers*'s skipper had a communications buoy up on a wire. He hadn't flooded tubes yet, but he was prepared to. So far, though, the only message from Hamilton, FD, on the subject of the Balboan fleet was, "Wait."

*And so*, thought the captain, *I wait for . . . well, for what?*

"Skipper?" said Communications. "I've got something on GNN . . . you know we check that, too, because . . ."

Meredith made a *can it and get to the point* gesture.

"Yes, sir. Sir, my Spanish is not of the best . . ."

"Mine is," said the captain, walking across the deck to take over the headphones. He listened a couple of minutes, then said, "Holy shit. Why the hell . . ."

### BdL *Dos Lindas,* mouth of the Paquera Gulf, Santa Josefina, Terra Nova

*Dos Lindas* had offered to make its own facilities available to GNN and the *First Landing Times.* The newscaster and the writer had both tried to be polite in their refusal. Even so, the unvarnished fact was that they carried better comms in a suitcase than the *classis*'s flagship ported in several cabins. Only in terms of redundancy and encryption did the carrier have anything on the civilians' packages.

Fosa had led them on a small tour, himself. It began on the hangar deck where the Turbo-finches were being disarmed and rendered inoperative. Much the same thing was happening with most of the Yakamov helicopters, though the three on antisubmarine duty at the moment were still out and active. The ordnance the planes and helicopters had carried were carted off, some of it literally on carts, to the storage sections set aside for them.

From the hangar deck Fosa had taken the pressies on deck where a crew from Intelligence had two honest-to-God burn barrels going, with flames lancing up from them, the plastic-scented smoke from code books and maps rising to the sky in a trail behind the ship. Their cameras had busily recorded everything, sending it live to their home's base, in the case of GNN, and in the form of photos and short blurbs, for the *First Landing Times.*

Then Fosa had brought them to his day cabin via the bridge, letting the cameras sweep around to see walls bare of maps. One of the radio men was broadcasting something in the clear to the Port Authority at *Puerto Bruselas.* The newsmen spoke Spanish well enough, of course; that's how they'd gotten assigned to this gig. But they had a hard time crediting what they were hearing. Thus, in Fosa's day cabin, the one from GNN asked, incredulously, "You're really having your fleet interned? On your own initiative? I can't . . . I don't understand."

"There's no sense in wasting men's lives fruitlessly," said Fosa, for the camera. "The corrupt Zhong Empire and even more corrupt and hypocritical Tauran Union are in cahoots as only the worst conspiratorial thieves can be. I can handle the Zhong. But my fleet has no chance against the four carriers the Taurans are bringing against us, each of them four times the size of mine.

"So, yes, my fleet is turning itself in for internment, voluntarily, in officially neutral Santa Josefina.

"You might make a note for your viewers and readers, gentlemen, that Santa Josefina, whose claim that we were a threat to them brought the Taurans into their country in the first place, giving rise to the guerilla war that has arisen there, will, upon internment, have complete control of the only way we could have logistically supported an invasion such as they feared. Let us see if they see sense from that and send the Taurans home."

# CHAPTER TWENTY-TWO

Whose game was empires and whose stakes were thrones,
Whose table earth, whose dice were human bones.
                              —Lord Byron, *Age of Bronze*

## Headquarters, *Tercio la Negrita*, Matama, Santa Josefina, Terra Nova

The few antennas for the headquarters' radios sprouted up from a school building in town. The headquarters, itself, was a good mile away, connected to those antennas by wire, as it was connected to the generators that provided power to the headquarters by wire. The building chosen was three stories, though the top two stories were empty barring only a set of quarters for Legate Salas and a few key staff. Admission was highly restrictive, though, in truth, Salas thought the restrictions silly. *Everyone in the goddamned town knows we're here.* Surely *the Taurans have at least* one *spy. Or maybe the spy's reporting the air defense, too. It's possible, I suppose, that when you're flying two-hundred-million-drachma airplanes, and hundred-million-drachma helicopter gunships that the prospect of losing one to a infantryman's bottle rocket or even a twin heavy machine gun is just more embarrassing than you can stand.*

Legate Salas really didn't understand any of it. He didn't understand why his headquarters hadn't been bombed and he didn't understand why any of them were alive and at large, nor why the port was still in his hands.

*They had us dead to rights. The cohort at Pelirojo was routed,* broken. The Casement *wasn't unloaded, and of what was unloaded, most was still somewhere around the port. They could have crushed us, totally and utterly. What in the name of God stopped them? Well . . . I suppose it wasn't anything to do with the name of God.*

That headquarters in town, though, was more of a planning headquarters. Salas's real command post was in a deep draw in the hills south of Highway Twenty-three, connected with the rear and the forward trace by radio and wire. Though it was reachable from the highway, he'd had his engineers cut a couple of smaller trails through the jungle, to avoid the command post's being spotted.

Salas's central position was stronger now than it had been, but not as useful for anything except guarding the port. He had two cohorts, one of them admittedly understrength after the drubbing it had received at Pelirojo. These were, minus one maniple in reserve, dug in along the western side of the broad river that ran to the Shimmering Sea almost precisely halfway between the Port of Matama and the town of Pelirojo. He had swamps to the south side of his defensive position and rugged mountain to the north. He might be outflanked by infantry here, but not by armor again.

*And I can deal with infantry that moves no faster than my own men do and carries no more firepower.*

*And supposedly I'm getting some replacement firepower. Though I'm still on my own for men and, since getting run out of Pelirojo, the volunteers haven't been forthcoming. And we're not quite in position to declare even a symbolic conscription.*

### *Campo de los Sapos*, Cristobal Province, Balboa, Terra Nova

Carrera watched one of Air Balboa's airships, the *Casamara*, being loaded with some containers—thirty of them, all told—out of Arraijan and a few dozen pallets that had been assembled on the spot and rigged for an amphibious parachute drop, one where the containers were waterproofed and floatation devices would kick in just after the parachutes opened. Inside the airship the overwhelming bulk of the seats, bunks, and cubicles had been knocked down and stashed along the flanks and forward, leaving a large cargo compartment in the center and forward of the broad loading ramp.

No one but the workers assembling the pallets and the loadmasters for the airship paid much attention to them. The guard around the containers, on the other hand, was fairly heavy. Most such were gone already, but these four had been held back for the day.

*And it is about time for "the day," thought Carrera. No sense in dawdling about it anymore. Indeed, Fernandez tells me that he senses the enemy getting close to some things they cannot be allowed to know. So . . . it's time to commence the war again. "The villainy they have taught me . . ."*

*Pity, about the classis of course, but what must be must be.*

*So what, if anything, are we missing? There must be something I have overlooked. If I were a better man I might be able to at least think of what. Ah, well; the staff tells me everything is in reasonable readiness. The ALTA is loaded and standing by. The shuttle flies. Robinson is suitably cowed. They shall bomb us, but we are prepared to counterbomb as needed. The TU may, when I order it, explode in ethnic violence. The legions and tercios are in place. Our rather large human minefield to the east is in position. Supplies are distributed, so they tell me. All is ready, so they tell me. And who am I to argue with them?*

*And they say too that the Zhong fleet is halfway across the sea, and the Taurans can sail any time. That built-in timing suits me well enough. Perfectly? No. Perfection in matters of war is the bugaboo of simple minds, and small ones. Lack of perfection costs lives, of course, but a fruitless attempt at an impossible perfection costs wars, which makes all the loss of life more fruitless still.*

*So today we cast the dice. In about four they will land. Such gentle dice, too . . . relatively speaking.*

*And let us hope that Lourdes, clever girl that she is, understands the full import of the message Raul and I sent her and her team.*

*I wish I could be sure that the idea of moving the nukes out of the island's bunkers and putting them on the bombardment freighters at sea was the right one. But I just don't know. The captains of those two would have five city-busters, each, which they would be instructed to launch on warning. And I am going to have to tell the TU that, if they attack the freighters after the freighters launch their conventional warheads, nukes will follow. I think I am, anyway. But, once they know about the gliders, how long until they figure out how to spot them? It's not like they don't have a metric shitpot of technological capability.*

*Hmmm . . . no, I think the nukes do not go to the ships. So where? Hmmm . . . there's one fair safe place. How about if I send them, their condors, and their launch crews to Sada? Yes, that might work.*

Seeing that loading was nearly finished, and having other people to see, Carrera went aboard the *Casamara* for a word with her captain, Reserve Tribune Emilio Soliz.

As he walked he reminded himself, *Parted out Mosaics, fueled and armed, on the airfield at Herrera International, soonest. With arrows.*

### Hotel *Cielo Dorado*, Aserri, Santa Josefina, Terra Nova

*I hope Patricio and Raul know what the hell they're doing*, thought Lourdes, as she, Triste, and Esterhazy stood. She'd made sure there were press in attendance, to include the two that had sailed with the *Dos Lindas*.

She would be leaving the country today, along with Triste. The woman Triste had brought with him, Warrant Officer Aragon, would be staying behind. So would Esterhazy. The latter had pointed out that, with a war in the offing that almost nobody expected Balboa to be able to win, the value of precious metal certificates and legionary drachma would be going through the floor. This would give him a change to recover them for the legion, at *centavos* on the drachma.

"There is nothing further to talk about," said Lourdes, seemingly out of the blue. "There will be no more return of prisoners, though all of your civilians still in our hands will be dropped off at the border over the next couple of days.

"Why no more?" she asked rhetorically. "The Zhong fleet has sailed. Zhong submarines have attacked our ships." Lourdes took a moment to glare in righteous indignation at the empress, who glared right back.

*Not as if I can blame you*, thought Lourdes. *In your circumstance, my people killed while trying to do a good deed . . . well . . . mistake or not I'd be more than a little angry. On the other hand, tough shit about your submarines.*

"The Tauran Union abets them in these crimes. The Tauran Union's national fleets stand on the other side of Cienfuegos, ready to pounce. They, too, have assembled an invasion fleet. Innocent citizens of our neighbor, Santa Josefina, have been wantonly slain by Tauran forces."

*And I know that's bullshit. If ever anyone took care to keep from "wantonly" killing noncombatants, it was the TU. Screw that, though; when the survival of the country is at stake, well . . . truth is always the first casualty of war.*

Lourdes looked left and right at her two companions, saying, "Gentlemen, let us get away from this place, out where free men and free women can breathe without the stench of Tauran and Zhong corruption."

To exasperated grunts, angry mutters, shocked gasps, and a large number of flashes, the three stormed out of the conference room without another word.

For long minutes, the other delegates had sat, stunned. Then, gradually, they'd dispersed to their various sections of the hotel. In the office suite set up in the Tauran, Zhong, and UEPF wing of the hotel, the major players from those groupings had gathered.

"Teach them a lesson," said Xingzhen. "Upstarts. Little arrogant beasts. Bomb them."

"Why don't *you* bomb them?" replied Janier. "You're the one whose ships and subs they sank."

"I would if I could," hissed the empress. "But my carriers can't do much. And what they can do is needed for the island. You, on the other hand, started all of this, you and your bureaucrats. And, besides, they sank yours, too, didn't they? You owe it to us to bomb them and you owe it to yourselves!"

"Hush, Empress," said Wallenstein. Looking away from Xingzhen and directly at Janier, she said, "You could bomb them. The question is, should you?"

"I should not," said Janier. "They are too damned dangerous."

Marguerite nodded, though not exactly in agreement. "They are dangerous, General, yes. But their power is quite limited and they know it. Think a moment upon the sequence of their actions. They introduce a small force into the southern part of this country. They leave this conference. Tauran troops inflict a defeat upon the troops of this clandestine incursion. They return to the conference, tails between their legs. The Zhong post submarines to watch their fleet.

They attack those—yes, I am certain they attacked first, even if I don't know how—then, panicking at what it has done, their fleet defects and interns itself. Worse, from their perspective, an entire battalion of the Santa Josefinan allies defects and crosses the border to go home.

"Don't you see the pattern?

"You don't want a war, General. All right, I can sympathize with that. But that war is probably inevitable unless we can cause the Balboans to back down in some substantial way. Based on how the Balboans act when pressed, you might well best avoid a war by being heavy handed, as we were here, in the town of Pelirojo."

"Even if that's true," said Janier, "how do we tell if they're really backing down or just manipulating us?"

"Still you take counsel of your fears," said Xingzhen. "Still you doubt even your doubts. These people are not supermen. Cut them and they bleed. Poison them and they die—"

"Wrong them," interjected Janier, to the surprise of both high admiral and empress, "and they shall revenge."

Marguerite played her ace. "They said no more prisoner return, General. This time, if I read the woman, Carrera's wife, well—"

"You read women very well," said the empress, with a subtle smile.

"Yes, I suppose," Marguerite nodded, not quite getting the joke. Janier understood it, but only let a smile, not quite so subtle as the empress's, play across his lips.

"In any case, if I read *her* well, this time she's serious . . . or she takes her instructions seriously. She knows her husband, if anyone does. If she believes he is giving back no more of your captives, we can take it as given that no more will be returned without some change in motivators.

"*That*, General, means you will be ordered to attack at some point, a point where the political pressure back in Taurus builds. Have the Balboans not already shown the ability to manipulate your press?"

"They have," conceded Janier. "And the bit with the death payments was especially wicked, giving us false casualty returns, just so they could pay a little money to some families, making us look cruel, heartless, and incompetent . . ."

*And push that down, NOW*, the general commanded himself. *That was the old you, vainglorious and foolish. Forget the personal hurts. Remember your duty to your country and the men who followed and follow your command.*

"What can they do to you in return?" the empress asked. "Here, in Santa Josefina, you have their measure. Here, you have proven you can beat them. They might be able to get at your fleets on the near side of Cienfuegos. They would have a hard time, noisy as their submarines are, at getting to them on the far side. You can bomb with impunity. If you do, they will be true to form and back down like whipped dogs . . ."

"What about my political masters?" Janier asked.

"Don't worry about them," said Marguerite. "They still do as commanded, pending my granting them the rejuvenation I've promised.

"Speaking of which, General," said the high admiral, "I am taking the empress with me to my ship for a few days, to strip a dozen or so years of off her. Why don't you come along . . ."

"For?"

"For the same."

"No," Janier shook his head. "Or not yet, anyway. Not while my men languish in captivity. Not while I am still in shame at my failures. Maybe someday, yes. Not yet, no."

"As you prefer. But you still need to prod the Balboans back to the peace conference."

"Let me think upon it."

"Don't think overlong, General," Marguerite said. "The orders will be coming from your political superiors shortly." *As in, once the swine see the rejuvenated empress.*


## Commercial Airship *Casamara*, over the Shimmering Sea, twelve miles southeast of Capitano, Balboa, Terra Nova

Along the deck there were twenty-seven pallets lined up in nine rows of three. Though rated for five tons, none of them held quite that, four tons of cargo being a fair average. The cargoes were held down by nets sewn of flat nylon straps. Further straps ran from rings around the edge of the pallet, twenty-two of them, though not all were used, to a centrally located parachute cluster atop the cargo. Straps ran from the parachute clusters rearward; they would not be hooked to the airship until just before pushing the cargo out, lest some butterfingered crewman trip over one and set off the parachutes inside the cargo bay.

The one hundred and eight tons was mixed, but most of it was closely related to losses suffered by the *Tercio la Negrita*, in Pelirojo. There were, for example, six new 160mm mortars, to replace the lost 160s, on six of the pallets, with seventy rounds, still in their dunnage, accompanying the guns. Another four pallets held an additional one hundred rounds each, for a total, on all pallets, of six hundred and eighty rounds of varying types. Most of the shells, more than three-quarters, were straight high explosive.

A total of three pallets brought in Gallic long-range 120mm mortars, six of them, and their ammunition, a total of just over a thousand rounds. These actually outranged the 160mm jobs, though a given shell wasn't nearly as potent. As good, they were rifled, hence much more accurate than the smoothbore 160s.

None of the *Tercio la Negrita*'s mortar crews had used these before; neither had anyone in Balboan service. They were captures, but, through administrative oversight, hadn't been listed as captured until late, nor classified until quite recently. Still, mortars were simple weapons, and usually quite similar to each other. Hence, hopefully, the guerillas would figure out the nuances on the job. And there were some manuals, albeit without translations. Ah, well, in any given tercio somebody usually spoke French.

Most of the other pallets were mixed, containing radios, rifles, machine guns, explosives, mines, grenades, night vision, ammunition, medical supplies, and whatnot, mixed into individual loads.

The pallets sat on strips of rollers, half-recessed into the deck. Normally these—the flip-floor system—were rotated over, hence covered up for passenger operations, with carpet overlaid. After all, the *Casamara* was a civil airship ninety-nine percent of the time. A look inside now would have given the lie to that, since every man and woman—there was one female regular from the Sixteenth Legion, Jan Sobieski, and four more militia among *Casamara*'s normal flight crew—was currently in legionary uniform.

## Matama, Santa Josefina, Terra Nova

The day was hot, overcast, and hazy. Even with the sun up, visibility was down substantially. Salas squinted against the sun's diffuse glare seeking out a particular airship, said to be still painted up in its civilian carrier colors.

If the port of Matama lacked for anything, it wasn't small and medium boats. Indeed, it had a fair share of large ones, half a dozen, impounded and their cargoes commandeered when Salas's men liberated the port. The large ones, however, weren't useful for this mission. Instead, Salas's support company had a couple of dozen fishing boats out, under crews mixed of local fisherfolk and men of the tercio's support cohort.

Salas, watching from the shore, wasn't too worried about Tauran intervention. The legion was keeping a large fighter contingent active along the border, even while the *Tercio la Virgen*, minus the one cohort that had crossed over, reassumed the same warlike posture they regularly did.

"That might not have failed yet," mused Salas, aloud, "but it's going to . . . and soon. Oh, well, probably no matter since the word is that the war also recommences soon, at which point posturing and demonstrations will become trivial. For today, anyway, we've got the overcast on our side."

"There, sir," said Salas's RTO, pointing into the haze at a shape his legate still couldn't see. Even as the RTO spoke and pointed, the radio's microphone sounded with the news from the boats scattered to seaward that the airship had begun disgorging cargo pallets. This was punctuated at least once when the parachute system failed and the flotation system *also* failed, probably from the shock of impact upon the sea.

*Whew,* though the legate, *who would have imagined young Mario could swear like that? I'm impressed.*

Salas had no real idea how many pallets had been dumped before the airship became visible to him, a dozen or so miles away. He could see, or thought he could, another seven come out the back end before the airship, lighter now, lifted through the clouds. No words were exchanged, but Salas offered a silent prayer for the safety of both ship and crew.

## Commercial Airship *Casamara*, over the Shimmering Sea, twelve miles southeast of Capitano, Balboa, Terra Nova

With the last of the pallets gone, Tribune Soliz took a look downward and watched the smaller boats hooking themselves up to the floating pallets and carting them off, across the water, towards Matama. Satisfied, he turned the command over to his number two, then sauntered down to the cargo deck. There, half a dozen men and one woman broke open the seals on the containers the airship had taken aboard and began removing from them ovoid shapes, long wings, cylindrical containers, balloons, and electronic components. The woman, like the men a member of the long-range bombardment *ala*, took inventory as the men emptied the containers. This wasn't because the components were too heavy for her; it was that she was senior . . . and, so would the men have happily agreed, a cast iron bitch.

*Ah, but she's our bitch.*

For the next two hours, Soliz watched the crews assemble the parts into the beginnings of condors, which were laid out on the deck and lightly tied down, a dozen of them. Carrera had informed Soliz that the cargos were of two types, one funny and the other funnier. He smiled to himself at imagining the consternation they would cause down range.

From each of them cables were run to a central computer. This, the airship's captain assumed, correctly, was the control or targeting box. Just what kind of target would be chosen, and where they would be, depended on a number of factors, some of which couldn't be known yet.

## Hotel *Cielo Dorado*, Aserri, Santa Josefina, Terra Nova

The orders came. Janier had never really had any doubt that the high admiral could persuade the TU's ruling clique of bureaucrats that the Balboans should be bombed. After the beating she'd administered to Monsieur Gaymard, Janier doubted she'd even had to have bribed him.

*Almost worth the price we're going to pay,* thought the general, *just to see that tall and lovely blond Amazon smashing his worthlessness against the wall and slapping him silly . . . "almost."* Janier mentally sighed. *What a shame she seems to prefer girls; for a while there I thought she might have been interested in me. No matter; I've lost all kinds of illusions of late.*

The orders included calling Janier home, to take over the direct command of the punitive force currently at sea and in Cienfuegos, as well as the invasion force that would hit the Balboans from one side while the Zhong hit them from the other.

*Well, if I have to bomb them, I'd better plan on bombing them well. They have an air force, and it's not contemptible, at least in numbers and, if that delectable Anglian captain—ah, no, she's a major now, isn't she? In any case, if she is to be believed, they are unlikely to be worthless in their training either.*

*Nor is their air defense umbrella worthless, either. And there are those rumors of lasers for air defense. Well . . . their carrier has them, why not the ground forces?*

*And, on the twin principles that one should never do an enemy a small injury and that it is not more moral to cut the dog's tail off an inch at a time, I'm sure I'd be better to make it a biggie, a thousand-sortie attack, such as this world hasn't seen since the end of the Great Global War.*

*Sadly for everybody, not least the people I am going to bomb, the Five Permanent Members of the Tauran Union Security Council have set the limit I can engage in; twenty-four sorties, exclusive of refueling.*

*Oh, well, we'll make the best of their foolishness.*

### Puerto Bruselas, Santa Josefina, Terra Nova

Corporal Sanchez, now wearing a nondescript uniform consisting of denim trousers, a dark blue shirt, and a blue baseball cap, brought his shotgun to "present arms" as Legate Roderigo Fosa departed the fenced-in area of the port behind which his fleet was interned. The legate had an apartment in town, where he was billeted, in accordance with the law on the subject. No one seemed to object; the Tauran commander, Marciano, had even been known to stop by for drinks from time to time.

Interestingly, Sanchez and the entire maniple to which he normally belonged had been hired by one of the local police poobahs, a lieutenant named Blanco, to secure the interned fleet. As far as it went, too, they *were* securing it. They were also fraternizing shamelessly with the crews, until Fosa stepped in and put a stop to that.

Even so, as he passed through the gate on his way home, after returning the salute, Fosa gave the corporal a wink, which Sanchez duly returned.

Just past the gate Fosa turned and looked over his fleet. Nearly every ship had somebody chipping paint or dabbing more paint on with a brush, or both.

*One of the nice things about internment,* he thought, *was that I get to repair all the damage and wear and tear that's built up. When we sail from this place, assuming we ever do, we'll be in our best shape in years. And the paint is the least of it.*

# PART III

# CHAPTER TWENTY-THREE

I am purely evil;
Hear the thrum
of my evil engine;
Evilly I come.
The stars are thick as flowers
In the meadows of July;
A fine night for murder
Winging through the sky.
—Ethel Mannin, *Song of the Bomber*

### *Casa Linda, Carretera InterColombiana,* **Balboa, Terra Nova**

From somewhere to the south, a smilodon or jaguar roared at the stars. Overhead, the Pentagram was visible, as was the moon Eris. *Antaniae* called out, *mnnnbt . . . mnnnbt . . . mnnnbt* as they searched for mates and prey, in the latter case preferably young and weak or blind . . . or stupid. Trixies, of course, one could not hear. Those intelligent proto-birds hunted the *antaniae* silently, only announcing their kills once made.

Most of the valuables and sentimental articles were long since stored deep in a cave halfway from the house to the beach. The people continued to sleep in the *Casa*, largely because the cave was a misery, cold, wet, and insect-ridden. It was also far too small to hold the household and its staff in anything but a standing or, for some of the women and girls, a sitting position. At that, the sitting position for them would mean a lot of wet feminine posteriors.

Ham was gone, sent off with Cano and Alena the witch to Valdivia. They'd keep him in a hotel, not too far from where a ship was expected, not too far from a refugee camp for children with a surprising number of boys each of whom boasted a remarkable degree of military bearing. Ham would join them eventually, but not yet, not when his presence might tip off somebody to something.

For the rest, all of Ham's thoroughly deflowered wives, five of whom were now pregnant, though not showing much, if at all, the Pashtun guards, a few of Carrera's personal and household staff . . . they all waited in their normal quarters for the word to run like hell for the shelter of the cave. There were several shoulder-fired antiaircraft missile teams around, but those were mostly to ward off helicopters, should the enemy get too daring. Oh, they might get a revenge shot in, but Carrera thought it unlikely.

*Still, one has to try.*

Complementing the missiles, there was a platoon of light antiaircraft guns, twin 23mm towed jobs. He had no great hopes for them, either.

Under gleaming moonlight from two of Terra Nova's moons, Bellona and Eris, sitting outside his quarters—he found no joy in his own bed, with Lourdes for the moment still in Santa Josefina—at his normal table on the elevated veranda, with his usual bottle of scotch still mostly full. A bucket of ice came with the scotch. He looked out to sea, then lifted the condensation-dripping glass to his lips. The sip barely qualified as a taste. He thought about drinking more—*as tired as I am after all these months I need the sleep*—but decided against it.

Carrera didn't have to see them to know that some of Ham's Pashtun guard stood silently just off the veranda. *Orders of Alena the witch? The boy? Or are the guards just in the habit?*

The glass door squealed open and a Pashtun stepped onto the veranda. "Sir," said the Pashtun, "father of the God, Iskandr, there is word from the . . . communications center? . . . yes, that . . . or through them from Lanza, commander of the air legion. This word is that there are aircraft, maybe twenty, maybe thirty, heading toward us. Lanza sends that he knows what he can and can't do, and that the traps are waiting."

"Excellent news, Sarbaz," said Carrera, recognizing the voice. He still held onto the glass. He wasn't sure where the word had come from. He could find that out later, in any case. The news was as welcome as expected.

"Please get everyone into the shelter. And alert the air defense people here."

The Pashtun gave a quick bow, announced, "I alerted them first, father of our lord." Then Sarbaz hurried off. In what seemed mere seconds, several long processions of people began winding from the house, the barracks, and several of the stand-alone quarters. None of the women, none of Ham's wives, none of the men or boys shed a tear. But Lourdes's latest and final, little Linda, sniffled loudly enough for Carrera, above, to hear.

The little girl cried, "But *why*, Pililak? Why do they want to hurt us?"

Ham's first consummated and—in his father's opinion—best wife answered, "Because they are slaves and we are free, beloved sister of my lord and husband." Ant's voice dripped pure venom as she finished, "Slaves always hate the free."

*Gotta love that girl. She's such a bitch but, after all is said and done, she's our bitch.*

Carrera stood then and turned to the two guards he'd known were behind him. "Loot the liquor cabinet," he ordered. "As much as you can carry, bring it to the cave."

"Yes, father of our lord. Glasses?"

"Too fancy; the bottles alone will do well enough."


### *Ciudad* Balboa, Balboa, Terra Nova

In theory, twenty-four sorties, exclusive of refueling, could carry an impressive load of ordnance, about one hundred and ninety tons. In practice, that was a rarely achieved dream. In the first place, the twenty-four aircraft used were not all fighter-bombers or attack-bombers. One was a propeller-driven early-warning and command bird, recognizable by the outsized dome, the radar, carried above it. Two—one Anglian, one Gaul—were set up for electronic warfare; these would prevent the Balboans from sensing the incoming air until late in the game, then would spoof them as to how many, and where, once it was obvious they were there. The electronic warfare birds would also make pursuit somewhat problematic, if the Balboans decided to try that, as they might.

It was believed that the Balboans could lift several hundred obsolete fighters. But it was also believed that, if they did, they would take some time getting airborne. Thus, two fighters were almost entirely devoted, eighteen of twenty-two hardpoints' worth, to air-to-air missiles. Every other plane carried two missiles on two hardpoints. Each of those also carried an additional two fuel tanks; given the range at which they were operating and the route they planned to take, this was only sensible. Everybody carried at least one homing antiradiation missile, for shutting down or shutting off enemy radar. Thus, the total air-to-ground ordnance was under ninety tons, most of it in the form of larger bombs.

The Gallic fighters, the *Tourmentes*, boasted a few more hardpoints, but their maximum ordnance load was within about one hundred kilograms of the Anglians' Sea Hurricanes.

Of the nineteen primarily bomb-carrying planes, two split off from the main body and stuck fairly close to the civil airport at *Ciudad Cervantes* and the military field at *Lago Sombrero*.

The planes avoided most Balboan radar by the expedient of coming in over the mountains on the eastern side of the country, by Santa Josefina. One of the electronic warfare planes blinded the civilian radar at *Ciudad* Cervantes's airport. Then they'd turned west, except for the one dedicated to cutting the runway at Cervantes, heading for the capital. The second EW plane took care of the radar for that approach. Whatever the effect of jamming the radar, and it surely had some, it didn't stop the Balboans from tossing up an impressive display of fireworks above the City as the Taurans approached.

*They probably had visual or aural warning passed on to them,* thought the leader of the Tauran strike package.

Visually impressive the Balboan cannon fire might have been, the bright green and red tracers arcing up into the night sky. But it was still a case of small bullet (or cannon shell), big sky. Nobody in the strike package was really all that impressed.

The first visual glimpse of the planes near the city probably came when some of them lit off their antiradiation, which was to say, anti-radar, missiles. Given that the Balboans were being jammed, even as they tried to use their radar to find targets for their guns and missiles, meant that few or none of those so targeted had clue one about the incoming HARMs until their radar dishes exploded in flame and shards of metal.

The first actual bombs to fall near the capital were rocket-assisted, Gaul-manufactured Oliphants. These runway cutters—resembling more narrow pipes with fairings and fins than more traditional ordnance—were released over Arnold Air Base at an altitude of a few hundred feet. They deployed small parachutes behind them which slowed them and also caused them to change angle to about forty-four degrees. Once they reached that angle, at which point the aircraft was long gone, a rocket in the tail fired, driving the bomb down into the concrete or asphalt of the runway. There, because of their narrowness, strength, and speed, they typically penetrated completely.

These did that. Then the larger charge in each of them exploded, creating a large crater and driving a much smaller charge very deep into the earth below the runway. When these exploded, the concrete was lifted up and moved. At that point, repair requirements changed from a few score hours of coolie labor to much, much heavier machinery for a much, much more difficult job.

In short, nobody but maybe a Cricket or Turbo-finch was going to be flying out of Arnold any time soon. Two planes, both Gallic *Tourmentes*, came back around to give Arnold a more thorough pasting, setting one airship alight, smashing several hangars and two barracks, and generally having a fine time.

With Arnold out, two planes cut left to take out the airfields at Brookings and *Campo de los Sapos*. Two more bore on for Herrera International. There were other airfields around the country, of course. But the six targeted—Cervantes, *Lago Sombrero*, Arnold, Brookings, *Campo de los Sapos*, and Herrera were expected to cripple the Balboans' ability to lift the kinds of waves of fighters that had been driving Marciano and his Anglian fighter jock, Squadron Commander Halpence, more or less batshit for quite some time now.

The Oliphants were mounted in clusters of four, with the clusters themselves affixed to the hardpoints. Each of the five aircraft involved in the runway cutting mission carried four clusters. They also carried on their remaining three (or five) hardpoints three (or five) bombs of between a quarter of a ton and a ton and a half. The bombs were satellite guided.

For the bombs, the two planes out to the east of the country, the ones targeted at Cervantes and *Lago Sombrero*, would eventually turn their attention to the buildings at the legion base that fanned out from all four corners formed by the intersection of runway and highway. For now though, the runways needed cutting. This was tougher than it sounded. All of those runways had been designed and built by the Federated States for their much heavier aircraft. They were also longer than the Balboans needed, meant to accommodate heavy transports and bombers rather than nimble little lightweight fighters. This meant that to cut the major airfields, they had to be chopped into sections smaller than the minimum take off run of a Mosaic-D. This meant they had to be cut into sections of five hundred meters or less. For something like *Lago Sombrero*, with its seventeen-hundred-and-thirty-five meter runway, this meant cutting it thrice; once would only have left two perfectly suitable airfields for the Mosaics. Twice would have left two or three.

Legate Thomas Broughton was pigheaded and a prick. Everyone knew it, to include himself. And he was proud of it. Being a prick went with the job: running the legion's *Escuela de Cazadores,* or Cazador School, a close cognate of the Federated States Army's Ranger School.

Broughton was also a bit on the short side, though his general prickishness didn't come from that. If it had, he'd have cheered up immeasurably at being in a country where he was middling tall in comparison. But no, he remained a prick.

Known to Carrera of old, and much appreciated for his qualities, he'd been hired expressly to set up and run the school. He got less credit for it than he deserved, really, since the Cazador School was the very soul of the legion. It was the thing that tied together all of the leadership corps of the legion. It was their sole source value system. It was their moral foundation.

It explained them, everything from their tactical approaches to their training philosophy to their almost incredible bloody-mindedness when it came to casualties.

Broughton didn't have or want much of a life outside of the school. His joy was in his work. That joy was a little truncated now, since the last graduating class had finished up and departed a week ago. When the school would open up again, no one knew. It couldn't even really be known *if* it would open up. If Balboa lost the war, clearly it would not.

In the interim, Broughton and the couple of hundred cadre and support troops he had at hand split their time between securing the school, doing the same for First Corps base, and conducting security patrolling along the InterColombian Highway, from the thin defensive line facing east, east of the Transitway, to about thirty miles west of the school. Though the school had begun with an entirely FSA cadre, they were almost all Balboan now.

The other cadre groupings, in the deep jungles down in *La Palma* and the high mountains by Hephaestus, had, in the former case, attached themselves to the *Tercio de los Indios*, and, in the second, to the Fifth Mountain Tercio. They were particularly useful to the latter, by serving as liaisons and advisors to the Lempiran and Valdivian cohorts attached to the Fifth.

Broughton, somewhat resentful at missing out on the major fighting against the TU, was making the best of it now, enjoying the security mission his school had been given. Still, that kind of fun was limited to begin with and became less fun with every increment of acquired routine.

For the nonce, with everything pretty quiet, the legate was tramping across the airfield to his quarters for a richly needed shower and change of uniform. For himself, he didn't much care about a stench that had long since overwhelmed his sense of smell. He figured he owed it to the troops, though, not to be sending them to hurl every time he walked in a room.

He'd sent a note to Carrera about a week ago, listing the ease of doing so very little as he had to, now, reminding him of his record, and requesting a reassignment to a line tercio, preferably as a cohort commander. Carrera had been about as gracious as expected in his answer: "Fuck off, Thomas. The school will be kicking in again as soon as we win the war. And I'll need you to run it. Worse, you're getting old. But . . . well . . . hell, if we have an opening, I'll put you on the list for a cohort . . . maybe a tercio. MAYBE."

That wasn't overly generous. For all practical purposes, Cazador school *was*, ordinarily, already a regiment.

*Best I can hope for*, thought Broughton, walking across the concrete of the airfield with his head down. He felt something, a kind of pressure or presence, behind him, and turned just in time to catch the organ-rattling roar of high-performance jet engines, and a series of flashes in the sky—*Rockets!*—lancing down at an angle to the surface of the planet. He barely had time to register that thought when the concrete began to shudder and rock like the area was experiencing a major earthquake.

Broughton found himself on hands and knees, shaking his head to clear it. The jet's had passed now, but . . .

*Fuckers will be back.*

Forcing himself to his feet, perhaps a bit too quickly, Broughton swayed still, then bent to throw up as sudden nausea overtook him. He found himself once again on hands and knees, remaining that way as he evacuated the contents of his stomach. The next time he stood more slowly and carefully.

*I am getting too old for this shit.*

One of the twin-barreled light antiaircraft guns scattered about the base began chattering a few hundred meters away, its thick tracers arcing up altogether too slowly to have a chance to catch anything.

Forcing the nausea back—*fuggit, been concussed before*—Broughton began to jog for the antiaircraft gun. Every brain-jarring step was an agony, a fresh wave of urgency to vomit. Twice, in fact, about once every hundred meters, he did stop to throw up. The third splurge was at the gun site, itself. Fortunately, he managed to turn away from the sandbags.

"Cease fire!" shouted Broughton at the gunners. "Cease-fucking-fire! You aren't even threatening shit, let along hitting it."

Reluctantly, the two-man crew present stopped their useless barrage. "Well what do we do then, sir?" asked the senior, Corporal Camacho, who wasn't even a Cazador instructor, but a cook.

"First, you go get the rest of the crew." Broughton heard some shouting from the direction of the school's barracks. The shouting was heard as if through the filter . . . or as an echo in a thick forest. *Well . . . sure . . . my eardrums are still vibrating. Only stands to reason.*

"Belay that," said the legate. "At least until we see what shows up on its own. Do you have wire to the other guns or to the air defense command post?"

"Only one other gun has a crew tonight, sir, and they're no more trained for it than we are. We got a week's worth of loading and aiming drill from one of the air defense types before he moved off with his regiment. It's just us cooks and I'm senior."

"Okay." *Toss 'em a bone? Yes.* "You've done well so far. But we want to try to get one of them, not just frighten them off. Where . . ."

Broughton was interrupted by the return of the attacking Tauran jet. This time it came first as the sound of straining jets, then with the *foompfoompfoompfoomp* of four rockets, each with its own flash. Only after that did the earthquake return, though at the far end of the airfield. And nobody saw it, anyway, since they were all belly flat to the ground.

"Maaan," observed Broughton, standing again, "when they want to fuck something up they don't do it by halfsies, do they?"

"Sir?" asked Corporal Camacho.

"Never mind, it was rhetorical. Now how about missiles? We always assign missiles to these things; 'Mass, Mix, Mobility, and Integration,' after all," he said, citing principles for the employment of air defense.

"I don't know shit about any of that, sir. I'm a cook. I know beans, potatoes, rice, and meat. Oh, and stew, when we mix 'em all with some veggies."

"'Course," agreed Broughton, more or less happily, as the nausea began to wane. "But the key thing is, do you have missiles?"

"Yes, sir. Privates Villa and Rocha have them, two each."

"Excellent. Now here's what I want—"

Someone interrupted from behind. "Legate Broughton?"

"Yeah. Who is it?"

"Chaplain Murillo, sir. I saw the shooting and figured I'd be as useful here as anywhere."

Broughton, who was surprisingly religious for being a prick, said, "Excellent. Now, Chaplain, I want you to work on a combination curse on aircraft and general blessing on missiles and cannon shells. Not much time, so hurry. And Camacho?"

"Here, sir."

"Once again, here's what I want . . ."

*** 

Sub Lieutenant Davies, operating a Sea Hurricane fighter-bomber off of HAMS *Indomitable*, laughed at the pitifully thin cannon fire rising behind the aircraft as it turned tightly for another run. The cannon fire cut off before he swept north to south down the length of the airfield. Nor did it resume as he emptied the second cluster of Oliphant runway cutters. *Two more to go*, he thought, as he slid over the hills and began a long sweeping turn. His display marked clearly for him when he was back on a proper course to ripple the field.

Just as Davies pushed the firing button two streams of tracers—one a little high, the other a little low, and either potentially quite dangerous—lashed up, whiplike, from the ground to his left. He instinctively pulled his stick to aim for the wider open space between the tracer streams, to his right. This ruined the shot completely, all four Oliphants smacking into the ground east of the airfield, between it and the main taxiway. The Oliphants threw up great geysers of dirt and rocks, but did no other harm.

As Davies continued on, approximately out to sea, a warning buzzer sounded. His infrared-guided missile countermeasure pod had self-activated on detection of a missile launch.

"Shit," said Davies to himself, "this was supposed to be easier than this."

His countermeasure pod also launched a couple of diversionary flares, even as it set up a pattern of IR emission to convince the—fairly stupid—missile that it was several meters over from where it actually was. This, for the most part worked; the missile veered a bit before exploding.

Unfortunately for the aircraft, the missile fired a continuous rod upon exploding. This was basically a circle of metal, serrated and folded, that expanded upon firing back out into the circle from which it had been formed. That metal circle clipped one of Davies's wings, sending a shudder through the aircraft, and setting off enough warning lights for a moderate-sized Christmas tree.

*And on that less than happy note*, thought the pilot, *let us to home. Shit!*

The attacking plane neither went down nor showed any sign of

THE RODS AND THE AXE

damage that Broughton could congratulate his gunners on. On the other hand, it didn't come back, either, as he'd expected it to.

*Showmanship,* thought Broughton, *the art of the commander.*

"Well done, boys," he said. And, in fact, it had been about as well done as one could expect. "Take a break, except for a gunner and assistant gunner per gun, and one man on the missiles."

For himself, he watched out, eyes sweeping the darkened, or rather, moonlit, which was to say unlit, sky. *What the hell; maybe one of them will silhouette himself.*

Davies's squadron mate from *Indomitable,* Lieutenant Saunders, finished up ruining the airfield at *Ciudad* Cervantes, then went on to his secondary mission, flattening the barracks and offices of First Corps, at *Lago Sombrero.* About halfway to the target, Saunders was appalled to hear his comrade, Davies, reporting in of enemy fire and taking damage. This was most unexpected. Saunders engaged his radar detectors, but sensed absolutely nothing. A quick call to Davies confirmed that a) yes, the other plane should make it back to the ship well enough, and b) no, there wasn't much defending the base but a couple of guns and some damned hard luck.

Fortified with that knowledge, Saunders bore in from the east.

The buildings were, for the most part, unoccupied, their normal denizens being somewhere between the capital and the Parilla Line, along *Rio Gatun.* Indeed, the reason the buildings were to be hit was not to kill anyone; it was to drive up the capital cost to Balboa of engaging in war with their betters, thus changing the logical calculation under which the Balboans should, again *logically,* make peace and give back all of their prisoners.

Janier had known, far, far better than his political masters, that logic was the last consideration in nearly everyone's mind that was engaged in war. Sadly, as the general told his AdC, Malcoeur, "Telling this to a politician who doesn't understand war and who really desperately doesn't *want* to understand it is an exercise in futility. So we do the best we can with what we have and ignore the bastards where possible."

Broughton was just about to send the gun and missile crews, who were, after all, primarily cooks, off to start on breakfast or, at least, on getting some sleep. Indeed, he'd just gotten the words, "Corporal Camacho, I want—" when a barracks in the middle of the southeastern quadrant of the base disintegrated, the wooden ruins immediately catching fire. Another barracks went up in smoke after that, then another. The gun crews couldn't see a damned thing, either; the plane was gone before the flames could illuminate its underside.

# CHAPTER TWENTY-FOUR

We could never learn to be brave and patient, if there
were only joy in the world.

—Helen Keller,
Letter to Dr. Oliver Wendell Holmes,
*The Story of My Life*

### Santa Cruz, Balboa, Terra Nova

Imagine a warehouse, outside of which is a concrete parking lot,
perhaps a bit larger than the warehouse calls for. Wide doors permit
access for anything up to fifty feet across, though they are currently
closed. Past the doors, inside, is a truck, a five-ton. The rating, five-
tons, refers only to what can be carried across country; on a good hard
surfaced road the truck can do double that, though for anything but
ammunition it's likely to cube out before it weights out. The truck had
no canvas top, nor is it carrying a normal cargo. Instead, the truck
carries a short rail, on a mechanism, through which the rail can be
raised or lowered. Right now it is lowered, parallel to the ground. The
truck has no side rails, as that central rail is a launch rail. Atop the
launch rail sits a Mosaic-D jet fighter. Old and rebuilt, and then
product improved—with, among other things, a new tail, twin-
barreled Gast gun, and a fairly decent avionics suite and radar—still
the fighter would have little or no chance one on one against any of the
Tauran planes that pounded Arnold Air Base to the west. Underneath
the fighter is a rocket, sufficient to get it airborne in a tiny instant.

The truck and plane combo is only one of six inside the warehouse. Six drivers are there, too, if the order should come to move out to the concrete and launch. A fuel truck also stands by, as does a truck full of air-to-air ordnance, missiles and belted cannon rounds. There is a maintenance truck there, as well, with a crew. Lastly there is a small command and control vehicle, with a shelter in the back. The shelter receives up-to-the-minute intelligence on the Tauran aerial attack or, rather, it would, if the system were up and operating. It is not, and the cluster of people standing in the shelter looking down at an empty display screen clench their fists with their frustration.

To the west, down the hill and across the stream that is the natural border between the air base and the area of the town, an airship burned merrily. This was not because of the use of hydrogen as a lifting gas. The airship used helium. Neither was it because of the dope used on the gaseous envelope. It didn't have the need, given modern materials. Rather, there was just a lot of plastic and natural fiber to the thing, plus fuel for its engines, and these were burning away, lending a flickering, smoky light to the base and even to the parts of the hill on which the town sits that faced the base.

Six pilots sat at the crest of that hill, a short jog to the warehouse, above where the airship burned. The pilots couldn't see the damage, even by the firelight, not even with the aid of the moons. But they'd seen the damage being done, as it was done, and known what it was. The concrete runway of Arnold Air Base wouldn't be lifting off or receiving any aircraft but helicopters or Crickets for a while.

The pilots weren't actually paying any attention to the airfield. They didn't need it, after all. The rockets slung under their planes and the rails that could be raised to near vertical meant that, given the authorization, *they* could take off in zero meters, almost straight up. The airfield meant almost nothing to them, though its fuel and ammunition facilities, which so far seemed unharmed, did. In this they were unwise. Although they could take off by means of their Zero Length Launch Systems, there would be no time to fix the damage to the airfield before their Mosaics ran out of fuel. There were emergency fields identified, of course, some hundreds of them. But no one really *wanted* to land on an unlit, dirt strip, in the night, possibly in the rainy season with the dirt turned to muck, and possibly under attack.

The pilots *were* paying attention to the attack on the city, to the west, well past the airfield and across the Transitway. Rather, they were paying attention to what they could see; waving streams of tracer-fists, rising futilely through the sky, the occasional launch of a missile—a loud *crack*, a streaking flame, then usually nothing—the irregular crump of bombs . . . and the sirens of fire trucks and ambulances.

One pilot wept in frustration at not being allowed to launch. One chewed his fist until it bled. One rocked, arms around knees. Three just sat immobile, glaring hate. Among the latter were Tribune Ordoñez, senior and therefore tasked to make sure none of his comrades could take off.

"Why won't they let us *go*?" demanded one of the glarers. "It's our fucking *job*!"

### *Tourmente* Number 21, off of *Charles Martel*, southwest of *Ciudad* Balboa, Balboa, Terra Nova

*Lieutenant de Vaisseau* Madon crossed the Transitway right over Florida Locks, then flew low, over Brookings Field. This had already been cut, so he had little concern for fighters lifting to engage him. This, if anything, was a disappointment. Madon rather longed for an aerial victory, so rare had they become.

There were clouds over Brookings, their undersides lit by a faint orange glow. Clearly something was afire down below. This was none of Madon's concern, however.

Past Brookings he cut northwest, towards the City. Madon passed between two skyscrapers, limiting his exposure to both missiles and cannon, because being shot down by the Balboan air defense would have been just too humiliating. These forces were now beginning to show some limited signs of coordination, or at least of getting manned up to strength. He resolved to make maximum use of the contours of the city.

Two or possibly three times, search radars set off warning buzzers in Madon's ears. The buzzing never lasted, so his tactic might have been working. *Or maybe they're just not that good.*

Madon swung out over the *Mar Furioso*, briefly, then pulled his stick to the left, aiming for Herrera International. He was, in effect, the second wave to hit the airport, the first having trashed the runway, then bombed the terminal. By the light of the flaming terminal, enhanced in his plane's own night-vision display, he saw twenty-three or twenty-four aircraft lined up. Had they not been so widely spaced they'd have been a perfect target. As it was, they were nearly so.

Letting his targeting computer see the grounded planes, Madon armed his 30mm cannon. He only carried enough ammunition for twenty-five seconds' worth of fire, as the slowest possible rate. The Gaul pushed his stick forward, fired, fired, fired; *brrrp . . . brrrp . . . brrrp*—and was rewarded with the very satisfying sight of a Mosaic-D fighter explosively disintegrating in his field of view. It had, apparently, been fueled and armed.

Madon leveled off, then let go a single two-hundred-and-fifty-kilogram bomb. That, he could not see hit, but he did get to see still more orange reflections—not so dim ones, either—off the clouds above.

The Gallic pilot didn't realize several things. One was that the spacing of the aircraft was only partly to reduce vulnerability. Another was that not one of the aircraft could fly; they were parted out derelicts, permissible to use as bomb, rocket, and cannon magnets because the legion had found Mosaic-Ds so cheap. The third thing was that they were out there as distraction and bait. In his concentration on his targets, he hadn't noticed that there were four quad 14.5mm machine guns, eight twin 23mm cannon, two single-barrel 57mm guns, and a few light missiles all waiting for somebody to get into position where he just *had* to fly through the area on which they'd all been targeted.

Thus Madon, really through no particular fault of his own, flew smack into a wall of antiaircraft fire that approached the solid. He didn't have time to bail out—he didn't even have time to scream—before he and his *Tourmente* disintegrated in a fuel-fired mix of blood, bone, brain, plastic, copper, and steel.

It made quite a show over the airfield.


### The Cave, *Casa* Linda, *Carretera InterColombiana*, Balboa, Terra Nova

One of the defining features of modern life on the planet of Terra Nova was the quest for certainty, amongst bureaucracy. In many cases, and perhaps most, where military forces were concerned, that quest for certainty worked out to be a quest for the illusion of certainty. To a large extent, this began at political levels and worked its way down with the fear that, God forbid, some politician should ask a question to which a general or admiral had no answer. To avert this, subordinate staffs and commanders often became little but information gatherers, to feed the information—true or false didn't always matter—to higher commanders and staffs so that no one would be embarrassed by the questions of politicians, so that politicians would be safe from the ignorant questions of the press.

There would probably have been some advantages to this if, in fact, certainty were possible. It never was, so all the efforts, all the bloating of staffs, all the bloating of officer corps, all the reduction in average quality, was simply a waste.

Though, at least, flag officers were not usually embarrassed by the questions of politicians, for whatever good that may have been.

Carrera was both fortunate and fatalistic. He didn't care, personally, about things he could not do a damned thing to address. Hence, he didn't ask for continuous input of usually spurious instant information that he couldn't do a freaking thing with, anyway. Nor did he really have to report to anyone; his commander, President Parilla, had good cause to trust him. Those factors meant smaller, higher-quality staffs and fewer, but better commanders, who could be better trusted to do the right and effective thing with the information *they* had. Better still, since said staffs and commanders were not perpetually nagged for useless information, they could concentrate on doing, rather than reporting.

Thus, it didn't bother him in the slightest to sit in an almost unlit, damp cave, surrounded by staff, friends, and family—to include his twelve daughters-in-law—just enjoying the company . . . and the booze Sarbaz had brought along, too, of course.

Pili, or Ant, as de facto first wife of the "god" Iskandr, hence senior to all, took charge of the children, leading them in singing songs both of Balboa and of her own tribe back in Pashtia. Ordinarily, that would have been the job of Alena, the green-eyed witch.

*Still, little Ant is filling in nicely*, thought Carrera.

Two of Ham's wives, Mehmood and Sahiba, both a little older than the boy and unusually tall, Lourdes levels of tall, sat to either side of Carrera. Every now and again he'd pass them the bottle, since they were known not to be pregnant. This was a lack that weighed heavily upon them, as it did on all of the Pashtian girls Ham hadn't managed yet to knock up. Still, Carrera wondered why these two sat on either side. Then it hit him, *They're the biggest. They self-selected to sit here to protect me, father of their lord and master. Jesus, is that a humbling thought. They slept around the boy's bed to guard him, when he was younger. They flank me now.*

*Note to self: Professor Ruiz and his propaganda ministry; TV show on devoted young girls, of exceptional bravery, soonest. Hmmm . . .*

"Have either of you two thought about joining the *Tercio Amazona*?" he asked Mehmood and Sahiba.

"Oh, yes, father of our lord," Sahiba, the red-maned, answered. "After we each have two or three babies that live, by which time we will be old enough to join. Then we can accompany our lord on his great crusade."

"Great crusade?" Carrera asked, with a sense of dread that his deepest plans had been compromised.

"Oh, yes," Sahiba enthused. "It was written long ago, seven signs, of which Pililak was the sixth, seven signs by which we would know our hour had come. After that, then Iskandr reborn shall lead his people back to their proper home."

"Ummm . . . what's the seventh sign?" asked Carrera, with a decidedly sinking feeling.

"It is a mystery," answered Sahiba. "As written, it says that 'Iskandr shall strike the snake in his den.' Do you understand it, father of our lord?"

*Only too fucking well,* thought Carrera. *Ah, bullshit; it's all coincidence. But then . . . but then . . . Cassandra did, after all, speak truth to the Trojans.*

He said, however, "Oh, no, daughter-in-law. I'm not of the mystic sort. I don't understand it at all."

## HAMS *Indomitable*, South of Cienfuegos, Shimmering Sea, Terra Nova

"Wave him off," said the airwing commander. "Doesn't he see what kind of shape he's in?"

The landing signals officer sent that directly to the pilot of the inbound plane, Davies, who obeyed but promptly called in to register his objection.

"We only have so many of these fucking planes," said Davies. "This one can be fixed and there is no replacement available. For Christ's bloody sake, they closed the assembly line as a cost saving measure last year. I haven't heard it's been reopened, have you?

"Now if you don't trust my ability to get it in, let me go last, strike the other aircraft below, clear the flight deck, and *then* let me come in."

"Wait, out," the LSO replied.

Davies wasn't either as confident or as enthusiastic as he let on.

Right after taking the hit, which was, admittedly, not all that bad, he'd had a time of it fighting for control of the aircraft. Half that battle was fighting for control of himself, as fear and the adrenaline rush of being hit set his hands to shaking.

He'd won both battles, of which the latter was the tougher. The Sea Hurricane had fought its way over the mountains, then descended to a few hundred meters above sea level. There, Davies had dumped his remaining ordnance, except for the air-to-air missiles. Those he'd dump once he was close enough to the mother ship to be sure of defense beyond self-defense. Not that, what with the new and unpleasant vibration the plane was giving, he had a lot of confidence on his ability to win a dog fight, even with one of Balboa's obsolescent fighters.

A visual inspection was impossible, even under the twin moons showing. And the most his instruments would tell him was that he was missing a chunk of his starboard side wing, but not how much of a chunk.

He began to suspect the chunk was large when the vibration began to grow to an alarming level. He could still control the plane, but it was an exercise that was both physically and mentally demanding, one that further threatened to become exhausting.

By the time he checked in with Cienfuegan air control, and crossed its central chain of mountains, the threat of exhaustion was fast becoming a reality. He throttled down his speed, which helped some, but there was still a sense of vibration there, slowly shaking apart both plane and pilot.

***

The reduced throttle had Davies still in the air when the sun popped over the horizon. With that, he could look over his right shoulder . . . and be appalled. Whatever damage whatever had hit him had done, the damage he'd done to the wing by continuing to fly the plane—*Not that I had a bloody fucking lot of choice!*—was worse still. As if to punctuate, a piece of the skin near the wing's edge peeled off and fluttered away as Davies watched. He could hardly feel that, what with the bucking of the plane.

Then he heard from the landing signals officer, "Abort!" Ah, but one should never discount the pull of Anglian propriety, stiff with upperlippedness, and amplified by Davies really, really dreading the prospect of both ejection and a dip in the shark-infested sea. Davies tried very hard to be allowed to land.

The planes and helicopters were struck below. And the sub lieutenant *did* have a point. Landed, there was a fair chance of fixing the plane. Ditched, there was no chance at all.

"All right, Davies," agreed the landing signals officer, "we'll let you come in. Emergency crews are standing by. Good luck."

On the plus side, weather was good, "Case I," as they said. On the negative side, the Sea Hurricane was being an absolute cunt, control-wise.

Davies's radio informed him, "Below glideslope. Left of centerline."

He pulled up slightly, and shifted to the right, until informed that he was in the proper position. The shuddering of the plane told him he didn't have a lot of time or opportunity left.

There was an automated landing system that, ordinarily, made carrier landings much safer than they'd otherwise be. Davies tried that, only to discover that the system wasn't quite up to dealing with random damage and an unresponsive and stiff plane, seemingly on the verge of falling apart in midair. He took command back from the ship's computer and informed the LSO he was coming in under his own control.

It was one of those cases where the pilot really deserved a safe landing, but fate's fickle finger, randomness's reaming rod, perversity's pulsating prong, just all combined at one time to fuck him. His approach was good, right inside the crosshairs. He was right over the deck, descending fast. And then—Finger!—the plane yawed slightly to port. He corrected, or rather, overcorrected, and was aimed just a bit to starboard. Rod!—he applied throttle, in case he had to take off after missing the wires. His landing gear hit, unevenly, and—Prong!—he bounced up, completely missing the wires. Unfortunately, that starboard yaw, now combined with three-quarters throttle, launched him into the rear of the forward tower, the one that sailed the ship. He didn't smack head on, but that wing, already damaged disappeared.

Davies, stunned silly, bounced to port, with his plane spinning uncontrollably around him. Automatically, knowing he'd missed the wire, he applied full throttle. Then he looked down at the deck, seemingly spinning past, *above* him, and screamed like a little girl. He saw his port wing disintegrate on the flight deck. It slowed his plane's spinning. Slightly.

Still screaming, as soon as he sensed open sky above, Davies reached for the eject. In a case of terror-induced adrenaline versus centrifugal force, terror won. He grasped the ejection lever and pulled. The little girl screams stopped, to be replaced by screams of pain, as the ejection seat subjected the pilot to about fourteen Gs, which was almost fine, and a compression fracture of one vertebra, which was not.

### Intersection, Via Santa Josefina and Via Belisario Carrera, *Ciudad* Balboa, Balboa, Terra Nova

A tranzitree trunk, ordinarily ornamental, if deadly, now leafless and stripped of its lesser branches, stuck up from a thick layer of rubble and broken glass. Above the tranzitree, the front of the building was sheared off. Its rubble and shattered glass lay across the sidewalk, past the tranzitree, and out into the streets. The mess of concrete, rebar, plaster, plastic, fabric, wires . . . all the components of a normal office building remaining, were left exposed to the elements. There were believed to be bodies in there, at least two of them. A sniffer dog, her head moving from side to side, walked gingerly with her handler over the wreckage. She was a specialist in searching for corpses and living victims buried under rubble such as this. There were also a dozen armed guards, surrounding the area, civilly clad but unreasonably heavily armed. These were men from Fernandez's organization. So were the ones loading the computers and files—dangerous work, given the state of the building—into trucks and carting them away.

Carrera and Parilla had split up the spots they intended to visit, the latter taking the more or less civil zones of damage, while the former went for the military and quasi-military. There was, however, an area that was officially civil, but in practice, military, or, more specifically, research and development for the military.

Balboa Yacht Corporation had never, not even once, built or even designed a true yacht, though there had been some early work done by some of its marine architects in designing things that looked like yachts, but mounted enough firepower to sink anything shy of a warship.

It had happened, of course, that some very rich folk or their minions had come to inquire about having a yacht built. Whenever anyone had tried that, there was a set of front offices, all manned by people on Fernandez's organizational payroll, to tell the prospective commodore: "Oh, no, *señor*, we are much too busy—Julio, you lazy swine, did you finish the drawings for the duke of Belgravia?—as I was saying, *señor*, we could not hope to—Marissa, you wretch, I said get in touch with Borchadt Marine Engines *now!*—Where was I, *señor*?" and keep up with that routine more or less indefinitely. They'd never had to, because the prospective buyer would invariably walk off in disgust within, at most, twenty minutes.

That had taken place in a suite of front offices, a cover for the rear ones, where the real work had been done, as, indeed, the entire company had been a front for what it really was, a wing of *Obras Zorilleras*, the legion's R&D arm.

Some of those real offices, the ones where real work had been done, now lay exposed by chewed off walls. Surveying the damage, Carrera decided that the formerly hidden offices didn't look like that or like anything suspicious; they looked completely unremarkable amidst the general ruin.

Miguel Lanza, the commander of the Sixteenth Aviation Legion, coughed behind Carrera, then said, "Sorry it took so long, *Duque*. I was looking over the damage to the airfields, when I heard."

"No problem, Miguel," Carrera assured him. "How bad are they?"

"We can fix them by blasting and bulldozing the concrete shards, then filling with gravel and covering with steel planking. Take a few days, though."

"Don't," said Carrera. "Rather, don't fix most of them past the ability to keep them looking unfixed and unserviceable . . . except maybe for one or two places where you can fix them completely, provided you hide it. We wouldn't want our friends to run out of targets, now, would we?"

Lanza nodded, saying, "I understand." He hesitated for a moment and asked, "Did they know about this, *Duque*? I mean, did they know what it was? And if they did, what does it mean?"

"You figure it out, Miguel. The city, not even including the whole metro area, is almost three hundred square kilometers. It has tens of thousands of buildings. Every other bomb they dropped that I've heard of had a valid—not necessarily a legitimate, but a valid—reason for being bombed. What are the odds that this one bomb, out of hundreds that hit where they were supposed to, was just a fluke, given what this has meant to us?"

"Shitty," Lanza said.

"Yep, shitty. They knew . . ."

As Lanza had, someone else announced himself from behind Carrera and the aviator. "Sir?"

"Yes, Jamie." James Soult was Carrera's driver and friend.

Soult proffered a block of paper on a clipboard with some writing on the paper. "Got the list of damage. Casualties weren't too bad, under a hundred and fifty dead and injured both, reported so far, though that can be expected to rise. It was more than half civilians. Here's the list of facilities they hit."

Carrera took the clipboard—the legion had a positive prejudice against using computers where a) pen and ink would do, and b) electronic security could not be guaranteed. As he took it, he thought, *A hundred and fifty. The Federated States' equivalent would have been fifteen thousand. Heavy . . . heavy . . . but . . . if you will the end, you will the means, and you will the price, too.*

Soult's clipboard didn't have a by-name list of the dead, though it did mention places where groups of people had been hurt and killed. From that it wasn't hard for Carrera to figure out which were military and which civilian. The only surprise was that one civil apartment building had been hit, accounting for about half of the civilian dead and injured.

*Hmmm . . . well . . . okay, if they hit an inoffensive apartment building maybe this one could have been a fluke. Problems are that I can't treat it as a fluke and I must retaliate for the apartment building.*

"I've got a secure link up with the *Casamara*," said Soult, "and the target list for Condors is in the car."

# CHAPTER TWENTY-FIVE

Retaliation is related to nature and instinct, not to law.
Law, by definition, cannot obey the same rules as nature.
    —Albert Camus, "Reflections on the Guillotine"

**Militarized Airship *Casamara*, over the southern Shimmering Sea**

About midocean, Tribune Soliz, the commander of the *Casamara*, had ordered displayed on the ship, from six angles, the gold eagle of the Sixteenth Legion. The displays weren't especially large, of course. Indeed, being no bigger than any other military aircraft's roundel, they were essentially lost against the sheer bulk of an airship. They could also, in a pinch, be hidden, too. Soliz didn't expect that to be necessary.

*We've never quite fit into the law of war anyway, being neither ship nor aircraft. Sure, there are provisions that ships, when armed, ought to declare themselves as auxiliary cruisers. Sadly, for the legalistic, we are not a true ship and the treaty was never extended to cover airships.*

*'Course, we've always been a pain in the ass for the customs folk, too, and nobody ever got around to fixing that.*

Like all of his crew, Soliz wore the uniform of the legion. In his case, being the captain, this was dress whites. Most wore battledress that did something less than a great job of making them blend in with *Casamara*'s pastel walls and carpets.

Soliz felt something less than guilty about not identifying his command as an instrument of war. *They can see it if they board us. Not that they really can board us, hence that continuing sense of annoyance from the customs people; but they could, in theory. And if they did, if they got past the hidden machine guns and the men with shoulder-fired antiaircraft missiles I've got out on the exterior catwalks' corners, they could see that we're all in uniform, nice and proper. And besides, did those murdering fucks from the Tauran Union illuminate their wing and tail flashes so they could be seen at night when they came to kill our people and destroy our property? They did not! So fuck 'em.*

Soliz, wearing his very distinctive whites, left the bridge and went to the catwalks that encircled the airship. Normally these were fully Plexiglassed or otherwise fenced in, to protect the passengers from falling overboard. For the most part they still were, but several sections had been removed to allow fire from the machine guns and missiles.

To get to the machine gun crews, or to expose them, would have required cutting through some thin material along the flanks, bow, and stern. Soliz wasn't too concerned with them, anyway. They were warm and dry, inside *Casamara*. No, he was mostly concerned with the four three-man missile crews at the corners, where a dozen meters of Plexiglas sheets had been removed to allow firing to flank and stern or bow without the backblast damaging the ship. He'd verbally drilled the crews, personally, before issuing the missiles. Even so, he wanted to remind them. Hence, Soliz's sojourn out to the catwalks.

Having checked with the forward port missile men, Soliz, shivering because—*What the fuck was I thinking wearing this thin white shit out in the open? Man, it is* cold *out here!*—of the open catwalks, walked aft. There were stationed three men, all heavily bundled against the cold. One of the three men on duty sat on a passenger bench. The other two scanned continuously through huge binoculars that just happened to be mounted there, as if they were solely for the enjoyment of the passengers, when passengers were carried. The missiles remained in their cases on the deck, though Soliz could see that the tops were ajar already, for easy access.

He stood there for a few moments, shivering while chatting with the troops. Then, duty done, Soliz ducked back into the shelter of the airship, walked a dozen meters down the corridor, and turned right to go to the cargo—sometimes the passenger—deck.

In the center of the cargo deck was a kind of mobile cradle, mounted on roller rails bolted to the logistic track, or L-track, tie-down rails along the deck. The cradle seemed to Soliz to be a very good fit for the single Condor auxiliary-propelled glider that rested on it, hence also for the other eleven still resting on the deck. There was, he noticed, a thin, plastic-covered steel cable attached to both the rear of the cradle and the deck, with the excess rolled up neatly between them.

Technically, the rolling cradle wasn't necessary; the crew could have manhandled the gliders out the rear cargo ramp. This way was safer though.

*And why not?* thought Soliz. *The legion takes so many risks in every other activity, why not a little safety for the men where we can have it? Especially where it costs just about nothing?*

Soliz already knew the targets; the data for them had been selected from documents in his safe, based on certain inputs from home and the Global News Network.

Even though he knew the targets, Soliz went and stood behind one of the Condor crew, the woman, as she input targeting data into a computer linked directly to one of the gliders.

On one side of the screen were the numbers one through twelve, a target type, a location, a time of strike, and an approach, where that made a difference. It didn't, always. Only eleven of those seemed to be complete. On the other side of the screen were displayed eleven empty sections and the twelfth, still full of data. Between those two was a map, the caption of which gave a code for the survey section and the major feature, in this case, the city of Lumière, capital of Gaul and, in some ways, of the entire Tauran Union, however much certain unimportant attributes—like the corrupt, rubber stamp of a Tauran Parliament—had been shunted elsewhere.

Soliz silently skipped over the right side of the display, in no particular order, *Soccer game, Altstadt . . . MB . . . Tauran Parliament . . . FMB . . . Throtmanni, Sachsen, MB . . . Kaiserswerth, Auto plant . . . FMTIB . . . Lumière, athletic event, MB . . . Lumière, Gaul, Tauran Defense Headquarters, FMB-I . . . Muddybrook, Anglia . . . SCIB . . . Nemossos, Gaul . . . FMB-I . . .*

The woman, Sergeant Vera Dzhugashvili, was a daughter of one of the Volgan officers of the Twenty-second Tercio, by his wife, also a Volgan. Soliz had never met either of Vera's parents, but still had to admit, from a purely aesthetic point of view, that the match was a prime piece—*Okay, pun intended,* he admitted to himself—of evidence in favor of Volgan women.

Green eyed, of a height to match Soliz's own, blond, slender . . . *Ah, crap, if I keep thinking this way we'll both get in trouble. Still, what a great ass. Not much tit, but a truly spectacular bottom.* He thought, *both,* because he was pretty sure the sergeant was interested, too. But nothing could be done until one or the other was out of service. The sergeant had joined at age nineteen, not so long after her family had moved to Balboa to man the legion's opposing force regiment. She probably could have been an officer or centurion, thought Soliz, or even a pilot warrant officer, if she'd gone through Cazador School, for selection. Sadly, it was only recently that a female Cazador class had been opened, once annually. That was closed for the duration of the war. It was unlikely she'd ever rise above the rank of optio. And the legion could be literal death on that kind of mixed marriage.

*That rule's got to change,* thought Soliz. *Now, with full mobilization, we've got to come up with something less restrictive. On the other hand, now, with full mobilization, we've got opportunities for corruption, favoritism, abuse of office, and de facto prostitution like never before. So maybe not. For sure, there's no glib and easy answer. But, damn, is she pretty!*

"Sir," asked the sergeant, "any idea why of four MBs, two are targeted at Sachsen but only one each at Anglia and Gaul?"

Soliz shrugged, then answered, "My best guess, and it's only a guess, is that Anglia and the frogs are used to hooligans, while Sachsen has a higher opinion of itself, possibly an unreasonably high opinion of itself, and so is likely to be more mortified when publically shamed."

"Oh . . . okay, that makes sense," Vera agreed. "I guess." She pushed a final key, then said, "Anyway, we're ready, sir."

Soliz looked out and saw that the night was fast descending. "How close are we to the launch window?"

Vera glanced at her display and answered, "Twenty-one minutes."

"Okay, commencing in twenty-one minutes, launch . . . one every five minutes. And let's see how those bastards like it."

Vera felt a little shiver pass through at the skipper's words. *It's so damned unfair. He already looks delicious and smells just right. Does he have to* sound *so damned perfect, too?*

## Condor One, over the Southern Shimmering Sea

The carriage slid easily down the rails to edge of the open loading platform. As soon as it reached that edge, a set of blocks abruptly stopped it, allowing the Condor to fly free.

For a moment, the Condor dropped. But its long, thin wings quickly bit into the air, generating enough lift to turn the drop into a long, shallow glide. The glider's GLS antenna was already out, and its active computer—though nothing special, to be sure—knew its objective, the course to take to that, and the final approach. The computer also received, through the same antenna, updated weather data to include wind, which ranged favorable from this direction, this time of year. Wind would be especially important at the target.

The glider had been launched with its auxiliary power—a mast bearing a propeller—already set. This engaged sixty seconds after launch. After that, the gliding was done for a while, while the propeller lifted the thing to an altitude of four miles, then cut off. For the next several hours, the glider would, in fact, glide toward its target.

By the time Condor Two departed the airship, Condor One was well out of the way. By the time the last of the twelve was airborne, on its own, the *Casamara* was an easy hundred and twenty kilometers from the initial launch point. Thereupon, the airship turned due west for Volga, where it would deliver the crew from the long-range bombardment squadron to a nice little dacha, then continue on in a circumnavigation of the planet until it reached Santander, west of Balboa. There it was to intern itself . . . for a while.

## Hotel *Cielo Dorado*, Aserri, Santa Josefina, Terra Nova

"It's Commander Khan, the husband," Esmeralda announced to the high admiral, shaking her awake gently. The empress barely stirred until the shaking became rather less gentle. "High Admiral, the commander says it's important. He's not given to panic or exaggeration."

"Oh, all right," Marguerite answered, finally stirring from her bed.

Esmeralda saw that she was naked, frankly magnificent, and had an interesting pattern of delicate-looking bite marks on her breasts. Totally unself-conscious of any of that, the high admiral stood, stretched, and then took the communicator from Esmeralda's proffering hand.

*No sense in disturbing Xingzhen,* thought the high admiral. *I'll take it in the other room.* Esmeralda followed dutifully.

"Are you alone, High Admiral?" asked Khan's voice, once Marguerite answered.

"Yes . . . well, except for Esma."

"She can hear this," was Khan's judgment. "High Admiral, do you remember a couple of days ago, that airship that resupplied the guerillas in Santa Josefina?"

"Yes, sure."

"Well . . . I put a skimmer on it, just in case. I have visual of the airship launching a dozen or so . . . gliders. Yes, I am serious, gliders. But not just gliders, High Admiral.

"Right now, *Spirit of Brotherhood* is over Taurus. It cannot see the glider by radar. Lidar is highly problematic. At least the limited returns we get show something that ought not be. We only have it on visual and, by the time I was notified, there was only one we had via the skimmer. It's a glider, of course; it's following the winds for the most part. So I can't say where it will come down."

"So what is it?" asked Wallenstein. "Or what are they?"

Khan hesitated a moment, then said, "I am guessing here . . . but I think this is how a nuclear warhead was delivered to Hajar without anyone noticing it. I would suspect these are delivering nukes to a dozen Tauran cities . . ."

*Oh, elder gods,* thought Wallenstein, feeling a sudden attack of something like panic. *Could he do that? Would he do that? He only had ten warheads though . . . well, ten I know about. He could have had more. But nukes? I could see him nuking the Salafi Ikhwan and those who supported it. It even worked out well for humanity, if not so well for the population of Hajar. But ten cities, or twelve, over some light bombing? No, he's a nut but he's not that bad of a nut.*

"Don't think so," Wallenstein said. "So go ahead and assume not and give me the other analysis."

"Just enough to provoke and humiliate them, High Admiral.

Carrera wants this war as much as we do, and if there's any better measure of his basic lunacy I don't know what it could be. If not nukes then those are—I am guessing, of course—high-explosive-armed gliders."

"And we can't see them by any technical means?" asked the high admiral. She asked herself, *Will this help nudge the Taurans to the war they're afraid of? Oh, yes.*

"No," answered Khan. "Only visual."

"Then the TU can't see them either?"

"We think we're still ahead of them in radar, lidar, and computer analysis, yes, High Admiral. So, no, High Admiral, they probably can't. At least we're ahead of them in those ships where the radar and lidar still worked and those we've been able to restore since your elevation to Class One and loosening of the purse strings."

Wallenstein thought for a bit, then thought some more, then asked Khan, "How long until these things reach somewhere worth hitting?"

"Half a day or so, High Admiral. There's no particular hurry."

"My instincts," she said, "tell me to ignore this, in the same general way that any enemy, making a mistake, ought not be interrupted. I'm going to continue thinking about it, but unless you hear from me otherwise, ignore this and make sure no whisper leaves the fleet that we saw a damned thing."

"Roger, High Admiral. Wilco."


### Condor One, over Lumière, Gaul, Terra Nova

The gliders all had a pecking order and a presumptive time of arrival over their targets. Each on-board computer was also able to plug into the local global net, via a cellular connection, to coordinate, to the limited extent they had to coordinate. Condor One, also number one in the pecking order, was launched first and was first over its target. As soon as it was, it adopted a fairly high-level circular holding pattern, well away from well-travelled air routes. It also dialed into a site set up by Khalid, the use of which the assassin had never a clue to. The gist of its message was, "I am here. I am in charge. Notify when in position."

## Condor Twelve, over Altstadt, Sachsen, Terra Nova

The last one in position was Twelve, which had acquired its number by virtue of when it was expected to arrive on target. It duly checked in to Khalid's website, reporting, "I am here and ready." Twelve's brother, Eleven, was also over the city, though its target type was very different. It had also reported in a few minutes earlier. Thereupon One said to all the rest, "Numbers Twelve, Nine, and Five, execute in three minutes. Numbers One, Two, Three, Four, Six, Seven, Eight, Ten, and Eleven, execute in five minutes."

All sent back digital, "Wilcos," immediately, except for Number Six, which was a little slow. Six floated over an oil refinery in Tuscany. Eventually, it, too, reported in.

## *Sicherheitsgruppen* Park, Throtmanni, Sachsen, Terra Nova

It was a huge stadium with a soccer game ongoing.

Soccer had, unsurprisingly, been carried to the new world from the very beginning and kept intact since then. It was unsurprising because, where many other outdoor sports, and not a few indoor ones, required massive quantities of equipment, soccer required a ball. Everything else could be manufactured on site, if necessary.

Soccer was, from some points of view, a perfect social sport; it encouraged a tie, no winners, no losers. For some, like the Federated States, this was anathema. But for Taurans it worked very well indeed.

That is to say, it worked well for a large number, even a large majority, of Taurans. There were those, though, for whom anything but victory was as impermissible a concept as it was in the FSC.

And then there were those who just liked a good fight better than anything except a good riot. These went to soccer games, invariably in groups, sometimes very large groups, on the not unreasonable premise that self-fulfilling prophecies are called that because they're destined to be fulfilled.

With Condor Nine floating lazily and easily above the stadium, unseen or ignored among the crowds, Gallic and Sachsen hooligan clubs took turns singing their national anthems, tossing unsavory ethnic epithets and similarly themed chants at each other, and generally engaging in the brotherly banter that had been at the core of soccer hooliganism on two worlds over more than five centuries. Before that it had been the core of the legal concept of "chance medley," which was another way of saying, "young men like to, indeed are compelled to, fight and you can't stop it."

In a crowd of eighty-three thousand, though, the presence of not more than a thousand hooligans, combined, was thought to be a minor threat.

Nine received the word from One, via the website. It made a final read of the wind and weather, calculated its path from its own position and altitude, and then began a spiraling descent over the open portions of the stadium. Nine passed its eighteen-meter wingspan easily between the widely set yellow pylons over the stadium. Many in the crowd now *did* look up, some even pointing at the spectacle of the graceful glider coming so low.

Then came a flash, a great puff of smoke, and the vision of the glider disintegrating. The wings, so light as to be harmless, flew off to the sides, then began to flutter down alone, spinning into the seating areas on either side. The small engine that separated out was heavier, dangerously heavy in fact. But soccer players are not noted for the slowness of their reactions. Neither are the referees who judge the play of the games. These saw the rapidly falling engine and stepped nimbly out of the way. The other pieces, the spun carbon fiber shell, the polyurethane embedded with its uncountable millions of randomized tiny concave-convex chips, the bits of shattered fuel tank, all sank slowly to the artificial turf of the stadium.

And when all that had cleared, and the crowd looked up, all that they saw was a cloud, and not an especially thin one, of brightly colored rectangular pieces of paper, fluttering down like . . .

Possibly the first to discern the nature of the attack was a camera and news crew, sending a live broadcast of the game to audiences and Gaul and Sachsen, both. The crew had two cameras, two cameramen, and two sportscasters, one Sachsen, the other Gaul, in each case. There was also a foreman of sort, an Anglian, who was the only man completely free to step outside the glassed-in booth.

He grabbed one of the fluttering pieces of paper, saw what it was, and said, "Christ! Becken and Franck are no longer the highest paid men on that field."

"It's fucking MONEY!" screamed one of the soccer hooligans of the Sachsen side, as he snatched one of the fluttering greenish pieces out of the air. Less certain, after the first impulse, he felt it between thumb and fingers . . . *Yep, pure cotton.*

"It's a fucking hundred Tauro note!" the hooligan screamed.

"They're all large notes," said one of his compatriots, softly, gazing with wonder at another Tauro bill, this one a yellow two hundred, graced with the image of a mythical bridge.

They'd been looking down at the notes. Spontaneously, they both started to look up to where the money had come from. One the way, their eyes, the eyes of forty thousand people, caught about forty thousand Gauls beginning to stream onto the field, where most of the money was blizzarding down.

With a gasp of outraged shock and horror, roughly five hundred Sachsen soccer hooligans charged onto the field. With no more than a moment's delay, thirty-nine thousand, five hundred, give or take, solid, upright, honest, law-abiding Sachsen citizens joined them where they met forty thousand-odd Gauls in a battle the likes of which the continent had not seen since the close of the Great Global War, generations before.

Thanas had only one recognized talent. He was just emerging from the service area, under the grandstands, where he'd spent the last hour and change in a men's room exercising it, giving oral sex to a fairly large selection of fairly random men, few of whom spoke German all that well. Ignoring his first, sensibly cowardly, instinct to run from the hubbub, he hesitated just that fraction of a second before his innate cowardice could take over. Thus, he was caught up in the flood of the mob until it spilled over the playing field walls, dragging him with it.

Unlike those who were leaping over, eager to come to grips with the hated, and now doubly hated, Gaul, Thanas didn't want to go. This caused him to land not on his feet, but on his shoulder, which broke.

He screamed like a baby with a long unchanged diaper. This wasn't helped when he realized how much danger he was in and really *did* need a diaper, or at least an underwear, change. For a moment, as the crowd surged past him, leaving him alone, he tried to scramble over the walls but, one armed, just couldn't do it. He'd probably have been well enough off if he'd simply lain down again. Standing, he drew the attention of three other young men who, since they'd started off in the cheap seats, hadn't a prayer of getting to either the bulk of the money or the nexus of the action. Those young men weren't at all happy about it. They were also members of the same hooligan club, a fact easily discerned by their severe haircuts, black club uniform, heavy pull-on boots, and displays of archaic silver insignia few in Sachsen could have identified.

These three took one look at Thanas, decided—not with reason—*Schwul*, and, feeling the desperate need to beat someone to death, began to stalk him.

Thanas slammed his back to the wall and put up his one good arm. The first of the hooligans to reach him grabbed his hand and bent in downward, so abruptly that the wrist broke, leaving the hand flapping. Thanas opened his mouth to scream, but a fist wearing multiple rings smashed into it, breaking off several teeth. Tears running from his eyes, Thanas sank to the turf, vainly trying to protect his savaged face with his useless arms. A kick to the chest pulled the arms away from his head automatically. Gagging and choking and gasping for air, he rolled over on his side. The next kick was to his head, after which Thanas knew nothing at all as the three hooligans stomped and kicked him to rags and pulp.

And the cameras caught it all.

# CHAPTER TWENTY-SIX

The contest on our side is not one of rivalry or vengeance,
but of endurance. It is not those who can inflict the most,
but those who can suffer the most who will conquer.
—Mayor Terence MacSwiney, Lord Mayor of Cork,
October 25, 1920

### Tauran Defense Agency Headquarters, Lumière, Gaul, Terra Nova

Condor One had already gone off over the local stadium, Josephine
Park, with effects not dissimilar to, if not quite as satisfying as, those
from the *Sicherheitsgruppen* Park, in Sachsen. This was only to be
expected, given that the former had only just over half the number of
the latter. On the other hand, what the participants lacked in numbers
they made up for in brainpan-spattering enthusiasm; the two teams
playing were Anglian and Gallic, and those two groups detested and
hated each other from very far back.

Not every target, though, was moral, as were the four stadium-
aimed money attacks. There were others en route, both economic and
military, plus one reprisal.

Three were purely military. One of these was the Tauran Union
Defense Agency Headquarters.

The lower windows were barred but the upper ones were not. The
bars dated to a simpler day. Now they were retained mostly for
sentiment's sake. Khalid had noted them, and noted as well their

absence above. He'd actually had to spend an extra day in the city to find out if the bars mattered. "They do," he'd been told.

As it turned out, though, they didn't. The office he wanted, that of Lady Elisabeth Ashworth, was on one of the upper floors of the ancient building. Her windows were not barred. Still, it had taken another *two* days to determine that they were also not special, not bulletproof. "Does that matter?" he'd asked. "Bloody fucking right, it does," he'd been answered.

It had been hard enough to find the right office window; the interior layout of the office had been beyond Khalid's ability and beyond the time he had, having wasted so much, to devote to it.

Lady Ashworth sat at her accustomed chair, behind her massive desk, facing the window and doing precisely nothing. She hadn't a clue, not the first clue, *what* to do. A pure party hack, ennobled as part of a backroom deal, with no education to speak of and no ability beyond self-aggrandizement that anyone had seen much real evidence for, she was a useless time server, drawing a check well above her abilities to earn. *Any* check, so it was widely believed, would have been above her abilities.

Besides, the staff spoke mostly French while she had nothing but lower-class English to see her through. She was as isolated by that as by anything.

Staring out the broad window, mindlessly, Lady Ashworth didn't understand just what that circular thing growing in the window was. The wings gave her the beginning of a clue, but that beginning hadn't grown to a certainty before the window bowed in, then broke into thousands of shards.

The shards slashed Ashworth's face, but before blood could flow, the thing had torn off its own wings, smacked into that massive desk, and pushed both bureau and bureaucrat back against the wall, pinning her and breaking her spine at the same time. Already fishlike of visage, the woman's mouth opened and closed in agony like a fish tossed on the shore and suffocating.

She barely noticed when a series of tiny explosive charges blew away four small sections of the thing pinning her and her desk.

And, of course, since she spoke not a word of French in a largely French-speaking building, she had no clue what it meant when the aircraft—she was dimly coming to awareness that it was an aircraft—squealed, squelched, and a sultry feminine voice said:

"*Votre attention s'il-vous-plaît, je suis une bombe à retardement de cinq minutes. Votre attention s'il-vous-plaît, je suis une bombe à retardement de cinq minutes. Veuillez évacuer la zone. Je suis une bombe à retardement de cinq minutes. Veuillez évacuer la zone. Je suis une grande bombe à retardement de cinq minutes. Mon délai de détonation a été fixé au maximum à cinq minutes mais pourrait bien y être inférieur. Sortez d'ici sur-le-champ. Quatre minutes cinquante-cinq . . . quatre minutes cinquante . . . une minute . . . cinquante-neuf . . . cinquante-huit . . . cinq . . . quatre . . . trois . . . deux . . . adieu.*"

Ashworth was fortunate that the charge killed her outright—and so thoroughly that no trace of her body was ever found—because the charge was mixed explosive and incendiary, a self-contained "shake and bake," and had she not died from the blast she'd likely have burned to death, as did some numbers of people, civil and military, and the TU Defense Agency Headquarters, anyway.

## Phaeton Factory, Kaiserswerth, Sachsen, Terra Nova

There were only a handful of carbon fiber looms on the planet. One of these, the simplest and cheapest, by far, wove the relatively simple interior shells of the Condor gliders. Another was in Yamato, where it was used in the manufacture of very expensive automobiles. But the best and the latest, needless to say also the most expensive, was at the Kaiserswerth Phaeton factory, making even more expensive automobiles.

Not Khalid, but another of Fernandez's operatives had rather brazenly taken a tour of the plant, offered by the company, itself, to get the details just right. He'd paced the distance to the loom from a known point.

No one outside of Phaeton corporate headquarters knew quite what the loom cost. One measure was that there were, in fact, only two of that caliber. The other was the price of the cars produced, which was simply staggering.

Although called a carbon fiber loom, in fact there was more to the process than this, a big chunk being impregnating the material produced by the loom with resin and plastic, both of which were rather flammable. Then, too, the value of the entire factory dwarfed the cost of the loom, so clearly it had to go.

Thus, the warhead on the Condor that crashed through the roof consisted of high explosive, the brisance of which was to shatter the loom, a thermobaric charge, to blow out the walls and do maximum structural damage, while releasing any chemicals held, and a magnesium based incendiary device, rather a pair of them, to set it all alight.

No Sachsen workers, however, were hurt. The condor crashed the roof, blasted out the panels covering the speakers, and then played a recorded message from a German-speaking female from the legion. Where Lourdes had spoken in her own sexy and sultry way, the German version had a tone like orders to assemble in the showers. Translated, it went, "Attention, please. I am a Five Minute Bomb. Attention, please. I am a five minute bomb. Evacuate the area quickly. I am a Five Minute Bomb. Evacuate the area quickly. I am a *large* five minute bomb. My delay is fixed at a maximum of five-minutes. It could be less. Leave the area *now!* Four minutes, fifty-nine seconds . . ."

No cameras caught that. But the word got around, and lost little or nothing in the telling.

### Militarized Airship *Casamara,* over Tuscany and heading west, Terra Nova

Soliz called in everyone but the missile crews to watch the Global News Network's coverage of the bombing on the big screen inside the passenger lounge. He had the bartender pour drinks and the cooks bring in some light finger foods, then toasted the success of the raid.

Behind him, on the screen, the images changed from soccer riot to burning headquarters to badly damaged, roof-sagging factory, back to riot, and so on. The crew certainly enjoyed seeing the success of their mission, especially the smoking ruins of the Tauran Union Defense Agency Headquarters. And the scenes from the four soccer games baited into bloody riots were just precious. The crew cheered lustily, in fact, until the screen showed rescue workers taking bodies, some of them very small bodies, from an apartment building in Anglia struck in reprisal for the one hit in Balboa. GNN keyed on that for long minutes, bringing in a battery of "experts," many of them dismally ignorant, to discuss it.

"But they're hardly being fair," said Sergeant Vera Dzhugashvili. "It's not like they didn't bomb us *first*."

If Soliz hadn't been in love with her already, he became so when the immigrant girl said, "us."

"Sergeant," he said, "when I take you to Volga and drop off you people of the Sixteenth and the eighteen Condors the airship still carries, you can disable the warning to evacuate systems for some of them. The *Duque* told me before we left home that GNN would be informed that its coverage would be even handed—as ours, by the way, will not be—or it would be declared an organ of an enemy government and engaged without warning. You do know how to disable the warning systems, right?"

"Yes, sir," the sergeant said. "Though it's more a question of not arming them than of disarming them."

"Excellent." Soliz glanced at his watch. "We have eighteen hours. Our man on the ground in the pertinent part of Volga, the town of Prokhorovka, is waiting. I need all of you to finish preparing the remaining cargo, and yourselves, for parachute drop."

Vera Dzhugashvili went suddenly pale.

"Is there a problem, Sergeant?" Soliz asked.

"They've drilled me on the procedures, sure, sir, but I've never jumped before. So, yes, you might say there's a problem. Sir."

"Then rejoice, Sergeant; you get your jump wings with one jump, rather than five."


### Hotel *Cielo Dorado*, Aserri, Santa Josefina, Terra Nova

Oddly, it was the hints and tips given by Aragon that let Esmeralda lie so facilely when Janier asked about the source of the bombs. "Surely, your fleet could see them," the Gallic general insisted. "You have five hundred years of progress on us. There is no way you did not."

"I'm just a cabin girl, sir," she replied. "I'm hardly privy to things like that. I am sure, though, that if the high admiral had seen them coming, she'd have let you know."

Janier nodded. On the face of it, it made sense. *But then*, he thought, *if Wallenstein did know, and had warned me, I'd have to have done something. That would have saved the life of that idiotic Anglian tart, "Lady" Ashworth. I cannot imagine any damage the Balboans did that would be greater than the benefit of being rid of that time-serving, incompetent twat. Even so, I had better check with lovely Marguerite.*

"Where is the high admiral?" Janier asked.

Esmeralda lowered her head demurely and, looking up with big brown eyes, under long lashes, gave a knowing smile. It was a smile that said, *In bed with the empress.* This wasn't impossible, of course, but as far as she knew it also wasn't true. What the lie gave her was a chance, a little time, to get to her chief and tell her that Janier had his suspicions.

"We saw it after the event, General," Wallenstein lied. "By tracking back through records in the computer we were able to see where each bomb came from."

"But not in time to prevent the attacks?" the Gaul asked, though it was closer to an accusation.

Wallenstein shook her head. "We have a massive array of sensors aimed at your planet, of course, but to make any sense of the data requires a human being. Five hundred years of progress hasn't changed that. The number of human crew we have for the purpose is limited. So, yes, once we knew to look to track back, it was easy to identify the source. But to see it in advance? No, that was beyond our *human* capabilities."

"I see. All right, then; that is something my superiors can accept." His tone did not suggest it was something *he* necessarily accepted. "And, then too, it rid me of the baleful influence of that fool, Lady Ashton."

"Speaking of which, General," asked the high admiral, "who would you like to replace the late, lamented Lady Ashton? I can put in a good word for someone."

"Nobody," answered the Gaul, without a moment's hesitation. "Anyone in there is an idler wheel, a device that reverses motion. Without one, there is only me. And, while I have my flaws, all too recently all too well shown, I am still better than any civilian bureaucrat or political hack. Can you do that for me, High Admiral?"

"That's tougher," she admitted. "Easier said than done. But I'll try, General. Of course. That will be easier if the people who run the Tauran Union are convinced that the bombs were in no way the fault of United Earth."

"I'll try," the general answered, with a smile that was almost an echo of Esmeralda's, an hour earlier.

Wallenstein asked, "If I do have to permit the appointment of a replacement, though, would Uni Wiglan do? She's usually easy to work with, in my experience."

Janier considered that, finally agreeing that, if there had to be a replacement, the Wiglan woman would do well enough.

### East of Prokhorovka, Elevation Four Hundred Meters, Airship *Casamara*, Terra Nova

There were many synergistic reasons why, as Tribune Soliz had recently observed, customs agents the world over disliked, or hated, airships. Unlike both ships and aircraft, they didn't need any permanent facilities. At least, the newest ones didn't. And even the older versions really didn't need much. Thus, who knew where to monitor and search them? Where could they be searched, except at the distant field where they had loaded and where ground crews, air crews, and customs people might well be corrupt. And what if they stopped somewhere enroute?

Worse, they had cargo capacities that, if dwarfed by ocean-going vessels, in turn dwarfed those of airplanes. And helicopters? Like airships, those could go where they liked, but had cargo loads that were, in comparison, trivial. And expensive to deliver to boot.

Worse still was the ability of an airship, with some modern methods of remotely controlled or pre-guided precision parachuting, to saunter along parallel to a border, parachuting contraband over to the other side. That last ability, whether the cargoes were consumer goods, information, or arms, had had a not insignificant part to play in ending the rule of the Red Tsar.

At night, as it was now, the problems for the customs folks were worse still.

★★★

The shipping containers, even with their cargoes, weighed no more than a standard load for a droppable pallet. They were rigged differently, of course, given the lack of perimeter rings and the heavy corner shackles. Still, with a few differences in rigging procedure, the chute cluster that worked for one worked reasonably well for the other.

The other advantage for dropping from airship was that it was a very gentle drop, much more so than even an airplane that had dropped to just above stall speed. The downside of that was that it took the chutes longer to open, and required more elevation because of that.

"Make our elevation six hundred meters," Soliz ordered, as the airship crossed the Volgan border. "Heading . . ." Soliz consulted the wind data, then said, "Zero-six-four." The deck officer repeated that, then was echoed by all three coxswains, Height, Altitude, and Course, who answered, "Aye, aye, sir."

Soliz had to hope that the requisite bribes had been paid. Then again, from being the class of the planet for terrestrially bound aircraft, under Red Tsar and driven by tsarist paranoia, Volgan air defense had become something of a joke.

That was only a two-hundred-meter rise, to be achieved over ten miles, so the change in the angle of the deck was almost imperceptible. The helm announced and the watch officer repeated when the desired elevation had been reached.

Sergeant Dzhugashvili had gone positively pale as the time for jumping approached.

"I'm afraid I'll freeze," she'd whispered to Soliz. "No . . . I'm terrified I'll freeze up, sir."

"Is that what's really bothering you?" asked the tribune.

"Most of it, yes, sir. Of course, I'm not exactly thrilled over the jump, the fall, or the possibility of a sudden stop at the end. But the big thing is fearing I'll fail through my own weakness."

"I understand perfectly," the tribune said. "You know why?"

"No, sir."

"Because I felt *exactly,* and I mean *exactly,* the same way before my first jump—I started in the *Cazadores,* you know—and my sergeant told me what I'm going to tell you. 'Don't sweat that, Private Soliz,' he said to me. 'I'll be right behind you and if you look like you've frozen I'll pick you up and throw you out.'"

"There? Now doesn't that make you feel better, young Sergeant."

Vera considered that for a minute, searching inside herself. She had to admit that, "You know, sir, in an odd way, it does. It really *does*."

Soliz clapped her on the shoulder, saying, "I thought it might. Now let's go aft to cargo, we have some deliveries to make."

Vera stopped suddenly, just before the hatchway that led into cargo. The hatchway was closed. Soliz took one step further, then realized the woman wasn't following. He turned and started to say something. Whatever that something was, it was lost as Vera planted a kiss on him that very quickly grew wet.

When they finally came up for air, she said, "I've been wanting to do that ever since the second or third pallet came aboard. I didn't because . . ."

"Because," he finished, "one thing would have led to another, and that other to something else, and, somewhere about the middle of the Shimmering Sea, we'd have been caught doing something for which we could be shot."

"Yes, sir. That. Just that."

"Sad goddamned life," he said. "Sad rules we live under, my lovely Vera. Sad . . . but necessary."

"Sir, Emilio, the war won't last. In six months my time is up and I vote with my civil century. I become a full human being again. If we live . . ."

"I will find you, Vera. I *will* find you. Then we can continue the conversation under a more fitting setting."

"Good," she said. "See that you do. A private room would be more fitting. And now I really figure I can jump. I didn't want that going unsaid, in case the jump went bad. So come on, sir, my very dear, and be prepared to toss my—you will surely have noted—rather well-shaped bottom out of this airship."

One thing the legion was not especially short of was Volgans. The influx had begun with buying Volgan arms and hiring a cadre of instructors for them, at the very beginning. It had taken a big boost with the recruitment of the better part of a Volgan parachute regiment, the 351st Guards Airborne, to serve as an opposing force regiment. The 351st had been, at the time, just on the friendly side of starvation, so they'd been available cheap. Still, Carrera had put them on Balboan pay scales which were, in the Volgan terms of the day, rather generous.

Between the cadres and the paratroopers, the word had gone back to Volga, *Good soldiers, there's a decent living for you.* Many had come then. Some had gone back but more had stayed. Some whores had come too, and many of those had stayed. Some few of the whores had even joined the legion, to serve as something besides whores. Some of both, whores and soldiers, had fought on behalf of Balboa and the legion.

Fernandez almost never had enough foreigners for all of his various overseas interests. But he'd had Volgans and to spare.

Sergeant (Medically Retired) Pavlov had received crippling wounds on a raid inside Santander, years prior. The legion had kept him on, though, paid for all his medical care, and fitted him out with the best prosthetics available anywhere.

Still, he hadn't really been up to combat anymore, nor even peacetime training for it. Thus, after a little consultation with the rehabilitation section, and them consulting with a section of Fernandez's department, he'd been offered a position. It had paid better than his old job, too, mainly because it entailed elevation to warrant officer (nonleadership). The new warrant's only stipulation was that he never be used against his natural homeland. So far, he had not been, either.

Thus, too, he now found himself on a barren plain, looking upward. Around him thrummed the engines of a whole company's worth of heavy transport vehicles, with palletized load systems, that he'd rented for a fair consideration from the unit's regimental commander. The good colonel had even thrown a case of vodka into the deal, and one couldn't be fairer than that.

"*Praporschik,*" said the *starshina* or first sergeant, who had come with the trucks, "there it is." Pavlov could only barely make out the *starshina*'s pointing finger.

Pavlov looked east-northeast, to where a barely seen whalelike shape slowly and ponderously crossed the sky, blotting out large swaths of stars as it did. The airship, on its current course, should pass within about eight hundred meters, half a mile, of where the trucks waited.

Pavlov's local cell phone rang. It was a call from overseas, apparently. He, however, knew better.

"Hello, *Casamara*," he answered. "Pavlov here, awaiting my package. I see you."

"On the way," the airship answered.

With a great grunt, the crew of the *Casamara* gave the final shove that sent the container rolling down the floor flip system, to the ramp, and then tipping over that and disappearing into the night.

At command the crew of the long-range bombardment *ala* formed up in two short lines, on either side of the cargo bay; Vera Dzhugashvili went with the port side line. So did Soliz. She was in the second place in her line. None of them carried anything but their chutes and reserves; personal equipment had been loaded in the containers with the eighteen remaining Condors.

They were already standing. The jumpmaster, one of Soliz's crew, ordered, "Hook up!" He shouted from force of habit, though the sound inside the cargo bay of the airship was almost nil.

"Check your equipment . . . sound off for equipment check!"

"Nice ass, Vera," said the sergeant behind her as he slapped it. "Three okay!"

"All okay!"

"Stand on the ramp!"

And then, in just a few moments, they were walking off the ramp and disappearing into the night.

**Intelligence Annex, Tauran Defense Agency,
Lumière, Gaul, Terra Nova**

Jan was reasonably confident that she had her throwaway, sacrificial organization in the form of Rocaberti's partisans. They would, of course, be trained. Indeed, they'd be coming here for that training. Sadly, that would be a highly truncated course, consistent with what she thought Fernandez would estimate Tauran competence at, but long enough that neither the designated sacrificial victims nor the

Balboans would have good reason to believe they were anything but a genuine main effort.

That was old news, and essentially a done deal. What she'd been working on since was the real effort, the one for which the Rocabertians, as she thought of them, were the cover. She had had some success, so far. There was one La Platan junior diplomat— *Devastatingly charming,* she thought, *but far too young*—who had signed on in fear of the Timocracy spreading to La Plata and destroying the rule of his class. Then there was a Volgan journalist whom she considered, since he was only interested in money, the most reliable of the lot. A pacifist Tsarist-Marxist, who probably didn't know a lot of history but knew what she liked, had signed on, and she wished she could get that woman trained before the Kosmos started their peace missions. *Sadly, the first one of those leaves a few weeks at the latest. No way to get Sister Melinda trained in that time.*

The problem here was that these people had to be highly trained. That would take time. Since it would take time, she found herself having to do the nearly impossible, or trying to. *How the hell do I time it so that the Rocabertians last long enough to get the real operations in place?*

# CHAPTER TWENTY-SEVEN

Appear weak when you are strong, and strong
when you are weak.
                    —Sun Tzu, *The Art of War*

**Post Theater, Fort Williams, Balboa, Terra Nova**

*I hate this part,* thought the Anglian chaplain, Captain Williams. It wasn't immediately evident just why he should hate it, when the massed noncoms, and those barely human corporals, too, sang, slowly, deliberately, to all appearances sincerely:

> "There is a green hill far away
> Without a city wall,
> Where our dear Lord was crucified
> Who died to save us all . . ."

*And here's the part that I hate.*
The senior sergeant major shouted out, "Two, three, four," and all the ranks burst out with:

> "For he's a jolly good fellow.
> For he's a jolly good fellow . . ."

*Fucking heathens,* fumed the chaplain. *And there is precisely nothing I can do about it.*

★★★

Marqueli Mendoza, the petite and perfect, had learned to ignore the singing. She was a deeply religious woman—"And why not? Was not my husband's sight miraculously restored? Who but God could do that?"—and one never really knew what new kind of blasphemy the Anglians would come up with.

*I hope God has a sense of humor,* she thought, as the song reverberated through the walls.

In a small office in the back, with a guard present, Marqueli spoke to half a dozen men, four sergeants, one a Haarlemer, and two corporals, both Haarlemers.

"I'm sorry, boys," she said. "I really am. But no, under our laws we cannot take you on, not so long as the war is ongoing and you haven't made a formal renunciation of citizenship in your home countries that predates the war.

"I've got to tell you, too, that *I* don't understand why the laws are written the way they are. I talked to our senior staff judge advocate, Legate Puente-Pequeño, and he says it makes no sense to him. More specifically, he said, 'That's what you get when you get amateurs making law.'

"I'm not so sure he's right, though. The regulation that allows us to give medals for valor, even to our enemies? That, I have reason to believe, was deliberate. Why not this?"

"It's not just us, ma'am," said the Haarlemer sergeant. "We're just picked representatives. There's two hundred and twenty-seven men who want to swim the river, as we say. We'd be bloody damned valuable."

"I know," she said. "You said that before. But we can't accept you. We can't, in principle, claim the right to shoot any of ours that go over to the enemy . . . to the Tauran Union or Zhong Empire, and not accord the same right to our enemies.

"Then, too, consider the implications. Suppose we took you in. Then imagine we lose. That's the way the smart money says to bet it. What happens to you guys? You get shot? Or hanged? Or maybe just imprisoned. We can surrender on our own behalf, if we must. But we can't surrender, not ever, if it means people who've tried to help us would be punished more severely than we would. It would be wrong . . . un-Balboan . . . un-Legionary.

"So we can't do that."

The Haarlemer sergeant sighed. "Oh, well, it was worth a try."

"And I appreciate it, personally," she consoled him and them. "But it's not right and it's not fair to anybody. Maybe after the war."

She stopped then, listening to the service. Chaplain Williams was bringing matters to a close, so she said, "Back to your seats now, boys, quietly. I have an announcement to make to the group as soon as services are done."

" . . . you fucking lot. Siiittttt . . . fuckckckinggg . . . DOWN!"

"Thank you, Sergeant Major," Marqueli said.

She sighed, then said, "Boys, I have some good news and some bad news. First the good news; my course is over. What I can teach, in the time I've had to teach it, is done."

Marqueli smiled, gratified at the groans. Whether they groaned because the boys liked her, liked her teaching, or just liked looking at her, she couldn't say. If pressed, she'd have guessed that, for most of them, it was probably two out of three.

"Now the bad news. We're going to have to disperse you to various small prisoner camps, about fifty of them, we've set up in various places near *Ciudad* Balboa. I don't know why the dispersal; no one's confided in me on that.

"What you do when you get there is on you. You don't have to accept what I've taught here; I've tried to make that clear from the beginning. If you do accept it, you don't have to teach it, either at your next camp or when you finally go home. If you do decide to teach it you don't have to teach it my way, or any particular way.

"But I do hope you will at least think about what we've talked about here."

### *Palacio de las* Trixies, *Ciudad* Balboa, Balboa, Terra Nova

There was dread in the air, all across the city, dread at the terrible vengeance everyone assumed the Tauran Union would wreak after being bombed themselves. The mood, the sense on imminent destruction, extended even to the old city and the presidential palace. Even the trixies were unaccountably quiet.

In the president's office sat four men, all but the president standing. He, seated, looked over a map with some complex graphics drawn on it.

Raul Parilla shook his head doubtfully. "I don't know about this, Patricio," he said to Carrera. "It strikes me as dirty, even cowardly, to hide behind prisoners of war."

Between the two men was a map of the city and the area to its south, labeled "Log Base Alpha." On the map were any number of red crosses, which would ordinarily indicate a medical facility. In this case, many were medical. Many others were not.

"Oh, please, Mr. President. We're not going to hide behind anything. And nothing of any importance is within one hundred meters of one of those crosses. They can bomb us as much as they like. The only difference is they can't be sure, if they carelessly—or deliberately; these are Tauran Union hypocrites we're talking about—bomb one of our marked medical facilities that they're not bombing a camp with their own POWs in it. And they can't risk staging a POW rescue without risking a massacre of our wounded they would find *most* embarrassing.

"Best of all, they *must* use precision munitions, pricey and rare. Any unguided bombs they may drop risks our wounded, and their own prisoners."

"What if they don't have that many guided weapons?" asked the president.

"Fuck 'em," said Carrera, "that's their problem. They've got all the goddamned money in the world—a lot more than we have—let them spend it."

"What does JAG say?" asked Parilla, looking pointedly at Legate Puente-Pequeño who had come to the office with the *Duque*.

"Well," said the lawyer, "it's never been done before, in quite this way, so far as I am aware, but, taking the project piece by piece, there's nothing especially noteworthy and nothing at all illegal that I can see. There's nothing wrong with telling an enemy there are areas you are not going to use for a warlike purpose. Nothing wrong with telling them where your medical facilities are. Nothing wrong with letting them know where their own POWs are. Nothing wrong with giving them a range of areas where their POWs might be, provided we use none of those area for a warlike purpose.

"Maybe if they didn't have the option of putting a bomb in a fifty meter circle, it would be wrong, Mr. President, but they *do* have that option. We're not obligated to make their lives easier, you know."

"Still strikes me as . . . well . . . more dark than gray."

"War's a shitty business, Raul," said Carrera. "Lawfare doesn't make it better; it just makes it sneakier."

Parilla sighed, then asked, "How are we going to get this to the enemy?"

"Esterhazy, acting as a *parlementaire,* will pass a copy of this map over to them, this afternoon, just before he, Triste, Lourdes and party depart Santa Josefina. Additionally, we will send copies to the major news networks—"

"They'll never publish them," said the president.

"They will," insisted Professor Ruiz, the chief of propaganda, "because we're also putting them up on web sites hosted in several countries, none of which are wild about the Tauran Union or the Zhong."

"Zhong prisoners going there, too?" Parilla asked.

Carrera tapped two spots, circled such as to indicate large perimeters. "They're at these two, now." He shook his head. "We don't actually have that many military or naval prisoners. And those we do have are too valuable not to keep close tabs on. The eleven thousand or so Zhong civilians, we're going to give back just as soon as the Zhong land east of the city. They don't hurt us any and will add to the enemy's logistic burden, which is what will really secure that flank."

Parilla sat back, away from the map. "What's that phrase you dug out of that old book from Old Earth? Survival cancels out programming; something like that? Okay, you can do this.

"Now, since we're on the subject of the pounding we're going to take, talk to me about air defense."

Carrera cut off a semi-nasty retort; he'd briefed Parilla on the prospects of air defense several times already. It just didn't seem to sink in. *Oh, well, here we go again.*

"The more advanced fighters are allegedly soon going to be on the way from Zion, Mr. President, but I don't think we'll use them even if they arrive. The pilots aren't that well trained. No matter; I expect the Taurans to bribe Zion to keep them.

"We'll get better use out of our updated Mosaic-Ds, which our pilots *do* know how to use, and which we can launch without runways—"

Parilla interrupted, "You can launch them, yes, but you can't recover them without runways. And they're so *old*, our boys are going to be slaughtered."

"Raul," said Carrera, "we've been through this before. The Mosaics are all rough-field capable and we have a metric shitpot of rough fields. They are *still*, sixty years after first being fielded, the second tightest turning aircraft on this planet. And the TU doesn't have the tightest turning, the Federated States does. They've also been extensively upgraded in everything from weapons, to radar signature, to avionics. We're going to take them down, when we commit, two or three for every five. We can stand that. *They* can't.

"We have five tercios of air defense in the Eighteenth Legion. When the bombing starts again—and it will, pretty damned soon— their orders are to cease fire and go out of action and *hide* at the first near miss. They all have solid hides dug or built. We also have enough mock-ups of wrecks for most of them. The duckhunters come back into action at a time of our choosing. The Eighteenth has the SPLADs, about which the Taurans may know nothing and against which they are unlikely to have developed a defense."

The SPLADs were Self-Propelled Laser Air Defense, a system some would have called illegal, designed to blind pilots as painfully as possible, making them crash their aircraft.

"And we have Project Sarissa, which we will know is coming, when we decide to use it, and they will not.

"Lastly, we are dug in like termites. Over an area of ten thousand square kilometers, they would need to expend seventy million tons of bombs over a short period of time to *temporarily* neutralize us. They couldn't drop that many bombs in ten years.

"Mr. President," Carrera finished, "relax. Please. I have . . . oh, shit!"

The sirens began to blare all across the city. In places, those where the newest warning systems had been installed, voice commands rang out: "Take shelter. Enemy aircraft inbound. This is not a drill. Enemy aircraft inbound within fifteen minutes. This is not a drill. Enemy aircraft . . ."

Parilla's bodyguards bustled in to cart him away. From outside came the screech of presidential limousine tires, laying rubber.

"JAG," said Carrera, heart pounding and eyes flicking back and forth, nervously, "you come with me. Professor Ruiz, please accompany the president and first lady."

Once outside, Carrera let the presidential limousine depart first, waiting impatiently for it to clear the way. Then he and Puente-Pequeño mounted up in the much less ornate staff car—unlike the limo open to the air—where Warrant Officer Soult pulled out from his parking spot and began following the president to a shelter, but not the one under *Cerro Mina*. Crowds of nervous civilians, mostly women and children, flooded the streets, making the drive slow and difficult. Carrera scanned faces, seeing less than he'd have liked of determination and more than he wanted to see of terror.

*Well . . . it's a new experience to them,* he thought. *Though I'm not entirely sure how much it helps when it becomes a common experience.*

They lost sight of the limousine somewhere in the crowds ahead, a fact that raised Carrera's heart rate until they caught sight of it again, turning onto *Avenida Ascanio Arosemena*, which was half of *Avenida de la Victoria*.

A bomb unexpectedly exploded atop *Cerro Mina*, raising a long and drawn out wail of fear from the civilians who, herdlike, began flooding back into the city and away from the blast.

"What the . . ." began Puente-Pequeño.

"Either something stealthy that snuck in under the radar," answered Carrera, "or something jammed our radar to let something else sneak in. They went after the top of *Cerro Mina* because we have both radar and a heavy air defense missile battery up there, covering the city, with a battery of light self-propelled guns covering them. If they survived that, they should be—"

The air overhead erupted with the sound of multiple sails ripping, and those ripping fast, overlaid with organ-shaking *bangs* as the propellant in the heavy missiles expended itself *almost* as quickly as explosive in a cannon barrel. That sound, too, raised another long drawn out wail from the civilians.

*At least they're not panicking,* thought Carrera, *though, of course, Ruiz has pre-made recordings of very calm and determined-looking civilians going to their assigned shelters, complete with the sounds of aircraft and air defense women herding them in. And we've got teams out to record the damage as it comes in. And then there are the atrocity tapes.*

*Now, my personal opinion, is that the average Tauran is about like anybody else, and really won't give a shit about the damage done to us, real or, as in the atrocity tapes, acted. And the Tauran ruling class, the unelected bureaucrats, won't really give a shit, either. But between them is a class that doesn't rule, but decides who does. That class is sensitive, which is to say, weak, and will not be able to stand the damage they do to us.*

*So they're giving us ammunition to use against them. Silly bastards; they forget that, except when the Federated States leads, so it can take the blame, they can't sustain anything on their own that offends their sense of aesthetics.*

*I think . . . well, I hope.*

Still the loudspeakers blared, "Take shelter. Enemy aircraft inbound. This is not a drill. Enemy aircraft inbound within seven minutes. This is not a drill. Enemy aircraft . . ."

The car had to stop for the dense crowd. Soult turned around and said, "Boss, I'm never going to get through this in time for you to get to the shelter. It's not far, you can get out and trot there before their main attack gets here."

"What about you?" Carrera asked. "You can't ditch the car; the ambulances are going to need a clear path through."

"I'll stick with the car until the crowds clear."

"Fuck that shit," said Carrera. "There are things one doesn't care to live with. Saving one's own skin while leaving behind one's friend is among them. But Puente-Pequeño?"

"Yes, *Duque.*"

"You get out and go on ahead on foot."

Shaking his head, the lawyer replied, "To quote somebody or other, 'fuck that shit,' *Duque.*"

"Insubordinate bastard."

"Yes, *Duque.*"

Again, the air defense batteries on the hill overhead erupted in a mix of rapid light-cannon fire and a single blast from a launching missile. That was followed by two explosions that definitely were not from the defenders, the shockwave knocking the scurrying civilians to their knees or all fours and rocking Carrera's staff car.

The scampering crowd thinned enough for Soult to advance a few more meters. Catching sight of a thin opening between the row of parked cars, Carrera said, "Stick the son of a bitch in there! Crossways. Just so long as it's out of the road!"

Soult cut the wheel to the right, struck one of the parked cars, pushed it out of the way, and forced his way up and over the curb. In a flash, he, Carrera, and the JAG were out of the vehicle and hurrying forward. A large explosion hit the hill again. This one was big enough—most likely a thousand kilogrammer—to knock all three down, stunning them on the way to the asphalt.

"Enemy aircraft inbound. This is not a drill. Enemy aircraft inbound within three minutes. This is not a drill. Take shelter immediately. Enemy aircraft inbound . . ."

Standing, Puente-Pequeño caught sight of a little brown girl, no more than three, standing alone and crying. She took turns wiping at her eyes and at the snot running down her face. Ignoring the latter, the JAG trotted over and scooped the child up. He looked around for Soult and Carrera, only to find they had almost reached him. Again, the three men, now reinforced by a child, took off for the shelter.

*KaaaWHOOMF!* That last, apparently on the old *Comandancia* and current Second Corps headquarters was a whole new order of explosion. The blast shattered windows over a goodly chunk of the old city and sent a column of smoke rising high over the slums between the headquarters and the avenue. A chorus of screams and wails, mixed with an increasing number of police, fire, and ambulance sirens, arose ahead of the party.

*Shit,* thought Carrera, *the Taurans must be* pissed. *No sense of humor, those people.*

"Here, sir," announced Soult, upon arriving at a concrete opening, then turning and waiting for the lawyer and the *Duque* to show up.

The shelter was marked as such, both in words and in a graphic showing a wall turning away a blast. Because so much of the area had been destroyed during the Federated States' invasion of a generation prior, new buildings had been able to incorporate some very strong basements, deliberately designed as shelters. They wouldn't stop a deep penetrator, but they could stand up to almost anything else, and had within them life support sufficient to provide oxygen in the event of a firestorm.

Entering into the shelter, lit, if not well, by emergency lights lining the walls at just over head level, Carrera looked for a place to stand. Taking the JAG by the sleeve, he dragged both him and the little girl to it.

"You picked her up," said Carrera, "you get to ask for her mother. How'd she lose her mom, anyway?"

Puente-Pequeño shook his head. "She doesn't know, but from what she says I would suspect the crowd simply parted them and dragged the mother along with it."

"Okay, well see if you can . . ."

A woman walked up, bearing a very small baby in her arms. She gave Carrera a dirty look, and then a grateful one to the lawyer, then took the crying girl by the hand, dragging her off while scolding her without cease.

*Nice to be loved*, Carrera thought, sardonically.

The ground underfoot shook with another huge blast. Even through the thick concrete walls, the shockwave could be felt by the people sheltering within them.

Nodding to himself, Carrera stood up on the short platform he'd intended for the lawyer to use to find the girl's mother. The ground shook again, this time worse. This time, also, it raised a new bout of crying from the civilians who were, again, mostly women and children.

"I thought," said Carrera, loudly enough to be heard even in the recesses of the shelter, "that I ought to give you good people the chance to see if I am as big a son of a bitch as most of you probably think I am . . ."

### Joint Headquarters, 16th Aviation Legion/18th Air Defense Legion, *Ciudad* Balboa, Balboa, Terra Nova

Miguel Lanza, with both his own key staff and that of the duckhunters, felt his organs quivering under the aerial assault. The worst of it was when, so he guessed and so it later proved, the enemy dropped several penetrating bombs onto the thick piles of earth and metal over the concrete bunkers of the joint headquarters. Those had knocked people to their hands and knees, set some of them to vomiting, caused a couple to wet themselves, and generally been a most unpleasant experience.

The lights went out momentarily, but flicked back on again once the emergency power system kicked in.

The mission of the moment was more distasteful than any Lanza could recall. Little by little, he was taking the country's air defenses off line and hiding them, leaving everything open to a lashing from the air.

As he ordered the Air Defense Legion's chief of staff to take a battery of medium self-propelled out of action and hide them in bunkers, Lanza thought, *You are a soulless bastard, Patricio Carrera.*

# CHAPTER TWENTY-EIGHT

War is the unfolding of miscalculations.
—Barbara Tuchman, *The Guns of August*

## *Isla Real,* Balboa, Terra Nova

Lieutenant Sanders, flying a Sea Hurricane low over the sea, bearing a good seven tons of unguided munitions, really didn't get it. He'd dropped his bombs on the mainland for weeks now, not less than a sortie a day. At first the resistance from the ground had been fierce, and not especially ineffective. Between the four carriers, the bases on Cienfuegos, and the airfields in "neutral" Santa Josefina, the Tauran Union had been sending in a thousand sorties a day, carrying two or three thousand tons of ordnance. They'd lost better than forty aircraft to ground fire which was not, given rates of production of modern aircraft, long-term sustainable. The rate of loss probably would have been a lot worse except that they had apparently driven the Balboan air defense from the field . . . that, or destroyed it.

Saunders wasn't entirely convinced of the latter, but when he'd raised the objection with his wing commander he'd been pooh-poohed off.

He still wondered though, and about more things than one.

*I wonder if the reason I'm carrying unguided crap now is because we used up everything we had in the inventory trying to avoid bombing their field hospitals and our prisoners. Okay, that part I could get, if true and they'd admit that it's true.*

*What I don't get is why are the higher-ups so confident. How do we know their air defense umbrella is shredded? I know that three other pilots and myself made a claim on a missile launcher near Brookings. I am pretty sure they counted us each as having destroyed one. What if it was only one? Or what if it was none, a diversion, a dummy?*

*It's always been a problem with air forces, inflation of damage reports; don't the generals and admirals know that? Were they selected for something besides brains?*

*Hmmm . . . that's a stupid question, isn't it, Saunders? Next you'll be thinking that the Tauran Union's democracy deficit isn't a feature of the system.*

*And then the dipshits declared "air supremacy!" What the fuck is that supposed to mean, that the declaration is a victory? Jesus, popping champagne corks everywhere, and on the GNN cameras. Nearest to an explosion any of those pogues have been, I suppose.*

"Aaand . . . here's my target."

Saunders jerked his stick, just in case anybody on the other side hadn't heard that the TU had achieved "air supremacy," then pulled back and climbed upward, paralleling the slope of the central rise of the island. His targeting computer was already set for this target, a supposed mortar battery, well dug in, facing the northern beaches. At the proper time the computer, itself, released two one thousand pounders. The bombs kept a goodly portion of the course the Sea Hurricane had already been on. They flew up and over the hill, losing energy all the way, then reached the apogee of their arc and began a rapid descent.

The target was a series of turrets, set into concrete, with large muzzles pointing generally upward. What damage he did, Saunders had no clue. Supposedly someone was tracking battle damage from the air or space or both.

The pilot deftly punched in the number for his next target, noted the preferred approach on his screen, and brought his plane around for another pass.

*Hmmmph. Wonder why we're not bombing the city today. I suppose it could be those peace activists who chartered an airship and intend to occupy various points in Balboa as human shields. Yeah, that's likely it.*

**Herrera International Airport, *Ciudad* Balboa, Balboa, Terra Nova**

*Pax Vobiscum*, despite the use of a Latin title, and the presence of Catholic clergy, was not a Catholic organization. Oh, it had its share of mostly nominal Catholics in it, mostly liberation theologians, nuns in mini-skirts and see-throughs, that kind of thing. But, by and large, the organization was secular, and made up of citizens of the Tauran Union's member states supremely dedicated to preventing the use of force, even where that use was necessary to save life. They did this by physically placing themselves in positions to protect whatever it was they thought either their home countries or the Federated States might want to bomb, then defying those same powers to do so. It might have been noble and brave had there been the slightest chance that either the TU or FSC would take them up on their dares. As it was, though, it was safe and, better still, gave the membership of PV the chance to travel in style, screw all kind of grateful and admiring youngsters, and preen themselves on their courage.

In the case of Balboa, they'd have ridden to the rescue sooner, of course, had it been possible. This was the chance to stop a real war. But chartering airships—five star airships—and having them repainted in *Pax Vobiscum* colors took time. And both, of course, the five stars and the colors for advertising, were a lot more important in the big scheme of things than mere timeliness. Besides, if the TU managed to kill a slew of civilians in Balboa, while that killing had to stop upon the arrival of PV's martyrs, that would go to show how very important and effective PV was.

A couple of the senior Paxers had been invited up to the bridge by the airship's captain. They were listening as the captain made the call to the control tower, below.

"Herrera control, this is Anglian Airways Charter Eight Seven Seven, out of Mauer, Sachsen, with eight hundred and ninety-nine really annoying passengers. Can't you please take them off of our hands?"

It's possible that the captain lacked tact; a remarkable lack in an Anglian, to be sure.

"Eight Seven Seven, this is Herrera Control, are you requesting permission to land?"

"I thought I'd made that clear, Herrera Control."

"Just making sure. You *are* carrying *Pax Vobiscum,* are you not, Eight Seven Seven?"

Said the disembodied Anglian accent, "Sadly, yes."

"'Sadly,'" echoed the Spanish-accented voice from the ground, "it's not as simple as that. Assume a circular holding pattern, eight kilometers south of this port . . . hmmm . . . you're dynamic lift, so circle clockwise, altitude of thirty-five hundred feet, while I notify some people of your request. Note that the solar chimney that was there is currently dysfunctional and you won't be able to see the plume it used to put off. Lights are out, too. The peak of the tower's still there, though, except that now it's jagged."

"Roger, Herrera Control, eight kilometers south, thirty-five hundred feet, clockwise. And thanks for the tip."

"I say," said Sister Mary Magdalene, short-skirted and thin-shirted, "I don't think I like the sound of that. You would think they'd be pleased we've come to protect them."

"They're probably just concerned with the prospect that we have spies among our ranks, Sister," said Father Segundo; Leonardo Jon Oscar Segundo, in full, a steel-haired and seam-faced pastor of *an* old school, if not the traditional old school.

"But we . . ." The nun looked properly scandalized.

"No, of course not, Sister," the priest assured her. "But they can't know that, can they?"

"I suppose not, Father," agreed the short-skirted nun.

*Pity,* thought Puente-Pequeño, looking over the bare concrete floors of the Herrera International terminal, *that there wasn't time to set up tents. On the other hand, good thing we got the bloody carpets up.*

"Bloody," in this case, wasn't a minor Anglian vulgarity. Between the maniple of the Balboan Corps of Cadets that had been stationed here and the Gallic paras who had, finally, pretty much exterminated them, the old carpets had been soaked with blood. The other downside to using the terminal was lack of power for air conditioning. On the other hand, with the bulk of the windows blown out during the assaults of a couple of months prior, there was at least some breeze, sufficient to reduce the heat inside from impossible to merely miserable. That most of that heat came from just this side of melting tarmac of the runways and taxiways didn't help.

Walking across the bare concrete to a shattered window, Puente-Pequeño looked out at the five lines of mostly Taurans passing through some hastily set up "customs" check points, none of which actually cared in the slightest about routine tax collection or smuggling prevention. No, these agents were actually police detectives and they were gathering evidence: "Where is your citizenship? Is that where you vote? Is that where you pay taxes? What is your purpose in coming to Balboa? So you were aware that there is a war on, albeit under a temporary truce, between your home country and the alliance of which it is a part, and the Timocratic Republic of Balboa?"

The brief interviews were being taped, *Which should,* thought the staff judge advocate, *save some time.* A little more time was saved by separating out the eight hundred and ninety-nine peace activists into three groups: Taurans, who made up—by far—the biggest, citizens of the Federated States, and everyone else. From the furtive glances of the Taurans—*Well, from all of them, but especially the Taurans*—Puente-Pequeño had the impression that the fact of being separated and segregated was making them nervous.

*Perfectly understandable it is, too,* he thought.

As the lawyer watched, armed legionaries boarded the airship, to make sure it didn't go anywhere until released.

Father Leonardo Jon Oscar Segundo was neither unholy nor a hypocrite. Other Catholics in *Pax Vobiscum* may have been nominal; not he. He'd read the scripture diligently from boyhood, and from that early age he'd read in it things that seemed to completely pass by most of this fellow clergy and nearly all of those they served. He took seriously the admonition, "Put away your swords." He believed that the miracle of the loaves and fishes was more about sharing than about multiplication. And, while he truly believed in the life hereafter, he didn't think that absolved anyone from trying to make life in this world more just.

And he knew—he didn't delude himself about the matter—that most of the activists with him were more concerned with their perks and prestige than with anything else. Even Sister Mary Magdalene, who was better than most, had a streak of excessive concern with her own position.

*Okay, so maybe bricks without straw are not of the best, but they're better than no bricks at all.*

When the guards came and ordered the priest to follow them, he'd taken it in stride. Excessive militarism was hardly unique to Balboa, after all. He was a little more concerned when he found himself standing before a panel of three judges, was presented with a uniformed man, Warrant Officer Bonadies, who, the priest was informed, was his defense counsel, and then heard read off a criminal complaint charging him with treason.

*Treason? Treason against their enemies? These people are charging me with treason against the Tauran Union and my own Tuscany? That's . . .*

"How do you plead, Father Segundo?"

" . . . preposterous," the priest said, thinking aloud. "I mean . . ."

"The good father pleads not guilty," said the man assigned to his defense, Bonadies.

Thereafter the trial went very quickly, from the video recording of the reading of the activists' rights, to their admission that they were citizens of a country at war with Balboa. Bonadies made his objections here and there, but they were all obviously pretty pro forma.

It didn't really sink in with Father Segundo just how much trouble he was in until the three judges conferred for all of five minutes, without ever leaving the room, and the center one of the three, Judge Achurra, said, "And, so, however reluctantly, Father Segundo, this court finds you to be a citizen of Tuscany and of the Tauran Union, with which polities the Timocratic Republic finds itself at war. We have further examined the prospect that, you might, as a priest, have claimed extraterritoriality, even though you did not. Sadly, as your church, which is also ours, is based in Tuscany, and since Tuscany is also at war with us, a claim of extraterritoriality will not stand.

"We further find that, in coming here to interfere with the Tauran Union's war effort, you have attempted to give aid to it and Tuscany's enemies, those being ourselves. This is treason under our laws, which do not define treason only in regards to Balboa, but as a human phenomenon, applicable anywhere in the world and to almost any human being who holds citizenship somewhere, and over which we claim universal jurisdiction.

"Father, before you faint dead away, consider that if a Tauran court can claim jurisdiction over crimes against human rights, as they have, and if human rights, on the one hand, mean an obligation to respect those rights, on the other, this recognizes human obligations as a universal legal reality. There is no principled reason to restrict universal legal realities to merely the obligation to respect human rights. Among other obligations is also an obligation to be true to one's country.

"In other words, Father Segundo, your polity has claimed universal jurisdiction over human rights, hence of human obligations, while we claim universal jurisdiction over human obligations, which implicate human rights, the right of your fellow citizens not to have you betray them by betraying your common country."

The judge's voice grew very somber than as he said, "Thus this court has no recourse but to sentence you to death for treason to your country. And that doesn't even begin to address how we feel about the mortal insult directed toward our country by the implication that we can only be defended by hiding behind you and yours.

"Oh, and may God have mercy on your soul."

Father Segundo sat behind barbed wire, in what had probably been the luggage handling area of the terminal in a more peaceful and happier day. The parting words of his defense counsel, Bonadies, hadn't been a lot of comfort: "The sentence has to be approved by the president, who is a fair man. Thank God it doesn't have to be approved by Carrera, who is not a fair man. I think I can probably get you off with hanging, or maybe even firing squad, rather than crucifixion. Fortunately, no one tried to put on any evidence that this was not a first offense or it would be the cross for sure."

Almost as if they were worry beads, the priest's rosary beads made a soft clicking sound as he manipulated them. They'd have been reduced to worry beads, too, but for the "Ave Marias" and "Pater Nosters."

"When?" the priest had asked. "When will they execute me?"

Bonadies had shrugged, somewhat embarrassed. "Under normal civil criminal procedures, it would be a month or so. But this is wartime and there's not a lot of care being paid to the niceties. There are three courts set up. Each trial is taking about half an hour, with breaks. Thus, eighty or a hundred or so a day. Figure you have a week to ten days. Is there anyone you would like me to notify?"

Based on his attorney's perfunctory performance, Father Segundo was by no means certain that he would not be crucified. He, more than most outside of Balboa, had reason to know this would be the hardest possible death. As the wired-in area filled up with his fellow condemned, thus filled up with a load of shocked silly, weeping, screaming, and begging persons, the priest found himself praying less for his deliverance than for theirs.

Segundo spent a fair amount of time counseling the condemned. But when he wasn't doing that, or eating, or sleeping, he tried to puzzle through the justification the judge had given. If nothing else, it took his mind off the prospect of the mass crucifixion impending.

*Is it really true,* wondered Father Segundo, *does it really follow, that a claim of universal jurisdiction in defense of human rights also supports a claim of universal jurisdiction to defend human obligations? This may be the first time in my life I wished I'd become a Jesuit, and taken up the law, as some of them do.*

*But even without that training, I, I myself, have always held that people had a right to certain things: food, shelter, clothing, education, medical care. And, yes, surely, the judge was right in claiming that if someone has a right to something, then someone else has the obligation to provide that something. So, okay, there's a correlation between rights and obligations.*

*But there I stop. Countries are bullshit. No one has obligation one to any of them. So I feel. So I believe.*

*Ah, but what about those who believe differently? There are those who do not believe in the universal human right to food, shelter, clothing, education, and medical care. But I insist that they honor my belief in those rights. Am I being arrogant, unreasoning, and unfair in demanding others honor my beliefs and refusing to honor theirs, myself? What if I am? What if I am?*

*And if I am, and if I have accepted the principle of universal jurisdiction to support my beliefs, how can I deny them the principle of universal jurisdiction to support theirs? How can I, in principle, deny them that principle?*

*And if we have two opposed principles, how can I say which is right? Mine, just because it* is *mine? That's not a principle. Damn.*

### *Palacio de las* Trixies, *Ciudad* Balboa, Republic of Balboa, Terra Nova

The planes hadn't been hitting the city much, lately. Instead, the bulk of the bombing effort seemed to be directed at more purely military targets outside the capital's political and practical boundaries. And even there, the presence of so many thousands of Tauran POWs in little camps, indistinguishable from so many other facilities, had had a considerable dampening effect on how freely they were willing to bomb.

Thus, President Parilla could feel more or less comfortable in his own home. He'd still sent his wife away from the palace, just in case.

"I'm a superstitious man," he explained to Mrs. Parilla. "Worse, all my life I've had the feeling that the Almighty's sense of humor was perverse."

She hadn't gone with good grace, but she had gone.

So now Parilla had the place to himself and his staff. As a younger man—not necessarily that much younger, either—he'd probably have used the opportunity for some casual dalliance with one or two of the cuter maids. Now? *Too fucking old for that shit.*

"What was that, Mr. President?" asked Carrera.

"What? Was I thinking out loud?"

"Something about 'too fucking old,'" Carrera confirmed.

"Then I am getting to be too fucking old," the president said.

"Everyone does," said Puente-Pequeño. Then, taking off his glasses to polish and thinking about blood-stained carpets now gone from the terminal, he thought, sadly, *Well . . . no . . . not everyone does.*

"Anyway," Carrera continued, not wanting to make too much of the old man's slip, "we wrote the law as an oversight, as much as anything."

"The same way we ended up giving medals for valor to Sada's men in Sumer?" Parilla asked.

"Yes, Mr. President," said Carrera, "pretty much. Though that was an oversight that had a happy ending. This one, unless you do something, won't."

"Note, sir," said Puente-Pequeño, "that no lawyer had a hand in crafting this law. Your veterans did that on their own. And you have to expect a certain amount of legal idiocy when you permit that."

Carrera and Parilla both shrugged, indifferently, which caused the lawyer to roll his eyes.

"So anyway," asked the president, "how are these different from the Castilians?"

"Two ways, Mr. President," said Puente-Pequeño. "In the first place, the Castilians joined us and became our troops at a time when we were not at war with the TU, and after the TU's leadership here, the Gauls, had attacked their commander. That cut off any obligations between Muñoz-Infantes's unit and the TU. Second, we are not at war with Castile, which has limited itself to medical aid and such."

"Okay, and the individual immigrants from Taurus?"

"They're all pre-war. By joining us they went through formal renunciation of rights and obligation vis a vis their former countries."

Parilla wondered about that. *Every time you introduce a lawyer*, he thought, *things get complicated and the truth flees.*

Still, he couldn't see where the lawyer was precisely *wrong*, so, "What do you want me to do?"

Carrera replied, "We need all the condemned to get a conditional pardon, Raul. Just that."

"The condition being that they go away and never return?"

"On pain of death," answered Carrera. "We've held over but not refueled their airship. They can reach Santa Josefina, where we fully expect them to salve their pride by doing what we refused to permit them doing here."

"And we don't mind this?" the president asked.

"Not a bit," answered Carrera, smiling wickedly. "After all, officially the rebellion in Santa Josefina cannot be our war."

"So we get all the moral advantages of refusing to hide behind foreigners, and the Taurans over in Santa Josefina still get all the disadvantages of having their enemies able to hide behind their own traitors?"

"Evil, Mr. President, is it not?" asked the JAG.

"A little, yes," said Parilla, raising a frown on the lawyer's face. "But

. . . well, yes, I'll do it." Turning his attention back to Carrera he asked, "Now what are we going to do to humiliate the enemy about their bullshit announcement of 'air supremacy'? Swear to God, I am surprised they didn't put anyone's eye out, what with all the flying champagne corks."

"I think," said Carrera, "that they've had long enough to become complacent and that now a little humiliation is in order; that, and some disillusionment."

# CHAPTER TWENTY-NINE

Surprise is the master-key of war.
—B.H. Liddell Hart, *Thoughts on War*

**Santa Cruz, Balboa, Terra Nova**

Every day Tribune Ordoñez took a walk down to Arnold field, to check on the status of the damage. It wasn't all that far, after all, nor did he have anything better to do. The six truck-mounted aircraft in his flight already checked out as ready to go, while the solid fuel rockets underneath were so simple they were presumed to be wholly reliable.

At the airfield, the story on the surface never changed. The charred skeleton of the burned airship still sat, the rags of its singed fabric flapping in the breeze. The airfield itself had been well cut by the Oliphants; rough-field-capable or not, no Mosaics would be coming down along its roughly one-mile length without repairs, either to the airfield, beforehand, or to the plane, afterwards.

That said, there were Sixteenth Legion ground crews with dump trucks full of gravel and sections of perforated steel planking just waiting for the word to make some temporary repairs. Moreover, while the main runway was still cut, then Taurans hadn't paid a lot of attention to either the taxiways nor the parking lots nor the roads. Between those, there were no fewer than seven strips on Arnold Air Base, *alone*, of sufficient length and quality to recover aircraft. There were two more adequate lengths at Herrera International, plus another one at Brookings, though that last one was tricky, and slated to be used only as a last resort.

Even so, every day Ordoñez took his walk and consulted with the centurion in charge of the runway repair crews. "Less than two hours, Tribune," was the centurion's learned judgment, "provided you keep the enemy air off my back. I've had my boys rehearsing this for weeks now. We can blast away the rippled concrete and push it off line, fill every hole with gravel, and cover them with steel planking, in about eighty-seven minutes."

*And it might just be,* thought Ordoñez, *that all you will do is attract their fires, so that we can land on the alternate strips. But we'll still hope for the best and we will give you all the cover we can.*

*For now, we await the word. I can't say anything, but I think it's coming soon, in the next couple of days.*

Despite sneers from Carrera, the declaration of "air supremacy" on the part of the Taurans had definite and serious operational implications well over and above the televised mass popping of champagne corks on the part of generals, admirals, and bureaucrats . . . to the extent those differed. These implications were distinct, but synergetic.

In the first place, for so long as the Taurans perceived a credible air-to-air threat—not strong, just credible, it being such a potentially humiliating prospect to lose a hundred million Tauran airplanes to an obsolete aircraft costing less than a tenth of a percent of that—they had to carry a certain amount of air-to-air ordnance, both on aircraft dedicated to the aerial combat mission, and on others dedicated to the bombing campaign. That cut into ordnance carried for the campaign that mattered, bombing the upstart Balboans into the stone age.

Second, because of the threat of antiaircraft fire, both cannon and missile, whether radar guided, infrared homing, or Mark One eyeball directed, a certain weight of effort had to be directed to SEAD, or suppression of enemy air defense. These were also known as "Frenzied Ferrets." Moreover, still more had to keep the runways cut, while the Balboans were still trying to keep them repaired.

The threat from enemy ground and air remained conceptually, and as far as they could tell from the air or space, genuinely, fixed, so only so much had to be dedicated to it. But that amount didn't change with the size of the attack package. Thus, the Tauran air forces could most efficiently attack by sending in between four and ten attack packages of one hundred to two hundred and fifty aircraft each, of which ninety percent were bombing, rather than twenty or thirty, daily, of thirty to fifty aircraft each, of which about half would have had to have been dedicated to something besides bombing.

That limitation on numbers of strike packages also meant, in practice, that the enemy had eighty or ninety percent of each day totally free to do whatever they wanted, without any threat overhead to interfere. Worse, the big strike groups were predictable as to time. And the Taurans were pretty sure that observers were reporting as they assembled, too.

Worse, perhaps, than any of that, though, was what the major strikes were doing to the ground crews, to the aerial refuelers, to airframe maintenance, and to bomb load per aircraft committed to bombing. Assembly took time. Time took fuel. Fuel took up weight that otherwise could have gone to ordnance. And both the intensive prep and the intensive recovery were wearing the ground crews to a frazzle. This was especially bad on the carriers, two of which had already experienced fatal wrecks while recovering aircraft.

So, with the declaration of "air supremacy" the TU had been able to mount smaller packages, with less devoted to refueling, to aerial combat, or SEAD. Best of all, for the last several days there had *always* been an air raid in progress or en route, which was presumptively driving the Balboans crazy, wearing them out, and preventing their free and easy movement.

Not that they completely dispensed with SEAD or aerial ordnance, of course, but a strike package of forty aircraft might have only one electronic warfare bird in it, and maybe two with a load primarily configured for air-to-air, with the rest carrying a maximum of either one HARM, Homing Antiradiation Weapon, or one air-to-air missile, plus whatever they carried for the cannon.

It was all very efficient. It was not, however, without its weaknesses.

**Joint Headquarters, 16th Aviation Legion/18th Air Defense Legion, *Ciudad* Balboa, Balboa, Terra Nova**

The bunker complex had been built a goodly distance from the *Estado*

*Mayor* building. This was just as well, since the latter was now reduced to a chewed wall, smoking hulk with cascades of brick and tile occasionally pouring off. Rather than there being one bunker, the legion had put in half a dozen, with a certain amount of redundancy shared amongst them, thick walls and roofs, all of that under considerable dirt and a double layer of roughly 30mm thick hexagonal steel plates buried under the dirt.

Lanza, being senior and also having command of the more decisive arm, was in charge. At least he was when Carrera wasn't there. However, today Carrera *was* present, therefore . . .

"You're in charge, Lanza," said Carrera. "I just want to be here to witness giving these motherfuckers a healthy dose of fear and humiliation."

The first reports to come in were visual, from human observers using a mix of extraordinarily powerful binoculars, high-definition closed-circuit television cameras, thermal imagers, telescopes, and even the national observatory which, for whatever reason, the Taurans had elected not to target. These fed information to the command bunker, which some of Lanza's staff converted into a display on a large map board in the middle of an operating theaterlike room.

There was also a small fleet of Balboan-manned fishing boats operating off the northern coast of Cienfuegos, mixed in with other, civilian craft. Those, however, were being held in reserve for the day that much earlier warning would be required.

"Arrogant bastards," muttered Lanza at seeing the single package inbound. It was labeled with a formation number, the composition of the formation being shown on a large television screen on the wall. Lanza stated the number of aircraft aloud, "Forty-three, all in one close group. I wish I had a nuke to use."

*No comment*, thought Carrera. Turning to Lanza, he asked, "How are you going to handle it?"

Lanza pointed to the same map as held the enemy formation marker. Staff legionaries were emplacing sundry markers for air defense units, *lots of them*.

"They typically come in loaded heavy for ground attack." He looked at the board as it flashed an update. "Anglians, flying Goshawks. We know what they're capable of because the Federated

States tried to interest us in their Goshawk multirole fighters, the same planes the RAAF bought. That group probably carries two hundred and fifty tons or so."

"Sergeant Miller," announced a communications sergeant, "out on Guano Island, reports refuelers passing by heading north."

"Okay," said Lanza, "so light on fuel, heavy on ordnance. I wish we could sneak someone in to fuck with their tankers. Be a blast, *Duque*, to have the Taurans have to ditch in the sea, no?"

"The Condors?"

Lanza shook his head. "Nah. The aerial tankers never get out of range of the ground-based fighters on Cienfuegos. We'd just be asking to have the Condors hunted down and destroyed. Remember, they can't even take a close fly-by from a high-performance jet."

"Okay," Carrera shrugged. "just a thought."

Lanza rubbed at his chin, thinking. "On the other hand . . . well . . . you know, just pushing the tankers so far back that the planes hitting us couldn't reach them might be worth it."

"If you come up with a good proposal, I'll authorize it."

"Maybe for next time," Lanza said. "Anyway, the air defense—well, *most* of it; we couldn't rehearse that much without giving the game away—will be up in a few minutes. Everything active is coming on line, missiles, guns, and lasers. As soon as the Taurans cross the shore of the Shimmering Sea, I'll know whether they're going after Cristobal and Jimenez's boys, or either us, here, or Firebase Alpha, or the Island."

"What's most likely?" Carrera asked.

"Firebase Alpha or the Island," answered Lanza.

"Why?"

"Because that's where the Anglians nonnaval air usually hits. The naval air, Anglians and Frogs, plus Frog and Sachsen nonnaval air, typically go after Cristobal or us, and usually not together. No, I don't think I fully understand the logic of that. It might be nothing more than keeping apart people who don't speak the same language and don't necessarily like each other. Anyway . . . Oh, excuse me a moment, *Duque*."

Lanza went and consulted with the chief of staff of the Eighteenth, then came back. "They're ready, the duckhunters, I mean. Just waiting for the word . . . and . . ."—Lanza again made a quick glance at the screen—"Eighteenth, you are weapons free! Excuse me, again, *Duque*."

Lanza hurried down to the operating floor, so to speak, and picked up a microphone himself. Carrera could not, over the general hubbub, hear what the aviator was saying. It became obvious, though, as new markers appeared on the map table, then moved at super high speed out to the city's east and west flanks. Some curled around to move south, too, to take up a position between the enemy aerial armada and its bases on Cienfuegos.

"Someone's been paying attention to the battle tactics of the Nguni," Carrera muttered. "I see the horns of the buffalo growing out."

## Santa Cruz, Balboa, Terra Nova

Ordoñez sat, flight-suited and helmeted, under the closed canopy, within the exceedingly cramped space of his plane's cockpit. In such a simple, even primitive craft, there was no air conditioning. Sweat beaded up and rolled down the tribune's body.

The trucks were lined up in two rows of three, engines already idling. The jet engines were not on yet, and would not be truly engaged until the aircraft had received its great, four-second, kick in the ass to get airborne. At that point, they would either work or not. *And,* thought Ordoñez, *if not, I have a very small time to decide whether to try to start them or to punch out. I think, though, that no matter what, I try to start them. I've been preparing for this moment for years. I'd rather die than—*

The tribune felt the truck shudder, then start a jerky roll out of the wide warehouse doors, through the asphalt parking lot, then down the winding road to the beach. Ground crew hung along the sides by railings. Ahead, only the upper fraction of his body seen, the truck's co-driver manned a heavy machine gun, hands resting on spade grips while his eyes scanned the skies.

The truck came to a stop at a flat spot in the road a quarter of a mile or so from the off-white sands of the beach. As soon as it did the ground crew sprang into action, disconnecting cables from the airplane and engaging the small electric motor to elevate the launch rail. Looking left, to the other side of the road, Ordoñez saw a different crew spinning a couple of large cranks to manually elevate the rail.

*You can rehearse and test and test and rehearse, but when it comes down to it something always goes wrong. Always.*

With the elevation of his rail, Ordoñez lost sight of the ground crewman who would give the final order to send the Mosaics aloft. He couldn't even see the man whose finger was on the button, waiting to engage the rocket.

Ordoñez felt a sudden pain in his eyes, not too bad but enough to have him seeing spots and blinking for a few seconds. He was cleared to know about the SPLADs, the Self-Propelled Laser Air Defense systems. He also knew that they were dangerous to the eyes of everyone for miles around anywhere they were used. He had to trust—and did trust—his legate to know that, once the aircraft were airborne, the lasers had to cease fire.

"Five," sounded in the pilot's helmet. "Four."

*They wouldn't have fired those for no reason,* thought the tribune. He began scanning the skies for . . . *Ah, there he is, the poor bastard.* What elicited the sympathy was a single Tauran fighter-bomber, a Goshawk, Ordoñez thought, doing the mamba across the bright blue Balboan sky, probably because its agonized pilot was too busy scratching his own eyeballs out to control his plane or even to set an autopilot.

"Three." Ordoñez braced himself for what promised to be quite an experience. *I've only done this once before.* "Two." *Oh, shit!* "One!"

Suddenly, the pilot felt himself pressed back into his seat, while the skin of his face rippled from the acceleration. He counted, mentally, *One . . . two . . . there goes the jet . . . three . . . thank God . . . four . . .*

And then, having felt the jar of the rocket being jettisoned, Ordoñez was on his own, fighting to gain altitude while scanning around frantically for enemy aircraft. In his helmet he heard his five subordinate pilots reporting in one by one as they, too, achieved launch.

*Odds were,* thought the flight leader, *that we'd lose one in the launch phase. I wonder if that means that, because I didn't, someone else had to fail. God will have His little jokes.*

The six Mosaics of Ordoñez's little command assumed a loose formation, three pairs of two, each pair with one forward and one well staggered back and to the flank, with the three pairs forming a loose triangle in the sky. A quick scan in his long-range television told the tribune that there were maybe thirty-eight to forty enemy aircraft ahead, scattered to the winds as they scrambled to make a less tempting target for the ground-based air defense. He didn't have the impression that they'd yet figured out that just shy of two hundred fighters either were or soon would be airborne.

Ordoñez flicked a switch to arm the two missiles his Mosaic carried, both heat-seeking V-37s. These were not of the best or latest Volgan design, by any means, but they were highly upgraded versions of a competent design, very maneuverable and capable of seeing a target up to forty degrees off of the center line. This made it both easier to acquire a target and harder for the target to shake the missile once acquired. Being cryogenically cooled, the missile had a very good chance of acquiring even a fairly distant target, even from some angle other than behind.

A particular buzzer in his ears informed the tribune that his right missile had a lock. Flicking off a red safety, he depressed a button, sending the V-37 heat seeker off to glory. Other smoking lances from above and behind him told the flight leader that the rest of his flight's Mosaics had likewise launched.

*Maybe they'll hit something, eh, God?*

Of the six missiles launched, though, Ordoñez couldn't tell if a single one connected with a target. He did see a couple of what looked to be aerial explosions larger than the fifteen-pound warheads could account for, but whether that was his boys, some other unit, or ground-based air defense or their much larger warheads was just impossible to determine.

No matter; the tribune still had one missile, three cannon, and two hundred and forty rounds for the latter. He bore in.

### Joint Headquarters, 16th Aviation Legion/18th Air Defense Legion, *Ciudad* Balboa, Balboa, Terra Nova

"Weapons hold on the lasers!" Lanza ordered. "Weapons tight on everything else. We've got our own folks mixing it up in the air with the enemy now, people; let's not shoot any of them down, eh?"

"What's going on?" Carrera demanded.

"Well . . . reports always lie, but even discounting them, it looks like we got eight or nine of them, about half with the lasers, and the others from a mix of cannon and missile fire, aerial and ground. No real way for me to tell who's getting what; we're relying on ground observers who can see big explosions easier than fading smoke trails. There are so many radars operating, both in the air and from the ground, that it's become just a hash. That's even with identification friend or foe operating.

"One thing I *can* say, though," Lanza continued, "is that the enemy dropped all their ordnance pretty much anywhere they happened to be. Some of it will still do some harm, but whatever they intended to harm will probably get off scot-free."

Carrera looked past Lanza at the map board. He had the distinct impression, from the frantic way the crew was trying to move around the little markers, that this system was not really up to the demands of modern war. He wondered if anything could be, or if it was just going to be anarchy in the air from now on.

*If so,* he thought, *that will probably work to our advantage, since we do a better job than most in tolerating individuality. Well . . . slightly better, anyway.*


### Over *Ciudad* Balboa, Balboa, Terra Nova

The Goshawk ahead of Ordoñez outclassed his aircraft, ordinarily, in every particular but three. His Mosaic was so cheap that the cost would barely have paid for the tires on the Goshawk. The Mosaic could outturn a Goshawk, though not by much. The Mosaic carried a heavier cannon. Otherwise, the Goshawk could engage with missiles from almost any angle, provided it carried air-to-air missiles. If this one did, he'd already expended it or them. The Goshawk was almost twice as fast in straight and level flight, about nineteen hundred kilometers per hour to the Mosaic's mere eleven hundred. Ordinarily those differences would have been dispositive, the Goshawk would have raced ahead, leaving the Mosaic in its figurative dust, then donated Ordoñez a missile better than anything his plane could carry, let alone use. This would, eventually, have led to Mrs. Ordoñez receiving a "We deeply regret to inform you" letter.

Unless the ground-based air defense had done for them, somewhere overhead there were one or two Goshawks, configured for air-to-air, doing just that with any number of Balboan planes.

The plane Ordoñez had targeted, however, could not do that. He might or might not have had that missile. He couldn't use it now, not darting among the towers of the city. He might have been able to race away in the open sky. Down in the figurative weeds, where the screams of "My eyes! My eyes!" and "Missile! Missile!" had driven him, that was an excellent way to end up a part of something that couldn't fly at all. Worse, from the Tauran's point of view, the superior maneuverability of the Mosaic, coupled with Balboa's standard barbaric approach to the prospect of casualties in training, meant that Ordoñez was better equipped, psychologically, to push the limits of his aircraft than the Tauran was to push the limits of his.

*Or, I suppose, hers,* thought the tribune, nudging his stick just slightly to line up his cannon on the Tauran's tail. *Well, if so, fuck the bitch.*

The shattered windows of a skyscraper flashed by the tribune's cockpit. He paid it no mind, having eyes only for the Tauran ahead of him. *Brrrrp.* There went thirty rounds, every one of which missed. *Brrrrp.* Ordoñez was gratified to see some bits and pieces flying off the enemy aircraft. *Brrrp . . . brrrp. . . . brrrbrrrbrrrp.* Smoke began to pour out. Lazily, the Tauran Goshawk began to turn over, before diving down to smack into a parking lot at the base of a glass tower. Most of the plane dug a hole into the asphalt, but a portion drove through part of the ground floor of the same, dragging a tail of fire behind it and out the other side.

*Yessss!*

### Joint Headquarters, 16th Aviation Legion/18th Air Defense Legion, *Ciudad* Balboa, Balboa, Terra Nova

There had been two more markers on the plotting table, one showing a Tauran strike package assembling near Cienfuegos, the other showing one halfway to Balboa. The attack already inbound turned around, returning to its bases. Closer to home, aircraft were being landed, refueled, rearmed, and sent aloft again. The message to the

Taurans was, "Yeah, that's right. We kicked your asses. You want some more?"

"There'll be an amazing clusterfuck," said Lanza to Carrera, "as the enemy tries to improvise out of the routine schedule they let themselves fall into. Within the next several hours, they're going to have to recover two packages they didn't expect to have to, cancel several more, remove ordnance already loaded from the ones they had to cancel, scramble fuel tankers they didn't think they'd need from airfields already operating at capacity.

"Oh, and they're going to have to explain to the press and their governments just how a bunch of jungle runners like us managed to smack around their best, brightest, most sophisticated, and most expensive."

"What was the butcher's bill?" Carrera asked.

Lanza pointed at the display screen, explaining, "It's only a preliminary but, near as we know, so far, we got twenty-three of them for thirty-seven of us, plus some air defense trashed. 'Course, we had surprise this time, so you could expect a better performance than the planes' quality would suggest. Next time will be tougher, if there is a next time."

"No matter," said Carrera. "They're going to have to take us seriously from now on, lest they get embarrassed again. That means big packages, time to assemble, fuel instead of bombs, wear and tear, lots of air-to-air and SEAD ordnance, and virtual attrition bad enough to cut them down to about half as effective.

"This is . . . it's a victory, Miguel. Tell your boys and the duckhunters, both, 'well done' from both the president and me. I'll see about convening a quorum of the Senate to make some kind of unit commendation. But don't wait for it; tell them now."


### Arnold Air Base, Balboa, Terra Nova

Ordoñez and his three remaining pilots, surrounded by ground crew not needed for the moment, poured cheap sparkling wine over each other's heads. Even the loss of Timoteo and De Rosa couldn't dampen the mood.

The other ground crew busied themselves with cranking the planes back up the launch rail and the extension that, when erected, led to the ground, refueling them, and mounting new rockets to their undersides. When that was finished, the truck drivers loaded up the men needed, and took the Mosaics to the lines of bunkers east of the airfield, where ammunition rats mounted new missiles and filled the cannons' magazines.

Then it was off to a hide in the jungle far less comfortable than the one they'd hidden in before. That had to be considered compromised at this point.

# CHAPTER THIRTY

You are Athenians, who know by experience the difficulty of disembarking in the presence of an enemy, and that if a man is not frightened out of his wits at the splashing of oars and the threatening look of a ship bearing down upon him, but is determined to hold his ground, no force can move him. It is now your turn to be attacked, and I call on you to stand fast and not to let the enemy touch the beach at all. Thus you will save yourselves and the place.

—Demosthenes, at Pylos, 425 BC

## *Isla Real,* Balboa, Terra Nova

In the lulls between the enemy's aerial shitstorms, the Balboans had managed to tow away the unpowered training carrier to one of the docks at port. This wasn't to keep it from being sunk, necessarily, but to make it possible to recover it after it *was* sunk, something that would have been much tougher in the deeper water off the island. There was another reason, too, but that awaited events.

The big attacks on the island only came twice a day, now, but they *were* big, containing as many as two hundred and fifty aircraft, with as much as fifteen hundred tons of ordnance being dropped in the matter of an hour or so. Sometimes, in fact, the ordnance came down from planes flying in tightly controlled, but large formations, with the bulk of it landing within seconds. Those raids set the island to shaking as if undergoing an earthquake. They also tended to collapse trenches, set off mines, rip apart belts of barbed wire, and displace caltrops by anything up to miles.

Even so, except for people's nerves there were comparatively few casualties. Most of the positions on the island were too small to justify using a deep penetrator on, either as a matter of comparative cost or as a matter of operational effectiveness. A sortie that might drop a single deep penetrator could have, instead, carried several times that in more conventional tonnage. Though there were a few targets worth using a deep penetrator on.

They'd tried bombs guided by the Global Locating System before, both on the mainland and on the island. Six times they'd tried using the rare and expensive bombs with GLS guidance. Six times the bombs had gone anyplace but where they were supposed to. Finally, some clever analyst had done a check of certain radio broadcasts coming out of Balboa and determined that, at least during air raids, they were capturing the GLS's encrypted signal, delaying, it amplifying it, and rebroadcasting it. This voided the need to break the encryption. Figuring this out had been especially difficult because the Balboans used half-rhombic directional antennas to both boost the signal to overpowering strength and limit it to a couple of narrowly focused—about three degrees—broadcast areas. Outside of that area, or in its opposite direction, even detecting the stolen GLS signal was unlikely and difficult. The analyst who'd figured that out had deserved every accolade and commendation she had received.

The GLS itself, to include with the encrypted signal, gave off a time stamp, from each of its twenty-seven geosynchronous satellites. A comparison of the time stamps, each, in effect, saying, "At the tone, the time will be" gave one a precise location on or above the surface of the planet. What the analyst had discovered was that, in effect, the Balboans were changing the GLS's "At the tone the time will be" to "at the tone the time will have been," for systems that simply couldn't tell the difference between present, future, or future perfect tenses. With those differences, moving at the speed of light, for all the poor bomb knew it was over Taurus. Of *course* they missed their targets.

Bombing the half-rhombics hadn't done a bit of good either. They were cheap and plentiful, largely locally made out of spare commo wire and plastic what-nots.

Then the Taurans had tried inertial guidance, both on its own and as a check on the GLS. The problem with using it on its own was that errors built up in the guidance package. Sometimes these cancelled each other out, but more often they multiplied. For a large area target, inertial guidance was . . . acceptable. Balboa had precisely no targets that really suited. Nor did using it in conjunction with GLS help much; lost is lost. The best that inertial could do was get a bomb into the right general area.

They'd tried radar, very briefly. Something in the trees made it almost impossible. Some Anglian major, so said rumor control, insisted that the Balboans had been laying precisely cut strips of aluminized plastic in the trees for years, for precisely that purpose. Nobody believed it, though; who really thought that far ahead?

What had worked, finally, was the use of laser guidance and closed-circuit television guidance, either active or preprogrammed, depending on the precise circumstances of the targets. Laser was good—dangerous, because the plane had to stay exposed, but good—wherever the target could be targeted by laser. Triple canopy tended to screw those to the point where what should have been science was largely art. TV camera was also good, even through the jungle, but depended on having an identifiable reference point, which wasn't always available.

Still . . . sometimes it was.

The Tauravia Hurricane was about as capable a fighter bomber as existed anywhere on the planet. It was not ordinarily capable—rather its heavy hardpoints were not capable—of carrying the heavy, two-and-a-half-ton, deep penetrators. For that, a small number of planes had been modified, perhaps two dozen between the Anglian, Sachsen, and Tuscan air forces, together, of which a fraction had been sent to the war. These had their centerline hardpoints replaced with much heavier duty ones, which were affixed to the aircraft differently from normal heavy duty hardpoints. Those were for the two-and-a-half-ton penetrators.

Squadron Commander Halpence kept well out to sea on his flight from Julio Asunción Airport, in Santa Josefina, to the big fortress island the Balboans called the "*Isla Real.*" Higher headquarters had demanded it, now that the Balboans had shown both teeth and the willingness to bite in painful and humiliating ways. Still, with only the five thousand pounds of ordnance carried, which left plenty of capacity for two drop tanks, the only cost was time and a little wear and tear.

Where previously, Halpence and his squadron had had a semi-independent existence directly supporting Marciano's little pocket division, now, with the advent of whole wings at Julio Asunción and other airfields in Santa Josefina, and with those wings more group captains, air commodores, vice marshals, air marshals, colonels, generals, and at least two admirals, Halpence's brief sojourn into the joyous Never-Neverland of independent command had come to an end. Now, the only refuge from the idiocies of the higher command were in flight, and that in more senses than one.

Looking ahead, Halpence saw the island as if shrouded in smoke, as indeed it was. Above the smoke, like flies gathered above a corpse, or perhaps more like buzzards, Tauran aircraft circled, flittered, and more than occasionally dove down to deliver rockets, cannon fire, or bombs.

*As long as you don't obscure* my *target*, thought Halpence, *then, boys, have fun.*

There were eleven aircraft, in total, accompanying Halpence, of which four were modified to carry the heavy and deep penetrators. Of the bombs, themselves, only thirty-two had been delivered, which was very nearly the complete stockpile within all the air forces of the Tauran Union. That number, thirty-two, had been selected on the basis of one per coastal artillery gun turret on the island, of which there were sixteen, plus twelve for the heavy bunkers, and four spares. The number twelve was chosen, despite the fact that there were thirteen known very large and very deep bunkers on the island. One of these, however, the enemy had identified as either a POW holding pen or a medical facility; they refused to be more specific. In any case, that one was off limits.

Four of the other twelve, though, were in for a pasting today.

Rocket assist in deep penetration had never entirely caught on. A few heavy bombs used it, but, in the main, the complexity, reduction in payload, and probability of the bomb not being precisely aligned upon the rocket's firing mitigated against any widespread use. The bomb Halpence carried, for example, didn't have it. Instead, the bomb relied on mass, velocity, strength, and sharpness to achieve its penetration. A fuse ensured that it would go off somewhere in the depths of the body to be penetrated, generally in an open space as would indicate human facilities. The bomb could also be set to pass through several open spaces before detonating.

A quick check with the electronic warfare and Frenzied Ferret people confirmed that the Balboans' anti-GLS measures were not only fully operative, but switching from one emitter to another so quickly that there was essentially no chance to use an antiradiation missile on them . . . or, for that matter, to do anything worthwhile in the slightest to them.

Halpence mentally shrugged. *Right, no GLS-based targeting. And, however much one hates to admit it, it still has to be said, the motherfuckers are getting better the more we fight. So are we, of course, but they started at a lower level and are getting better, faster.*

Still, it wasn't all bad. Both Frenzied Ferrets and strategic recon (which Halpence was rapidly coming to suspect was code for "Earthpigs") said the Balboan air defense umbrella was down or, at least, not up. Accordingly, about forty kilometers out he pulled back on his stick to get enough altitude to use his penetrator to some good effect. The other eleven Hurricanes in the flight did likewise, though they spread out a bit more as they rose.

Halpence activated both the camera on the bomb and his ground attack computer. The enemy's anti-GLS measures seemed to be fixed along certain axes; if you weren't within one of those, your own GLS would work as well as ever. Of course, the Balboans also switched off regularly; predicting where GLS would work was always problematic. Still, for now, operating with the aid of the GLS, the computer, for the most part, took charge of both bomb and plane, guiding them in, locking the target image into the bomb's "brain," and releasing the bomb at the proper time.

*"Oh, I have slipped the surly bonds of Earth,"* thought the bomb . . . oh, no, it didn't. It was just a freaking bomb, not a poet. All it really "thought" was a bunch of numbers meaningful only to it, which numbers gave things like target position, its own speed, altitude and

position relative to the target. Some of those numbers created a sort of digital picture that could be matched to the picture seen by the camera in the nose.

In this case, the match was multifold. The bomb saw a large set of doors, themselves set in a concrete frame. It also saw both a road leading to the doors, and an intersection not far from them. Several trees planted after the bunker had been covered also formed a distinctive pattern. Lastly, a section of the base of the heavily damaged solar chimney that normally provided the island's electric power was within the camera's field of view. In short, the bomb had an excellent idea of where the target was and where it was to penetrate.

Once released from Halpence's modified Hurricane, the bomb used its own abilities to track down to the target. Its camera sent back a continuous signal to Halpence's plane, which Halpence could have used to guide it manually. Until it was obvious that the bomb needed that, though, the pilot figured it knew what it was doing.

The first strike on the earth pulverized the camera. At that point, though, it wasn't needed anyway. Straight and true the bomb plunged into the dirt and rock over the multistoried bunker. At that point, things got complex. Worse, they got complex in ways that the bomb couldn't tell anyone about and which would not necessarily be obvious to the outside viewer.

The first complexity came in the form of twin layers of hexagonal plates, something over an inch thick, that had been laid over the earth over the bunker in the course of covering it, once it had been substantially completed. The bomb's sharp nose touched one of the plates in the upper layer near its edge and simply tore through that edge at the cost of a little energy.

That, however, meant that it hit one of the plates in the second layer about ten inches from the center. There was no tearing though that; the bomb's sharp nose simply impaled itself onto the plate, forcing it to come along on its dive into the depths of the island.

If it had been a dead center hit, the plate would have increased the cross-sectional area, hence the resistance, by a factor of about three or four, dropping the bomb's usual penetration from perhaps thirty meters of mixed rock, dirt, and concrete to maybe seven to ten meters or so. Because of where it hit in this case, however, the plate caused the bomb to do something worse; it yawed. It yawed so much, in fact, that the cross section changed from about one hundred and sixty square inches to fifteen times that, for most of its brief subterranean journey. True, there were moments when it was pointed straight down, as it veered back and forth, but those moments were quite brief. And even there, the yawing sucked up energy, too.

That all sounds much more involved and complex than it really was. In fact, the bomb hit dirt. It effectively missed one plate then picked up a different one. The plate it speared itself to caused it to yaw one way, until resistance caused it to spring back and yaw the other. It slipped into the dirt, wore itself out, stopped, and went *boom*. A great spray of dirt and hexagonal steel plates was blown up into the air and to all sides. It took a lot longer for one of the plates to reach apogee than it had taken the bomb to go from the final "a" in "Kawabunga" to "*Boom*."

Down on the sixth floor of the bunker's twelve, a clerk turned to a radio operator and asked, "Did you feel something?"

Not every bunker of the four attacked had it quite so easy. One of them, dug into the north-northeastern face of Hill 287, and next nearest to the one Halpence had attacked, wasn't as fortunate. There, the bomb had plunged right in between two of the hexagonal steel plates, then glanced off another in the next layer down without spearing it. Rather, at that angle the bomb simply brushed the plate aside.

From there it had sliced through dirt and rock deftly and easily. Indeed, it had been made more easy by the cut-and-cover method of construction the Balboans had used to save time and expense. In short, the dirt and rock had been comparatively loose and soft.

The three-meter-thick roof of the bunker, all reinforced concrete, hadn't been able to do much more than slow the bomb down. Its sharp steel point—and steel of the highest grade, too—punched right through concrete and rebar almost as easily as if they were not there. The most that could be said was that the roof slowed the bomb. It never had a chance of stopping it.

Inside, a massive spray of spalling had erupted into the bunker's top floor, killing several and wounding almost two dozen. They'd just begun to realize what had happened and to scream when the tail of the bomb passed through the floor. Indeed, while that tail was still about midway between floor and ceiling, the bomb's sharp nose was sending another spray of spalling into the third floor down, the tenth floor. That spray, however, had little of the energy of the first. The bomb was noticeably slowing. Rather, it would have been noticeable if anyone had had the presence of mind not to be shitting themselves as the bomb passed by.

Continuing on through the six, seventh, eighth, and ninth floors, in the opposite order, the bomb finally came to rest there, with its nose dug about half a foot into the concrete of the sixth floor's floor. Thereupon, it met its detonation parameters and promptly set off its six hundred pounds of high explosive.

The explosion ripped the thick steel casing into shards, even as it drove the nose on a fiery spear downward, though two more floors. The nose itself didn't kill anybody. The spalling did, but only a few. However, that fiery spear shaft created a concussive shock through the holes into floors four and five sufficient to kill all forty-seven people currently working there.

The shards from the main casing, meanwhile, created a blizzard of flying steel on floors six and seven, and a lesser storm on floor eight. None of that really mattered, as the blast alone was enough to scour those floors free of human life, and also took care of the trixie that one of the supply detachments on floor seven kept as a mascot.

The blast from those floors more leaked than flooded into floor ten through the hole gouged by the bomb. It was a mere fraction of the blast, and even that fraction entered the tenth floor more slowly than was strictly inconsistent with life. Eleven got off almost scot free, minus a few killed by the initial spalling, while the top floor lost nobody to blast. This was not necessarily a good thing, as the agony-induced screaming from people with chunks of concrete imbedded in their guts was worse on them and the remainder than death might have been.

Power went out and with it the elevator. There were steps linking the floors but the blast doors were pretty much slammed shut and wouldn't be opened any time soon. Meanwhile, noxious fumes from the explosion, in the absence of any method of clearing them, crept from floor to floor, sending the miserable creatures still living there to horrid, choking deaths.

## Fixed Turret 177, *Isla Real*, Balboa, Terra Nova

Their regiment was the *Tercio Santa Cecelia*, but just about everyone called them "Adios Patria." As in, "We have met the enemy. Goodbye, Fatherland."

Sergeant Rafael de la Mesa sat in the commander's hatch of his turret. He couldn't stand; he'd lost the ability long ago. That was how he'd ended up in the *Tercio Santa Cecelia*, the regiment for those less than whole of mind and body.

The turret had come from an old Volgan tank, not really suitable for standing in line of battle *as a tank* anymore. Bought for little above scrap metal value, the old tanks had had their turrets removed and a thick-walled casemate built up over them. In these had been mounted milled-out medium artillery pieces, firing either shaped charges or ninety-pound lumps of High Explosive, Plastic. The shaped charges might or might not penetrate the best of modern tanks from the frontal arc. The HEP, however, could pretty much be counted on to slap a tank's crew to death.

Instead of commanding one of those tank destroyers, SPATHAs, they were called, or, better still, a real tank, de la Mesa had only the turret and its concrete surround.

*Oh, well,* thought de la Mesa, *one does the best one can with what one has. Dammit.*

The sergeant had lost the use of his lower body when a tow cable had snapped, with him a little too close. The cable hadn't been enough to cut him in two—nor were the days few when he'd wished it had—but it had severed his spine, roughly and completely, and in a way that modern medicine, as practiced on Terra Nova, could not rebuild.

The sergeant's little command was larger than a tank. It would not, however, be travelling except insofar as an enemy bomb might move it. Even then, the concrete was set on what was called a "raft," to keep even a near miss from overturning it.

There were a few different configurations for the fixed turrets. In the case of de la Mesa's, it was a two-floor arrangement, with walls a meter and a half thick, and a bowed roof a bit thicker, built of high-quality concrete with rebar and a crushed coral aggregate. Inside the concrete, hollow plastic objects of various sizes and shapes ensured that neither a direct hit with a tank's main gun's penetrator nor from a HEP charge would cause much spalling. They also helped with the concussion, as did the plywood paneling that lined the walls and the rubber matting on the floors. The turret position was several years old. Already the trees transplanted around it had grown to the point of providing adequate shelter from the sun, through most of the day, if not at high noon. A camouflage and radar-scattering screen erected between the trees helped there. None of the trees was closer than nine meters from the turret, thus allowing full traverse. There were some gaps in the earth and concrete through which ball-mounted machine guns could fire, to supplement the fires of the infantry maniple in the position behind, and what looked like pipes—they were more complex than that—for sending live grenades outside. De la Mesa had tried to teach the boys to use the grenade dispensers, but except for Juan, he thought the process just too dangerous for them and for the turret's continued existence.

De la Mesa's crew consisted of four men. These were himself, Pablo, Juan, and Julio. He was crippled in body. The last three were all victims of Down's Syndrome. At first, de la Mesa had resented his charges deeply. Their flawed condition was a reminder of his own. With the passage of time, though, and a realization on his part that the boys worshipped the ground he rolled on, he'd come to accept them for their virtues. Not least of these was a boundless capacity for love.

Juan was the least defective of the lot, at least in some ways. He served as the gunner. It had taken some work on the sergeant's part to convince the boy—Juan was only twenty, chronologically—that it was not only all right but necessary and praiseworthy to use the cannon and machine gun to kill other human beings.

*And if it turns out he just can't do it when the time comes? Well . . . I can gun from my station if I must.*

Julio was probably the most severely damaged. Even letting him enlist had taken the testimony of several legionary psychologists that, inarticulate or not, he could understand the oath well enough. In fact, though, there were birds and proto-birds on Terra Nova with IQs estimated to be higher than Julio's. Julio was the loader for the main gun, a job that required strength but not much in the way of intelligence or coordination. He didn't actually load the gun, but rather the carousel below it, which fed rounds to the gun as the gunner or commander selected them.

Julio tended to cry a lot when the bombs fell. To combat that, de la Mesa had taught the boys several songs. Their singing was by no means good, but it still served the purposed of keeping them from a mind-numbing terror they were otherwise ill equipped to deal with.

Last came Pablo, who had been with de la Mesa the longest. Pablo wasn't clever enough to gun, but was too clever to waste on merely loading. Instead, he did the running to the cook house for the four, plus kept the generator for the turret traverse, the lights, and the air filtration going. He also did the laundry, by hand, made the beds down in the lower level, and generally cleaned up. It was also Pablo, usually assisted by Julio, who moved de la Mesa out of his command chair, to his wheelchair, or down below to sleep.

*At least I can still wipe my own ass. Frankly, a couple of the boys aren't too fastidious about things like that for themselves. If I didn't nag, this place would be intolerable.*

"Would you like some breakfast, Sergeant?" Pablo asked from down below. On seeing de la Mesa's hand come down, he placed the sergeant's aluminum mess kit into his hands, making especially sure to wrap the hand in such a way as to secure both plates.

Next Pablo passed up a clean knife and fork from the sergeant's own kit. It had taken both some work on the sergeant's part and a severe case of the gastro-intestinals to convince Pablo of the importance of clean mess gear. Now he was at least as fanatical on the matter as was de la Mesa, himself.

De la Mesa didn't initially hear the shriek of the engines of the attacking jets. Out of the corner of one eye he saw two long, slender, and dark objects falling through the sky. Then he heard the jets and instinctively reached down to drop his command seat into the turret. He left his own head out of the turret, albeit just barely. Just as instinctively, he used his command override to swivel the turret in the direction he'd seen the bombs fall. The first one he saw hit raised such a flash and such a plume of metal, rocks, and dirt that de la Mesa instinctively crossed himself, thinking everyone in that bunker was probably dead.

He expected the other one to be as bad, but was gratified to see no great blast erupting from the island where that bomb slid into the ground. De la Mesa was terribly surprised then, when a score of ambulances and a fair amount of construction machinery collected at the second bunker, while ignoring the first hit.

He thought, *Maybe they know everyone from the first strike is dead.*

# CHAPTER THIRTY-ONE

All the gods are dead except the god of war.
—Eldridge Cleaver, *Soul on Ice*

### Xing Zhong Guo Aircraft Carrier *Luyang, Mar Furioso*, Terra Nova

Paranoia was something of a Zhong trait anyway. It was also a highly admirable trait for commanders at sea. *Hai Jun Yi Ji Shang Jiang*, or Fleet Admiral Wanyan Liang had it in an even more than normally Zhong or naval degree. Indeed, it was said among the crews of any ship he'd ever commanded that, if one opened up a dictionary to the word "paranoia," there would be a two-by-three-inch glossy of Lieutenant, or Commander, or Captain, or Admiral Wanyan.

With the fleet he'd been given, Wanyan not only could afford to be paranoid; he *had* to be. He was carrying virtually the entire Zhong Marine Corps, plus two corps from the army, escorted by all that was left of Zhong naval aviation and about two-thirds of the surface and submarine fleets. In other words, Admiral Wanyan had command of his empire's future, of its chance to carve out its own place in the sun. In those circumstances, anything less than paranoia would have constituted gross dereliction of duty.

Wanyan left the running of his flagship, the *Luyang*, for the most part to her captain. His concerns were simply too great in scope to allow more than cursory concern for the carrier. Neither could he pay any particular attention to the other carrier, the *Jiangwei*, following behind at a distance of about four miles. Both of those had been stripped of almost all their rotary craft, and those distributed among the destroyers of the fleet, in order to make room for more fighter-bombers.

The destroyers and frigates were grouped into six main divisions, one of them holding about half of all the destroyers and frigates available. That large grouping had the point of the fleet's advance, the individual ships serving as base for the antisubmarine helicopters, even as they alternated passive listening with frantic dashes to and fro, while pinging like mad.

Two more groups held the flanks, but echeloned back somewhat from the point group. In theory that might have allowed an enemy submarine to slip in. In practice, Wanyan would have liked to have seen them try it, since the bulk of the nonnuclear submarine force he brought with him was guarding those gaps diligently.

A fourth group took up the rear. Group Five was entirely air defense, and operated both to the flanks of the carriers and amphibious group, as well as between them. The final group was made up of the latest antisubmarine warfare destroyers and frigates, Wanyan's personal hammer to smash any threat that was found by any of the other, screening groups.

One would have expected Fleet Admiral Wanyan to be just thrilled about the size of his command. He might have been, too, except that, *Gods, so many of my ships are so old. And so many, especially among the amphibious vessels, have been pressed into a service for which they were not designed. And we have reason to believe the enemy is, if small, both clever and ruthless. Worse, it may be that their submarines are nearly undetectable. I keep running through the reports of the survivors of our engagements with them. And Mao Zedong's captain, Liu? I've known him since he was a Shao Wei. He's convinced the Balboans maneuvered, without being detected, behind him and fired themselves on their own ships. Backing up Liu is the conduct of the Federated States, who act convinced that we fired first. The fact that they are so convinced means they were witnesses or, rather, had a witness. The fact that they believe it also means they didn't detect the Balboans who, per Liu, are certainly the ones who fired first.*

*Unless it was the Federated States, itself, that fired first. They are wicked, and evil, and . . . and my paranoia is getting the better of me.*

### *Batería* Pedro *el Cholo, Isla Real,* Balboa, Terra Nova

The bronze plaque by the rolled-open steel doors proclaimed the battery was named for an Indian, a man without surname, who had been a follower of Belisario Carrera in his war of independence from Old Earth. Each of the eight batteries ringing the island was named for a different character from that long-ago conflict. Moving clockwise from Battery Pedro, one came to *Batería* Nandi Mkhize. Mkhize, a former UN Marine?—and a pure stunner of a Zulu girl—had deserted the UN to join Belisario and later married into the family. Past that was *Batería* Mitzilla Carrera, then *Batería* Juan Alvarez, Jr. Next, were one following the ring road around the island, one could have come by *Batería* Amita Kaur Bhago, another deserter from the UN to that old Carrera. After that came *Batería* Mendoza, just that, since nobody knew what old Mendoza's first name had been. It was even likely that there were two or three of them with the same last name. Then came *Batería* Isabel Cordoba. Lastly, before the ring road would return to *Batería* Pedro *el Cholo*, was *Batería* Oliver Rogers, who hadn't fought in the war but had arranged to buy guns for the rebels and ship them north. This was the same Rogers for whom the FSN had named a submarine.

A battery's normal armament consisted of two triple six-inch turrets, themselves removed from one of the cruisers scrapped by Carrera as not needed for naval efforts. The turrets sat atop artificial hills, the sodded and tree-planted dirt surmounting thick hollow cones of concrete. Behind the twin hills for the two turrets, various ammunition bunkers, twelve of them for each battery, were situated to either side of a rail line, a spur running from the ring that encircled the island about three kilometers inland from the coast. Typically, eight of those twelve bunkers were on the coast side, with their large steel loading doors facing toward the central massif, Hill 287. Short rail lines ran right from the main spur into the ammunition bunkers. The turrets themselves, while capable of all-round traverse, were oriented primarily to sea. Unseen, underground and connected by tunnels, were concrete headquarters, the fire direction center, and quarters and mess facilities for the battery's troops.

Of the sixteen triple turrets, every one had been knocked out by the air forces of the Tauran Union. Two of them, the Eighth Legion's engineers had managed to get back to duty, for a while. Then the Taurans had come by again and smashed them still more thoroughly.

The Taurans really hadn't had much choice about their targeting. The ammunition bunkers were much more numerous than the turrets, and just as hard to destroy. Even if they'd had enough suitable penetrators, there would have been other targets for those. Rail lines like those that ran between the bunkers and the turrets were notoriously hard to take out and keep down. And besides, the odds were good that each of the turrets had a fair-sized magazine below, such that taking out ammo bunkers or rail would have been pointless.

Legate Rigoberto Puercel, commander of the Corps which contained the Eighth Legion and the island it defended, accompanied by his engineer, a Sachsen immigrant named Fehrenbach, inspected the damage from the latest Tauran hit on one of the coastal batteries. There weren't any bodies, this time, which was a blessing. Previous strikes had scattered broken men and bits of men throughout the labyrinthine depths of the batteries. There had never been too many of them lost to air strikes by the batteries, the worst case having been Battery Cordoba where the battery's own crew of a baker's dozen had been supplemented by a reinforced infantry platoon seeking shelter. *That* had been an ugly scene, when Puercel had inspected it, less than half an hour after the strike.

This time? Nobody was killed, nor even hurt. After building an arrangement of connected tripods to lift the turret enough to set it back down in its ring, everyone had left for a beer. At two hundred and fifty-odd tons for a turret, they deserved the beer.

"Do we keep it up?" asked the engineer. "This one lasted about a day. It took four to recover her."

"You have anything better to do?" responded the legate.

"Well, no, not really," Fehrenbach admitted. "But the thing is, boss, that if they think we'll keep fixing the turrets, eventually they may well go after the ammunition bunkers, which, if detonated, we could not fix. That would be . . ."

"Stop fixing the turrets," said the legate. "Effective right this fucking minute we concede to the enemy that they've won that round."

*Because, God forbid they take out the "ammunition" bunkers. Then we'd be well and truly screwed.*

Now that the containers of "Log Base Alpha" were sorted out, Warrant Officer Han Siegel, wife of Sig Siegel, was officially the translator for the two hundred and change Cochinese immigrants who manned Batteries Pedro, Nandi, and Mitzi. She was tiny, lovely, and quite possibly the most ruthless, foul-mouthed bitch in four languages. She certainly spoke rudely enough to most of her countrymen.

Those Cochinese, former slave laborers for the Tsarist-Marxist regime, had been purchased by Siegel for more or less petty cash. Initially, he'd used them to package up certain light and heavy guns being bought from or through the Cochinese authorities, many of whom were relearning free enterprise with a vengeance. Then, since they'd learned how to take the guns apart, he'd brought them to Balboa to put them together again. There, faced with the fact that nobody would take them in, while Balboa had a military-only immigration policy, the Cochinese had volunteered en masse for the legion. Fair numbers had continued to come, too, egged on by glowing descriptions sent back home by the old Cochinese.

They'd been a real bargain. Not least because, among the two hundred plus males in the initial crew, every one was a former soldier, sailor, marine, or airman. That was how they'd ended up as slave laborers, they'd been on the losing side of the Cochinese civil war. Better, of those, fully fourteen had been through the Federated States Army's Ranger School. *That* meant they could be commissioned into the legion without going to Cazador School, for which they were all far too old. Technically, because of their age, the Cochinese could only be assigned to the Tercio Socrates. In practice, because of their experience and qualification, the Tercio Socrates, whose job it was to find military employment for those who joined late in life, had been able to form a heavy artillery group from the Cochinese, *under* their own officers and centurions, and *with* their own cooks, cooking a menu suitable for *them*. It was nearly ideal for everyone.

Everyone, not least the Cochinese, agreed that it was a mighty fine deal, and worth fighting to keep. And they intended to fight to keep it. After all, their wives, children, and grandchildren, though evacuated from the island with the rest of the civilians, still had their houses in the town Carrera had built for them on the island's southern side, from which they had, when not militarily employed, made a living fishing and selling the fish to the training brigade on the island.

The Cochinese, on the other hand, had never quite taken to Spanish. Rather, the elder ones who made up the heavy gun crews hadn't; the younger ones had adopted it just fine. That was where Han Siegel, who had a gift for languages, came in.

Sort of. Kind of. With some allowances being made.

"You faggots!" said the almost vanishingly tiny Cochinese girl, standing under artificial light atop an eighteen-centimeter gun. "You limp-wristed suckers of leprous cock! My husband's boss, which is to say *our* boss, is coming from the mainland for a visit and you think you can sleep?! Tribune Pham?!"

The tribune, a former air force pilot no longer really up to combat flying, sighed. Technically and legally, of course, he outranked the ever loving shit out of a warrant officer. In the real world, and especially the real world *he'd* grown up in, rank was a much more amorphous concept than that. Perhaps he outranked Han. Perhaps he outranked her husband. But her husband had the highest contacts imaginable in this context, old friendship with Carrera. Nobody for several countries around outranked Carrera, not even the presidents. At least that was Pham's reading of it. So, in practice, the bitch outranked him and he had to put up with her foul mouth.

"Here, Warrant Officer Siegel," the tribune answered.

"You need to get your take-it-up-the-ass-from-water-buffalo-and-donkeys crew of whores together and . . ."


### Estado Mayor, Ciudad Balboa, Balboa, Terra Nova

In two large places, the otherwise modern-looking, concrete and stone aedifice, was now blasted flat. The upper walls of most quadrants still looked to have been chewed by dinosaurs, by the dinos had grazed down a bit more. Some large sections were still perfectly useable, though most of the key functions had been moved underground and away. They were useable, but not safe to use.

Where spoil from the demolition had been thrown onto the asphalt and grass around the building, that had mostly been cleared into piles. Even in the piles, though, was a pattern, where a rather broad strip had been cleared to allow launching of Condors and Crickets, and several wide squares were open for helicopter landings. A glider sat on the strip, with a tow cable running from its nose to a winch some hundreds of feet away. Those winches existed all over the country, too, and were barely noticeable. A suspicious man might have thought they were there for a reason.

"Not a sub?" asked Carrera. The commander of the legion looked inexpressibly tired to both his chief of staff, Kuralski, who was worried about it, and Warrant Officer Rafael Montoya, who was not.

"Too dangerous," said Kuralski. "They've been targeting the sub pens and the water's too shallow for true stealth between here and the island."

"Yeah, but . . ."

"Don't 'yeah, but' me, Patrick," said the chief of staff. "You're the one who decided you just had to visit the *Isla Real*. This is the only safe way we've got to get you there. And it's not all that safe."

"Yes, it is," said Montoya, lightly tapping the sea-blue top of the glider resting atop the asphalt of the general staff building's parking lot. "We run a courier out to the island twice a day, me in the morning, just after daybreak and Casavetes just before nightfall. Less chance of showing up in a thermal that way. We think. There's precisely nothing unusual about this, that would key the Taurans to target the *Duque*.

"Moreover, since we've got the enemy back to having to assemble large strike packages, and given that the facilities—airfields terrestrial or naval, supplemented by aerial tankers—are limited, that means we know when they're coming, since it takes them so long to assemble. They won't be coming in the hour I'll have the *Duque* in the air.

"*Duque*," said Montoya, "trust me; I'll get you there safely enough and then I or Casavetes, depending on how long you decide to stay, will get you back."

There were four methods of launching a Condor, five if one counted dumping them out the loading ramp of an airship. The other four, the four available to Carrera and Montoya, were over the edge of a cliff, via the balloon launch system, self-launching with the on-board propeller (or jet, a few Condors had small jet engines), and the winch. The winch had all kinds of disadvantages. But it had, for the present purposes, two big advantages.

"I don't have to carry fuel so I can carry you, *Duque*," explained Montoya from the pilot's seat to Carrera, scrunched in the back. "It's not as noticeable as a big-assed balloon. And it doesn't put out any heat, like using the auxiliary motor would, so it's unlikely to get picked up on the thermal imager."

"Works for me," said the big—compared to Montoya he was big— ex-gringo in the back. "Let's go."

"Roger." Montoya looked out the port side, raising a single inquisitive thumb. The ground controller held up a palm—*hold on a sec*—while he checked with intel to ensure the air was free overhead. When he pulled his right hand away from his headset he gave the pilot an answering thumbs up, then aimed a knife-hand at the winch operator, a few dozen meters away. Ground control also shouted something to the winch operator at the same time, but Montoya couldn't make out what it was.

The cable leading from a recessed fixture in the nose of the Condor went taut in a small fraction of a second. The glider immediately began to move towards the winch, though in a matter of mere yards it became airborne, leaving the wheeled cradle on which it had rested behind and below. The winch continued to pull until Montoya decided he had enough altitude, whereupon he cut the tow rope, which fell with a gently curving grace, below.

"Wow," said Carrera, "that was smooth."

"It's even smoother off a ship," said Montoya. Then he added, "Oh . . . I'm not supposed to talk about that."

Carrera gave a small chuckle. "And just *what*, Warrant Officer Montoya, do you think there is about your recon flights to Atlantis Base that I am not privy to?"

"Ah . . . good point, *Duque*. Even so . . ."

"Yeah, don't worry about it. Just get me to the island. In the interim, and as a demonstration of the boundless trust I have in you"—Carrera chuckled again—"I'm taking a nap."

"*Duque! Duque*, wake up! We have a problem."

From the back seat came a barely intelligible, "I wasn't sleeping Sergeant," followed in a few moments by a, "What the fuck?"

Montoya, who had had his own "I wasn't sleeping, Sergeant" moments in the past, tactfully ignored that, keying on the, "What the fuck?"

"Air raid in progress on the island. It's light, maybe twenty-five or thirty planes, but that's still twenty-five or thirty planes more than I can take on in this."

"How? I thought you checked . . ."

"Did. But we've only got good advanced warning to the south and east. These came from the north."

"Zhong?"

"Eighth Legion Headquarters says so," the pilot replied. "I asked them about putting up the air defense umbrella to see us safely in but they say they're not even on weapons tight but on a 'do not shoot' order and only *you* can lift it."

Carrera considered that, then said, "Yeah . . . I could, but . . . no . . . we can't." At Montoya's questioning cough, he explained, "The Taurans must land and be defeated to win and end the war, Montoya. They need the Zhong to have landed to feel they'd got a fair chance of success. The Zhong need—or may need and so I have to bet it this way—the confidence they'll get from having their own air component in the war or they won't—at least might not—land. If we lift and unmask against the Zhong, and we could, we'll smash their carrier aviation capability. Then they don't land. Or we look like we could have smashed them but didn't for, no doubt, nefarious reasons of our own. Then the Zhong don't land either. Then the Taurans don't land. Then the bombing and embargoes—blockade, too—continue until we're in the economic stone age. We *have* to entice them to a fight to the finish, then fight them to a finish, beat them, and break them, before that happens.

"Can you get us in with the air raid ongoing? Failing that, can you get us back to the mainland? Failing even *that*, can you get us onto one of the other islands?"

"Maybe, no, and maybe, *Duque*, in exactly that order. We're too low and too far from the mainland, and I'm not likely to find any good updrafts out here. So forget that. I'm not carrying enough fuel to make it back under our own power so forget that, too.

"As for the main island or one of the others? It's possible. It's also risky. *Duque*, they don't have to shoot us down. These things are fairly fragile; just flying close could tear our wings off."

"Try for the main island, then. Or *Isla* San Juan or Santa Paloma. Puercel could retrieve us from either of those."

"*Si, Duque.*"

"Could have sworn someone said, 'safe,'" said Carrera.

"What? You've never been wrong, sir?"

Flying above the island, Zhao Hai and Fan Shenlu, flying Serg-83s configured for air-to-air combat, overwatched their comrades below, bombing and strafing, The senior, Zhao, took the lead with his wingman, Fan, behind and to the left. Both were nervous since, should the Balboans decide to surge—presuming they were able still to surge; something the Tauran pigs vehemently denied—they would be toast. They could fight off equal numbers. But their aircraft were really not a whit more capable than the Balboans' ancient Mosaic-Ds. A big surge?

*We'd be dead*, thought Zhao. *On the other hand, no guts, no glory . . . no kills, no glory . . . and I see an easy kill down below.*

The senior pilot ordered Fan, "Stay here. I'm going down to knock off that courier. Be back in a few."

"Roger."

"Oh, shit," muttered Montoya. He'd been keeping half an eye's worth of attention on the two circling Zhong planes ahead and above, hoping like hell they wouldn't notice him and his slender, blue-topped glider.

"What is it?" Carrera asked, then agreed, "Shit!" when Montoya told him. "What do we do?"

"I don't think he can get a lock on us," Montoya said. "We're basically radar invisible and within a fraction of a degree of ambient temperature. If he could have locked on us he would have already; it's not like he's in any doubt about whose side we are. So if he's coming, he's coming with eyeballs and guns. I can—well, *maybe* I can—outmaneuver him.

"You feel ballsy, *Duque*?"

"Do I have a choice?"

"Not really."

"Then I feel ballsy as hell. Do your job, Warrant Officer Montoya."

Zhao had missiles. *No good. The thing might as well not even be there.* Zhao had a gunsight/fire computer integral to his heads up display, but it was a generation too advanced to deal with the radar invisible glider at ambient temperature. It was almost like a tyrannosaur . . . hunting a mouse. They just lived in different worlds.

What Zhao had that might work were a Mark One calibrated eyeball, plus two hundred and fifty rounds of 23mm, feeding to a dual cannon in a pod slung underwing.

Adjusting his throttle down to bring him to just a bit above stall speed, Zhao lined up his Serg-83 on a point ahead of the glider, then tapped off a long burst from his cannon . . .

Only to discover that the frigging glider had veered off before the rounds reached the chosen spot. *Which was fucking wrong anyway, since I'm trained to aim at something more high performance.* Zhao pulled up, nearly skimming the crests of the waves, while looking about frantically for his quarry.

"Nicely done," said Carrera, with a calm he in no way felt. Trying to be helpful, Carrera scanned the sky for their pursuer. "Eight o'clock," he said. "Level."

"Ooo . . . level," echoed Montoya. "Not good. With the sea to guide him and restrict us, he only has to aim in one dimension. Soooo . . ." The pilot yanked back on the stick, turning energy into altitude, then jammed the stick forward, plunging at a sharp angle toward the sea. Carrera didn't even notice his stomach attempting to crawl out of his mouth at the image of dozens of fist-sized balls of fire passing overhead. The enemy jet passed close enough to see the whites of the pilot's narrowed eyes. In the turbulence the glider bucked. Carrera thought he felt something inside it give way.

Montoya yanked back on his stick, pulling into level flight a short distance above the waves. "How well can you swim, *Duque?*"

"So, so. Why?"

"What you just felt was some carbon fibers and polyurethane in the wing . . . right wing, I think . . . giving way. Take a look."

Carrera looked to starboard, then to port, and then to starboard again. No doubt about it, the right wing was fluttering in a way the left one was not.

"One more close pass and it's coming off," Montoya said. "The beach is about two hundred meters to our front. There's a small encampment there so we can probably get some help if we need it. We need to dunk and swim for it."

"But why?"

Montoya snorted. "Because the enemy will probably be happy with the confirmed kill and will leave us alone if he's got that. Pilots are weird about things like that."

"Okay . . . do it."

"Gotta make it look flashy," announced Montoya. "Hang on! Gonna be rough!"

To confirm that, he put his damaged wing down into the water. It duly ripped off, just at the juncture between wing and body. The glider spun like a pinwheel, tail over nose over tail, until the outside half of the port-side wing likewise dipped into the water and tore off, letting the thing plunge into the sea. It didn't even quite sink, but settled, then bobbed a few inches up and down, with the waves and its own bounce.

Montoya unbuckled himself, then popped the canopy off, knelt on his own seat, and turned around to help Carrera. That was dutiful, but unnecessary. Carrera was climbing out onto the remnants of the port wing before Montoya could so much as ask, "*Duque*, are you all right?"

"Swim for it, goddamnit!" said Carrera, over his shoulder. "The motherfucker's coming back!"

# CHAPTER THIRTY-TWO

The best executive is the one who has sense enough to pick good men to do what he wants done, and self-restraint to keep from meddling with them while they do it.
—Theodore Roosevelt

**Camp Penthesileia, *Isla Real*, Balboa, Terra Nova**

The Zhong aircraft had departed even more suddenly than Carrera and Montoya had become aware of them. Now, more or less peacefully and safely, the two sat on fine white sand, just a few dozen meters away from the edge of the surf. Peaceful and safe or not, their lungs still strained to pull in enough air to make up for their exertion.

Behind them were abandoned tiki torches stuck in the sand in a circle around a fire pit. Farther inland, though not far inland, were a fair number of houses, some of them now bombed-out wrecks, that Carrera recognized as, "Housing, Tribune level, two or three children, Type C." He pulled up in his mind the best recollection of the map of the island, then matched that to where he thought they'd been when they'd splashed in.

"This is where we put the Amazons while they were between courses," Carrera announced. "I wanted them to have someplace nice to call home, after what we put the poor things through."

Montoya just accepted that without any real question or interest. If the women had still been there, he'd have been a lot more interested.

For reasons not entirely comprehensible to Carrera, the Zhong pilot did let them swim away, though he made sure to put a couple of bursts into the general vicinity of the drifting Condor.

"Gun cameras," said Montoya. "Bet you it was his gun cameras."

"Huh?" asked Carrera, after a bout of coughing up some of the water he'd gotten in his lungs.

"The cameras probably only activate when the guns are actually firing. He needs proof of the kill, so he fires at the hulk. The firing activates the camera so he can prove to his unit that there was a hulk."

"Why do you suppose he didn't go after us?"

Montoya shook his head. "Knights of the air syndrome would be my best guess," said the warrant, "but it's not a guess I've got a lot of confidence in, *Duque*."

They heard a cough from behind them, then turned and saw a legionary in battle dress but with a mess hat on. The cook or KP, whichever he was, had a rifle slung across his back.

"We've still got some leftovers from breakfast, if you gentlemen are . . ." The man took a double take, then snapped to attention. "We can make you something special, *Duque*."

"No need," said Carrera. "But if you guys—what unit, by the way?"

"Second Cohort, Twelfth Infantry Tercio, *Duque*. Mess Corporal Alvarez, at your service, *Duque!*"

"Great, Corporal Alvarez. I'm not actually hungry, but if you guys have a tin of ration rum, I could use a fucking drink." Carrera held out one hand to demonstrate. The hand trembled slightly. "Montoya?"

"Concur entirely, sir. A drink. Maybe three."

"Yes, sir," said Alvarez. "If you would follow . . ." He stopped when Montoya shook his head. *Oh, yeah. Right. People after near-death experiences, especially people who are trembling, just might not walk too well.*

"*Duque*," said Alvarez, "I shall be back in a moment, with drinks."

As it turned out, Alvarez arrived later than indicated, about thirty seconds before Legate Puercel did, himself. Puercel seemed bitter, somehow, though Carrera let it ride until he'd managed to choke down a healthy dose of the rum-laced fruit juice provided by the mess.

Carrera probably didn't help matters initially when he told Alvarez to lead Montoya to the mess and Montoya to start making arrangements for the return journey. Alvarez left an opened coffee can with the rum and juice, resting in the sand.

The silence lasted long enough to become uncomfortable after the departure of the pilot and cook. Finally Puercel broke it: "I don't understand what I've done so wrong as to justify you coming here to take over."

"What?" asked Carrera. "What the fuck are you talking about?"

"Isn't that why you're here? To relieve me and take over yourself? Because you think I'm not good enough?"

Carrera blinked a few times in disbelief, that, and disappointment. *Where did these guys get the idea . . . shit.* He filled up his own cup from Alvarez's can, then passed it over with the words, "You need this more than me if you're that stressed out. Friend, I wouldn't have put you here or left you in command this long if I didn't have faith in you."

"But you're *here*," said Puercel, rather needlessly. He didn't, for the nonce, raise the cup to his lips. "What other reason . . . ?"

"Three reasons," said Carrera. "One is to share the burden with you and your men, since you're the ones getting the worst pounding from the Zhong and Taurans." He gestured generally out to sea where the remains of Montoya's Condor still bobbed above the waves. "Second, inspection and getting a sense of the troops. I have to know they'll stand . . . and before you go into a tizzy, remember that I know you didn't train most of them yourself, so knock off the defensive bullshit. Third, to make sure that if there's anything you need from the mainland—anything we can give you, I mean—you will get it."

"There's a fourth reason," Carrera said, contradicting the previously given number. "Can you guess what it is?"

"Relief was my guess," said the legate. At that, he did take a generous drink from the cup.

"Dipshit," Carrera said, though he said it genially. "I'm here to take the blame if it all goes to shit. You know? So that you can fight the battle without worrying about your reputation. Whatever goes wrong you can blame on me."

"Oh," said Puercel, feeling rather ashamed.

"Oh," echoed Carrera, not without a trace of sarcasm. *Though, and I will never breathe a word of this, the very fact that you've got troops you didn't train, that don't know or trust you, means you do need me here, because they do know and trust me and they'll fight the better if they do think I'm in active command.*

"Now, young Legate," said Carrera, "if you would arrange a car and a driver for me, along with an escorting officer you can spare?"

"Yes, sir."

"Oh, and see if somebody can get my bag out of the wreck of that glider, too, would you? It's not worth risking a life over, but if it can be done safely . . ."

### Batería **Pedro** *el Cholo, Isla Real,* **Balboa, Terra Nova**

The vehicle provided by Puercel was hidden in the lee of a couple of wrecked gun turrets. Leaving the temporary AdC, Signifer Torres, behind with the driver, Carrera stepped out onto concrete pavement with a rail line running through it, leading from a large set of doors to a similar set in the artificial hill below the wrecked gun turret.

"Sig sends his love, Han," Carrera said to the incredibly tiny and, if rumor was to be believed, incredibly foul-mouthed and vicious bitch the legion had inherited when Siegel bought her contract from the Cochinese brothel that had held it. There were only a few people in the legion who knew Han's origins, and none of those were talking. This was not only a courtesy to their comrade, Siegel, but also to her. And, what the hell, it was hardly her fault she'd been sold as a young girl. Moreover, she'd been doing excellent work for the legion and for Balboa for quite a few years now. Perhaps more important, still, she was privy to any number of secrets.

"He also says that you are to keep your head down and come home to him safely, once the war is over."

The tiny woman—tiny but shapely, almost a Cochinese version of Marqueli Mendoza, and similarly pretty—flushed with a mix of embarrassment, warmth, and gratitude. "Tell him back, please, *Duque,* that I miss him terribly and I would appreciate it if he would be very careful, as well. Also that you be careful with him, because he's the only one I have."

Not for the first time, Carrera was impressed with the woman's ability with languages. She had an accent, yes, but it was barely discernible. Also not for the first time he wondered if he ought have her transferred to Fernandez's crew.

"I'll do my best," answered Carrera, "though the Taurans may have other ideas. Now what am I looking for here?"

"This battery and the next one clockwise are manned by Cochinese under Tribune Pham. They're all here, now.

"He's pretty good, though I'd never tell him that to his face, especially for an air jockey turned into an artilleryman. His people aren't bad, either, though they're almost all pretty old. They've only got a couple of people cleared for the special shells . . . well . . . four, in total. No, wait. Five with Pham. And me, but I'm only cleared to know about them, not how to use them."

Carrera tried reading the subtext there, and was by no means sure he got it. *She treats them badly. Politics or vindictiveness or just plain personality? Maybe some of all three. And, after all, she probably hates the side that let the Tsarist-Marxists win the war in Cochin, which is what led to her being sold to become a whore. Poor thing. It's a sad fucking universe. But holding it against the people who lost, if that's what's going on, is . . . bad policy and probably unjust, too.*

"Okay," he said, "introduce me."

After a brisk nod, Han turned and led Carrera into a side door to one of the "ammunition" bunkers. The door was thick steel, and stepped to fit snugly into a matching steel frame.

One the other side, as soon as Carrera made his appearance, a series of sharp commands rang out in a language he didn't understand. He really didn't need to. The actions of the aged, bowed, leather-faced and weathered troops told of the commands' import.

One old man, almost as tiny as Han, turned to face Carrera, rendering a hand salute and shouting something in Cochinese. Carrera returned the salute, and ordered, "At ease."

Just as he didn't need to understand Cochinese to understand Tribune Pham's order, so Pham could tell quite well from the tone that Carrera had ordered him to put his men in a more relaxed position. He ordered them to Parade Rest on the theory of better safe than sorry.

Han seemed quite nervous. Carrera noticed it, and asked, "You've never done this before, have you Han?"

"No, *Duque*. What do I do?"

"Just follow along . . . translate back and forth. It's not hard."

The woman nodded understanding though her face said she still wasn't sure.

Pham, Carrera would have judged as being maybe eighty-five years old. Siegel, though, had said none of them here were over maybe sixty-five. It was life in the reeducation camps that had put so many years on them.

Whatever Pham's face looked like, his posture was immaculate and his handshake firm.

"Lead me through," Carrera said, with Han translating. Pham noticed that she left off her usual honorifics.

"He doesn't know how you address us, does he?" Pham asked in his own language. "Hmmm . . . I wonder if one of us doesn't have enough Spanish or English to explain it to him."

Which was actually the reason Han had been nervous. What? Do a little translating to and from languages she was utterly comfortable in? No big deal. Let the big boss find out she'd been verbally abusing *his* troops. Her husband had dropped a couple of hints here and there, without really meaning to and without any idea that they were necessary, that Carrera could be a real bastard.

"I'm sure one of us does," finished Pham.

"Honored grandfather," said Han, "I am sure we can work something out that will not require bringing unpleasant matters to the attention of people who do not necessarily understand the intricacies of our culture and—"

"Shut up, whore," said Pham, sensing the weakened position immediately and instinctively. "Your job is to translate and nothing but. Learn your place."

"Yes, honored grandfather . . ."

Carrera left the battery sure of two things. One was that, when the time came, at Puercel's command, the Cochinese would—if any of them were left alive and they had even a single 18cm gun working—put out the fire. They'd lost one home and made another; they were ready to die before giving that up. This was especially true since so many of them had sons and daughters, or grandsons and granddaughters, serving in the more mobile elements of the legion.

The other was that there was something going on there with

Siegel's wife that he didn't quite understand. *Note to self; detach one of the younger, bilingual Cochinese to translating duties. Pull Han Siegel back to the mainland and give her to Fernandez's department. I may not know what's going on, but I'm pretty sure that fixes most all of it, and without any hurt feelings.*

### Near Fixed Turret 177, *Isla Real*, Balboa, Terra Nova

Carrera's light vehicle arrived at the trail leading to a series of turrets manned by the *Tercio Santa Cecelia* just as the air raid sirens sounded. His temporary aide, listening to the radio, announced, "It's a big one, *Duque*. Twenty or thirty Zhong, over two hundred from Santa Josefina, and twice that from Cienfuegos and the enemy fleets near it."

"Pull the car under cover and leave it," he ordered. "We'll take shelter in the fortifications down the trail."

The driver jerked the wheel to the right, pulling the vehicle under the trees but also nearly into a drainage ditch the trees covered. The gently sloping, concrete-lined ditch was more than half-full of foul, stagnant-looking water, suggesting that somewhere downhill from it, there was a bomb-induced blockage in the system.

Springing out of the car, the small party began trotting down a trail that was clear at ground level, but somewhat obscure from above. On the other hand, the trees had already been thinned out quite a bit all across the island, and some places more than others.

The sign by the trail read, "T-177," and pointed to the left. There was a well-worn trail in that direction, as well. Carrera hesitated, in a moment of some doubt. The fixed turret positions were not precisely roomy. Then the first bombs hit perhaps a kilometer away, or a bit less.

"Fuck it," he said, "we can live with cramped." He scampered down that second trail, followed by the other two. At length, they came to a mound of dirt with what appeared to be a tank turret atop it. The turret was reinforced with concrete, and a concrete frame set in the dirt indicated the way inside. There was a field telephone, a simple sound-powered version, hung beside the frame. Next to the phone, the thick metal door was surprisingly open. Indeed, someone was leaving even as Carrera and his party arrived.

"Have you seen Pablo?" asked the mongoloid boy trying to make his way out the door.

"No, son," Carrera answered. "But you need to go inside. Pablo will be fine." *My ass. A six-hundred-and-fifty-plane raid? Maybe as much as three or four thousand tons of bombs? Anybody caught outside solid shelter is not all that likely to live at all, let alone be "fine." But there's no sense in throwing good after bad.*

"People say I look stupid, sir," said Juan, shaking his head firmly, "but I'm not as stupid as I look. Pablo is my friend and he's out there and he won't be fine. I'm going to him."

*And this,* thought Carrera, *is where a decent human being would either go with the boy or send him to shelter and go look alone. And maybe I'm decent and maybe I'm not, but the stakes are too big for me to go with him.*

Carrera looked at the aide.

"I'll go with him," said Signifer Torres. At that, Carrera nodded, half in giving permission and half in appreciation: *Thanks for picking up my cross, Torres. I don't know if you're a better man than I am but you're a good one. And probably a better human being, where that differs.*

"Sergeant de la Mesa, sir," reported the turret commander. "Late of Fourth Mechanized Tercio, now of"—the sergeant's eyes scanned around the concrete of the position—"*Adios Patria.*"

Carrera gave a thin smile as he took a seat on a bench resting against a wall. "Is that what you call yourselves?"

De la Mesa seemed slightly taken aback. "I think it's what everyone calls us, *Duque.*"

"May be," Carrera conceded. "Used to be I could get to know all the units, all the officers and centurions, most of the noncoms and even some of the rank and file. Now? Now I haven't a prayer. I can't even blame . . ."

The ground outside must have been deluged with bombs, at that instant. The plywood lining the concrete walls seemed to reverberate, cans and other things flying off shelves, and a queasiness-inducing series of vibrations causing everyone's internal organs to ripple alarmingly. Farther from the entrance, the one retarded boy remaining in the position began to wail. The lights flickered, were replaced by battery-powered ones, came back, flickered, then went dead. At that the boy began to wail more loudly still.

*To my dying day,* thought Carrera, *I will wonder whether I did the right thing in opening up the legion to all the disabled who could demonstrate ability to understand the oath.*

"Pablo," said the sergeant, "the one who was outside, usually keeps up the internal generator. When he gets back . . ."

Carrera gave a look that as much as said, "Nobody's getting back."

Surprisingly then, the sound-powered phone on the inside of the concrete position began to chatter.

De le Mesa gestured at his own withered legs. "Sir, if you could?"

Carrera sprang up and began turning the wheel that opened the door. It was of a naval design, and may even have been salvaged from one of the Volgan heavy cruisers, the sisters of the *Tadeo Kurita,* that he'd ordered scrapped to provide steel for the island's defenses. With about three-fourths of a turn the wheel, the restraining bars came out from the steel sides, allowing him to pull the door open.

On the other side were Signifer Torres, a mongoloid boy Carrera hadn't seen before, holding between them the limp body of the boy he had seen, leaving the position to look for Pablo.

Carrera guided them in, Torres first, followed by the limp boy, then the one he assumed was Pablo. As soon as they were inside and safe, he pushed the heavy door shut and spun the wheel again to lock it in place.

The wailing cut off. As if rising from the ground, the final boy of the crew sprang out and began to fuss over the limp boy, whom Torres said was called "Juan."

"He'll be all right," the signifer said. "Nothing broken. No bleeding that I could find. He just took a bad wallop from a flying piece of tree. Wish I could say the same for the car, sir. It's scrap, last I saw it. Or it will be, if we ever figure out how to get it out of the tree."

"Cost of doing business," said Carrera, stoically. "Besides, your legate will shit us a new one."

The previously unconscious boy began to stir, then gave off a moan.

"Pablo," asked de la Mesa, "are you all right?"

Pablo forced himself to nod. "Just a little scared, Sergeant. And a little sorry. I lost our breakfast on the way."

"Screw breakfast," said the sergeant, "as long as you're here. Why don't you break open one of the emergency ration boxes, then get the generator started?"

"I'll see to it, Sergeant," the boy said weakly.

Another string of bombs came in, but not as close as the last one. The bunker shook, of course, but the sickening organ rippling was barely noticeable. That, however, was followed by a series of blasts that were *much* closer. Julio screamed. Juan moaned. Even Pablo, who seemed too innocent for it, cursed. Glasses broke inside. And for some reason, a noticeable bulge appeared in the plywood paneling. De le Mesa looked nervously upward, his eyes questing for some indication that his turret had been deranged.

"This is the worst so far," the sergeant said. "I don't think we're worth a precision munition, but sheer bloody chance might do for us, even so, at this density. And . . ."

"Yes?" asked Carrera.

"Can you feel that, *Duque*?"

"Feel what?"

"The regular pounding. Airplanes bombing don't produce regular shocks. That's naval gunfire."

"Maybe so," said Carrera, trying to pick up the regular shocks de la Mesa claimed. *Maybe so, after all.* He then thought, *How do you measure the value of a pickle to morale, or the benefit of a "for whoso shares his blood with me"?*

"But . . . sergeant . . . boys . . . signifer . . . legionary . . . if I've got to die somewhere, there's no place I'd rather be and nobody's company I'd rather be in.

"Now who's got a deck of cards?"

Under de la Mesa's guidance, the other three, assisted by Torres and Carrera's driver, were using a tree trunk to tap to turret back into its proper position. It hadn't been damaged, exactly, but one of the all too near misses had deranged it a bit so that it didn't rest quite evenly in the ring. The tapping—which more closely resembled battering ramming—might or might not work, but since the turret couldn't turn at all now, there wasn't much to be lost.

"We're really going to have to put up a tripod and lift it," said Legate Puercel, like Carrera watching the proceedings.

"Yeah, I think so too," Carrera agreed.

"Have you seen enough, *Duque?*" Puercel asked.

"I think so. Well . . . no, there is one other thing . . ."

"Your old house? Quarters One?" Puercel asked.

"Was it that obvious?"

The legate shook his head, doubtfully. "You don't want to see it. There's nothing there to see but some charred wood and a few graves for some trixies. Most of the old cantonment area is smashed pretty badly, but I think they put a special effort into your house."

Carrera felt a sudden sinking of his heart. That house . . . that house . . . so many good memories in its walls and now . . .

*I wanted to retire there. Shit.*

"I'm sorry, *Duque*. It's not even a ruin anymore."

"Fuck it," Carrera said. "Take me to headquarters."

### Forward Observer Position Twenty-six, Hill 287, Isla Real, Balboa, Terra Nova

"Fuck it!" said Corporal Leon. "Just fuck it! God obviously hates me."

The reason for the corporal's outburst was all around him. As he sat atop the dirt covering his bunker, he was more or less evenly surrounded by a jagged-edged concrete cylinder, blasted off of the island's solar chimney, and, by fluke, landed around him. In other words, in order to see to do his job, when the time came, he was going to have to leave the safety of his bunker and peer over the top of the cylinder. This was, in every way, likely to be a lot more dangerous than what he'd been faced with before.

Leon's radio-telephone operator, a Cochinese-descended private, Private Loi, who had come to Balboa early enough to pick up Spanish well, tsked. "Not nice to take the Lord's name in vain, Corporal. Not nice at all. Besides, could have been worse. Could have landed *on* us, and driven the whole bunker underground. Suffocation then. No, no, Corporal, God, as the song goes, loves his faithful young soldiers."

Leon, who remembered the terror he'd felt when several hundred tons of concrete had landed almost atop him, was not to be mollified. "I'm a corporal. You're a private. If I say God hates me . . ."

"Then he must really love me, Corporal."

"Asshole."

### Wreck MV *Sadducee* (Zion Registry), *Isla Real*, Balboa, Terra Nova

They'd been waiting for a raid like this, one that would produce a hit or, at least, a near enough miss that the skeleton crew aboard the small coastal freighter could scuttle without it being obvious that it was deliberate. They'd gotten that and, before the smoke had cleared, the ship's keel had settled into the sandy bottom.

Now a flurry of activity was going on. Small boats were moving to extract the noncritical load the ship had been carrying. As each boat went out, though, it left behind a couple of engineers who set to work making nonobvious modifications to the ship. These ranged from cutting a couple of gashes in the hull, which were obvious but not necessarily suspicious, to building very strong positions inside to take advantage of the gashes, to unpacking and welding to the interior decks sundry crew-served weapons. The engineers also turned the noncritical parts of the ship, and anything that allowed access to the fighting positions, into a nightmarish maze of barbed wire and booby traps.

As the engineers finished and left, infantry took their place, still under the guise of removing cargo. The engineers had to move on; *Sadducee* had a sister on the eastern side of the island that needed similar preparations.

# CHAPTER THIRTY-THREE

Issue in doubt.
> —Major John F. Schoettel, USMC,
> Betio Island (Tarawa),
> 20 November 1943

## Xing Zhong Guo Aircraft Carrier *Luyang, Mar Furioso,* Terra Nova

The carrier had a light cruiser alongside, the *Taizhou.* She was the only gunned cruiser in the Zhong navy and, though not packing quite the broadside, in terms of throw weight over time, of the Balboans' *Tadeo Kurita,* she still packed some punch of her own, with nine admittedly slow-firing 180mm guns in three triple turrets.

She even had a modicum of armor, though that was much less than *Kurita* carried. Still, what she had was better than nothing, lots more than the carriers mounted, and in a platform that, unlike the carriers, could be expended. For these reasons, Admiral Wanyan had ordered it alongside, in order to transfer his flag from the *Luyang,* which would stay a considerable distance from the enemy fortress, to *Taizhou,* which would come in close enough for the admiral to see and command the landing.

The admiral's staff had transferred over the night before, just after the final issue of orders to the subordinate commanders or, rather, to those subordinate commander who would be involved in the landing. There'd been no need to bring in the Zhong army, as this would be a Marine show.

As the admiral made his transfer in his own pinnace, he could hear all around, in the distance, the sounds of marine diesels, as the invasion fleet formed up for the landing and moved closer to shore.

*Always a tradeoff,* thought Wanyan, *between security for the ships supporting the landing force and getting the troops ashore in numbers, quickly enough. And I can't risk using helicopters for troop landing until we have a secure place to bring them in. It's not like trying to land on a lightly defended section of coast, where the big threat is the counterattack from elsewhere. Then it's worthwhile to use helicopter to seal off the beach from reinforcement and to delay the enemy's response. Here, though? That island is thick with the enemy, and anybody I land deep—to the extent the concept has any meaning at all on an island twenty kilometers by thirteen—will just be a gift to the enemy.*

The Zhong Marines, a part of the army rather than of the navy, were something special. Everyone knew it, not least the Marines themselves. Already it was a considerable honor to be selected for military service among the Zhong, with only ten percent of the young men coming of age every year meeting the army's strict standards. The Marines, on the other hand, skimmed off only a couple percent of that already highly select crew.

Tough, strong, brave, well-trained, well-led, patriotic, dedicated . . . the Marines were also well-equipped for the task, with each of the two divisions fielding a regiment each of light amphibious tanks and artillery, a mechanized regiment, three light infantry regiments, a commando battalion, an engineer battalion, an air defense battalion, and a generous slice of headquarters and support troops.

Indeed, if the Zhong Marine Corps had a serious weakness, it wasn't internal, but in the odds and ends they'd had to scrape together to transport themselves and the regular corps, and get them to the beaches. For example, the two regiments of light tanks, between them, numbered over two hundred combat vehicles. Did the Zhong Navy have the capability of moving by sea the two hundred light tanks and four hundred or so other armored vehicles contained in their Marine Corps? Clearly. Could they launch two hundred amphibious light tanks and four hundred IFVs into the sea? Not a chance; the total portage capability with floodable decks for launching tanks and infantry carriers was about three hundred and fifty. And that wasn't accounting for the twelve hundred or so nonarmored vehicles, either.

They were an armed force used to making do, however, and they worked around their limitations in various ways. Some vehicles were carried on landing craft that would be lowered over the side on davits. In two cases the larger ships carried barges that, even now, crews were assembling to carry some equipment forward. Some were contained in landing ships that would have to beach themselves to let their cargo roll off.

The problems with the infantry were possibly worse. The eighteen battalions of light infantry and two each of commandos and engineers needed the equivalent of three hundred and fifty-odd landing craft loads, exclusive of extra supplies, and without any of their own vehicles. The latter two categories would roughly quadruple needs even at the Zhong's generally austere scales of supply and equipment.

What did they have? Admiral Wanyan could count on sixteen largish air cushion vehicles and one hundred and seven landing craft suitable for getting a platoon ashore . . . slowly.

It was factors like those that made amphibious operations the most problematic military operations there were. Just getting ashore was so complex that there was rarely enough time—or justifiable optimism— to plan ahead for what would be done once the force was ashore. Fortunately, for island attacks, that was rarely all that much of a problem. Simply being ashore and surviving usually meant the island was taken.

This island was not quite of such a small size. Admiral Wanyan expected a certain amount of both maneuver and attrition after establishing his beachheads, to finish the job.

*At least that's what I told the idiots at the war ministry. Personally, I think my Marines will be able to hold formation in a telephone booth by the time this island falls. That doesn't matter though; we can always rebuild the Marine Corps. But this island, giving us a stranglehold over the most important waterway on the planet? Worth every drop of blood.*

The *Taizhou* was a much smaller vessel than the *Luyang*. One could feel it in the way the ship rocked. Not that the admiral was likely to get seasick, but it was a different sensation. The strange sensation become much more pronounced when *Taizhou* swung her three triple turrets to starboard and flung the first of many broadsides at Beach Red, just west of the *Isla Real*'s tadpole's tail.

## Fixed Turret 177, *Isla Real*, Balboa, Terra Nova

De la Mesa popped the hatch and cranked his seat up enough to let his eyes peep over the rim of the cupola. The hatch remained above his head, providing a fair degree of a protection from an overhead burst. When he'd first occupied this position with his three charges, he'd not been able to see the sea for all the trees. Now he could see the sand of the beach, the white-churned surf, and, if he cared to drop back below and check through his commander's sight, the Zhong formations churning in.

He could also see the wrecked freighter, the MV *Sadducee*—well one of them; he'd heard there were two, the other being the MV *Nimrod*—that had been caught in an air raid and sunk. He'd never been told, but he was pretty sure that that freighter was a lot less abandoned than it had been made to look. If his guess was right . . .

*Poor bastards are going to be walking through the surf on our side of the reef, that, or clustered along the beach facing inland, and they're going to take it from a flank they don't expect or from the rear. Jesus, what a slaughter just a squad or two could make from there.*

De la Mesa reached up to adjust the hatch a bit. As he did, he noticed that his right hand was trembling. He remembered something he'd read once in one of the legion-published books that tended to sit in unit libraries. To paraphrase, *I'm not trembling like an eager race horse; I'm scared out of my wits.*

The sight of a line of smoke, rising above the dunes, didn't help his state of nerves in the slightest. Rather, it made them worse. So, for that matter, did the sudden sound of chattering machine guns from all along the beach. That, he believed, was mostly the unmanned, water-cooled machine gun bunkers, firing from a cradle that captured a portion of their recoil energy and converted it into movement left and right by means of a toothed crossbar running between the legs of their tripods. These, he had been told, had about forty minutes' worth of ammunition, and would keep spitting that out until they ran out, or were destroyed. Though remotely controlled—*and I wonder for how many the wires have been cut or the antenna knocked down*—these were based on the type of overengineered guns used in the early stages of the Great Global War, supplemented with a semi-automatic cocking mechanism that could clear stoppages. If they killed anyone, it would be a fluke. But they could be counted on to make the enemy nervous and attract an undue portion of his attention.

Inside, with the hatch down, de la Mesa wouldn't be able to hear. Still, he hated not being able to see. He dropped his chair down, closing the hatch above, then settled his eyes into the thermal sight.

*My, isn't that quite the show?*

As far as de la Mesa could see, all across the horizon, a mass of enemy ships, amphibious vehicles, and landing craft crawled across the water. One of the forward landing craft in his field of view apparently hit a nutcracker, a kind of antismall boat mine, that blew the front several meters upward, even as it blew the ramp completely off. Soldiers—*well, Marines, I suppose*—were flung off into the water in all manner of sprawling and undignified death.

*That was some bad luck,* the sergeant thought. *We actually don't have that many nutcrackers out, I understand.*

In the thermal sight, de la Mesa saw what seemed to be thousands of tracers crawling across the horizon. The resolution in the sight wasn't enough to distinguish water spouts rising from the sea, but he assumed they were there and were probably terrifying the enemy. He did see any number of landing craft that he could have engaged with success, but the orders were not to engage the landing craft until authorized to do so. He didn't understand why that would be.

*I'm a sergeant. I guess that means I'm also a mushroom; kept in the dark and fed bullshit.*

Then he saw it, the first target that was within his little command's authority to engage at any time. A tank. De la Mesa hadn't noticed it at first, perhaps because the hull was mostly submerged, the turret small, and the little that showed was hidden by the waves. Whatever it was, the thing was clear enough now as it crawled up onto the sand, its gun belching flame at targets the gunner probably didn't know were just unmanned machine guns.

"Gunner! HEAT! Tank!" They had some sabot ammunition, in case a heavy managed to get ashore. But the turret had much more High Explosive, Antitank, since it would do for both antiarmor and antipersonnel engagements.

Juan, seated below and on the other side of the turret, echoed the command. The turret slewed slightly, with an almost imperceptible whine. Julio, the loader, not really aware of what was going on outside but much happier doing the job to which de la Mesa had drilled him numb, filled the carousel.

"Target!" announced Juan.

"Fire!"

The turret didn't rock backward as a tank might have. Still, even though the HEAT rounds were undercharged as compared with the sabot, the whole position shuddered with the recoil. What happened downrange happened too quickly for either de la Mesa or Juan to pick out the individual steps. One second the Zhong light tank was slinking across the sand, hesitantly, as if expecting a mine. The next second after that there appeared a mixed red and black flower blooming on the turret, just left of the gun; the next the turret was flying into the air on a column of flame, spinning over and over like some frying pan in a rather odd juggling act.

As to the light tank's crew? *Well, probably vaporized.*

"Well done, Juan," said the sergeant. "Good shooting."

The young and not too badly mentally retarded gunner looked away from his sight, giving the sergeant a grateful look.

"You done good, boy," de la Mesa added, for emphasis, then, "Gunner! Canister! Infantry!"

## Zhong Light Cruiser *Taizhou*, Mar Furioso, Terra Nova

Wanyan stared at the map while staff officers busied themselves with making marks on it that he was pretty sure bore little relation to any detailed reality. *What matter that they call off "first wave one hundred percent ashore" when half or more of those are floating face down in the surf? I suppose that's mostly "ashore," but it hardly suggests progress.*

There were three beaches targeted for the landing. West of the tadpole's tail was Beach Red, which was outflanked automatically by the tail. The tail, therefore, was Beach Green, and was, so far, the only place taken that Wanyan was confident of holding. That said, it was taking a fearsome pounding from the enemy's armored, turreted heavy and concrete-revetted super heavy mortars, farther inland. So far, the number of reported landed were only just keeping ahead of the number of reported dead and medevacs. Still, Green had to be held or Red became an impossibility.

Beach Orange was southeast of the tail and, by all reports, a horror story. Listening to the reports from the commanders, or sometimes just their radio-telephone operators, if those were all that remained, was heartbreaking. One conversation in particular stuck with Wanyan. That was where a young private kept apologizing over the radio for interrupting the report by dropping his microphone, but, "I'm sorry . . . I'm so sorry . . . I'm trying . . . really I am . . . but I only have the one finger and thumb on my remaining arm. I'm so sorry . . ."

Two things in particular bothered Wanyan. One was that forward progress seemed to be held up by a minefield that the engineers simply couldn't get a handle on. They had both magnetic and radar mine detectors, as good as any on the planet, but they kept alerting on things that just weren't there. A thousand false positives to an actual mine detection was a common phenomenon, but this was approaching twenty or thirty times that. And when the engineers grew disgusted and tried pushing forward, while ignoring the false positives? Boom. "Medic!"

The other thing was on the approach to Beach Red. Though there was no flanking fire, and though the edge of the shore had been cleared of the enemy, Marines wading in were *still* being bowled over like ninepins. Wanyan had developed a suspicion, though, one sufficient to generate orders.

## Wreck MV *Sadducee* (Zion Registry), *Isla Real*, Balboa, Terra Nova

Centurion Alba, Tenth Infantry Tercio, had one platoon with him on the wreck. There'd been more, mostly engineers—coming, going, and occasionally staying for a few days—in the period of time since it had been "wrecked." In fact, it never had been more than scratched by the Zhong or Taurans. It had been set out, partially unloaded, hoping for a near miss. When it came, that near miss had been used as an excuse to scuttle it. Then the engineers had proceeded to turn it into a little steel fortress, capable of covering the coast to the east and south.

One of those preparations had involved cutting a ragged rent in the hull's side, just above normal high water and facing the coast of the tadpole's tail and the beach to its west. That artificial tear in the hull was so close to high water that strong waves sometimes partially washed into the hulk.

Well behind the ragged cut, almost on the other side of the hull, two water-cooled machine guns sat on tripods welded to the steel of the decking. Except for the water cooling, these were middle-weight guns, at .34 caliber, heavier than the M-26 light machine gun that was really just a heavy step up from the standard legionary rifle, but still lighter than the .41 caliber guns that graced most vehicles. With the water cooling, of course, they could fire for *hours*.

The rent was highly irregular, rising with an almost vertical tear such that the rightmost gun could fire at high trajectory at the tadpole's tail, about a mile away. He did so, in medium long bursts, not so much in the expectation of hitting something smaller than the island, but in the anticipation of making people on the tail more nervous than they would be just from the deluge of heavy mortar shells they were already suffering under. There is something about direct fire that is somehow more nerve wracking, at least for some people, than the random chance of indirect.

Watching through the rent in almost exactly the same angle as one of the machine gunners, Alba saw a long snaking line of Zhong Marines wading through water that was just above waist deep for most of them. One of the obstacles the Zhong faced in their perilous wade was a thick, almost solid, carpet of bodies, rising and falling rhythmically with the surf.

The gunner shook his head with disgust. "Oh, fuck it," he said, then used his left hand to depress the butterfly trigger of his -34. The gun began spitting out a stream of high-velocity lead at a rate of somewhere between four hundred and five hundred rounds per minute. The gunner tapped the gun with his right, more or less gently, causing it to traverse along the line of the advancing Zhong, knocking most of them from their feet to join the carpet of bodies already built up in the waves.

Within the steel confines of the hull, the muzzle blast was like a continuing series of blows to the face. That was anticipated; the platoon manning the ship was connected by headphones and an intercom system.

"This isn't fucking war," said the gunner, ceasing fire for lack of targets. "This is just murder."

"When did I tell you there was a huge amount of difference?" asked Alba.

"Never, Centurion, but I never expected to—"

The ship's hull shuddered with the impact of a high explosive round. "Pay no attention," said Alba, with a confidence greater than he actually felt. "The engineers built us positions to take a few hits."

*I hope.*

## Headquarters, Eighth Fortress Legion, *Isla Real,* Balboa, Terra Nova

Down in the bottom floor of the oldest of the deep shelters dug into the island's bowels, Carrera and Puercel stood staring down at a three-dimensional model of the island and its fortifications. The model itself had been put together by a team of Sitnikov's cadets.

At fifteen by twenty-five meters, the terrain model filled up over half of the shelter's bottom deck. It was by built-in sections, sitting well above the floor, held on wheeled carts. The carts had been moved, leaving a gap between the bulk of the island and the area the enemy had obviously targeted for his landing, so that staff officers and noncoms could mark the known and presumed positions, friendly and enemy.

The floor was also marked, though those markings were traced from the model's approximate center, Hill 287. On the floor were not only representations of the Zhong ships, hundreds of them, but also arcs were painted in the blue and marked with artillery calibers: "122mm . . . 152mm . . . 160mm . . . 240mm . . . 180mm . . . 180mm ERRB." That latter referred to "Extended Range, Reduced Bore," the sabot-mounted, laser-guided shells that could reach out more than two and a half times the 180's normal range, and have a fair prospect of hitting a target the size of a ship when they got there. Though the floor wasn't marked that way, there was also a limited number of ERRB-BB, the last two letters standing for "Base Bleed," which had certain advantages over rocket assist and added considerably to the already impressive range.

Virtually the entire Zhong fleet was within the latter arc. Lines of advance for landing craft were also drawn to the three identifiable beaches. As Carrera and Puercel watched, somebody placed a Zhong flag atop one of the larger surface combatants, the light cruiser which could only be the *Taizhou*.

"I have my doubts," said Carrera.

Thereupon, Puercel called over the staff officer who had emplaced the tiny flag. Replied the staff type, "Analysis of radio traffic, sir, says that only that cruiser, or either one of the carriers, could be their admiral's flagship."

Legate Puercel looked questioningly at Carrera, who said, "Sure, it could be. But we don't have the ability to unencrypt Zhong secure radio, so we have no idea what the traffic we're picking up say, only a volume of traffic. And between aircraft and requests for fire from the cruiser, *sure* there's more radio traffic." Turning to the staff officer, Carrera asked, "is there any correlation between radio traffic from the cruiser and the cruiser firing in support of the landing."

"Yes, *Duque,* some. But we've also seen bursts of radio traffic that correlated to changes in direction of columns of landing craft, changing of targeting parameters from attacking aircraft . . . sir, I'll bet my rank on it; that's the flagship."

"Okay," Carrera conceded, "it could well be." Turning back to Puercel, he said, "Now the question for you, Legate, is, 'Do you target the cruiser first, to get rid of their commander, or leave it alone, so he and his staff can add confusion when things begin to go badly wrong?' Well?"

"No it isn't," said Puercel. "The question is, is it worthwhile to get that fucking cruiser before it can go after my 180s?"

"Well . . . your show," said Carrera. "Decide and do it."

"Time then, *Duque*?"

"Like I told you when I first arrived and just told you again now, '*your* show.'"

Puercel scanned the walls for the intelligence charts posted there. Over half of the enemy Marine Corps was either landed or en route. Over three-fourths of his surface combatant fleet was in range of the island's artillery. Every purpose-built amphib known to be in commission in the Zhong Navy was in range. And the estimate of how much air they could put up in the next two hours was not especially intimidating.

"*Your* show," Carrera repeated.

*For the rest of my life,* thought Puercel, *I will be reliving this moment. My grandchildren and great-grandchildren, if I live that long, will grow up on stories of it. This is the supreme moment of my life.*

*So don't blow it.*

"Air defense umbrella, up!" the legate ordered. "Get our own RPVs out there."

"I'll have the heavy-missile batteries on the mainland unmask, as well," Carrera said.

# CHAPTER THIRTY-FOUR

A ship's a fool to fight a fort.
—Lord Horatio Nelson

**Zhong Light Cruiser *Taizhou*, *Mar Furioso*, Terra Nova**

There wasn't any particular shortage of remotely piloted vehicles in the Zhong armed force. Nor was there any shortage in Admiral Wanyan's invasion fleet. What there was, or, rather, what had developed in the last four or five minutes, was a shortage of information that the RPVs in the air had been providing. There was no shortage of clues as to why this had happened; two of the seven hovering above the island had sent back videos of massive walls of tracers appearing in front of them, just before going off the air.

It would only be a matter of minutes, eight or ten of them, at the most, before visual coverage of the island was restored. Already, replacement RPVs were winging in from the *Taizhou* and several destroyers. But it was disturbing to the admiral that now, just at this key moment, the enemy had elected to unmask his air defense. Wanyan had already called off the aircraft from the two carriers, waiting until a proper package could be assembled to take on the Balboan air defense. At that, better to wait until naval gunfire . . .

**Batería Pedro *el Cholo*, *Isla Real*, Balboa, Terra Nova**

Tribune Pham stood beside the concrete-set rails that led from the bunker behind him. Through the open doors of the bunker, with a great rumbling sound, emerged the twenty-three-ton, 180mm cannon that had hidden within for *years*. To either side of it, from two other "ammunition" bunkers, two further guns were dragged by small "shunter" locomotives, called, locally, "mules." Others were being moved out other steel doors to take a position either behind the ammunition bunkers or, in a few cases, along the ring railroad that encompassed the island. In total, sixty-four 180mm guns had been sent to the island and put on Volgan-designed and -built railway carriages. Almost all of these could be used.

The presence of turntables, such as still existed for some of the old Federated States railway guns, long since abandoned, would have been a dead giveaway. Instead, the rails had been laid out in several almost parallel curves leading to the ruined turret of the battery. This allowed a fair degree of effective traverse, all on its own. Still, even with the built-in traverse of the railway mounting, only some four and a half degrees each way, the guns were quite restricted in the arc they could cover. Conversely, with over sixty of them in action, from all around the island's perimeter, and able to fire either front or rear, every arc was covered by, on average five guns.

While Pham had ears only for the rumble of the rolling guns, he had eyes only for the sky, for the enemy RPVs that would spot his batteries, and for aircraft that would come in with explosive and liquid fire to destroy the guns and men.

For a moment, he wished earnestly for the little bitch of a trollop, Warrant Officer Siegel, to put a little foul-mouthed fire under the asses of his crews. Then he saw the first gun in position elevating up to about forty degrees and decided that she probably wasn't really needed.

"Sir," announced one of his men from the shelter of the bunker, behind, "Battery Mkhize says it has its first gun up. For the rest they say another two to five minutes."

"Let me know when they're all up," said Pham. "Both batteries."

"Sir!"

**Zhong LPD *Qin Shan*, *Mar Furioso*, Terra Nova**

Major Wu took what he firmly expected to be a last look at the miniature portrait he carried in his wallet of his wife, Jiao. *I wish I could have promised to return to you, my so very dear, but I cannot make a promise I cannot be sure to keep.*

Wu was slated to go in by landing craft with the first wave from his battalion, though it would be a later wave from regiment's perspective. Casualties were expected to be immense, just shy of one hundred percent. Wu suspected, not without reason, that casualties actually *were* expected to be one hundred percent, but that the staff was simply lying about it, in the interests of morale.

He put on a good face, did the major, for someone who was scared to death. That was scared *to* death, not *of* death. What terrified him wasn't the prospect of dying, but the probable futility of it.

*Oh, ancestors,* Wu prayed, *do not let your heir die uselessly and ingloriously, in the water. For the glory of our clan and our name, see me, at least, to shore, where I can strike a blow before I die.*

### Headquarters, Eighth Fortress Legion, *Isla Real*, Balboa, Terra Nova

While Puercel kept his attention glued to the displays showing heavy batteries coming on line, Carrera paid more attention to the physical depiction of the Zhong fleet on the concrete floor.

*That,* thought Carrera, *is probably because he's concerned with defending this island while I am a lot more worried about winning the war and winning it in such a way that it's worth the winning, which is something the good legate probably couldn't give a good goddamn about.*

Carrera listened with limited attention as Puercel, bypassing the Eighth Legion commander, gave instructions directly to his attached subordinate, the commander of the Twelfth Coastal Defense Artillery Brigade.

The big thing ordered Carrera tended to agree on. The fucking Zhong cruiser must go. He had to pause for a minute to translate unit designations into personal information. He was pleased to see the old men of the Cochinese artillery would get first crack at the cruiser. They hated the Zhong about as much as they hated the Gauls.

One of the display charts on the wall showed which batteries and which dedicated forward observers would be engaging which targets. Little flags for those were placed on the simplistic wooden ship models dotting the floor. Though the shells would be laser guided, there were limits to what laser guidance could do. The guns would still have to be directed the old-fashioned way and aimed the old-fashioned way to get their guns within laser correctable limits.

It seemed to take forever, though a check of a watch would have shown the target assignment process as being a matter of under ten minutes. Still, the time came when the display of the eight heavy batteries, batteries the Zhong certainly thought wrecked, showed each with a target, and each target ready to be lased by a forward observer, or RPV, or laser designator mounted under a barrage balloon.

"The Zhong carriers are never going to come in range," said Puercel to Carrera. The latter just shrugged. *Nothing to be done.*

"Paint," ordered Puercel.


## Zhong LPD *Qin Shan, Mar Furioso,* Terra Nova

Standing just behind the ramp of the landing craft, Wu turned around to see the ship still disgorging its fighting cargo, landing craft and amphibious vehicles pouring from the well deck. He heard occasional faint cries, orders, shouted out over the roar of engines and the splash of the waves, natural and artificial.

The LDP represented safety. The direction of the landing craft, however, represented duty. Wu tore his eyes from the former and, exposing no more than those eyes and the top of his helmeted head, turned his attention to the smoke-shrouded, jungle-clad island to the south-southeast. There were other landing craft there, as well as amphibious armored personnel carriers and light tanks. They seemed to Wu to be forming a rough line and staying there.

*Hmmm . . . beach obstacle of some kind, or maybe a reef.* A great blast shook the air and water. Wu felt it first through his feet. *Engineers clearing the way. Good boys!*

The landing craft seemed to speed across the water, though Wu knew it was capable of no more than twelve knots. Part of the sensation of speed came from the continuous bouncing of the hull, up, down, up, down, up . . .

Wu caught himself barely in time, shutting off his urge to vomit through sheer will power. Behind him, he heard someone else whose will either failed or who tried to exercise it too late. *Blaaaghghgh.*

*And that's why I'm up front*, thought Wu, *up where the stench won't reach me . . . because in the presence of a strong smell of vomit, even the best will can fail. And that would . . .*

The thought was cut off as Wu felt a sudden pain in both of his eyes. He blinked but the pain remained. He ducked down, behind the ramp. This was just as well, as from somewhere on the island machine-gun fire began to lance out, ringing off steel hulls and ramps or raising small geysers in the sea.

### Zhong Light Cruiser *Taizhou, Mar Furioso,* Terra Nova

"Admiral, we're being lased," announced one of Wanyan's operations people, clutching a headset tightly. "Five . . . no . . . six other ships also report they're receiving laser energy. Not especially powerful, all of it is consistent with range finding or target designation."

That sailor suddenly went white as whatever report he'd just received through his headset. "Sir . . . we have . . . a lot . . . an awful lot . . . of artillery rising from the island. The trajectories don't match anything in the database, but if they're not some kind of bluff, then . . ."

"What, dammit?" demanded the admiral.

"They . . . they can range . . . they can range . . . if it's not a bluff they can range . . ."

"WHAT!"

"Between seventy and one hundred kiloyards. And . . . Admiral? It looks like we're a prime target."

Wanyan was about to say, "Ignore it; nobody can hit at that distance." Then he recalled the other common purpose of lasers and wanted to say, instead, "Shit! Bring her about. Turn the fleet about. Smoke." Lastly, he remembered that, come right down to it, his cruiser, the destroyers, and the frigates couldn't take the island, but the infantry still waiting in the assault transports could, while the poor bastards on or heading to the beach still needed his fires.

*And, after all, fuck it; at least I have some armor. And we can use smoke.*

### *Batería* Pedro *el Cholo,* Isla Real, Balboa, Terra Nova

The two batteries between them manned sixteen guns. One of those, Pham was disgusted to learn, over on Battery Mkhize, was apparently defective. Rather, its railroad mount was. The mount disintegrated under the stress of recoil. Where the shell went . . . it was going to be short.

*Let's hope the infantry blame it on the enemy.*

Being artillery, Pham only had two medics for one battery and one for the other, another two in an aid station, and two men in a single light wheeled vehicle for evacuation. That vehicle, siren blaring, raced to the position of the shattered gun mount and began treating the wounded, of which there were far too many for the one ambulance to deal with.

Both Battery Pedro *el Cholo* and Battery Mkhize had been directed by the Twelfth CDA Brigade headquarters to put their fire on the enemy's single cruiser. It had, so the intel types said, between fifty millimeters and one hundred and fifty millimeters of armor, depending on where. Most of the ship, the waterline belt, the main turrets, and the barbettes, carried seventy millimeters. Pham thought it likely they could get through that. He was certain they could punch through the deck's lousy two inches.

*Provided the fucking shells hit, of course.* That was a problem. Of the sixteen shells fired in this first volley, one destroyed the carriage of the gun that fired it. The remaining fifteen? It didn't cheer Pham any that both the defective railway carriage and the shells were the product of Volgan workmanship. It was often quite good, lately, to be sure. But one could never tell when residual socialist principles of production would join socialist principles of accounting to produce a mess.

### Zhong Light Cruiser *Taizhou, Mar Furioso,* Terra Nova

Even without using base bleed or rocket assist, themselves, the cruiser's guns outranged what the shorter, land-bound 180mm guns could do by about eight kilometers, unless the latter were firing either

RAP or BB. Even so, she wasn't at maximum range, but at perhaps two-thirds of that, a bit over twenty-five kilometers, from the summit of Hill 287. Range-probable error increased greatly after certain ranges and, since *Taizhou* was firing dangerously close to her own men, desperately trying to carve out a beachhead ashore, it seemed worth it to avoid blasting friendlies.

Fifteen shells were targeted at *Taizhou*, though the radar wasn't quite good enough to distinguish several from several others. Still, the nine the cruiser initially thought were incoming were bad enough. Of the fifteen, four went awry, gods-alone knew why. In any case, between the island and the ship, they went into the drink. That was actually less cheering to *Taizhou*'s captain and Admiral Wanyan than it might have been. Two of the four were shells they hadn't been able to detect initially. *And how many more are there that we can't see?*

Of the remaining eleven, of which the ship could see, "Seven, no, nine . . . no, eight . . . no, seven," one hit the conning tower a glancing blow, which the tower's six full inches of good-quality steel armor just shrugged off. The shell flew off, exploding well away in the distance.

"Good girl," said the captain, patting his ship affectionately.

Four shells landed in the water—three to port and one to starboard—close enough to drench any crewman who happened to be on deck when they detonated down in the depths. They were not close enough to buckle the hull, or even inconvenience it.

Two did hit the water close enough to the hull to cause the ship to spring a couple of leaks. They were nothing serious, though; damage control would have had the leaks under control in minutes.

Another shell hit the bow, ahead of the waterline belt of armor. The metal here was thin and weak enough that the arrow shell passed almost completely through before it detonated. The damage was more obvious than real, since the bow remained intact from just a few feet above the water line. Not even the ship's speed was likely to be affected. The jackstaff, on the other hand, was a total loss.

One shell no one had a clue to. It simply disappeared, unreckoned and unrecognized.

The last two, though, hit Y Turret, the sternmost 180mm triple. Of these, one was, like the hit on the con, something of a glancing blow. Unlike the first case, however, the shell, 122mm in diameter and roughly a meter and three quarters long, didn't dive off into the sea.

Instead, it punched through the deck armor, passed through several more decks, and exploded next to the mechanism controlling the portside rudder. This really didn't matter, though, because the other shell did *not* glance off. Instead it penetrated the turret roof, one of the recoil mechanisms, the deck below, the deck below that, and finally set itself off in the magazine below Y Turret.

The explosion started large and grew larger, as first the roughly nine kilograms of HE inside the shell went off, which set off about one hundred bags of propellant, which in turn set off several dozen shells each as powerful as the Balboan shell that had achieved penetration.

### Headquarters, Eighth Fortress Legion, *Isla Real*, Balboa, Terra Nova

Puercel and Carrera, along with the bulk of the legate's headquarters command, saw the result on one of the wall-mounted plasma screens, being fed by a hovering RPV. Though it was being recorded for posterity and propaganda, which recording would allow slow-motion and detailed analysis of the events, from the point of view of those watching now it all seemed to unfold in an instant. There was a flash of light as the shell forced its way into the enemy turret, but almost instantly, that turret was blown into the air, even as the ship's stern quarters was severed—just like that, just that quickly . . . as if by an invisible, albeit ragged-bladed, guillotine—being blown rearward even as the forward sections were blasted forward.

"Hooolllyyy shshshiiiittt!" said one of the headquarters troops, giving voice to the common feeling.

Then the room reverberated with cheers. "Got 'em . . . hahaha . . . fuckers . . . teach you . . . hahaha!"

Puercel didn't join in the cheers. Staring at the markers for the Zhong fleet on the floor, the legate wondered, *Do I have them give it another volley or what? I don't see it being able to fire in that condition, the thing's immobile and unstable. But if it is their command and control ship . . .*

He looked at Carrera, who simply said, "It's written somewhere: Never do an enemy a small injury."

"Fire until she sinks or is burning stem to stern," ordered Puercel.

**Beach Green Two, *Isla Real*, Balboa, Terra Nova**

Wu found what the obstacle was the hard way, though not the hardest way. The hardest way was the landing craft to his right, which hit a mine and had its forward third nearly disintegrated in a fiery cloud. His craft, on the other hand, merely hit a sharpened I-beam, driven into the sea bottom, that punched through the thin hull, causing the boat to impale itself as it lifted out of the water.

Wu was about to order the coxswain to drop the ramp when a series of bullets, striking close together, stitched across the ramp's forward side. He had a momentary vision of massacre inside the boat as a machine gun simply concentrated its fire on the opening that would be left by the dropping of the ramp.

"Over the side!" the major shouted. "Get over the side and wade in!"

**Zhong Light Cruiser *Taizhou*, *Mar Furioso*, Terra Nova**

Even through the armor, the blast was enough to send Wanyan and his entire staff to the deck, then let them rise puking and shaking, and wiping blood from under noses. Some remained on the deck, holding broken limbs stationary or trying to staunch the flow of blood from split scalps or exposed bone splinters. One of the men on Wanyan's staff was beating a radio with his fist. The admiral assumed the radio was out.

The admiral knew he had a serious decision to make. *Do I transfer my flag or tough it out here?* Unsteadily, he walked across the swaying and bobbing deck to the hatchway. This he undogged and passed through, then climbed up a series of ladders to topside. Then, once topside, Wanyan was better able to assess the damage. It was bad. *All the antennas are gone, it seems. All the radar dishes twisted and knocked over. The conning tower is . . . bent. I must see if the captain survived . . .*

Neither of the remaining turrets was firing. *Cowardice or . . .*

As Wanyan made his way forward, he scanned to sea. *Taizhou* was clearly not the only ship hit. It was too far to identify individual ships with the unaided eye, but there were at least five columns of smoke rising from the gunlines, between the cruiser and the island. Even as Wanyan watched, one of the columns of smoke was replaced by a great explosion, while two more columns began to rise.

A destroyer of one of the newer classes pulled up alongside. Wanyan noted that it pulled up in the lee of the greater ship, on the side facing away from the storm of fire from shore. "Ahoy, *Taizhou*, can we assist? This is the *Yiyang*, standing by to assist."

*Wise captain*, thought the admiral.

Already, sailors of the *Taizhou* were bringing their wounded comrades up and helping them across to the destroyer.

A fresh salvo came in. Wanyan didn't try to count the hits, though they were many. Since a couple of the hits seemed to be on or around the turrets, and since there were explosions from below that made the ship jump and quiver, and since the whole thing didn't go up in a fiery flash, Wanyan decided that the lack of fire from the remaining turrets probably meant that the captain, or the surviving senior officers, or perhaps some clever ensign on damage control, had ordered the magazines flooded.

*And that, assuming I survive, is how my report will read.*

*But survival? That is a tricky proposition.*

"Ahoy, *Yiyang*," shouted the admiral across the gap. "This is Wanyan. I am transferring my flag to you. Prepare to receive and assume duties . . ."

### Batería Pedro el Cholo, Isla Real, Balboa, Terra Nova

The guns' rate of fire was actually quite slow, a round a minute for the first three minutes, a round every two minutes thereafter. In fact, though, it was that quick only for a stationary target, which the two Cochinese batteries didn't have anymore. Relaying the guns for a moving target was quite intricate and time consuming, reducing their practical volume of fire to about one round every five or six minutes.

Content that the guns would be well served, Tribune Pham sauntered into the ammunition bunker to oversee the fire direction center. This took data—generally polar data, a direction and distance from the forward observers, plus target type, direction, and speed—and converted it into charge, elevation and deflection data for the guns. He'd been drilling both gun crews and FDC silly, ever since they'd assumed their molelike existence, in the dark and damp concrete shelter.

"New target, *Dai Uy*," announced the FDC chief, using their own language's rough equivalent for Pham's Balboan rank. "The bitch finally sank."

"What's this one? Both batteries or just one?"

"Splitting both batteries, *Dai Uy*. Two troopships each for us and Battery Mkhize. We should . . ."

Whatever the FDC chief was about to say was lost as a flurry of shells—ten or fifteen, was Pham's impression—landed on or around the pads outside the ammunition bunkers. A crescendo of screams arose immediately following. The tribune raced outside to assess the damage. His first thought was, *Thank Jesus for defilade.* The hill to the north, behind which half the battery sheltered, was covered with thick black smoke where many of the shells had impacted.

Even so, enough had come in to do some damage. One of the 180mm carriages was overturned, and at least a dozen men in Pham's view were down, dead or wounded; he couldn't say, really.

*Except for Thieu,* thought the tribune, with a mental *tsk. Missing the top half of one's head generally means dead. Unless you're a general, in which case, of course, brains aren't really needed.*


## UEPF *Spirit of Peace,* in orbit over Terra Nova

Marguerite had taken the empress aboard her shuttle and up to her flagship once it became obvious that the peace conference had successfully failed to bring about peace. She wanted to watch the action from that vantage point, of course, but as importantly she wanted to gift her true love with a dozen or so years off her true age. The Taurans could use the lesson of that, as well.

Unsurprisingly, Xingzhen was already so utterly beautiful that the rejuvenation added nothing to her looks at all, even if it made her look slightly younger. Still, *A dozen years off her age is a dozen more years*

*I can have her in my bed, a fine dozen years indeed. That is, it will be fine if she doesn't have a stroke over the disaster unfolding below.*

Xingzhen, not just shaken but visibly shaking, asked the high admiral, "Can you get me communication with my admiral, below? Most men are weaklings and insistence is usually the fix."

### Zhong Destroyer *Yiyang, Mar Furioso,* Terra Nova

Aboard the *Yiyang,* Wanyan and what had been saved from his staff took over CIC, pushing the ship's own captain up to the bridge. Being back in communication, hence able to evaluate the damage, led Wanyan inexorably to several unpleasant conclusions. Of these, the worst were that the assault on the island was a lost cause, the Marines landed there already doomed. He could not extract any substantial numbers of them, and he could not risk the ships that would have had to stay, oh, way too close to the island, to do so. Maybe they could hang on to the tadpole's tail and maybe he could keep them supplied there.

*Maybe. For a while. It will be hard. Even for just a while.*

*And, no doubt, the Taurans could be bribed into taking out that damned artillery that's made such a hash of us. But so what? I cannot take the island without the Marines and they will not survive the time it takes for the Taurans to do that. So the island campaign is a failure, no matter what.*

*But we can still rescue something. We can—*

Wanyan's operations officer, reduced to manning a radio even while preparing and issuing orders, stood up to attention at the desk he'd taken over.

"Admiral," said Ops, pointing at the huge radio set resting in front of him, "it's Her Imperial Majesty. She's calling from . . ." Ops turned eyes and that single finger skyward. With the other hand Ops took off his headset and passed it over to Admiral Wanyan.

"Yes, Your Majesty?" said Wanyan.

The empress immediately launched into a shrieking condemnation of the Navy, the Imperial Marine Corps, and Wanyan himself. She finished with, "You will not retreat. You will take that island. If not, let none come back alive, especially to include yourself."

Quietly, hopelessly, the admiral answered, "Yes, Your Majesty. Whatever can be done shall be done. Or I will not come back alive."

### Headquarters, Eighth Fortress Legion, *Isla Real*, Balboa, Terra Nova

By ones and twos, fives and tens, the floor-bound ship markers that had begun to turn away from the island began turning back.

*Now I wonder why that is,* thought Carrera. *You have to know your plan's in ruin. Civilian interference? War may be too important a matter to leave to generals, as that Old Earth frog said, but it's far too important a matter to leave to civilians, except to the question of war or peace. And not even always then.*

*But a fight to a finish is what you're ordered to, are you? That works well for me, if I've weighed the matter well and properly. For I do not think you could take this island with ten times the force if you had ten years to do it in. What you need to take it is what nobody has anymore, or I'd certainly not have put so much effort into trying to hold the place.*

*I confess, if you had what's needed, a dozen heavily armored, great-gunned Dreadnoughts, things that could economically shatter my concrete, and take and shrug off my artillery . . . well . . . I don't know what I'd have done.*

Carrera was torn from his reveries by Puercel, speaking on a radio to the commander of Tenth Tercio. "Hold off for now," the fortress commander ordered. "For as long as they want to keep feeding men into the sausage grinder, we'll keep turning the crank. But I need you and your men to hold and shelter down, for the time when cranking's not enough and we have to stuff them into the casing."

### Beach Green Two, *Isla Real*, Balboa, Terra Nova

For Wu and those with him, the wade forward was a sheer nightmare. Nothing in training had prepared them for it, for the crack of the bullets, the geysering spouts of water . . . most especially not for the red-leaking men floating in the surf. By the time he reached shore the major had barely the strength to throw himself onto the sand. To his left and right front were two tanks, one simply seemed dead while the other's turret was off, lying nearby. The latter light tank burned furiously.

There Wu lay for long moments, behind three piled bodies, waiting for his soul to return to his body. Gradually the major became aware of the presence of others, others who lived, and who were as weakened and stuck as he was. Then he became aware of the deadly *crumpcrumpCRUMP* of incoming mortars. Lastly he became aware of some reserve of strength inside himself, hitherto hidden. He thought for a moment upon the source. Then he found it; it was duty. And not just duty to himself and his men, but to his wife and unborn child.

Wu stood, shakily at first. He steadied. His first attempt at speech since leaving the landing craft came out as an inarticulate croak. Wu felt expectant eyes upon him. *He heard his old retired father's voice: "The men will do anything you ask, if you will just tell them."*

Glancing back and forth, Wu saw a sergeant who carried a good reputation in the battalion. Sergeant Li must have understood what the major intended; he nodded encouragingly and stiffened as if for a leap upwards and forward.

Wu swallowed, found his voice, and shouted, "There are only two kinds of people who are staying on this beach: the dead and those who are going to die. Marines! On your fucking feet and follow me!"

# CHAPTER THIRTY-FIVE

I had hoped we were hurling a wildcat into the shore, but all we got was a stranded whale.
—Winston Churchill, *Closing the Ring*

### *Batería* **Pedro** *el Cholo, Isla Real,* **Balboa, Terra Nova**

The Zhong weren't taking their lumps without dishing out a few, too. Pham was down to six guns, here at Battery Pedro, and four guns at Battery Mkhize. He'd lost enough men wounded that he'd had to ask for backup support from the legionary medical cohort, itself being overwhelmed by the number of casualties among the gunners of the Twelfth Brigade. The tribune didn't have any idea as to whether his two batteries were having it harder or easier than the other six, around the island.

*Plenty of hard to go around,* he thought, *enough hard for everybody to have their share.*

And the dead? Each was a little piece torn out of Pham's soul. *So much we went through together, old friends,* thought the tribune. *The old war . . . the slave labor camp they called a reeducation center . . . the starvation, the beatings. Now to have you die here, in this place so far from the country of our birth . . .*

An ambulance's siren sounded, indistinct through what remained of the jungle, after distortion by the hills, and amidst the general pounding of both outgoing and incoming shells. *Be a wonder if the ride over what remains of the roads doesn't kill them,* thought the tribune.

445

He turned his attention to the loading, as an ammunition carrier trundled behind gun three, lifting by crane a one-hundred-and-eighty pound arrow shell from its rack and feeding it onto a ramp on the railway carriage. Two powder bags followed. Two ammunition bearers first struggled to hold the shell and bags in place, then rolled them to an indentation in the center of the ammunition ramp. They left a gap between the shell and the bags.

The crew waited until the gun was depressed to the angle required for loading, then one of the ammo haulers pushed a lever. A round steel cylinder lifted from the ammunition rack, then swept forward, pushing the shell up the loading ramp and into the chamber. After the shell was chambered, and the rammer returned to its hidden position, the ammo rats moved the powder bags up to the position the shell had just vacated. The powder then followed the shell into the gun.

The whole time the gun chief, Sergeant Loi, one of the few men in Pham's two batteries who had actually begun military life as a gun bunny, kept up a steady stream of chatter. This served to keep up the crew's morale even as it effectively kept them in time with the dance of the guns, which in this case included a moving dance floor, as the shunters pulled them back into position for their next salvo.

Not for the first time since opening fire, not for the first time since being assigned here by Tercio Socrates, Pham wondered whether they shouldn't be shooting and scooting, returning to the shelter of the bunkers during reloading and only emerging to fire.

*It would sure reduce our vulnerability in any given piece of time,* he thought. *Would the cost in time be so high we'd lose the battle? Fail to sink enough ships to lose? Not my decision, anyway; the powers that be decided that we'd be better off firing more, faster, than living longer. Oh, well, what the fuck? It's not like we're not all old men anyway.*

With a synchronized whine—at least it seemed synchronized to Pham—all four barrels he could see began to rise as the crewmen spun elevating wheels. Sergeant Loi bent over a gunner's sight, the gunner leaning away, and nodded satisfaction. Loi faced Pham, raising one arm to signify ready to fire. One by one, the other three did the same, even as the two he could not see reported in via field telephone.

"Fire!"

**Forward Observer Position Twenty-six, ruins of Solar Chimney, Hill 287, *Isla Real*, Balboa, Terra Nova**

In one of those little flukes that so bedevil a rational approach to war, Corporal Leon's bunker was still perfectly fine. It was also, as an observation position, perfectly useless, since its view of sea and shore was entirely blocked off by a cylindrical section of concrete, blown from the tower and embedded in the ground all around the bunker. The concrete had cracked, too, and there were a few gaps. Unfortunately, those gaps faced uphill, away from the enemy, not downhill, toward him.

"God hates me," said Leon, standing on a pile of dirt thrown up against the inner face of the concrete cylinder, aiming downrange with his laser designator. He never took his cheek away from the stock of his laser.

"Oh, knock it off, Corporal," said Leon's radio-telephone operator, who was also Sergeant Loi's grandson, as good a Catholic as his grandfather, and a better one than Leon. "If God hated you, you would be dead and in Hell already."

"Don't try to cheer me up, Loi," said the corporal. "God's just saving me for a worse death. You, too, for that matter."

"You need a break, Corporal?" the Cochinese-Balboan asked. It was true that, standing up with his head exposed was riskier for Leon than manning a radio in the lee of the shrapnel storm for Loi the younger.

"Nah," answered the corporal. "You just keep your ear glued to the radio and tell me when to lase."

The laser, perched atop the chewed concrete wall of the sundered cylinder, looked approximately like a rifle pregnant with triplets. It had an optical scope atop, just like the legion's standard F-26, too. Through that, Leon kept his crosshairs on the target.

There were any number of ways to organize and task organize forward observers, most of which had been tried at one time or another, on both of the planets that knew Man. Generally the issue was a trade off, never an entirely satisfactory one, between quality of training, moral integration with the units supported, making sure there were always enough observers to support the training of the guns, administrative depth, redundancy. All of those factors had some weight, but ability to mass fires was usually the biggie.

In the case of the Twelfth Coastal Defense Artillery Brigade's heavy railway guns, these factors were of little import. Especially was massing fires irrelevant; the guns were arranged in a circle, with limited ability to traverse, such that real massing of fires was not really possible.

Instead, the batteries had two sections of sea to cover. The forward observers were allocated to the guns to cover those sections of sea. And they trained only with their own guns. The waste came in with the FOs who happened to be facing the wrong way, but that waste was also a measure of militarily critical redundancy, so . . .

There were also separate units of observers, with special skills, such as the few tiny teams out on the smaller islands of the archipelago of which the *Isla Real* was a part, the ones controlling the laser designators mounted to the barrage balloons, and the PRV crews.

Each of the eight batteries had, by now, over the last forty-five minutes, engaged seven to twelve targets. In one case, two batteries had gone after one target, but those two batteries were now allocating their fires to different ships. In no case had any battery stopped firing until its target was obviously out of the war. No ship, once targeted, had managed to escape out of range. From where Leon stood, he could shift his scope a few degrees left or right and see anywhere from two to four ships dead in the water, and another two burning oil slicks spreading out atop the waves. Leon had the sense, if not a precise image, of living men burning in or drowning under those slicks. *God help the poor bastards*, was his thought.

"Time of flight three minutes, forty-six seconds, Corporal," announced Loi. "They will give a one-minute warning and a splash thirty seconds out."

"Roger," answered Leon, tightening his grip on his designator and aiming directly at the target he'd been, in an obverse twist of normal procedure, directed to. It was an assault transport, a Landing Platform Dock, still belching forth cargoes and men via landing craft and air cushioned vehicles from its hidden well deck. Helicopters sat on the

THE RODS AND THE AXE

one third-length flight deck, rotors churning, troops filing up from below to board. The LPD's single three-inch gun, mounted forward, was still gamely tossing its pitiful shells forward in support of the Marines bleeding their way forward, ashore.

"Shot, Corporal."

"Roger."

More impressive than the single gun were the four multibarreled rocket launchers. They'd used them against the railway guns, not without effect, but seemed to have run out of or run low on ammunition for them.

"One minute, Corporal . . . splash in thirty, Corporal."

Leon depressed the laser's trigger. If it was strong enough when it reached the target to bother anyone's eyes, he couldn't tell. *Besides, with all the smoke in the air I'm not sure they could tell if it was a laser bringing forth tears or all the nasty shit in the air.*

A part of Leon was gratified to see one of the helicopters finish loading and take off. Its place was immediately taken by another, with yet more troops shuffling out to board. Wounded were taken from the second one, some on stretchers, some ambulatory with help, and taken below. *Sorry, guys.*

"Splash," said Loi, prompting Leon to begin painting the ship, stern to stem.

## Zhong LPD *Qin Shan, Mar Furioso,* Terra Nova

The LPD had no armor. There was steel enough to keep the water out, steel enough to keep the hull from buckling, but of actual armor there was none. The ship was also much bigger, at nearly twenty-thousand tons, than the light cruiser, somewhat longer but much higher and broader in beam. That meant bigger targets for the laser-guided shells which were, at best, competent rather than brilliant. Six shells had been launched from Battery Pedro *el Cholo.* Two hit close by the hull, causing leaks when they exploded. Four went right into the ship.

Shell number one wasn't so bad. It hit just under the open compartment in which one of the ship's two pinnaces normally rested. Fortunately, both of those were off on beach control duty, guiding in the air cushion vehicles, landing craft, and amphibious armored vehicles as they struggled with surf, smoke, confusion, and fear. That shell punched right through the thin hull, leaving a ragged ellipse behind it, then detonated in an empty section of corridor. Not that there were no casualties; the high-explosive filler shattered the sturdy steel of the shell, sending pieces large and small flying and ricocheting down the corridor until they either ran out of energy, which took a while, or buried themselves in something soft, yielding, screaming and leaky.

Shell two hit close by the hull, plunged in about thirty feet, then detonated. The resultant gas bubble, when it tried to push through the hull, wasn't up to the full rigors of the job. But it did cause a welded juncture to buckle and twist, letting water bubble in.

Number three hit the flight deck, but penetrated it without exploding. Instead, it went off just off to the side and slightly over an air cushioned vehicle, as it was loading a fresh platoon of Marines. Eardrums were blasted, arms and legs torn off, eyes gouged, entrails spilled, and skulls shattered. It seemed as if forty men, including the crew of the hovercraft, screamed as one man or, rather, one huge-lunged little girl. Even the ones who weren't hit shrieked in horror at being covered in the gore of their comrades.

One steel shard penetrated the unarmored hovercraft's engine compartment for the impeller, killing that engine and letting the whole contraption settle into the water underneath. The lost noise of the engine was approximately replaced by that from the wounded and terrorized.

Number four hit the flight deck and, rather than penetrating, malfunctioned and exploded without delay. Seven Zhong Marines were bowled over, suffering anything from minor flesh wounds to dismemberment to disembowelment. The blast was enough to tip the nearest helicopter halfway over, causing the blade to decapitate one Marine before it, too, shattered, sending shards into the bodies of still others.

Shell five was another water strike, though far enough out as not to do any serious damage of its own. It did serve to worsen the leak from two, albeit only slightly.

Six, a truly aberrant one, hit forward of the 76mm turret, penetrated, exploded, but did no serious damage. It was so insignificant that damage control didn't even bother sending a team but only one evaluator who said, in effect, "Fuck it."

*Qin Shan* was a *big* ship. The detonation of just a bit over a hundred pounds of explosive was not going to take it down, barring a serious fluke.

### Forward Observer Position Twenty-six, ruins of Solar Chimney, Hill 287, *Isla Real,* Balboa, Terra Nova

*You'll get that on a big bitch like that,* fumed Leon. He might feel sorry for his targets, but that wasn't enough to make him forget that they *were* targets.

"Repeat," he told Loi to pass on. "Continuous repeat until I say stop. Tell the guns their shooting's good, it's just a big son of a bitch and is going to take some killing."

"Roger." The RTO passed the word onto *Batería* Pedro *el Cholo,* whose own FDC simply answered, "Roger . . . shot over . . ."

"Shot, out," answered Loi. Three and a quarter minutes passed before Pedro announced, "Splash, over."

"Shot over." The battery was actually firing faster than the time of flight.

"Splash, out."

Still standing on the ad hoc parapet formed from the solar tower's fragment of chimney, Leon began painting the enemy ship with his laser as soon as he heard the "splash." He mentally counted down from thirty, whereupon he saw two black flowers bloom atop the superstructure, and three more narrow plumes of fire and smoke shoot up through newly made holes in the exterior decking. He suspected the sixth shell had overshot, coming down on the far side of the ship, and probably too far away to do a bit of good.

"Shot over . . . splash . . ."

"Tell them to stop giving me the shots," said Leon. "It's more confusing than it's worth . . . it's nothing *but* confusing, as a matter of fact. Just give me the splashes."

"Splash," said Loi.

Over four shells hit aboard, as far as Corporal Leon could see. They all hit, for whatever reason, on the short flight deck over the well deck.

There must have been a fuel line there, or maybe a fuel tank. Whatever it was, a brilliant fire, red and orange, punctuated by black, grew up, covering the entire flight deck.

*I'd be very surprised*, thought Leon, *if that doesn't make the well deck inoperable, too.* "Call higher and report we've got a major fire on our target. Ask if they want us to switch to a new target."

Loi answered after a few moments' consultation with his radio, "They say, 'Pound the cunt until she sinks.' They're very definite about it."

Thought Leon, *Of course the fucking rear echelon cunts who don't have to see the work can be ruthless. But those men down there and their ship are not "cunts," they're just regular guys like me, caught up in something fucked up by their higher.* He sighed, *Oh, well . . . since I am caught up in it.*

"Splash . . ."

## Zhong LPD *Qin Shan, Mar Furioso*, Terra Nova

*Qin Shan*'s captain had a serious problem. Almost all the Marines were offloaded, true, but an absolutely *huge* proportion of his ship's cube was devoted to supplies. That, with the well deck blocked by a wrecked hovercraft, he couldn't unload in anything like the needed fashion. He'd, in fact, stopped offloading supplies completely. He'd had to, even before the well deck became an inferno of dripping, burning fuel, because the far worse problem was, with a crew of a mere one hundred and twenty: *Damage control. What in the name of Heaven were the idiots thinking, that a crew of one hundred and twenty could handle this kind of accumulating damage to a ship this size? Fucking morons; I can hear them now: "Oh, nothing will get through to damage the ship," and "Oh, you've got all those Marines aboard; use them." Fuckheads. Cocksuckers. The Marines are supposed to be fucking gone at the precise time they're mostly likely to be needed. Not that they'd be any fucking use because it's not their fucking job.*

Shells were still coming in in salvoes, some exploding inside the well deck, sending their shards flying and ricocheting in all directions. From a sheltered position forward of the well deck the skipper looked over the damage, his number two standing beside and behind him. It wasn't all a horror story. Besides the bodies, crisped and bent into fetal positions, the ruins of the hovercraft, and the bent and jagged tears in the fabric of the ship, damage control parties were trying to wash the burning fuel out the back of the well deck. They had managed to get the flow of fuel cut.

"Go back to the bridge," the captain ordered. "Call fleet and tell them I *am* pulling out of here. They can shoot or hang me later if they want. With luck, we might even make it for them to wreak vengeance upon my body. As is, we're nothing but a highly lucrative target. Tell them that, if we make it, I'll come back when I can still do my job."

The 76mm gun, mounted in its own turret, on its own little plinth, well forward, was silent for the moment. It was perfectly healthy; the reason for cessation of fire was that the thing was overheated, after firing its last seventy-five-round burst in support of the ship's own Marines. It would be a full thirty minutes before it cooled enough to fire. At least, that's what the book said. The gun's chief was skeptical. *Thirty minutes to cool after firing one such burst, yes. But that was our third. And the gun had hardly cooled enough after we finished our second. It's not going to be in action again for a full hour, possibly longer.*

Since he had the time, the gun cooling to its own schedule and he not being dragged off *yet* for damage control, the chief stepped out on the deck and listened. He could hear the distinctive whine of numerous incoming heavy shells, along with frequent largish explosions as those found targets. What he didn't hear was a whole hell of a lot of outgoing fire.

*We're so fucked! Fucked! Someone's going to* pay *for this.*

### Zhong Destroyer *Yiyang, Mar Furioso,* Terra Nova

The senior man left at Orange seemed to be a major who had started out as the executive officer of a battalion but was now elevated to the command of a regiment. The major was an honest man and, if he lived, if they *both* lived, Wanyan was determined to raise him to the rank suitable to the command he'd inherited. Or higher. "Whatever mortal man can do," said Major Wu, "our men are doing. We have corporals commanding companies and a lieutenant leading a battalion, magnificently. But I don't know if we can do *this.*"

Better than a mere gun chief, Admiral Wanyan had a very good idea of the state of his fleet. *A third of my destroyers and frigates sunk. A preposterous percentage of my actual combat landing capability sunk or is in such bad shape that only a major overhaul will render them fit for duty again. In some cases, of course, they're fit only for scrapping.*

*The empress is a silly spoiled bitch. Easy for her to say, "Let none come back alive." Cunt knows no better. But it's on my soul if, in fact, we are utterly destroyed here.*

*How many decades has it taken for us to build up a fleet able to defend our own waters? Five? Six? No, seven full decades. Throw it all away on a whore's whim? I don't think so. We've tried hard enough, done all that men can be expected to do. And, after all, ninety percent of the Marine Corps, maybe more by now, are ashore as the bitch demanded.*

Wanyan felt like weeping for his doomed Marines. *I can't even support them. Fucking useless little three-inch popguns the bureaucrats and designer-fools insisted on arming us with? And even the five-inchers aren't much.*

*Ah, what a pity the Federated States wouldn't sell us a couple of their remaining battleships . . . not that we could have returned them to service in less than several years, of course.*

*What to do; what to do? My life is forfeit if I order a withdrawal in defiance of the empress and tell the Marines to surrender at their own discretion. Worse, my end would be very trying, indeed.*

### Fixed Turret 177, *Isla Real*, Balboa, Terra Nova

For quite a while, de la Mesa had been able to sense small-arms fire coming from the infantry maniple to his rear. It had never been quite as ferocious as he'd expected, largely, he believed, because the infantry had taken serious losses during the preliminary aerial bombardment. Still, it had been enough to keep the Zhong Marines at bay, even as the turret, sited as it was, had been key to filtering them down to a rate of entry into the area no greater than the infantry could handle.

*For a while, anyway,* though de la Mesa. *Give the Zhong their due;*

*they're tough and they're brave and they're resourceful and determined. If someone's willing to pay the price, and competent Marines of whatever nationality are always willing to pay the price, you can break machine guns by throwing bodies at them.*

Now, sadly, there was no fire coming from the supporting and support infantry behind de la Mesa's turret. He still had communication with the rear, via radio. Something, likely an artillery shell, had cut the land line. And even the radio was spotty; de la Mesa suspected a half-cut antenna, blowing with the breeze, sometimes with a good connection and sometimes not.

He asked Julio, "Is the carousel full?" and on being told, "Yes, Sergeant," said, "Juan, forget gunning. I can gun alone. Go man the machine gun covering the door. Pablo? Julio?"

"Yes, Sergeant . . . yes, Sergeant?"

"Go man the other two guns. We're on our own, I think, but we've got to hang on until the counterattack drives the Zhong into the sea."

That last was, so far as de la Mesa knew, a pure fabrication. There wasn't going to be a counterattack, at least as far as he knew. But they did need to buy time for the grunts to reestablish the defense, farther inland.

# CHAPTER THIRTY-SIX

It is better to be wise after the event than not wise at
all, and wisdom after one event may lead to wisdom
before another.
—Air Marshal John C. Slessor, *Air Power and Armies*

**Near the juncture, Beach Green One and Orange Two
(the base of the Tadpole's Tail),** *Isla Real*, **Balboa, Terra Nova**

Three dozen very tough and fit-looking Zhong Marines were hunkered
down in a trench with the major who had ended up in command of the
entire regiment. That they were dirty, and tired, perhaps a bit wired
from adrenaline, and a few of them lightly wounded, did not detract in
the slightest from the impression of sheer toughness. Their
commander, a senior sergeant, Li, had taken a look at some of the
Balboan positions already captured or found destroyed. He had some
insights into them, though he wasn't sure he'd seen anything like the
major had described.

*It's not much,* thought Major Wu, looking the "company" over,
*but it's all I can assemble on short notice. And Sergeant Li is worth forty
men alone.*

It seemed to Major Wu that the enemy mortar fire had slackened
somewhat, maybe even quite a bit. Whether that was because the
mortars were running low on ammunition, because they had been
taken out by the Tauran aircraft that were beginning to reappear in
some small numbers, because the guns had grown too hot to fire for

the nonce, or for some other reason, Wu couldn't begin to guess. He was happy enough for the nonce just to be able to stick his head above ground without the substantial risk of it being torn raggedly from his shoulders.

That's how Wu's late commander had bought it, sticking his head up from a captured Balboan trench; a flying steel shard had simply sliced that head away, leaving a ragged stump of a neck gushing blood for a few moments like an obscene bottle of sparkling red wine.

Named Zixu, after a famous presumed ancestor, the major stood fairly tall for a Zhong, at about five feet, ten inches. This, in his view, made it all the more surprising that he was still alive. *Big targets die soonest.*

The sound of helicopters, not en mass but continuous, sounded from the north. In the eye of the shell storm, more Imperial Marines were being fed into the grinder. As the helicopters unloaded, medical teams led or carried or simply prodded the wounded in the direction of safety. Each one that came in left almost as full.

*I hope Private Fa makes it,* thought Wu. He'd found the private wandering alone, missing an arm which someone had crudely tournequetted off, and holding in his "good" hand, by his thumb and one remaining finger, a radio handset from which ran some severed wire. The private had kept apologizing into the handset, unaware that it was no longer connected to the radio. Wu had detailed a man to lead Fa to the airfield. Fa had initially refused, until Wu told him his radio needed repair. That had seemed adequate reason to the RTO, where the loss of an arm and three fingers had not.

Even now Wu shook his head, musing, *Where do we get them, these kids who'll give every ounce or everything they have for the country? The Imperial family has done nothing I can see to deserve it. But . . . perhaps the merit is in the innate virtue of our common folks.*

A single heavy mortar shell sailed over head. The major first heard its rattling passage, then looked up and actually saw the malevolent thing, arcing slowly across the azure sky. *Big bastard,* thought the major. *Fortunately, they've stopped being so lavish in expending them.*

*One nice thing about the enemy running out of mortar shells, or whatever is slowing down their pounding of us,* thought Wu, looking north toward the airfield, *is that at least we can bring in some troops by air and evacuate our wounded the same way.*

A salvo of shells flying overhead with the sound of a passing freight train reminded Wu that evacuation did not mean safety. As long as the Zhong were trying to use helicopters to land troops, or ships to disgorge supplies or men, the ships and helicopters remained legitimate targets, no matter how many wounded might be aboard.

*Hmmph! Maybe when every bunk for a given ship is filled with a bleeding man they'll get the idea and fucking leave.*

Wu pulled his dripping but acetated map from a cargo pocket and looked it over. *Sometime the map, itself, suggests a solution.* He'd passed through most of the area of the Tail since landing, moving north to south through a maze of cratered runway, wrecked buildings, fire, smoke, bodies, and whatnot. There were even a few buildings standing, though no one was quite brave enough to occupy them. The Balboans had a nasty tendency to booby-trap everything they didn't intend to physically hold.

Wu was situated on the western side of the Tail, more or less facing the ruined ship and the small island the map called "Saint Elmo's." Between him and those features bobbed more Zhong dead than he cared to think about. The carpet of floating bodies wasn't quite solid— *Well, in spots it is*—but, had the bodies been unsinkable, it wouldn't have been hard to have walked and jumped from one to the other to reach the distant island from the Tail. The ship was still there, and still in enemy hands, too. They'd tried blasting it, to no noticeable effect, and tried storming it. The latter effort had fizzled out amidst a hurricane of heavy shellfire, called in by the wreck's defenders on themselves.

*Which, too,* thought the major, *is an indicator that they are very well protected, indeed. Bastards.*

There was firing to Wu's right front, at Beach Red. He thought he heard more of the enemy's frightfully rapid firing rifles and light machine guns than he did of his own side's more moderately paced weapons.

*Counterattack,* thought Wu, correctly assessing the fire. He looked over the literally thousands of bodies in the bay formed by the Tail and Beach Red and added the thought, *No way they can hold. No way at all. Which means Red is as good as lost. There is only Orange, to my left, and my own boys, here. And I cannot support Orange, nor it me, because there is a position between us that simply refuses to give in.*

Wu turned to the senior sergeant in command of the group he'd assembled. "Now," said Wu to Li. "Now, while the shell storm's eye passes over us. Go eliminate that position between us and Beach Orange."

### Turret 177, *Isla Real*, Balboa, Terra Nova

The position had been very strongly built. It was essentially invulnerable to any practical amount of high explosive that the Zhong could deliver, to include in the form of HEAT. A main battle tank's long rod penetrator could have gotten through the dirt and concrete, but so far the Zhong hadn't been able to bring one up. *It's possible,* thought Sergeant de la Mesa, *that their Marines don't have anything but light tanks. Oh, and a shitpot of very tough infantry.*

Though strongly built and, to a degree, protected even against a chemical attack, the position did have its weaknesses. It wasn't a submarine, nor even one of the very elaborate deep shelters. It could not produce its own air. Filter and purify? Yes. Produce? No. It also had the ability to draw air very locally, essentially from a vent in the roof. That, however, had been foreseen as not quite enough, a bit of foresight de la Mesa particularly appreciated when the Zhong had used flamethrowers against every exposed bit of surface or pipe. There was also a pipe that went underground back to behind the now lost infantry position. When the possibility of gaining oxygen through the roof vent was cut off, the filters automatically began sucking in air from elsewhere. As a third backup, there were also oxygen candles, though those did, in fact, create so much heat that they were a very last resort.

The secondary weakness was related. The turret traversed primarily by electric power provided by the local generator. That required oxygen. Cut off the air, and the generator would stop. There were batteries, but they were not up to traversing the turret for very long, or very quickly at all.

De la Mesa swung the turret around in a great three-sixty circle, seeing nothing distinctly. That would have been fine, except that he had the impression of things, men, he supposed, dropping out of his vision just as the gun and sight reached them.

"And if it came to a fucking race," he muttered, "a sharp Zhong sprinter could run around the turret faster, a lot faster, than I can traverse it."

De la Mesa released his grip on the sight, then reached for the wheel that raised and lowered his own chair. He began spinning it with an arm that had grown terribly strong from long practice. Also by long practice, he knew when to stop. About a quarter of an inch before his helmet would have hit the inside of the commander's hatch, he stopped the spinning crank dead.

Up there de la Mesa could see through the five cupola-mounted periscopic vision blocks, one of which was infrared capable. Those had dead zones, too, but with the flip of a retaining latch, the cupola itself could be rotated. De la Mesa flipped, rotated, and—

"Oh, shit!" There, right in front of the side periscope, the sergeant saw two boots standing next to his turret. The vision of the boots was replaced first by a camouflage-clothed ass and then by what looked for all the world like a shaped charge, pointed down onto the gun mantlet. He saw a hand reach for the charge, then pull something. A stream of smoke began to rise.

*Crap! No way to be sure to get rid of it except to remove it by hand. No way in time, anyway!*

"Boys!" screamed de la Mesa. "Drop the machine guns, go below, and lock the access hatch!" He gave Juan, Julio, and Pablo a few seconds to comply. Then he bent down and took an antipersonnel grenade from a basket inside the turret that held several. Holding the grenade in his left hand, he pulled the pin with his right. The ring was still around his forefinger as de la Mesa popped the hatch and tossed the grenade outside, generally in the direction of the gun's muzzle. Before the grenade could explode—*if it had been possible I'd have cooked it off*—de la Mesa had his pistol out of his shoulder rig and transferred to his left hand. Then he began cranking the chair wheel again, pushing himself up through the hatch. The first thing he saw was a blue-camouflage-clad Zhong Marine, reaching for his own rifle. He shot at the Marine, missed—*Damned left hand*—shot, missed—*motherfucker*—shot and this time hit. The Marine flipped backwards, landing on the slope of earth in front of the mantlet.

Stunned, shocked, and badly hurt, the Zhong looked left and saw something green and roughly egg-shaped. *Oh, shit,* thought the Zhong, just as the grenade exploded next to him.

De la Mesa pushed the chair as high as it would go. High enough that he took some like fragments of wire from his own grenade when it went off. That was as nothing, though, compared to the danger represented by the charge getting ready to go boom sitting over the gun mantlet. *Lose that and we are not only useless; we're indefensible. Fuck!*

A burst of bullets whined by, two of them singing off the armor. They were close enough for de la Mesa to feel the passage on his exposed neck. He bent over, putting as much of the angle of the turret between him and his assailants as possible. Using arms that were unusually strong, for having to do so much of the work of legs, de la Mesa hauled himself out of the hatch and across the turret's top.

Being insensate below the waste, the sergeant didn't actually notice when his right foot caught on something. By main force, he pulled himself free, breaking his own foot in the process. In the breaking free, that leg below the knee shot up vertically. A Zhong machine gunner promptly blew it off, from about mid-calf down. De la Mesa felt that as a series of blows, transmitted up his body, but without pain. On the other hand, he did feel suddenly vastly weak, as blood gushed from his stump.

De la Mesa continued slithering forth on his rapidly failing body.

Sergeant Li *saw* it.

*I saw the* goddamned *leg fly off. The fucking Balboan acted like he didn't even feel it or care if he did. Whatever these fuckers use for drugs I want some . . . didn't even care. Shit, these boys are too tough for Mrs. Li's son.*

The most galling part, to de la Mesa, once he reached the shaped charge, was how easily he could have dislodged it and the sapper who'd set it without exposing himself to—*let us be honest here; I am a dead man*—the enemy's fire. Basically, with his fast-fading strength, his simply brushed the charge away. It fell over, and rolled down to where lay the much-perforated body of the sapper who set it. Boom. Arms and legs and flying guts everywhere.

Some of the body pieces landed across de la Mesa. He was distantly aware of them, but really didn't much care. The blood flowing from his leg had slowed, but not so much from coagulation as sheer drop in volume and blood pressure. He wasn't dead, not quite, but the end couldn't be too far off. In any case, as his consciousness faded and he dreamed the dream of having the use of his lower body back, his enemy, Sergeant Li of the Imperial Marine Corps' stormed forward with two other men.

The Zhong pulled a grenade from his load-carrying equipment, then flicked off the safety clip and pulled the pin. He was about to drop it down the open hatch when his eye came to rest on the wounded Balboan.

"Take him," he told the two men with him. "Get him to shelter; tourniquet his leg, and get him to the medics. Can you do that?"

"Yes, Sergeant."

Li waited until the Balboan and his own men were clear, then let the grenade's spoon fly off, counting, "One thousand . . . two thousand," before slamming the grenade in and rolling down the slope.

The blast, when it came, was quite muffled. Li crawled up to the hatch and repeated his attack. Again, the blast was muffled.

*Hmmm . . . while it might be emotionally satisfying to blow the fucking thing sky high, it just might take me with it. Then, too . . .*

Li looked back in the direction of the island's interior. *Then, too, pretty good fields of fire all around. And while that enemy position back there has its gun ports facing the wrong way, it's still fine shelter from their shells. And we can fix the collapsed trenches back good as new.*

*I need to make a suggestion to the major . . .*


## Zhong Destroyer *Yiyang*, *Mar Furioso*, Terra Nova

*Why is it,* mused the admiral, *that every time I've just about resolved to give up this mess and sacrifice myself to preserve my command and my subordinates, somebody like Wu comes along and makes sticking it out that much more reasonable a prospect? Life is just so unfair, especially unfair if that high-born whore of an empress was right. Ah, well, and they say that the stopped clock . . . oh, to hell with it.*

*Wu says he's managed to scrape together about five thousand men, hale and otherwise, more support than combat, but willing to try. He's says there are a lot more around, but they're so disorganized it's going to be a while before he can round them up and get some use out of them. He tells me the reason Beach Red doesn't answer is that Red Two was obliterated and Red One retreated into his area. He says there's a brigadier general there and two colonels, but one of the colonels is a loggie, the other is badly wounded, and the brigadier is essentially catatonic, except for screaming fits at random intervals. Note to self, on my own authority relieve the brigadier general and brevet Wu to colonel with date of rank to about four hundred years ago.*

Wanyan snapped orders to his adjutant to do just that, except modified to give Wu just sufficient date of rank to tell the loggie what to do.

*I can hardly blame the major . . . no, the colonel, now . . . for not being able to be more precise about what he's got available. He's got mortars and some artillery. Some armor. He says he'll hold.*

*Okay, the boy's done wonders so far. If he says he'll hold I am inclined to believe him. So . . . can I go to the empress and present this as a tactical matter. We pull back out of range and come in only at night to reinforce and resupply. Now . . . how do I go about this? Remembering that if I don't save the empress's face she'll have mine cut off and fed to ants. Or, worse, fed to ants while I'm still wearing it.*

## UEPF *Spirit of Peace*, in orbit over Terra Nova

Even Wallenstein became mildly nauseated at the fawning hyperbole in the Zhong admiral's message to the empress. "Brilliant, goddesslike leadership . . . unequaled craft . . . military planning a model to be studied by the ages . . ." and those—every one credited to Xingzhen— were the more restrained passages. The nausea passed as the message was read aloud and in full. Wanyan, down below, didn't use such tactless words. Still, what it boiled down to was, "All right, you were possibly right so far, your fragrancy. We have a beachhead where I was ready to give up; points to you.But if I stay here until those fucking guns are silenced, I will lose my fleet, lose my beachhead, and lose my life. That will be a light burden for me, sweetness, because I'll be dead. You, on the other hand, will have to live with loss of face . . . conversely, with a hold on the island that can be expanded, which hold will serve to fix the enemy formations facing the Furious Ocean, I can, despite our disasters, move on past Phase Two, to Phase Three, landing on the mainland to establish a base from which we can drive west. P.S. any ships that can't speed out of range are going to be sunk. Nothing to be done. The enemy's artillery is *that* powerful."

The empress looked questioningly at Marguerite. *Should I accept this or should I not?* Marguerite, in turn, looked at Khan, the husband.

"I think your admiral's approach is sound, Your Majesty," said Khan. As an Old Earther, he clearly outranked any of the locals. But as the high admiral's lover and, if Khan, the wife, was correct, the love of her long and rather wicked life, the Zhong empress was just as clearly someone not to annoy.

Xingzhen considered this, then sent back, "You have our permission, thou good and faithful servant."


## Zhong Destroyer *Yiyang*, *Mar Furioso*, Terra Nova

"Flank speed," ordered the admiral, "in any direction that takes you away from the island. Get out. Run away. Do not stop to tow. Do not stop for survivors, though you can drop them boats if they need it. But get out."

The *Yiyang* heeled over hard as her captain spun her to starboard, then put on all possible speed. A salvo of shells landed not far behind, indicating very strongly that the destroyer had been targeted for destruction, itself. The *Yiyang* began a series of sharp direction changes, which would leave it within the still undetermined firing arc of the enemy for longer, but reduce the odds of a hit somewhat.

The destroyer's captain was pretty sure they were screwed anyway, but no new salvoes came in. Instead, a lumbering LDP, several miles ahead of the *Yiyang* was suddenly deluged with shells. Nor was it four or six or eight or sixteen, no; at least thirty-eight, by the captain's own count, hit on and around her. The LPD stopped dead in the water, burning along her entire length. With a second volley, quite possibly as large as the first, she blew up.

"They shot at us," whispered the ship's exec, "while they thought we—with our miserable one gun—were an immediate threat. With us turning tail, they can go after the long-term threat. We're not going to get more than a double handful of amphib's out of this alive and afloat."

"I know," said the captain, wanting to weep at the loss to his country's fleet. "Oh, I know."

### Turret 177, *Isla Real*, Balboa, Terra Nova

*So they can make mistakes, too*, thought Wu. *That's highly comforting to know.*

Wu stood on the upper floor of the concrete structure, next to the turret basket. From the carousel at the base of that basket, some men were removing the cannon's shells and projectiles, and carrying them gently and carefully outside. The reason for that was the couple of engineers whom Wu had had scrounge a shaped charge, and who were about to use that charge to blast through the thick steel door that seemed to lead to a level below. The charge was set to cut through the center of the wheel, itself mounted just above the center of the door. That, Sergeant Li had believed, would give the best chance of getting the door open.

Wu had tried to get anyone who might be down there to come up and surrender, banging repeatedly on the steel with the butt of a broken rifle. There'd been no answer and, under the circumstances, no risk could be allowed. If someone were down there, they'd die down there.

*Sad . . . but I have my own to worry about; them, and my wife and unborn child. And my duties to those are infinitely greater than to an enemy who refuses to give himself up.*

Juan, Julio, and Pablo waited below where their sergeant had sent them for safety. Juan fervently prayed that Sergeant de la Mesa, too, was safe. But he doubted it; you could feel the cannon, even down here, when it went off. There hadn't been a tremor since shortly after they'd come below.

The cubicle in which the boys sat was about three meters on a side, and two meters high, with a few projections at floor level holding rations, fuel, and ammunition. One wall held four fold-up bunks while the opposite wall was taken up with concrete stairs, leading to the fighting level. Juan had heard some banging coming from the steel door, but had paid it no mind. The sergeant had said they'd be safe here, and so here, safe, they would stay.

★★★

The mistake Wu had found comforting was in the form of a counterattack, in what he estimated to be two-battalion strength, supported by a company of tanks and a company of what he tended to think of as assault guns, though the shells launched by those assault guns were something horrific, easily ten times the explosive power he'd have expected.

The counterattack had come in from two different directions. One had paralleled the eastern coast and driven north, trying to eliminate Beach Orange. The other had come in from the west, slicing diagonally across Red One and Two.

The two attacks hadn't been very well coordinated, either for timing or for fires. Worse, the second one had seemed to the major, who had been on site to witness its being driven off, genuinely amateurish. At least amateurish was the best word Wu could come up with to describe it.

*How else do you describe it,* wondered Wu, *when your enemy fails to follow his own artillery closely? When he runs into his own wire and doesn't know what to do about it? When he runs into his own minefields and can't find his own lanes through?*

In any case, that attack had been driven off handily, with better than a hundred of the enemy splayed out on the churned-up dirt or hanging obscenely from the wire. Of prisoners, too, there'd been a few, even a few unwounded ones. They were on their way north for evacuation and interrogation.

The other attack had been an altogether more dangerous affair, with the tanks and assault guns tightly supported by the infantry chewing their way across Beach Orange in a most professional and respectable manner. That attack hadn't been so much beaten off as withdrawn by the enemy himself, following the defeat of the Beach Red attack.

*I wonder, too, if they knew how very damned close it was, how close they came to pushing us into the sea.*

"We're ready, sir," said the senior of the engineers who had been setting the shaped charge. Wu nodded and proceeded to walk out the position's door, then to a nearby trench. Who knew, after all, what might be on the lower level of the position that the shaped charge might set off? Where he entered the trench, Sergeant Li waited, with a hand-picked team of four. They'd be the ones to go down into the lower level after the door's locking bars were cut.

From inside came a muffled shout, a Mandarin version of, "Fire in the hole! Fire in the hole! Fire in the hole!" On the last "hole," the engineers scurried out through the entrance portal, racing trippingly for the safety of the same trench.

The blast, when it came, was anticlimactic. If there'd been anything explosive on the lower level, the charge hadn't set it off.

Sergeant Li, without the need to be told, leapt from the trench, followed by his hand-picked team. Wu got up, too, but in a much more leisurely and dignified fashion. By the time he reached the door, Li was already there, and throwing up on the ground.

"Those bastards," muttered the sergeant. "Those ruthless fucking bastards. Even we . . . not even us . . . bastards."

# EPILOGUE

I

**Battery MacNamara, Fort Tecumseh (eastern extension), Balboa, Terra Nova**

It was marginally lighter by the guns than farther out in the jungle, but that was all it was, a marginal difference. The moons were low, low enough that the thick green canopy absorbed or defected almost all the light Hecate, Eris, and Bellona had to give.

*Antaniae* were thick in the jungle surrounding the concrete position, their low cries of *mnnnbt, mnnnbt, mnnnbt* setting everyone's teeth on edge, and giving every man's spine an unpleasant tingle. Trixies, clever proto-birds, almost as clever as man, hunted the packs of winged, septic-mouthed, flying reptiles, for the most part silently. Occasionally, though, one would raise the peculiar trixie cry of victory when it found one of the hated *antaniae* and began tearing it to shreds.

The *antaniae* were a more distant threat. Here, in the thickest part of the Shimmering Sea coast's jungle, mosquitoes were a greater annoyance and a more serious threat, at least to men. The *antaniae* concentrated on the young, the feebleminded, and the ill. Mosquitoes, bearing both Old Earth-derived diseases and some rarer ones found only on Terra Nova, went after everybody. And, while spraying helped, they were still thick enough to draw a pint to a quart of blood from a man, daily.

The battery, two 180mm guns on barbette carriages, with the

ammunition stored below and elevators to move it up to gun level, had almost no warning. The heavy air defense missile battery behind them fired at a target the gunners had neither a visual nor an audible clue to. Whether the surface-to-air missile hit or not the gunners never knew; three bombs hit the air defense battery, close enough together as to be barely distinguishable, while half a second later, two more thousand pounders scoured the surface of Battery MacNamara free of human life. That only represented a baker's dozen of dead, but it was also the ruin of both guns, taking the old battery out of action for the foreseeable future.

## II

### *Isla Santa Catalina*, **Balboa, Terra Nova**

The air was thick with helicopters, some carrying troops, and some with heavy guns slung on straps suspended from hooks, below. Still others carried supplies, in sling loads somewhat similar to the guns.

The island was already secure; for reasons Admiral Wanyan could only guess at, they hadn't made even a token defense, not even so much as to have laid out mines. His guess was, in any case, a fearsome one. *They didn't try because they don't like waste, or don't need to put on pointless shows to placate stupid politicians and stupider voters.*

*And it would have been a waste.* "He who would defend everything defends nothing."

*But it's also possible that they want us to have it. And I suspect that huge crowd of civilians inland of the other side of the straits has something to do with that.*

## III

### **Near Hephaestus, Balboa, Terra Nova, a few miles from the Balboan-Santa Josefinan border**

It was much like an assembly line, with the men and women of *Tercio la Virgen* filing through the tents, turning in their old uniforms, being issued a mix of new and civilian clothing, and turning in their weapons to have them replaced by captured Tauran ones. Then, by squads and platoons and maniples and cohorts, the tercio, minus the cohort already in Santa Josefina, "guarding" Carrera's *classis*, they disappeared into the fog and clouds of the mountain forest, heading for home.

Only the tanks and what minimal support they needed were staying in Balboa, though they were still putting on a demonstration on the Balboan side of the border.

*La Virgen* would stop on the way, just on the other side of the border, to build a safe haven should events turn against them. But they really weren't too worried about that. The Tauran forces in Santa Josefina were already stretched as thin as could be. The sudden materialization of a tercio on their southern flank, threatening their vitals, should be enough to send them reeling back to the capital, to keep a friendly government friendly and in power.

# IV

### Fifty-three kilometers southeast of Bjorvika, Hordaland

Under an overcast sky, two Xamari legionary immigrants and one native Balboan pushed the wheeled cart carrying the glider, sans wings, out into the open from the wooden barn in which it had been mostly reassembled. The BLS, or balloon launch system was already out there in the slush. The targeting computer sat atop the gas canisters for the BLS.

Each of the Xamaris went back into the barn, while the native Balboan hooked up the computer to the glider. The Xamaris came out with the wing, which they slid into place under the glider's body, then affixed it. While the Balboan fiddled with the computer, the Xamaris ran straps between the deflated balloon and certain hookups on the glider. These would disconnect at the glider's preset command, after which the balloon could go where the winds took it.

One by one, the Xamaris ran four of the five straps that came from the balloon to points on the steel carriage. Then they attached the fifth to the lifting ring atop the bird. The wires were hooked, one into a heavy-duty control that would cause the balloon to cut itself away from the four restraining straps, on command. The other went to the top of the Condor next to the ring. A hose was run from the tanks to the balloon.

One of the Xamaris turned a valve wheel to begin filling the balloon with hydrogen. This was much cheaper than helium. Moreover, since the balloon was a throwaway, who cared if it caught fire at some point?

Once the balloon was filled until it had *just* positive buoyancy, the Xamaro closed the valve. The balloon lifted until it was swaying unevenly over the glider. Once the restraining straps had grown taut, the crew stopped the filling and waited for word from the Balboan, still working the targeting computer.

"And . . . that does it," said the latter. He hit the enter button. Instantly, all four restraining straps, plus the cable, were cut loose. They cascaded to the ground around the Condor. Simultaneously, the balloon lurched upward, the Condor's wings bending under the acceleration and the air's resistance.

For a short time the three legionaries watched the glider lift, until it disappeared into the clouds overhead.

"Nothing to be done now," said the Balboan. "Go get your bags. Time to cross the border to neutral Scandza, then on to Volgan Republic."

"Where's the bomb going, Sergeant?" asked the elder of the Xamaris.

"No reason for you not to know, I suppose," replied the sergeant. "It's going to a Muslim neighborhood in the capital of Anglia. The idea is to start a riot."

"Oh."

# V

**MV *Alta* (Cochinese Registry), Saavedra, Valdivia, Terra Nova**

Ham came aboard with Alena the witch and about one hundred and twenty other boys. They came on in small packets, and by individuals, ostensibly unloading humanitarian supplies, with always a few less leaving than had come aboard.

The *Alta* had made a number of stops already, and had to make a number more. At each stop, some boys and, in a couple of cases, some numbers of men, had come aboard and disappeared into the ship's bowels, down where customs agents were occasionally bribed not to tread.

Legate Terry—"the Torch"—Johnson met them below. "Your father," he said to Hamilcar, "left me very specific instructions. You are attached to my staff as my aide de camp. He says he wants you to learn."

Ham nodded. The old man had told him as much. Ham also knew where, ultimately, they were bound for. Alena and her husband did not. Since he was aboard ship now, David Cano thought he could get away with asking, and did so.

Alena the witch just smiled.

In answer, Johnson led Cano to a map board, covered by green canvas. He pulled the canvas aside. Cano took one look, then turned to his wife and asked, not for the first time, "How the hell do you do that?"

## General Assembly, World League, First Landing, FSC, Terra Nova

Lourdes wasn't sure why the president of the Federated States hadn't propositioned her. In the event, she was both relieved and mildly insulted that the lecher of the southern hemisphere hadn't even tried.

*On the other hand, since we want the FSC neutral, and since, had he propositioned me, my telling him that his daughter would be kidnapped and thrown to a pack of sex-starved condemned prisoners would probably have made that tougher, it's surely just as well. Who knows, maybe the swine actually has some decency to him.*

*Okay, let's not be ridiculous. He no doubt has reasons of his own for getting me this speaking opportunity in front of the World League.*

To be continued . . .

# GLOSSARY

**AdC**    Aide de camp, an assistant to a senior officer.

**Adourgnac**    A Gallic brandy, alleged to have considerable medicinal value, produced from ten different kinds of grapes, of which the four principal ones are Maurice Baco, Cubzadais, Canut, and Trebbiano. There is an illegal digestif produced from the brandy that includes a highly dilute extract from the fruit of the Tranzitree, qv.

**Ala**    Plural: Alae. Latin: Wing, as in wing of cavalry. Air Wing in the legion. Similar to tercio, qv.

**Amid**    Arabic: Brigadier General.

**Antania**    Plural: Antaniae, septic-mouthed winged reptilians, possibly genengineered by the Noahs, also known as Moonbats.

**ARE-12P**    A Gallic infantry fighting vehicle.

**Artem-Mikhail-23-465 Aurochs**    An obsolescent jet fighter, though much updated.

**Artem-Mikhail 82**    Also known as "Mosaic-D"; an obsolete jet fighter, product improved in Balboan hands to be merely obsolescent.

**ASW**    Antisubmarine warfare.

**BdL**    Barco de la legion, ship of the legion.

**Bellona**    Moon of Terra Nova.

**Bolshiberry**    A fruit-bearing vine, believed to have been genengineered by the Noahs. The fruit is intensely poisonous to intelligent life.

**Caltrop**    A four-pointed jack with sharp, barbed ends. Thirty-eight per meter of front give defensive capability roughly equivalent to triple-standard concertina.

**Caltrop Projector**    A drum filled with caltrops, a linear-shaped charge, and low-explosive booster, to scatter caltrops over a wide area on command.

**Cazador**    Spanish: Hunter. Similar to Chasseur, Jaeger and Ranger. Light infantry, especially selected and trained. Also a combat leader selection course within the *Legion del Cid*.

**Chorley**    A grain of Terra Nova, apparently not native to Old Earth.

**Classis**    Latin: Fleet or naval squadron.

**Cohort**    Battalion, though in the legion these are large battalions.

**Conex**    Metal shipping container, generally $8 \times 8 \times 20$ feet or $8 \times 8 \times 40$ feet.

**Consensus**  When capitalized, the governing council of Old Earth, formerly the United Nations Security Council.

**Corona Civilis**  Latin: Civic Crown. One of approximately thirty-seven awards available in the legion for specific and noteworthy events. The Civic Crown is given for saving the life of a soldier on the battlefield at risk of one's own.

**Cricket**  A very short take-off and landing aircraft used by the legion, for some purposes, in place of more expensive helicopters.

**Diana**  A small magnet or flat metal plate intended to hide partially metal antipersonnel landmines by making everything give back the signature of a metal antipersonnel landmine.

**Dustoff**  Medical evacuation, typically by air.

**Eris**  Moon of Terra Nova.

**Escopeta**  Spanish: Shotgun.

**Estado Mayor**  Spanish: General staff and, by extension, the building which houses it.

**F-26**  The legion's standard assault rifle, in 6.5mm.

**FMB**  Five-Minute Bomb.

**FMB-I**  Five-Minute Bomb-Incendiary.

**FMTIB**  Five-Minute Thermobaric and Incendiary Bomb.

**FSD**  Federated States Drachma. Unit of money equivalent in value to 4.2 grams of silver.

| | |
|---|---|
| **GPR** | Ground-Penetrating Radar. |
| **Hecate** | Moon of Terra Nova. |
| **Hieros** | Shrine or temple. |
| **Huánuco** | A plant of Terra Nova from which an alkaloid substance is refined. |
| **I** | Roman number one. Chief Operations Officer, his office, and his staff section. |
| **Ia** | Operations Officer dealing mostly with fire and maneuver, his office and his section, S- or G-3. |
| **Ib** | Logistics Officer, his office and his section, S- or G-4. |
| **Ic** | Intelligence Officer, his office and his section, S- or G-2. |
| **II** | Adjutant, Personnel Officer, his office and his section, S- or G-1. |
| **IM-71** | A medium-lift cargo and troop carrying helicopter. |
| **Ikhwan** | Arabic: Brotherhood. |
| **Jaguar** | Volgan-built tank in legionary service. |
| **Jaguar II** | Improved Jaguar. |
| **Jizyah** | Special tax levied against non-Moslems living in Moslem lands. |
| **Karez** | Underground aqueduct system. |

| | |
|---|---|
| **Keffiyah** | Folded cloth Arab headdress. |
| **Klick** | Kilometer. Note: Democracy ends where the metric system begins. |
| **Kosmo** | Cosmopolitan Progressive. Similar to Tranzi on Old Earth. |
| **Liwa** | Arabic: Major General. |
| **Lorica** | Lightweight silk and liquid metal torso armor used by the legion. |
| **LOTS** | Logistics Over The Shore, which is to say without port facilities. |
| **LZ** | Landing Zone, a place where helicopters drop off troops and equipment. |
| **Maniple** | Company. |
| **Makkah al Jedidah** | Arabic: New Mecca. |
| **Mañana sera major** | Spanish: Balboan politico-military song meaning tomorrow will be better. |
| **MB** | Money Bomb. |
| **MRL** | Multiple Rocket Launcher. |
| **Mujahadin** | Arabic: Holy Warriors (singular: Mujahad). |
| **Mukhabarat** | Arabic: Secret Police. |
| **Mullah** | Holy man; sometimes holy, sometimes not. |
| **Na'ib 'Dabit** | Arabic: Sergeant Major. meaning |

**Naik**　　　　　Corporal.

**Naquib**　　　　Arabic: Captain.

**NGO**　　　　　Nongovernmental Organization.

**Noahs**　　　　Aliens that seeded Terra Nova with life, some from Old Earth, some possibly from other planets, some possibly genetically engineered, in the dim mists of prehistory. No definitive trace has ever been found of them.

**Ocelot**　　　　Volgan-built light-armored vehicle mounting a 100mm gun and capable of carrying a squad of infantry in the back.

**Meg**　　　　　Coastal Defense Submarine employed by the legion, also the shark, Carcharodon Megalodon, from which the submarine class draws its name.

**M-26**　　　　A heavy-barreled version of the F-26, serving as the legion's standard light machine gun.

**PMC**　　　　　Precious metal certificate. High-denomination legionary investment vehicle.

**Progressivine**　A fruit-bearing vine found on Terra Nova. Believed to have been genengineered by the Noahs. The fruit is intensely poisonous to intelligent life.

**Puma**　　　　A much-improved Balboan tank, built in Volga and modified in Zion and Balboa.

**Push**　　　　As in "tactical push." Radio frequency or frequency-hopping sequence, so called from the action of pushing the button that activates the transmitter.

| | |
|---|---|
| **PZ** | Pickup Zone. A place where helicopters pick up troops, equipment, and supplies to move them somewhere else. |
| **RGL** | Rocket Grenade Launcher. |
| **Roland** | A Gallic main battle tank, or MBT. |
| **RTO** | Radio-Telephone Operator. |
| **Satan Triumphant** | A hot pepper of Terra Nova, generally unfit for human consumption, although sometimes used in food preservation and refinable into a blister agent for chemical warfare. |
| **Sayidi** | Arabic form of respectful address, "Sir." |
| **SCIB** | Shaped Charge Incendiary Bomb. |
| **Sergeyevich-83** | Or Serg-83, a Volgan-designed, Zhong-built naval fighter bomber, capable of vertical take-off and landing, and of carrying an ordnance load of about two tons. |
| **SHEBSA** | *Servicio Helicoptores Balboenses*, S.A. Balboan Helicopter Service, part of the hidden reserve. |
| **Sochaux S4** | A Gallic four-wheel-drive light truck. |
| **SPATHA** | Self-Propelled Antitank Heavy Armor. A legionary tank destroyer, under development. |
| **SPLAD** | Self-Propelled Laser Air Defense. A developed legionary antiaircraft system. |
| **Subadar** | In ordinary use, a Major or Tribune III equivalent. |

| | |
|---|---|
| **Surah** | A chapter in the Koran, of which there are one hundred and fourteen. |
| **Tercio** | Spanish: Regiment. |
| **Tranzitree** | A fruit-bearing tree, believed to have been genengineered by the Noahs. The fruit is intensely poisonous to intelligent life. |
| **Trixie** | A species of archaeopteryx brought to Terra Nova by the Noahs. |
| **TUSF-B** | Tauran Union Security Force-Balboa. |
| **UEPF** | United Earth Peace Fleet, the military arm of the Consensus in space. |
| **Volcano** | A very large thermobaric bomb, set up by a seismic fuse. |
| **Yakamov** | A type of helicopter produced in Volga. It has no tail rotor. |

# LEGIONARY RANK EQUIVALENTS

**Dux, *Duque*:** Indefinite rank; depending on position it can indicate anything from a Major General to a Field Marshall. Duque usually indicates the senior commander on the field.

**Legate III:** Brigadier General or Major General. Per the contract between the *Legion del Cid* and the Federated States of Columbia, a Legate III, when his unit is in service to the Federated States, is entitled to the standing and courtesies of a Lieutenant General. Typically commands a deployed legion, when a separate legion is deployed, the air *ala* or the naval *classis,* or serves as an executive for a deployed corps.

**Legate II:** Colonel; typically commands a tercio in the rear or serves on staff if deployed.

**Legate I:** Lieutenant Colonel; typically commands a cohort or serves on staff.

**Tribune III:** Major; serves on staff or sometimes, if permitted to continue in command, commands a maniple.

**Tribune II:** Captain; typically commands a maniple.

**Tribune I:** First Lieutenant; typically serves as second in command of a maniple, commands a specialty platoon within the cohort's combat support maniple, or serves on staff.

**Signifer:** Second Lieutenant or Ensign; leads a platoon. Signifer is a temporary rank, and signifers are not considered part of the officer corps of the legion except as a matter of courtesy.

**Sergeant Major:** Sergeant Major with no necessary indication of level.

**First Centurion:** Senior noncommissioned officer of a maniple.

**Senior Centurion:** Master Sergeant, but almost always the senior man within a platoon.

**Centurion, J.G.:** Sergeant First Class; sometimes commands a platoon, but is usually the second in command.

**Optio:** Staff Sergeant; typically the second in command of a platoon.

**Sergeant:** Sergeant; typically leads a squad.

**Corporal:** Corporal; typically leads a team or crew or serves as second in command of a squad.

**Legionario**, or **Legionary**, or **Legionnaire:** private through specialist.

\*\*\*

Note that, in addition, under legion regulations adopted in the Anno Condita 471, a soldier may elect to take what is called "Triarius Status." This locks the soldier into whatever rank he may be, but allows pay raises for longevity to continue. It is one way the legion has used to flatten the rank pyramid in the interests of reducing careerism. Thus, one may sometimes hear or read of a "Triarius Tribune III," typically a major-equivalent who has decided, with legion accord, that his highest and best use is in a particular staff slot or commanding a particular maniple. Given that the legion—with fewer than three percent officers, including signifers—has the smallest officer corps of any significant military formation on Terra Nova, and a very flat promotion pyramid, the Triarius system seems, perhaps, overkill. Since adoption, regulations permit but do not require Triarius status legionaries to be promoted one rank upon retirement.